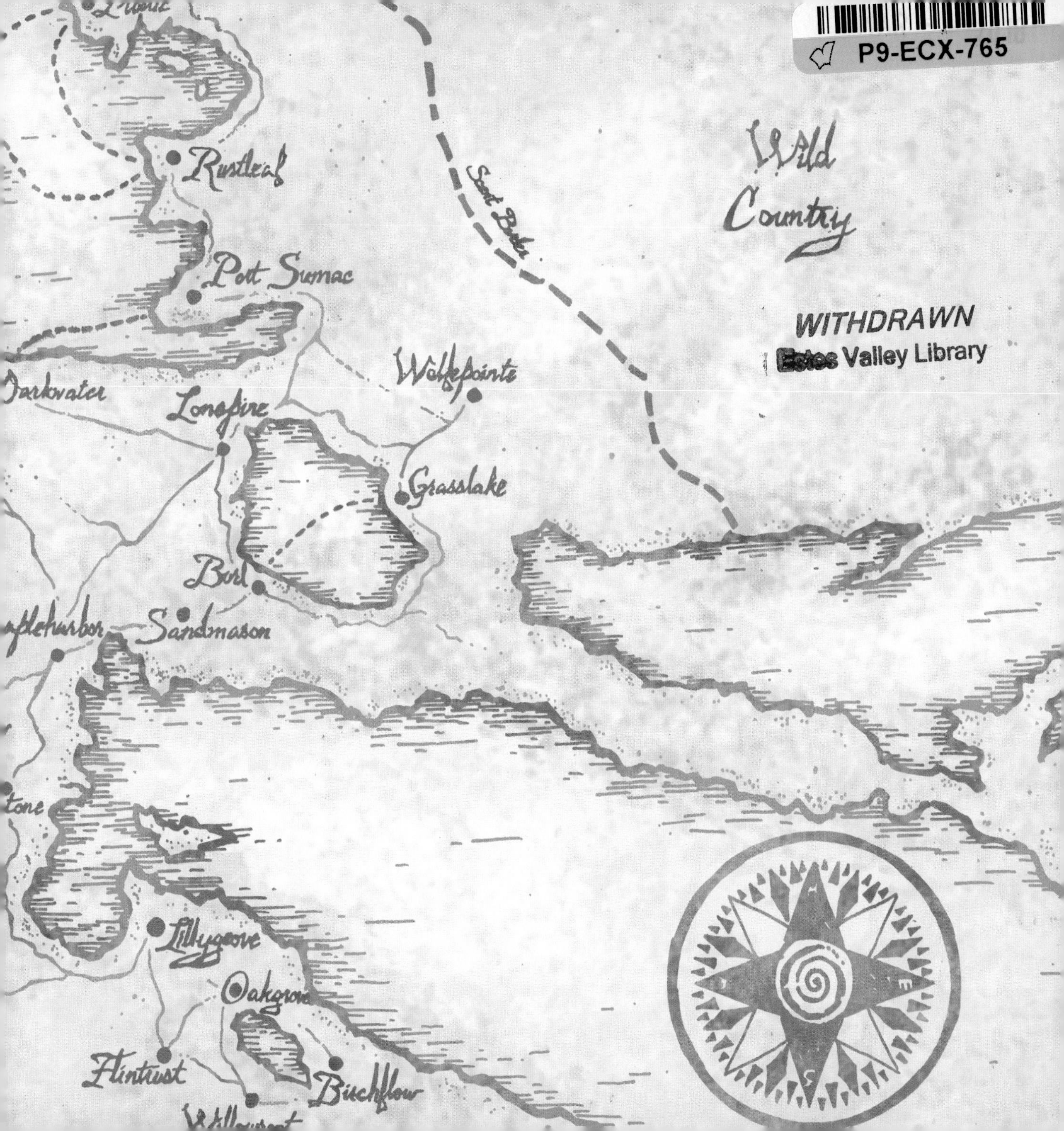
Rustleaf
Port Sumac
Wild Country
Wolfepointe
Lonespire
Grasslake
Borl
Sandmason
Lillygrove
Oakgrove
Flintrust
Birchflow

MOUSE GUARD™
WINTER 1152

Published by
ARCHAIA™

FOR MY WIFE JULIA

SPECIAL THANKS TO:

MY PARENTS, JESSE GLENN, MIKE DAVIS, EMERSON JONES,
SEYTH MIERSMA, JEREMY BASTIAN, NATE PRIDE, KATIE COOK,
GEOF DARROW, STAN SAKAI, CRAIG ROUSSEAU, SEAN WANG,
JANE IRWIN, MARK SMYLIE, BRIAN PETKASH, ERIC LYNCH,
AND JAMES GURNEY

MOUSE GUARD™
WINTER 1152

STORY & ART BY
DAVID PETERSEN

MOUSE GUARD: WINTER 1152, January 2018. Published by Archaia, a division of Boom Entertainment, Inc. Mouse Guard is ™ and © 2018 Oaklore Inc. Originally published in single magazine form as MOUSE GUARD: WINTER 1152, No. 1-6. ™ and © 2007-2009 Oaklore Inc. All Rights Reserved. Archaia™ and the Archaia logo are trademarks of Boom Entertainment, Inc., registered in various countries and categories. All characters, events, and institutions depicted herein are fictional. Any similarity between any of the names, characters, persons, events, and/or institutions in this publications to actual names, characters, and persons, whether living or dead, events, and/or institutions is unintended and purely coincidental.

BOOM! Studios, 5670 Wilshire Boulevard, Suite 450, Los Angeles, CA 90036-5679. Printed in China. Third Printing.

ISBN: 978-1-93238-674-5, eISBN: 978-1-61398-953-1

FOREWORD

EVERY MILE IS TWO IN WINTER.
—GEORGE HERBERT, JACULA PRUDENTUM (1651).

THE ICY SEASON HAS SETTLED OVER THE MOUSE TERRITORIES. THE MOUSE GUARD ARE SHORT OF FOOD AND MEDICINE. THE SMALL BAND OF ADVENTURERS HAS BEEN FORCED TO SPLIT UP, LEADING THEM TO TERRIBLE CHOICES.

EVERY GREAT SOCIETY LIVES UP TO ITS CHALLENGES, AND THE GUARDMICE ARE NO EXCEPTION. THEY SELFLESSLY CONFRONT THE WEATHER AND CHALLENGE THE PREDATORS. THEIR HEROISM, MEASURED AGAINST THE TRIALS OF WINTER, SHINES ALL THE MORE BRILLIANTLY.

DAVID PETERSEN'S TINY ACTORS PLAY OUT THEIR STORY OF COURAGE AND LOYALTY ON AN EPIC STAGE. WITH IMPECCABLE TASTE PETERSEN CHOOSES DRAMATIC CAMERA ANGLES AND STRIKING COMPOSITIONS, NOT MERELY TO TELL THE STORY, BUT TO EXPAND THE WORLD. THE COLORS TRANSITION FROM GOLDEN FIRELIGHT TO PALE BLUE MOONLIGHT. THERE ARE SNIPPETS OF OLD BALLADS, EPIC POEMS, AND TIMEWORN MAPS. THE EFFECT OF THIS ARTISTRY IS TO EXTEND THE STORY WORLD BEYOND THE FRAME OF THE COMIC PANELS SO THAT IT LIVES INSIDE OUR MINDS.

THE ELDER MOUSE CALANAWE TELLS HIS YOUNG COMPANION LIEAM, "YOU SHOULD ALWAYS AIM TO BE YOUR OWN MOUSE." PETERSEN HAS TRUSTED HIS ARTISTIC INSTINCTS, BECOME HIS OWN MOUSE, AND GIVEN US SOMETHING COMPLETELY NEW.

JAMES GURNEY
CREATOR OF DINOTOPIA

CONTENTS

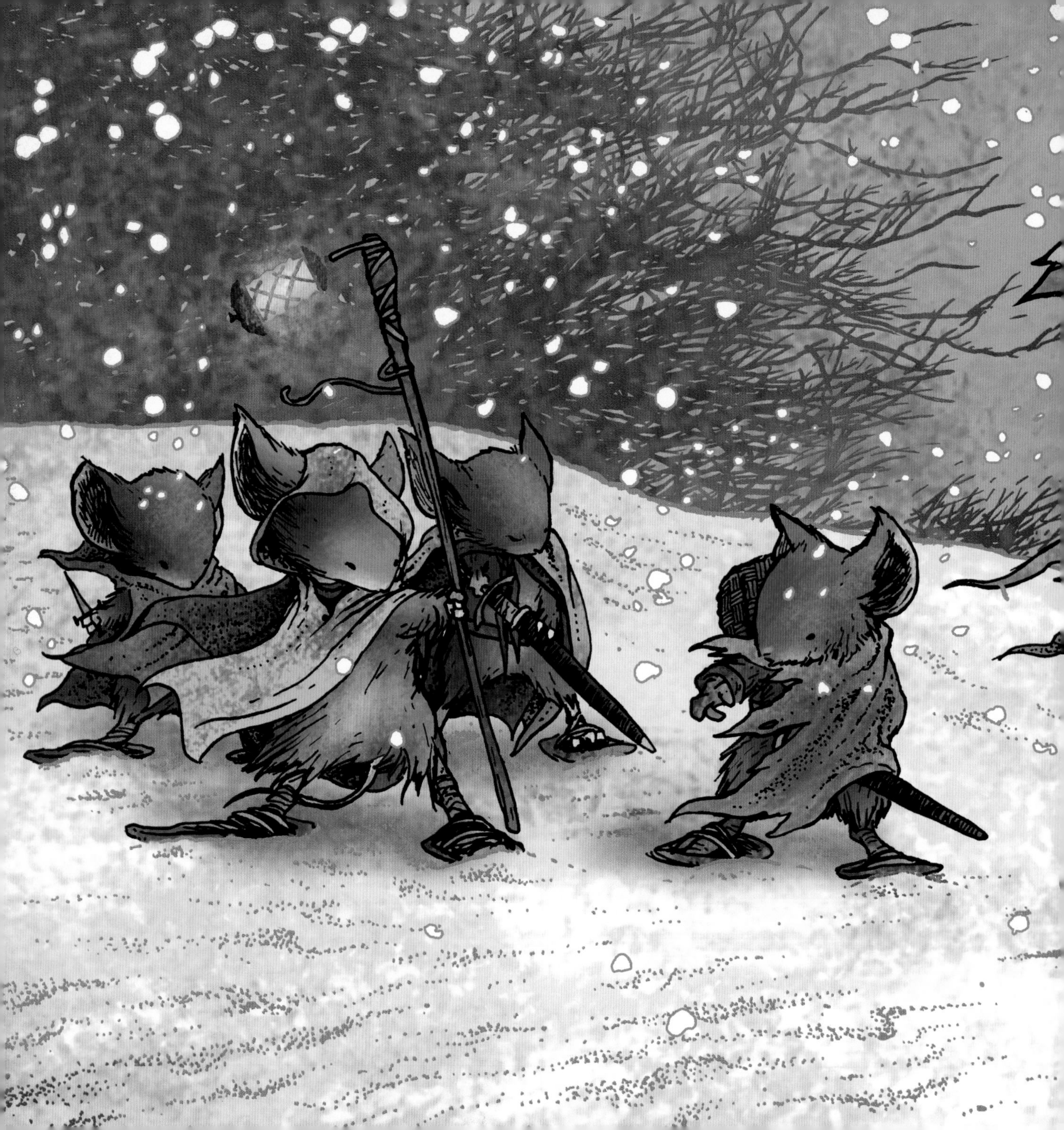

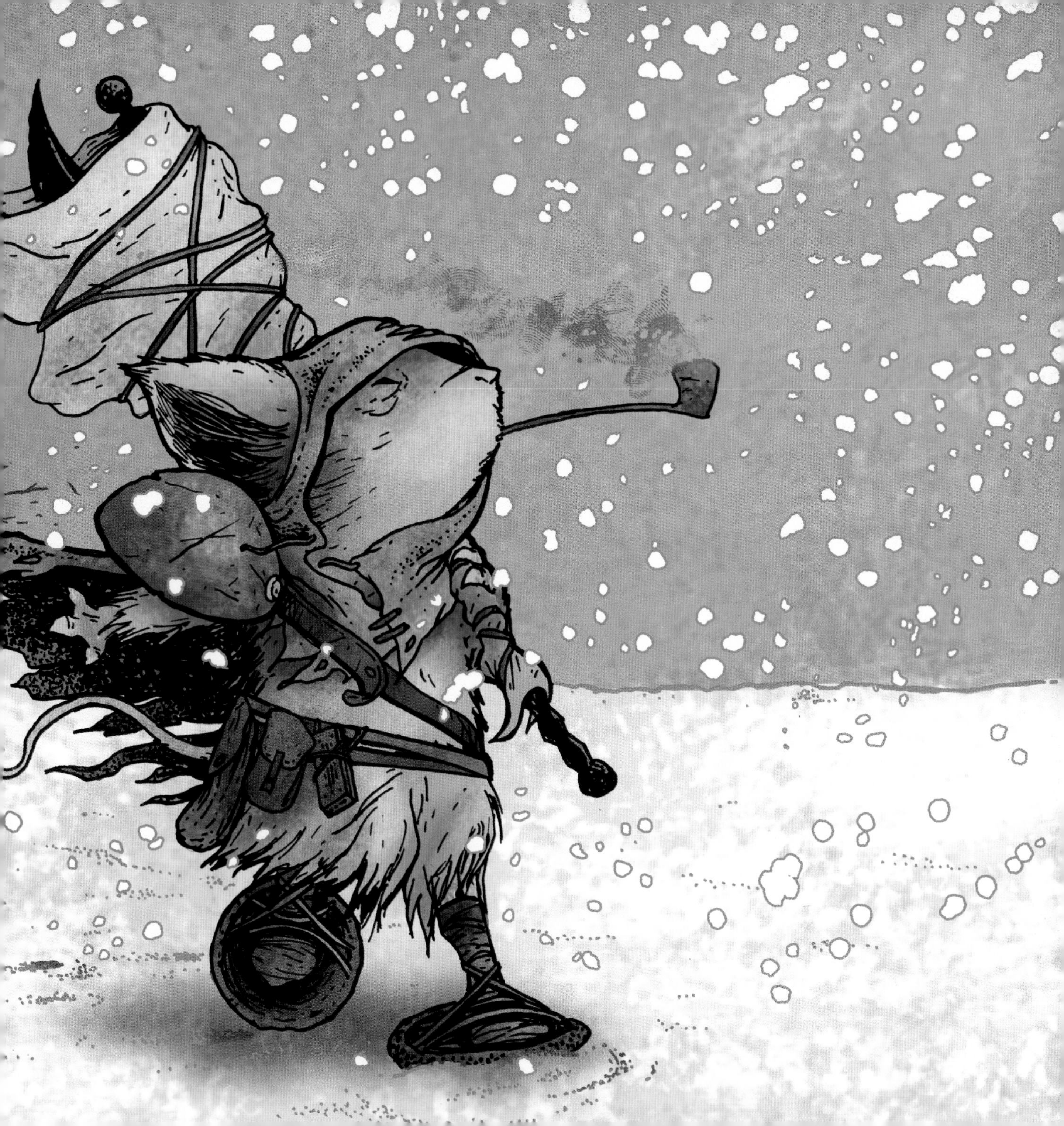

CHAPTER ONE

The Fall of 1152 left the Mouse Territories unprepared for Winter. The malcontent, Midnight, raised an army to breach the gates of Lockhaven and kill Gwendolyn, the Guard's matriarch.

As the seasons changed, underlying problems with food and medicine threatened the Mouse Territories themselves. Gwendolyn has scattered thirteen of her best Guardmice to act as ambassadors and gather immediate supplies.

'The winter skies are dark and drear.
Once green land is pale and severe.
Supplies are short and night is long.
Time stands still in it's bitter song.
Withered life sits frozen on the vine.
Is this the end of days for yours and mine?
'Tis but a season and such things turn.
Lack of preperation is a cold lesson to learn.'

-Poem by the Scribe Roibin in the Winter of 1152

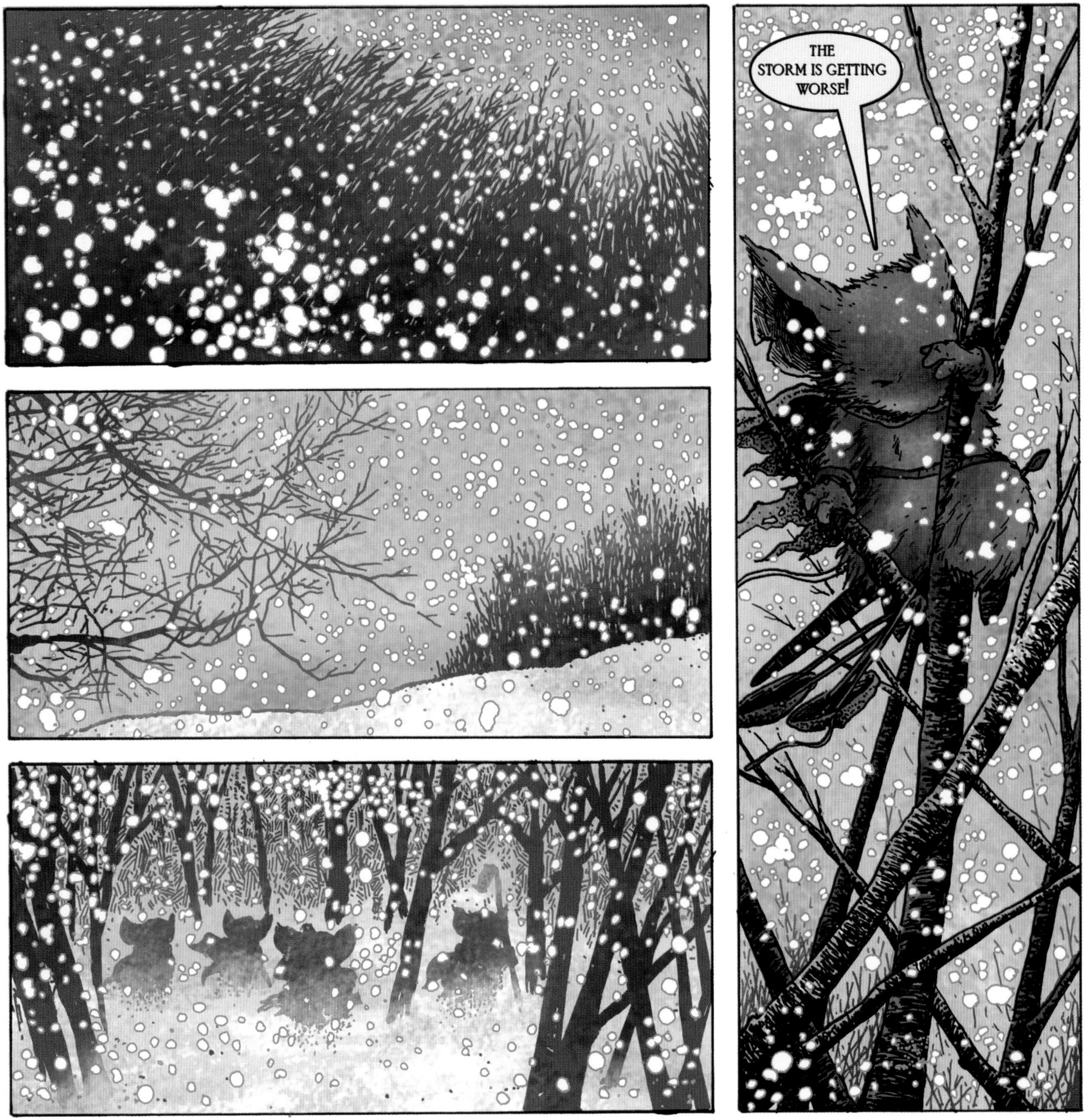
THE STORM IS GETTING WORSE!

WHAT IS THE PLAN, KENZIE?
WE HAVE ONE LAST CITY BEFORE WE MAKE FOR LOCKHAVEN.
SPRUCETUCK LIES JUST BEYOND THAT PLAIN.
BUT, IN THIS WEATHER, WITHOUT COVER, IT'S TOO DANGEROUS.

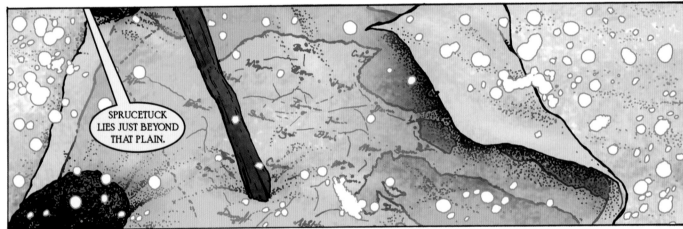

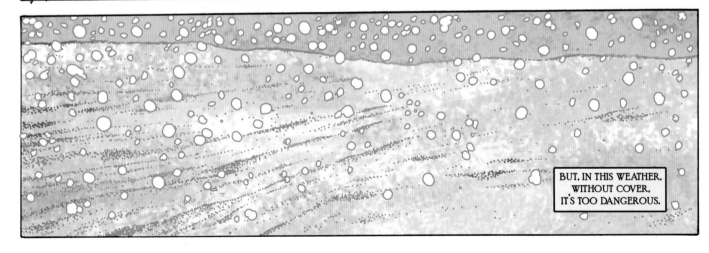

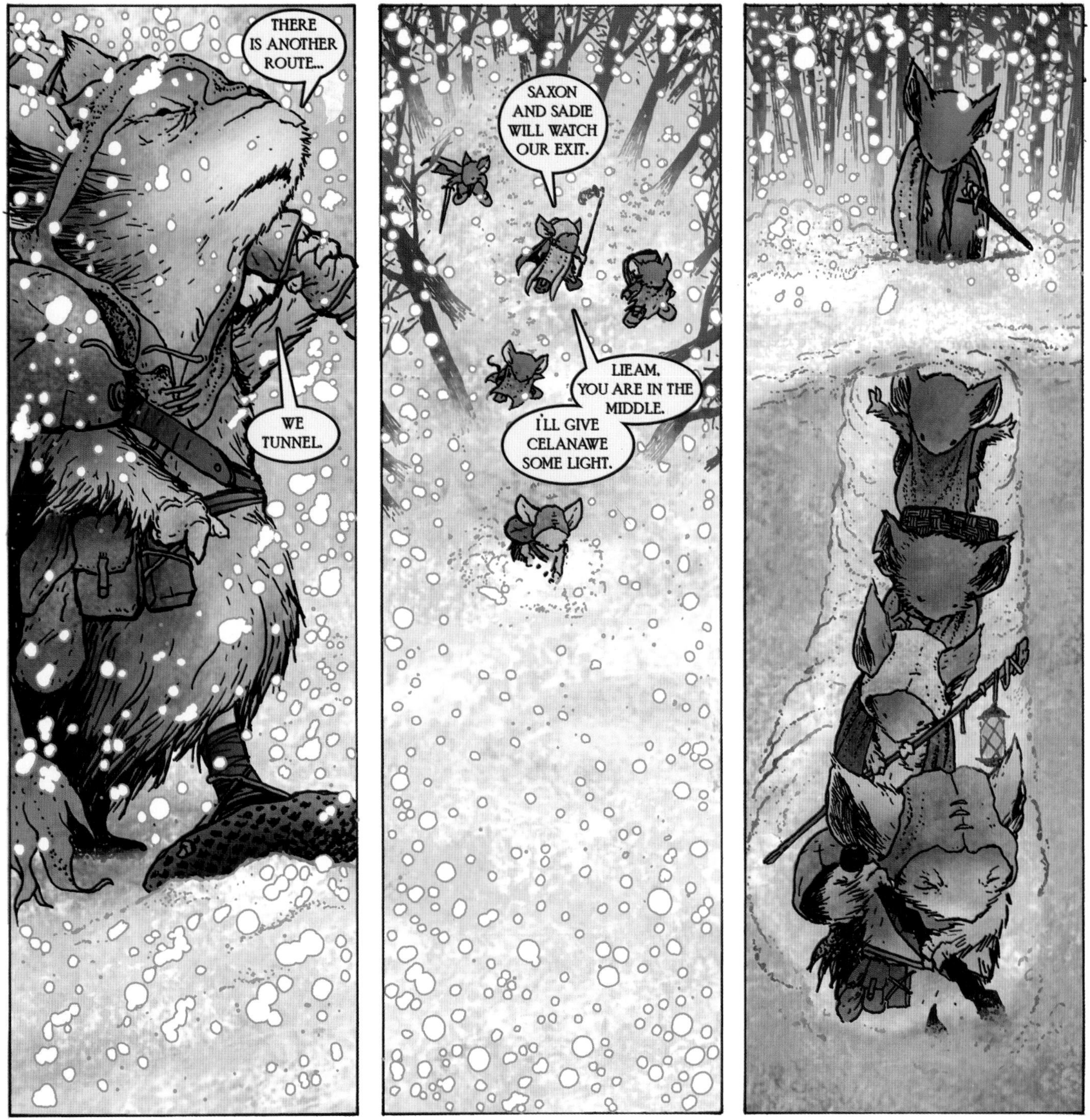
THERE IS ANOTHER ROUTE...
WE TUNNEL.
SAXON AND SADIE WILL WATCH OUR EXIT.
LIEAM, YOU ARE IN THE MIDDLE.
I'LL GIVE CELANAWE SOME LIGHT.

FOOLISH TO HIDE FROM A STORM...
WE HAVE BEEN DOWN HERE FOR AGES.
A SWORD CAN'T DEFEAT EVERYTHING, SAXON.
HEH, SOMETIMES IT TAKES AN AXE.
SHHH! WE DON'T NEED A FOX TO OVERHEAR YOU THREE AND TRAMPLE US.
!
?
WE ARE THROUGH TO SPRUCETUCK.

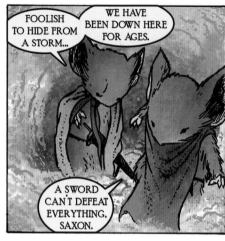

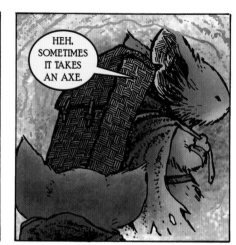

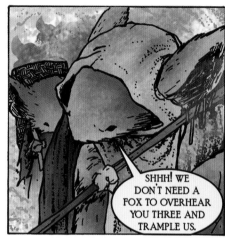

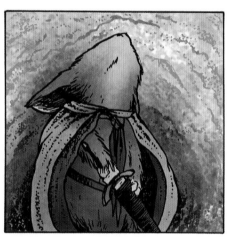

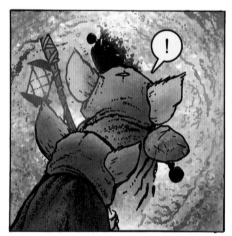

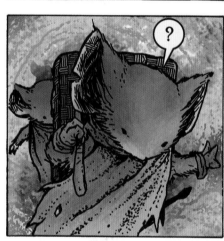

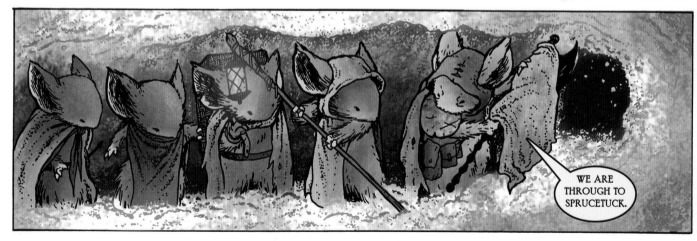

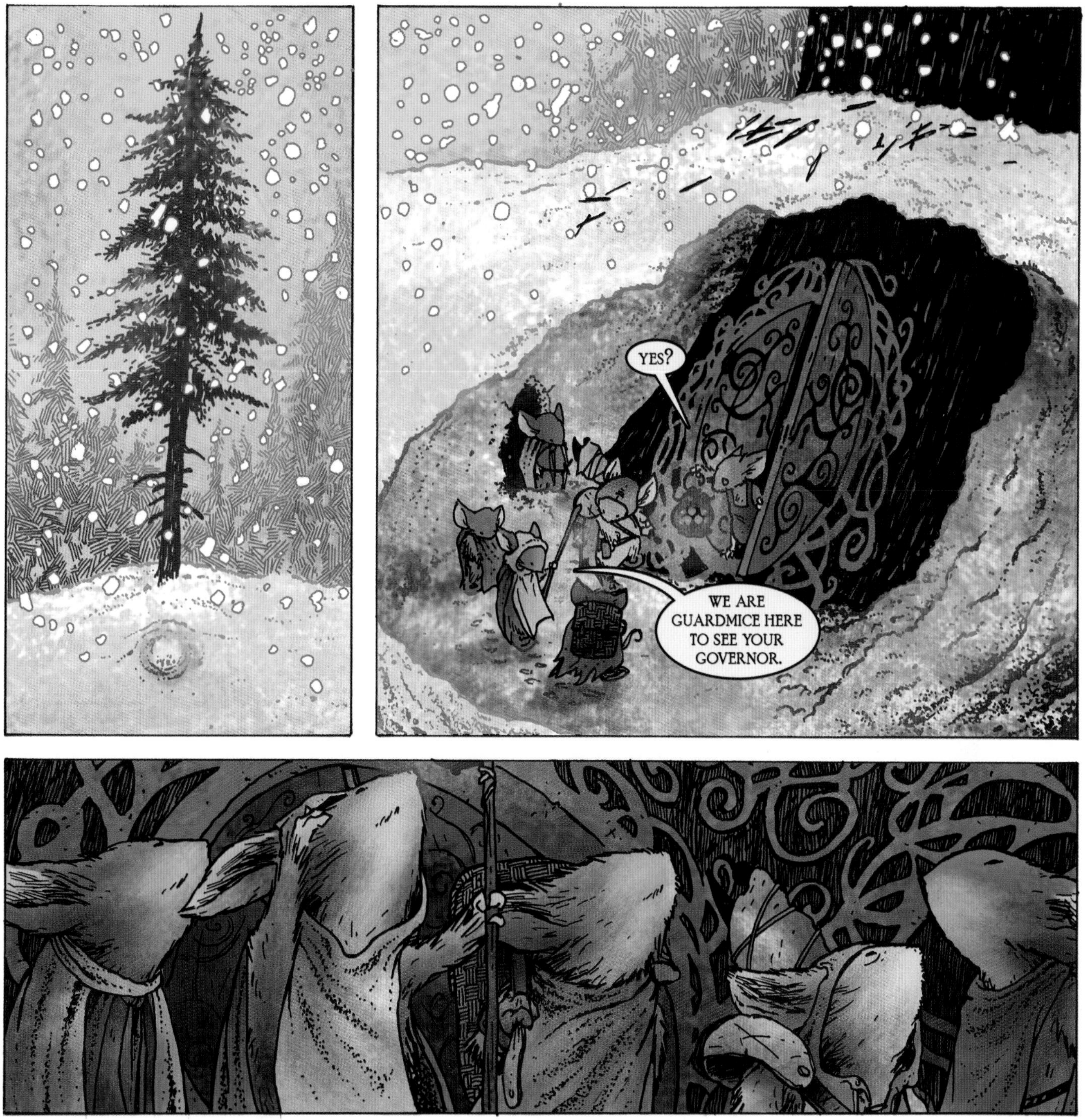
YES?
WE ARE GUARDMICE HERE TO SEE YOUR GOVERNOR.

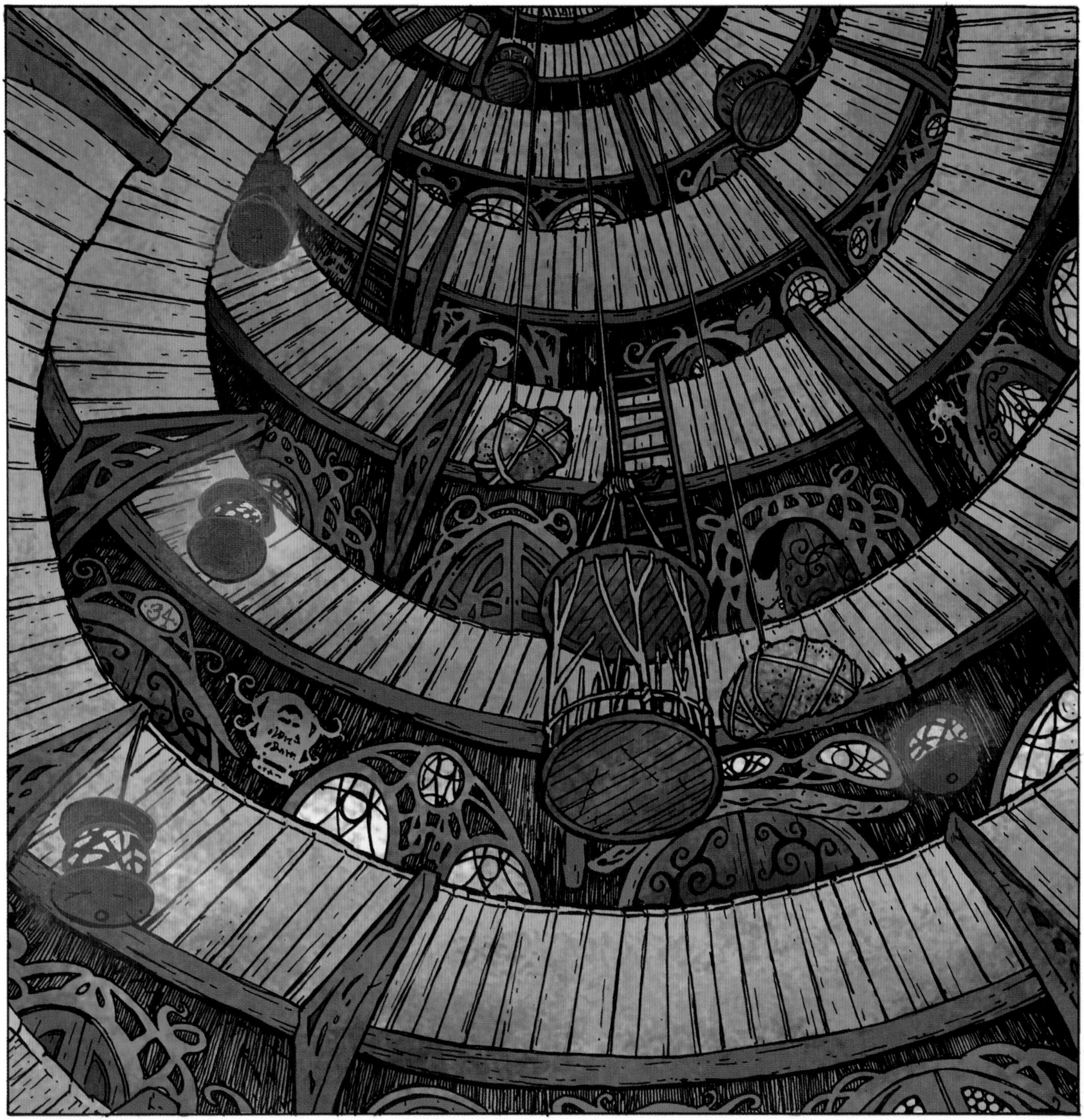
34

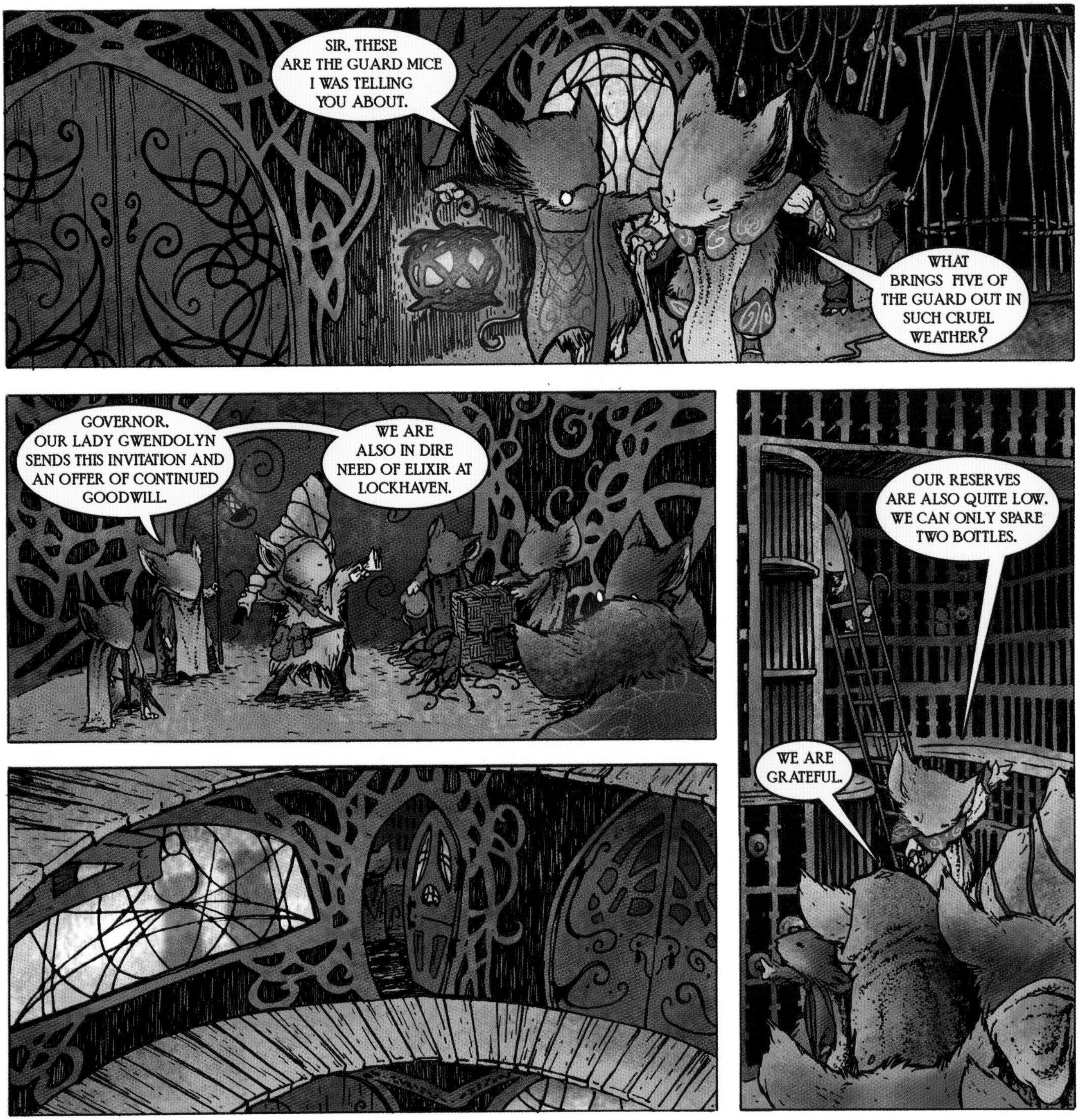
SIR, THESE ARE THE GUARD MICE I WAS TELLING YOU ABOUT.
WHAT BRINGS FIVE OF THE GUARD OUT IN SUCH CRUEL WEATHER?
GOVERNOR, OUR LADY GWENDOLYN SENDS THIS INVITATION AND AN OFFER OF CONTINUED GOODWILL.
WE ARE ALSO IN DIRE NEED OF ELIXIR AT LOCKHAVEN.
OUR RESERVES ARE ALSO QUITE LOW. WE CAN ONLY SPARE TWO BOTTLES.
WE ARE GRATEFUL.

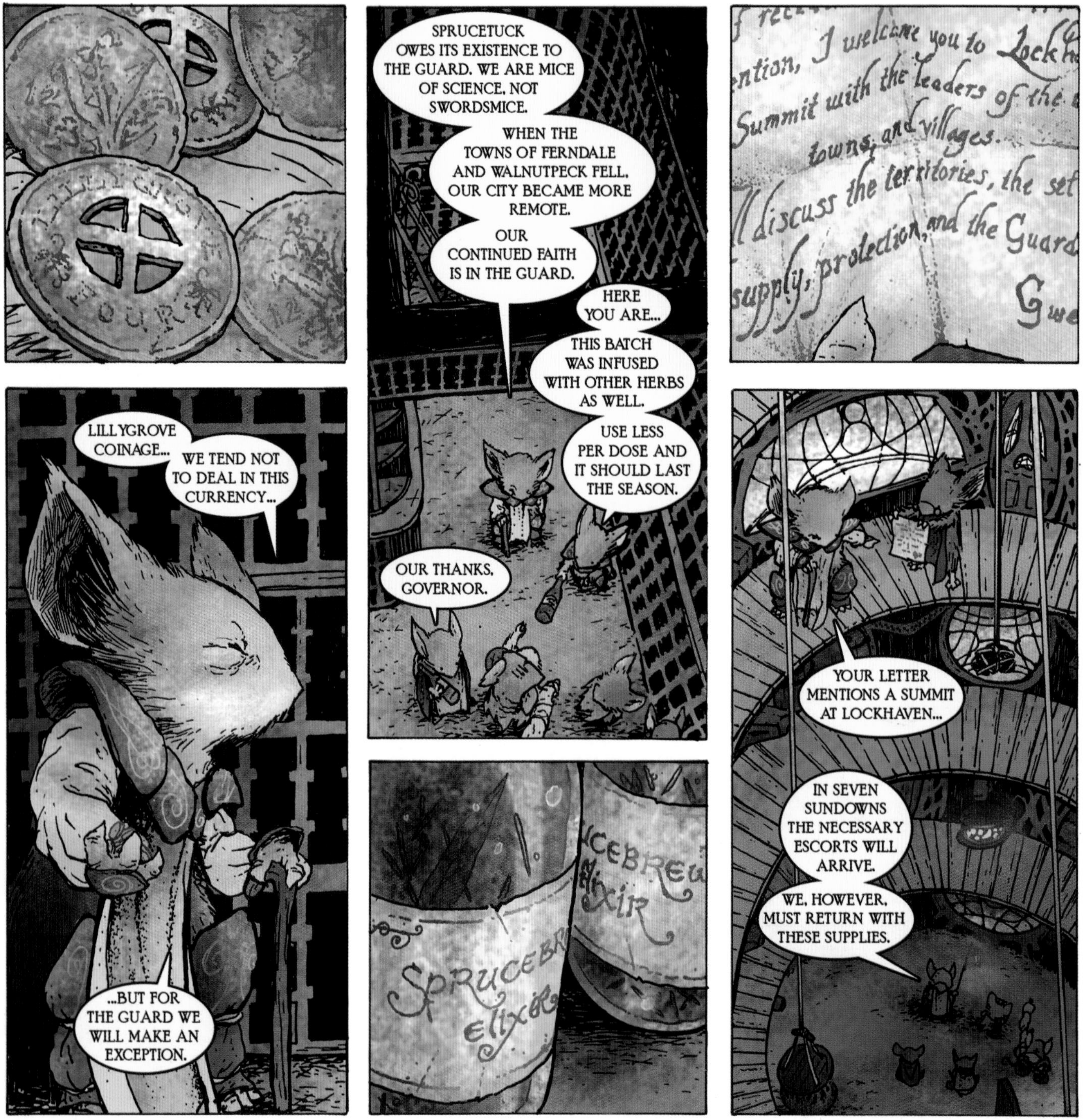
LILLYGROVE COINAGE...
WE TEND NOT TO DEAL IN THIS CURRENCY...
...BUT FOR THE GUARD WE WILL MAKE AN EXCEPTION.
SPRUCETUCK OWES ITS EXISTENCE TO THE GUARD. WE ARE MICE OF SCIENCE, NOT SWORDSMICE.
WHEN THE TOWNS OF FERNDALE AND WALNUTPECK FELL, OUR CITY BECAME MORE REMOTE.
OUR CONTINUED FAITH IS IN THE GUARD.
HERE YOU ARE...
THIS BATCH WAS INFUSED WITH OTHER HERBS AS WELL.
USE LESS PER DOSE AND IT SHOULD LAST THE SEASON.
OUR THANKS, GOVERNOR.
Sprucebrew Elixir
I welcome you to
Summit with the leaders of the
towns, and villages.
discuss the territories, the
supply, protection, and the
YOUR LETTER MENTIONS A SUMMIT AT LOCKHAVEN...
IN SEVEN SUNDOWNS THE NECESSARY ESCORTS WILL ARRIVE.
WE, HOWEVER, MUST RETURN WITH THESE SUPPLIES.

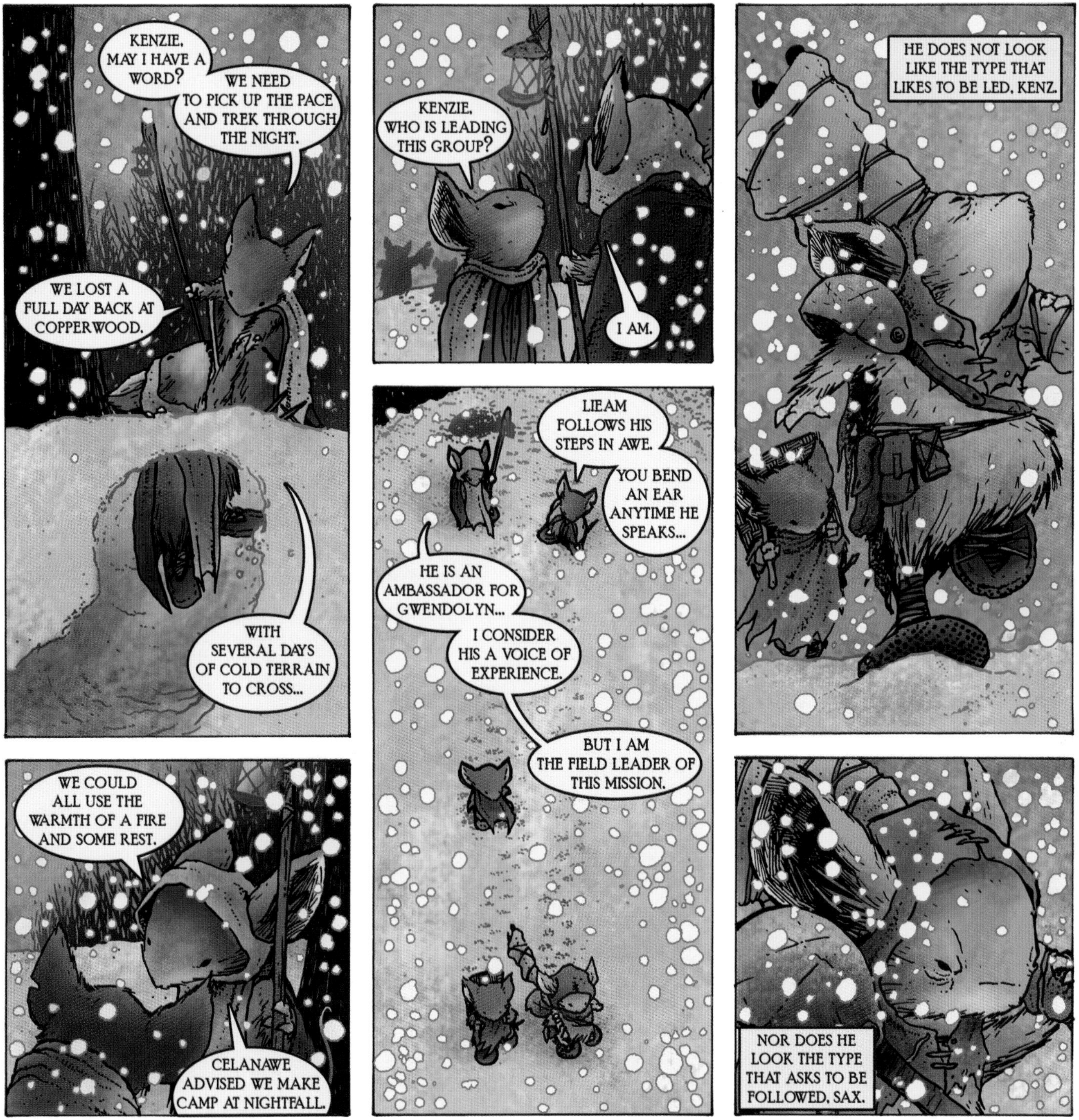
KENZIE, MAY I HAVE A WORD?
WE NEED TO PICK UP THE PACE AND TREK THROUGH THE NIGHT.
WE LOST A FULL DAY BACK AT COPPERWOOD.
WITH SEVERAL DAYS OF COLD TERRAIN TO CROSS...
WE COULD ALL USE THE WARMTH OF A FIRE AND SOME REST.
CELANAWE ADVISED WE MAKE CAMP AT NIGHTFALL.
KENZIE, WHO IS LEADING THIS GROUP?
I AM.
LIEAM FOLLOWS HIS STEPS IN AWE.
YOU BEND AN EAR ANYTIME HE SPEAKS...
HE IS AN AMBASSADOR FOR GWENDOLYN...
I CONSIDER HIS A VOICE OF EXPERIENCE.
BUT I AM THE FIELD LEADER OF THIS MISSION.
HE DOES NOT LOOK LIKE THE TYPE THAT LIKES TO BE LED, KENZ.
NOR DOES HE LOOK THE TYPE THAT ASKS TO BE FOLLOWED, SAX.

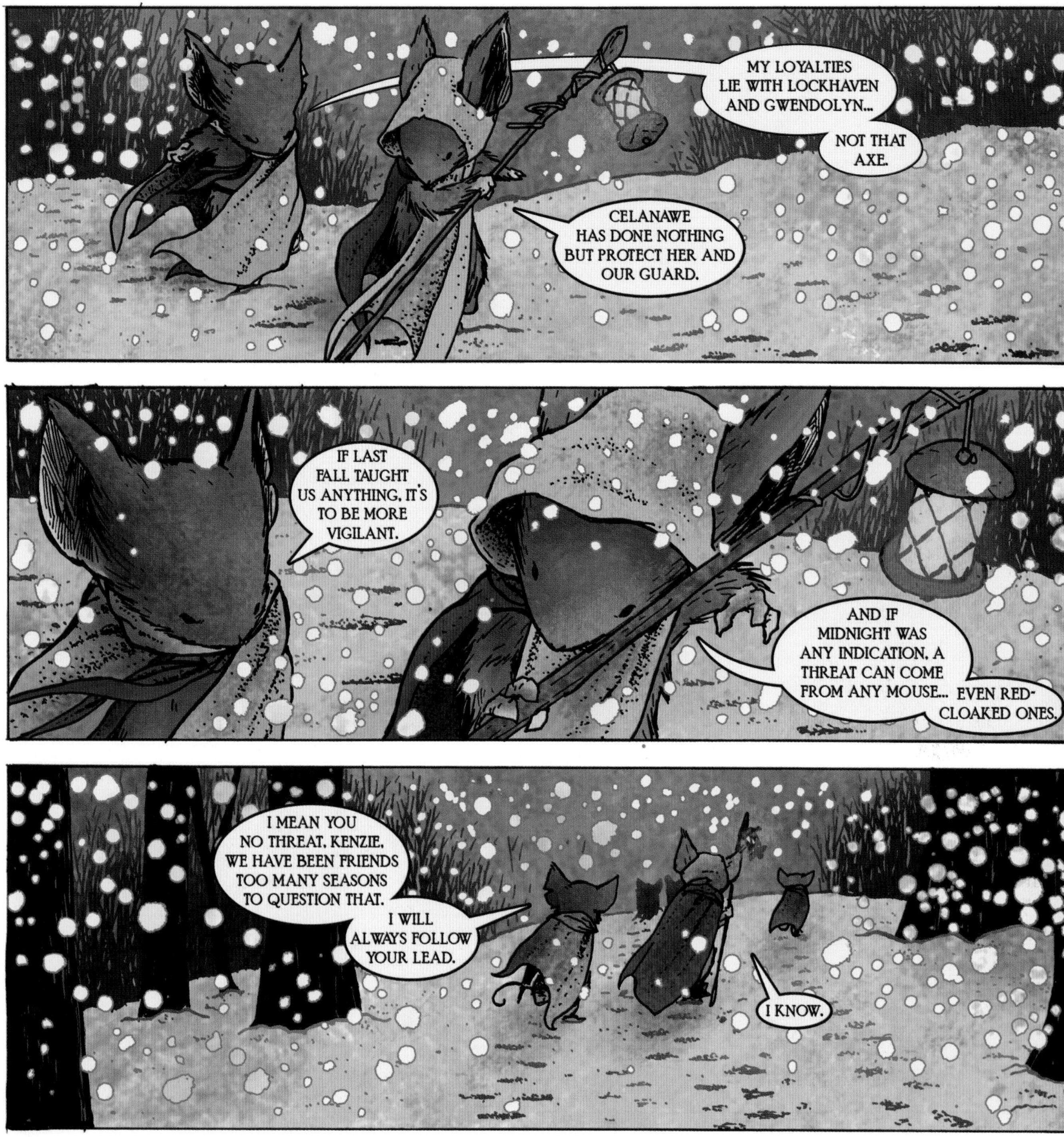
MY LOYALTIES LIE WITH LOCKHAVEN AND GWENDOLYN...
NOT THAT AXE.
CELANAWE HAS DONE NOTHING BUT PROTECT HER AND OUR GUARD.
IF LAST FALL TAUGHT US ANYTHING, IT'S TO BE MORE VIGILANT.
AND IF MIDNIGHT WAS ANY INDICATION, A THREAT CAN COME FROM ANY MOUSE...
EVEN RED-CLOAKED ONES.
I MEAN YOU NO THREAT, KENZIE. WE HAVE BEEN FRIENDS TOO MANY SEASONS TO QUESTION THAT.
I WILL ALWAYS FOLLOW YOUR LEAD.
I KNOW.

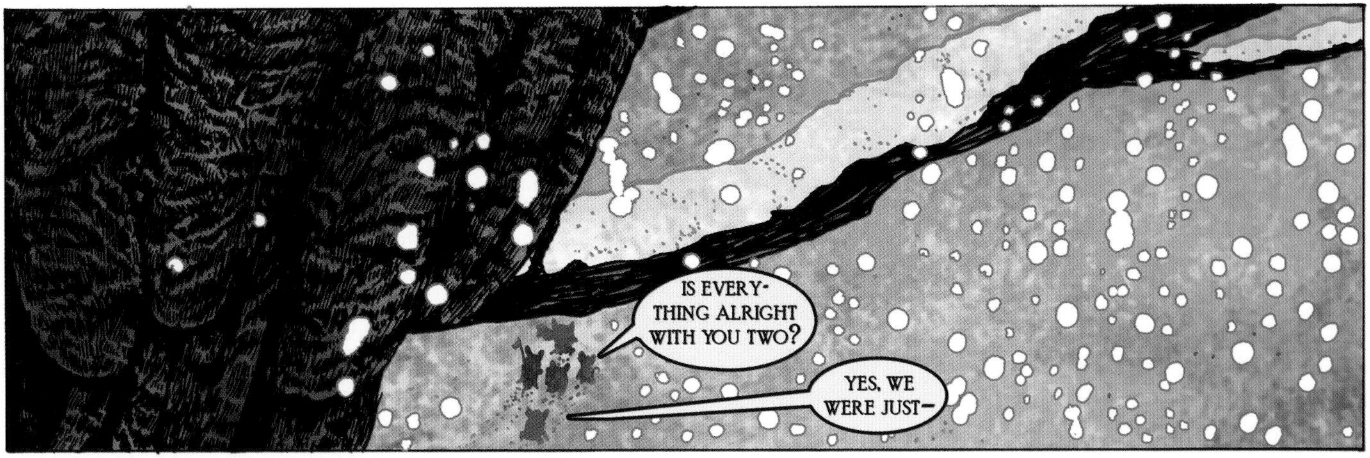
IS EVERY-THING ALRIGHT WITH YOU TWO?
YES, WE WERE JUST–

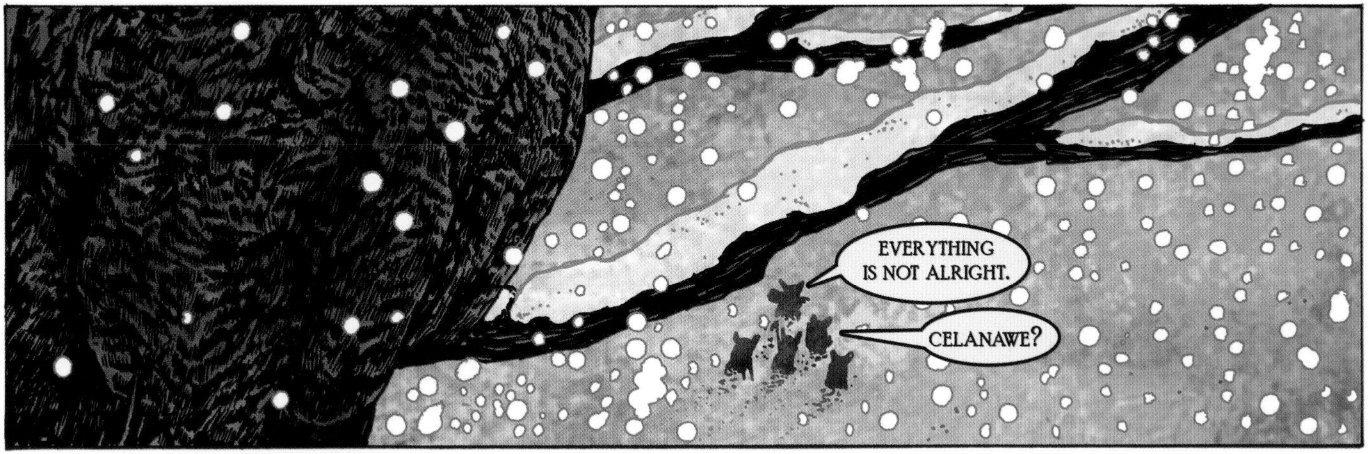
EVERYTHING IS NOT ALRIGHT.
CELANAWE?

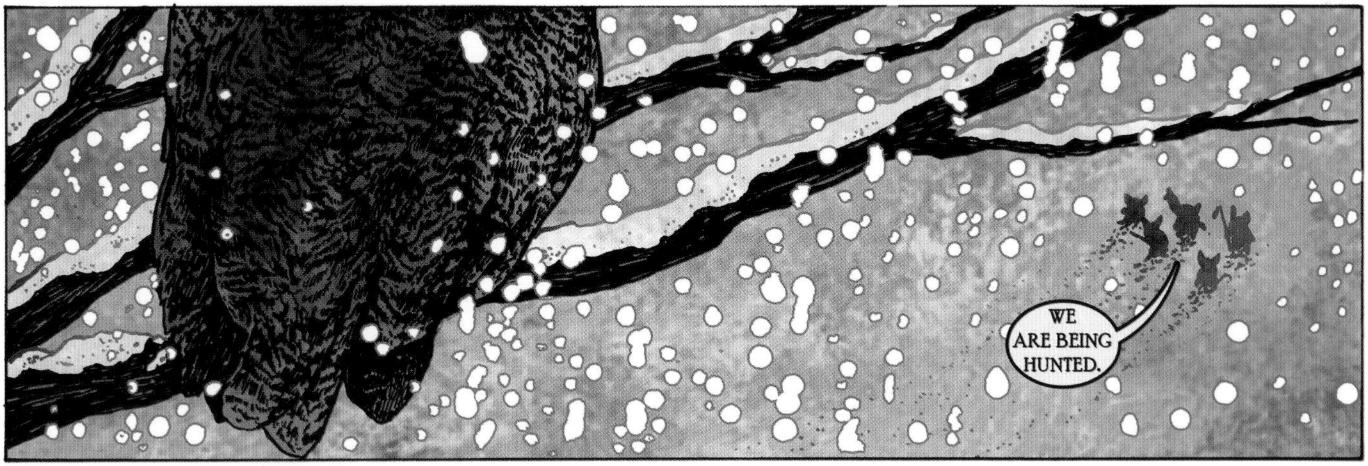
WE ARE BEING HUNTED.

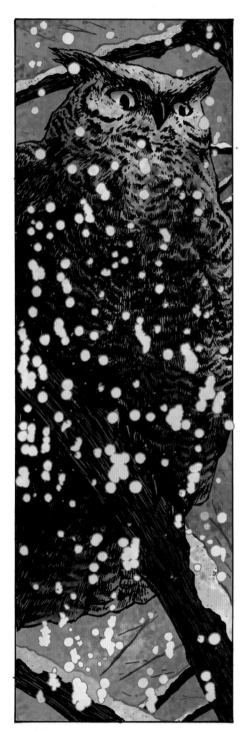

DRAW YOUR WEAPONS.

AND STAY TOGETHER.

SADIE! IT'LL PICK US OFF ONE AT A TIME IF WE SCATTER!

I DON'T INTEND TO LET IT GET THAT CLOSE...

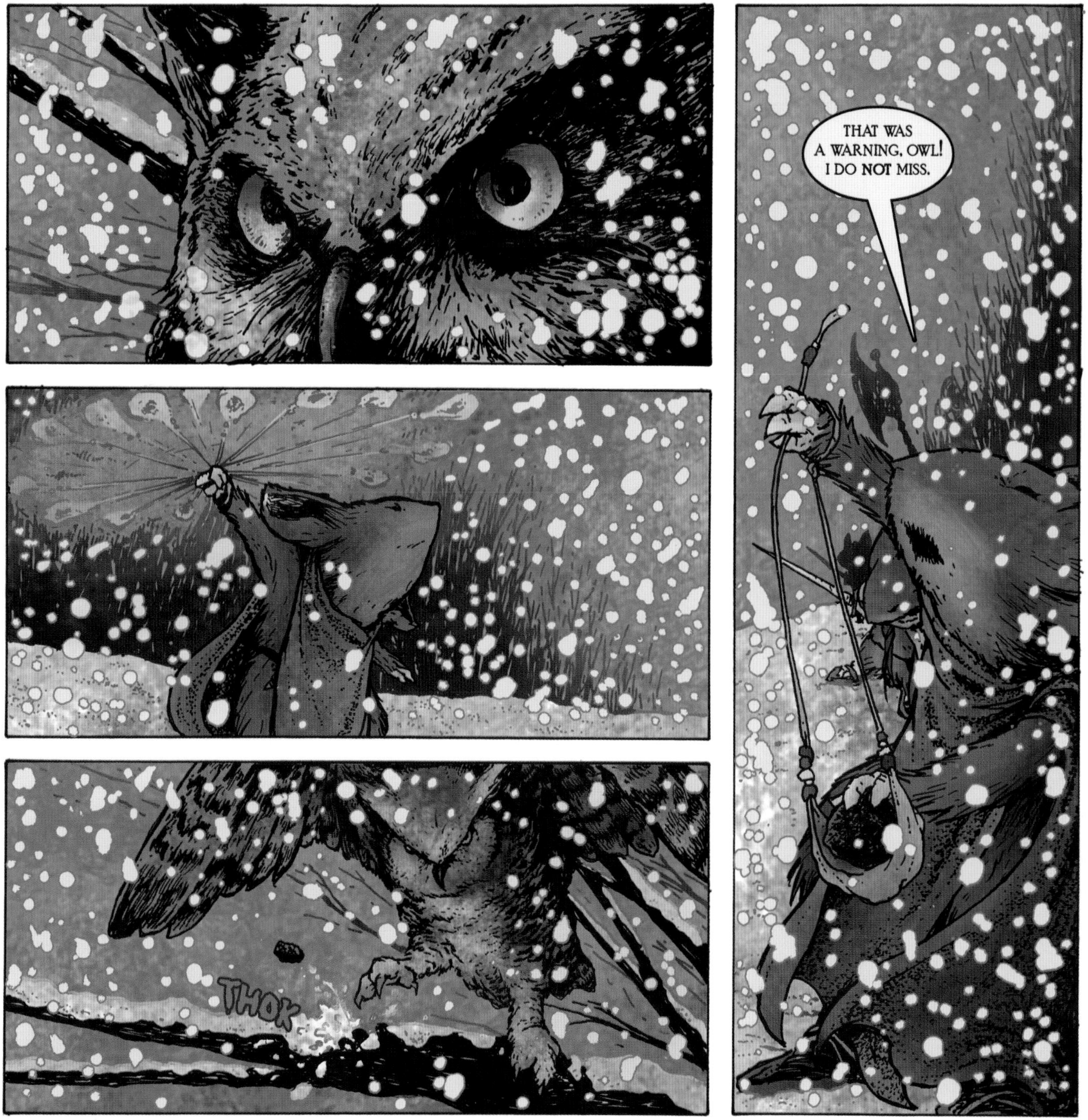
THOK
THAT WAS A WARNING, OWL! I DO NOT MISS.

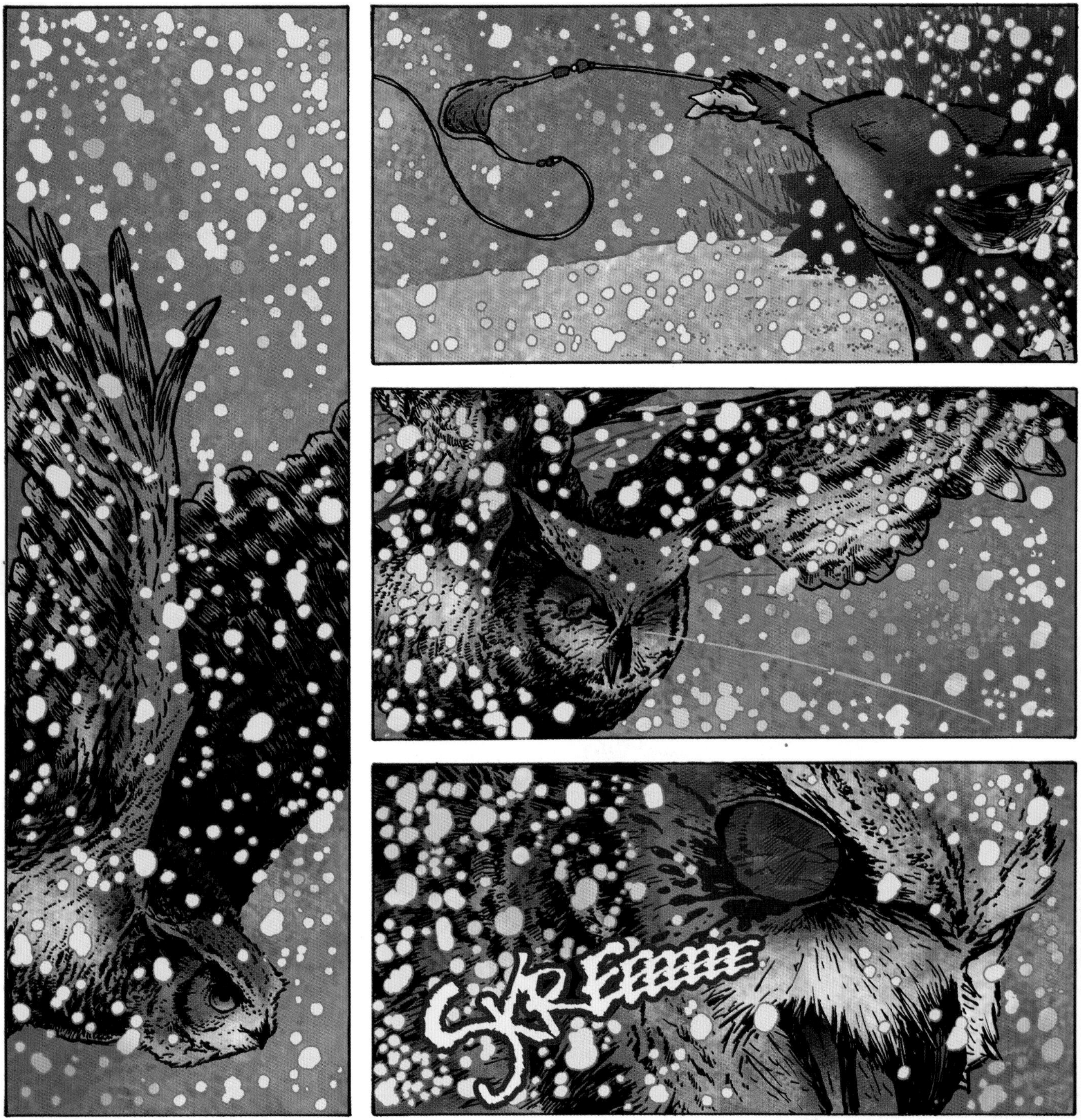
SKREEEEEEE

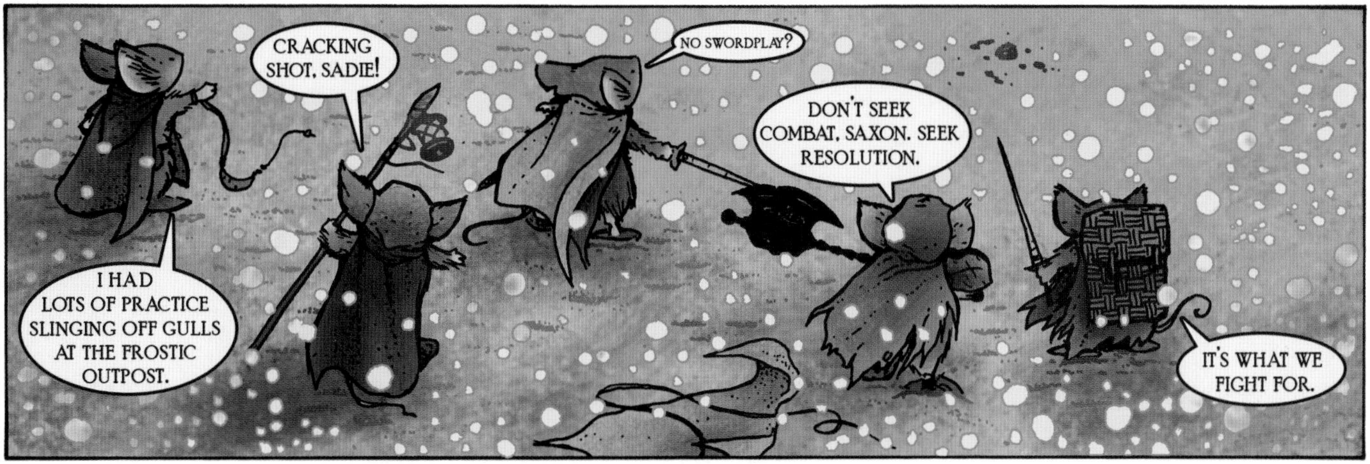
CRACKING SHOT, SADIE!
I HAD LOTS OF PRACTICE SLINGING OFF GULLS AT THE FROSTIC OUTPOST.
NO SWORDPLAY?
DON'T SEEK COMBAT, SAXON. SEEK RESOLUTION.
IT'S WHAT WE FIGHT FOR.

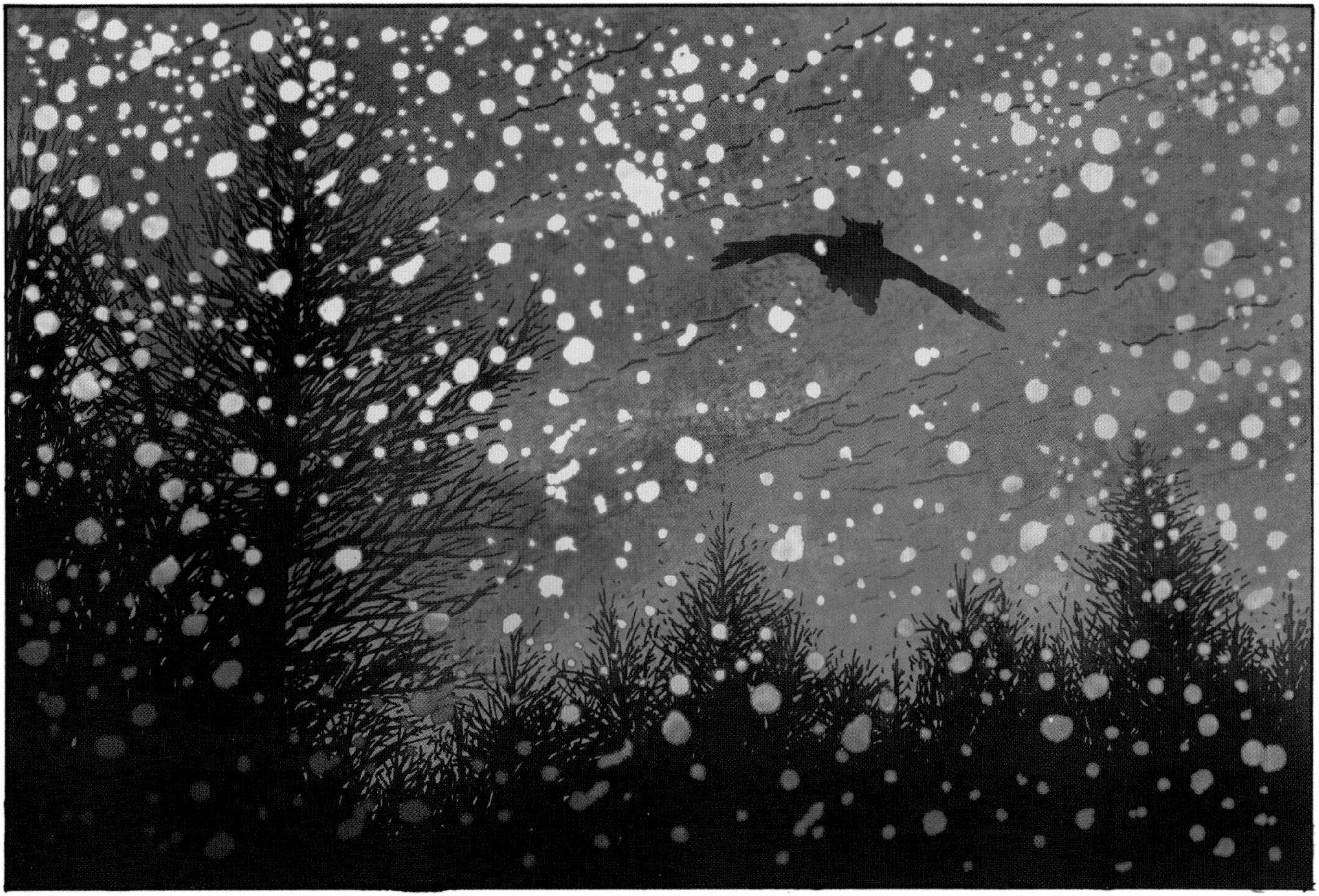

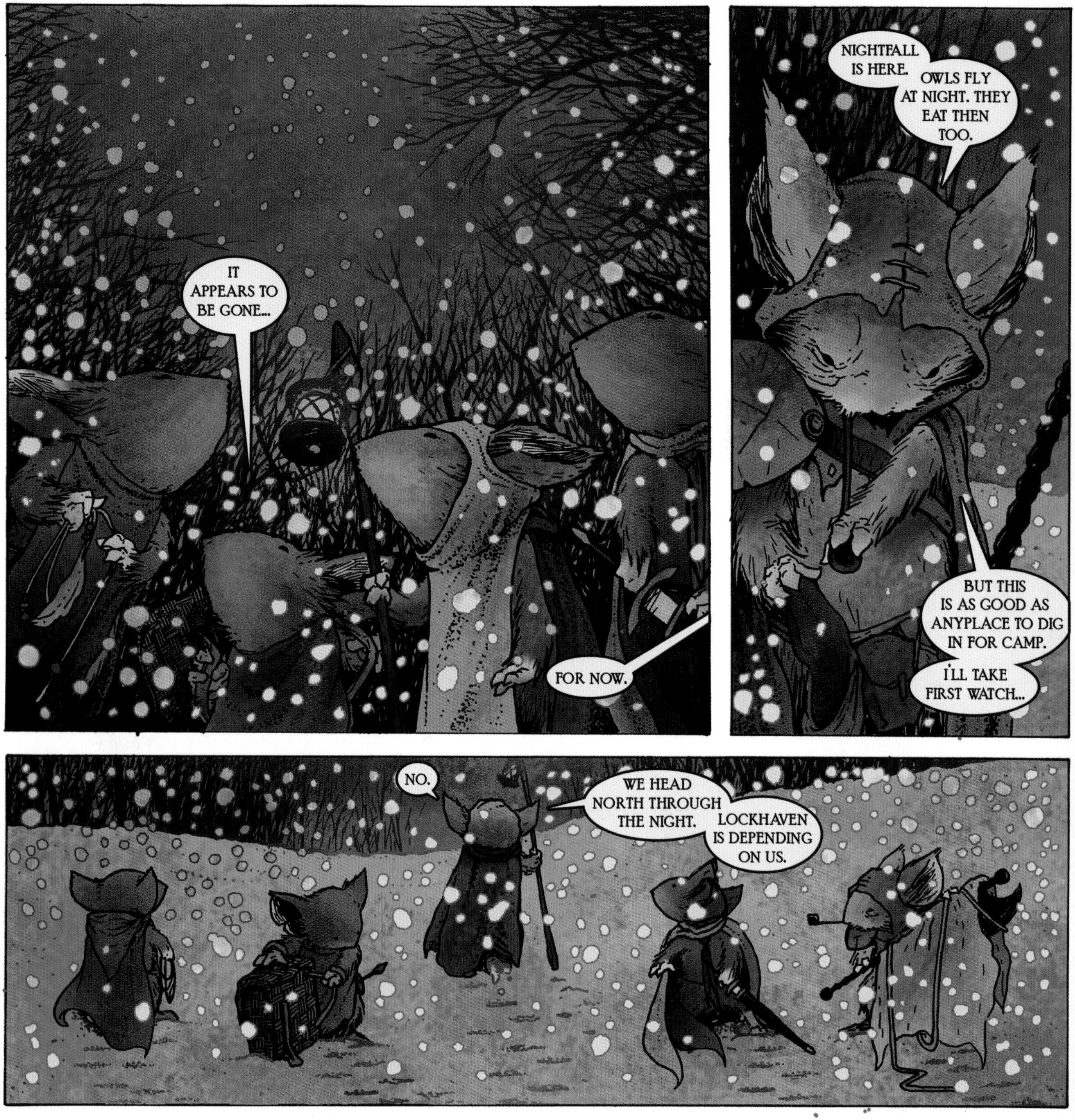
IT APPEARS TO BE GONE...
FOR NOW.
NIGHTFALL IS HERE.
OWLS FLY AT NIGHT. THEY EAT THEN TOO.
BUT THIS IS AS GOOD AS ANYPLACE TO DIG IN FOR CAMP.
I'LL TAKE FIRST WATCH...
NO.
WE HEAD NORTH THROUGH THE NIGHT.
LOCKHAVEN IS DEPENDING ON US.

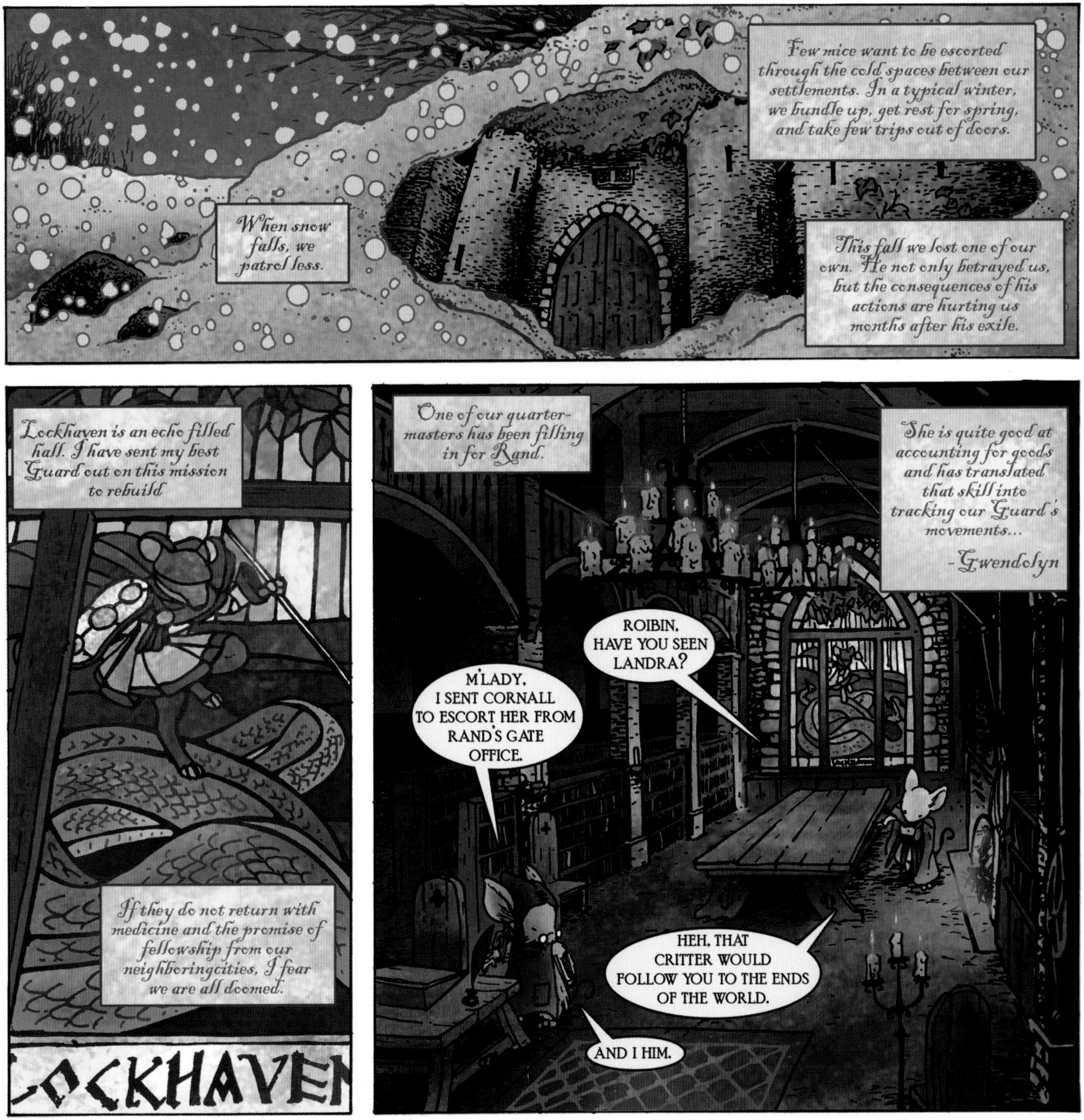
Few mice want to be escorted through the cold spaces between our settlements. In a typical winter, we bundle up, get rest for spring, and take few trips out of doors.
When snow falls, we patrol less.
This fall we lost one of our own. He not only betrayed us, but the consequences of his actions are hurting us months after his exile.
Lockhaven is an echo filled hall. I have sent my best Guard out on this mission to rebuild
If they do not return with medicine and the promise of fellowship from our neighboringcities, I fear we are all doomed.
LOCKHAVEN
One of our quartermasters has been filling in for Rand.
She is quite good at accounting for goods and has translated that skill into tracking our Guard's movements...
-Gwendolyn
ROIBIN, HAVE YOU SEEN LANDRA?
M'LADY, I SENT CORNALL TO ESCORT HER FROM RAND'S GATE OFFICE.
HEH, THAT CRITTER WOULD FOLLOW YOU TO THE ENDS OF THE WORLD.
AND I HIM.

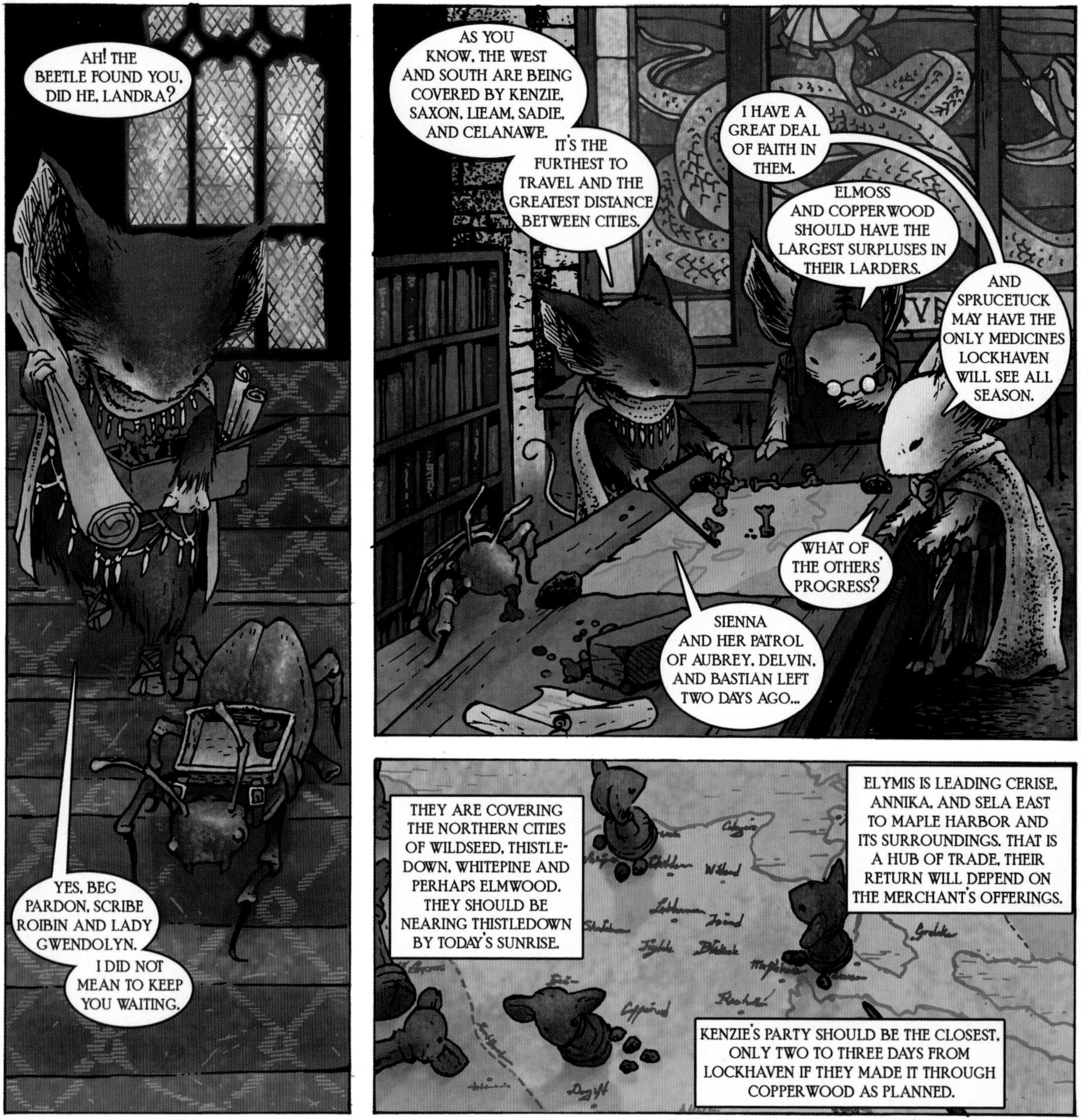
AH! THE BEETLE FOUND YOU, DID HE, LANDRA?
YES, BEG PARDON, SCRIBE ROIBIN AND LADY GWENDOLYN.
I DID NOT MEAN TO KEEP YOU WAITING.
AS YOU KNOW, THE WEST AND SOUTH ARE BEING COVERED BY KENZIE, SAXON, LIEAM, SADIE, AND CELANAWE.
IT'S THE FURTHEST TO TRAVEL AND THE GREATEST DISTANCE BETWEEN CITIES.
I HAVE A GREAT DEAL OF FAITH IN THEM.
ELMOSS AND COPPERWOOD SHOULD HAVE THE LARGEST SURPLUSES IN THEIR LARDERS.
AND SPRUCETUCK MAY HAVE THE ONLY MEDICINES LOCKHAVEN WILL SEE ALL SEASON.
WHAT OF THE OTHERS' PROGRESS?
SIENNA AND HER PATROL OF AUBREY, DELVIN, AND BASTIAN LEFT TWO DAYS AGO...
THEY ARE COVERING THE NORTHERN CITIES OF WILDSEED, THISTLE-DOWN, WHITEPINE AND PERHAPS ELMWOOD. THEY SHOULD BE NEARING THISTLEDOWN BY TODAY'S SUNRISE.
ELYMIS IS LEADING CERISE, ANNIKA, AND SELA EAST TO MAPLE HARBOR AND ITS SURROUNDINGS. THAT IS A HUB OF TRADE, THEIR RETURN WILL DEPEND ON THE MERCHANT'S OFFERINGS.
KENZIE'S PARTY SHOULD BE THE CLOSEST, ONLY TWO TO THREE DAYS FROM LOCKHAVEN IF THEY MADE IT THROUGH COPPERWOOD AS PLANNED.

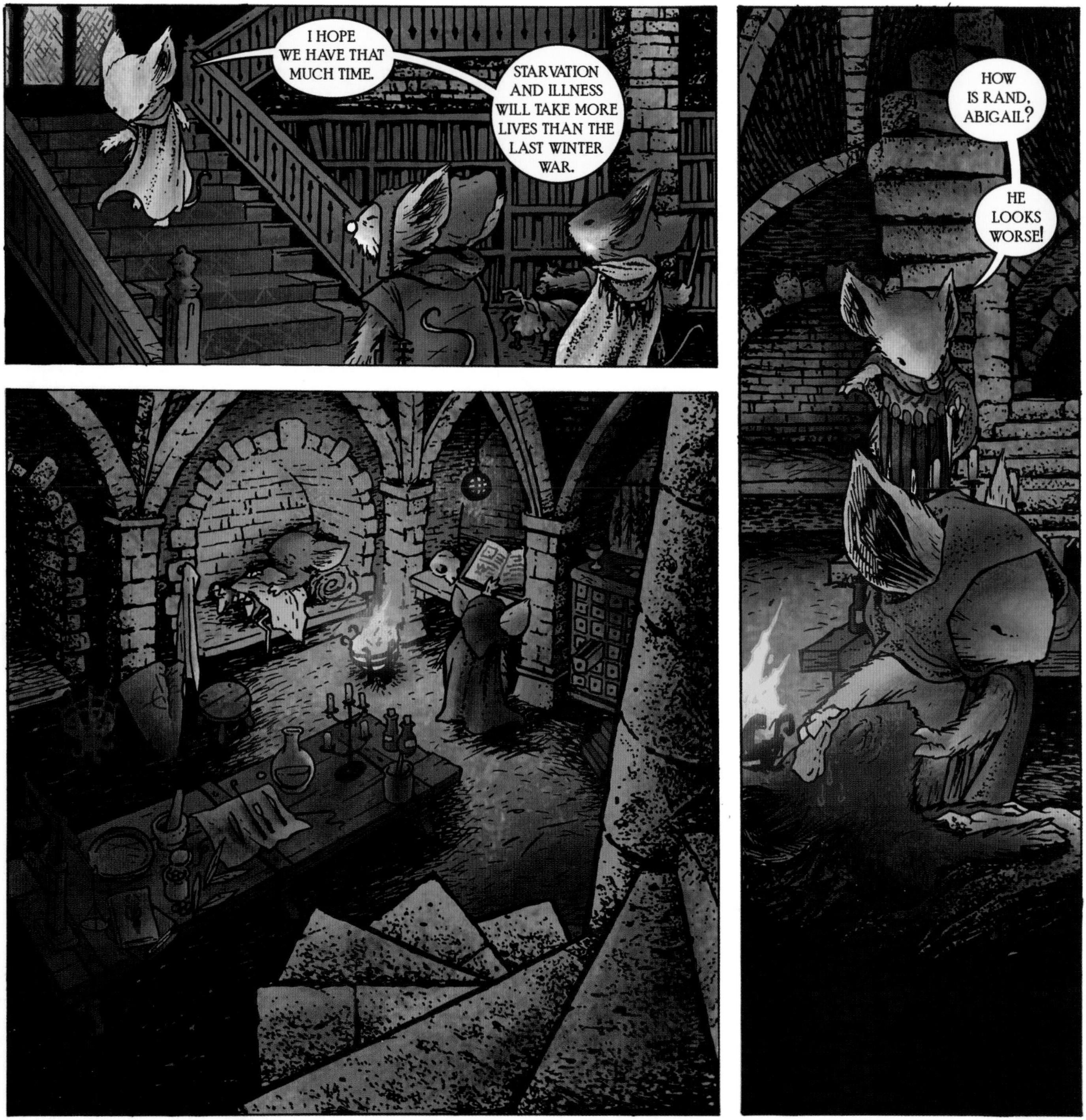
I HOPE WE HAVE THAT MUCH TIME.
STARVATION AND ILLNESS WILL TAKE MORE LIVES THAN THE LAST WINTER WAR.
HOW IS RAND, ABIGAIL?
HE LOOKS WORSE!

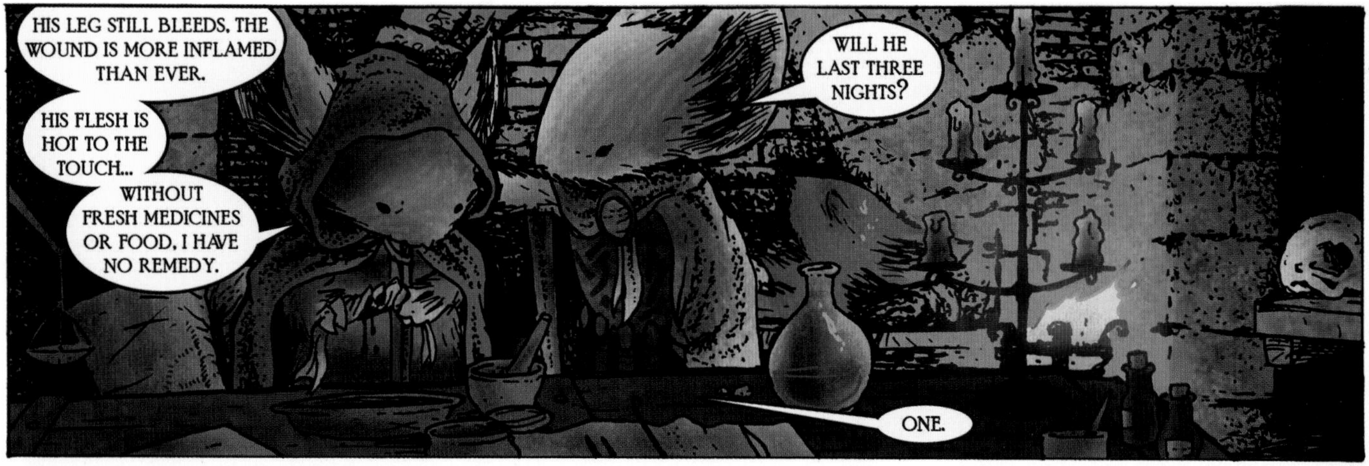
HIS LEG STILL BLEEDS. THE WOUND IS MORE INFLAMED THAN EVER.
HIS FLESH IS HOT TO THE TOUCH...
WITHOUT FRESH MEDICINES OR FOOD, I HAVE NO REMEDY.
WILL HE LAST THREE NIGHTS?
ONE.

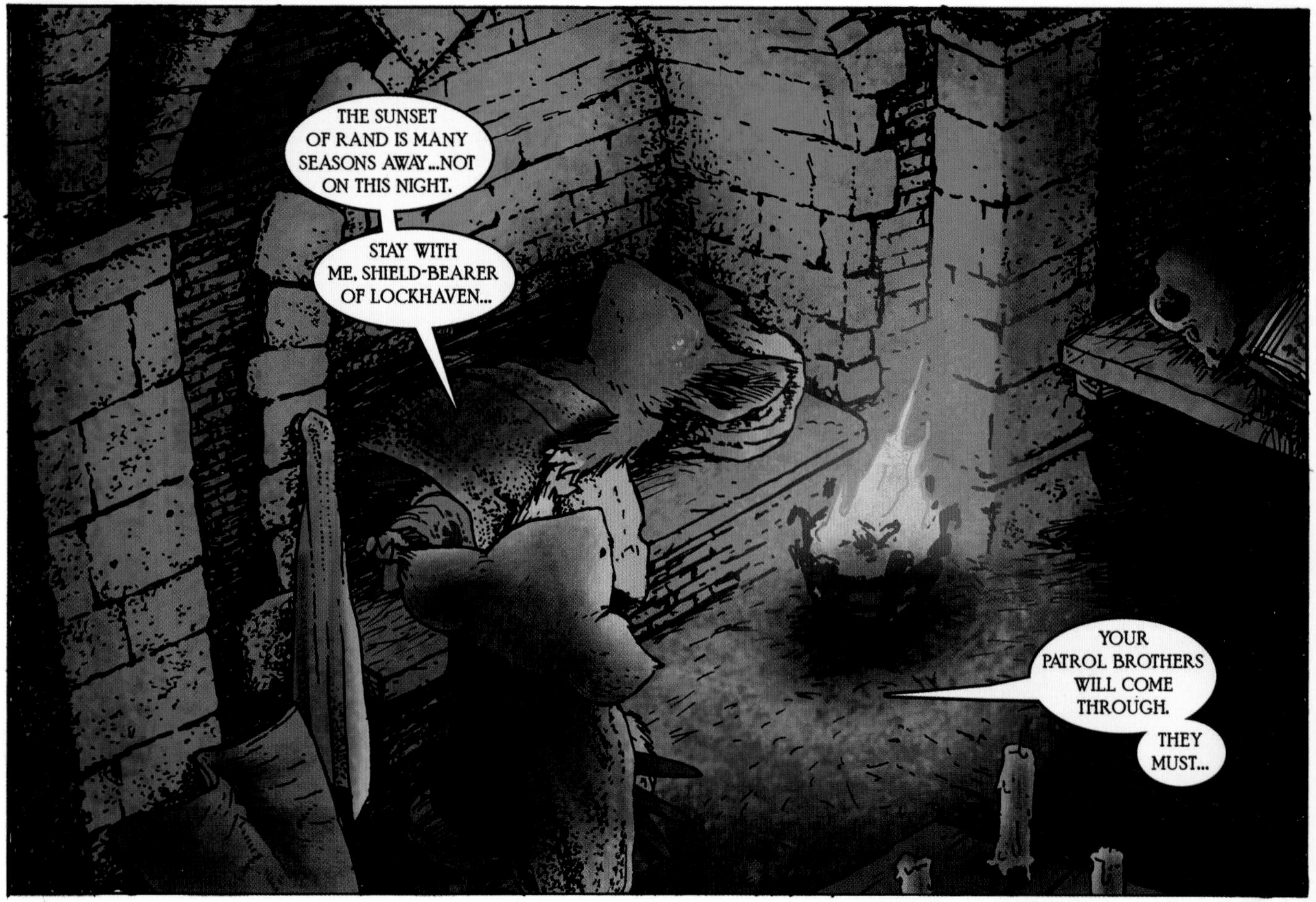
THE SUNSET OF RAND IS MANY SEASONS AWAY...NOT ON THIS NIGHT.
STAY WITH ME, SHIELD-BEARER OF LOCKHAVEN...
YOUR PATROL BROTHERS WILL COME THROUGH.
THEY MUST...

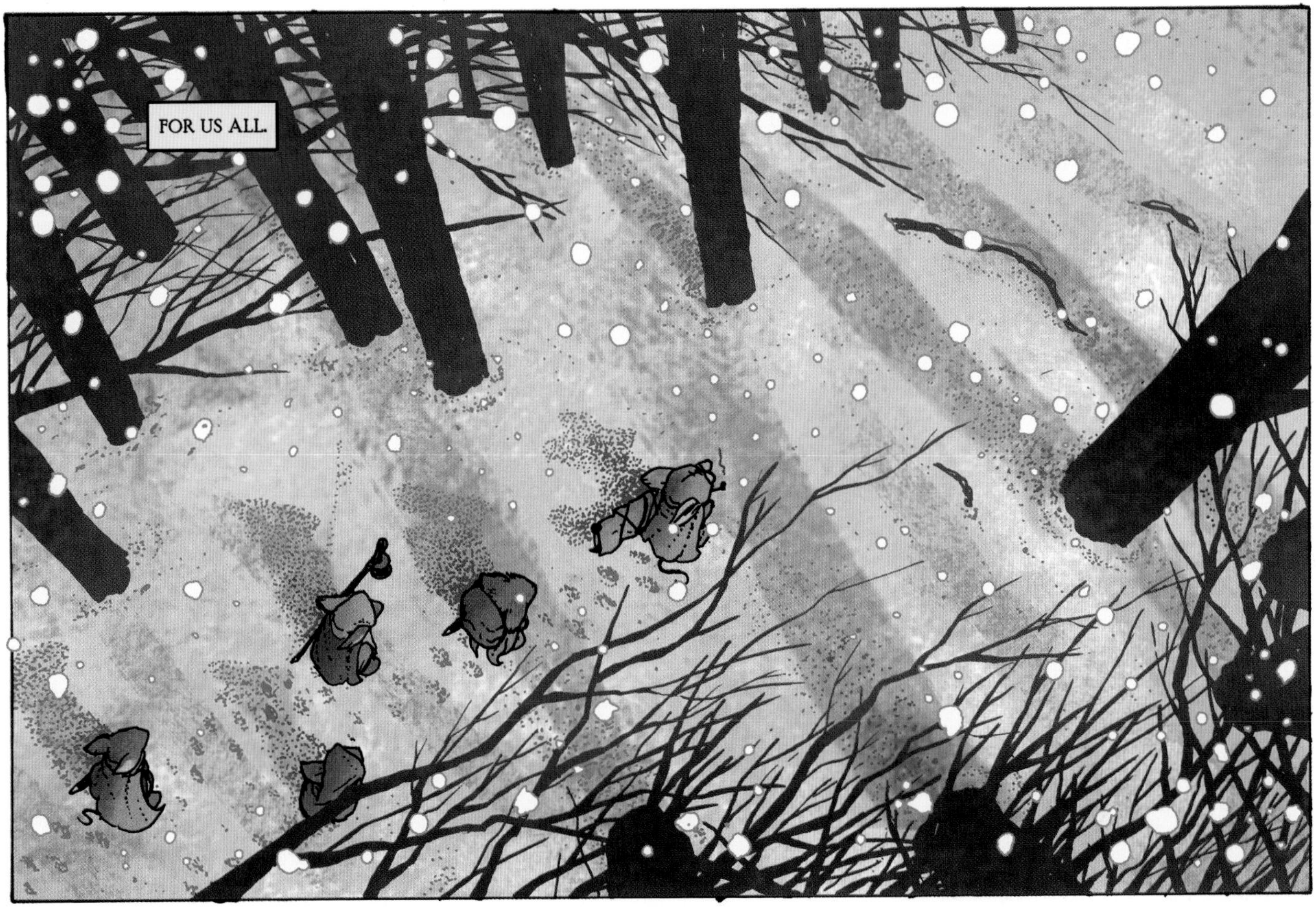
FOR US ALL.

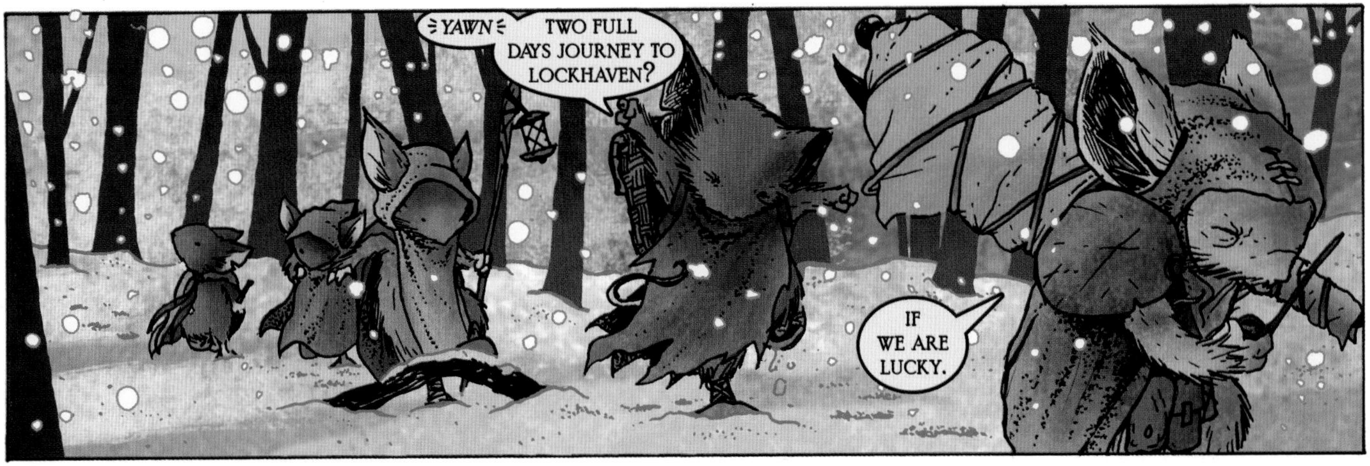
YAWN
TWO FULL DAYS JOURNEY TO LOCKHAVEN?
IF WE ARE LUCKY.

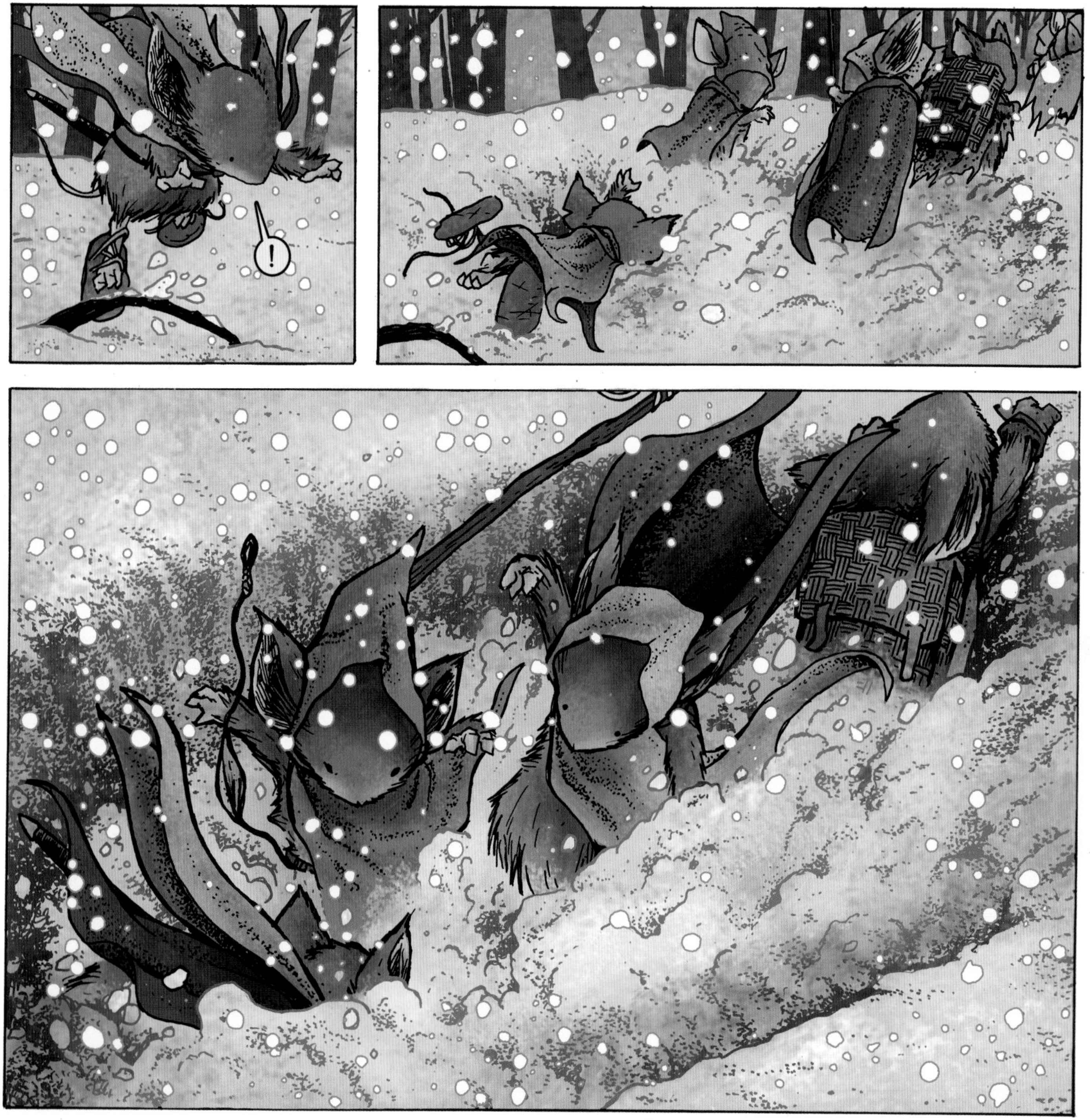
!

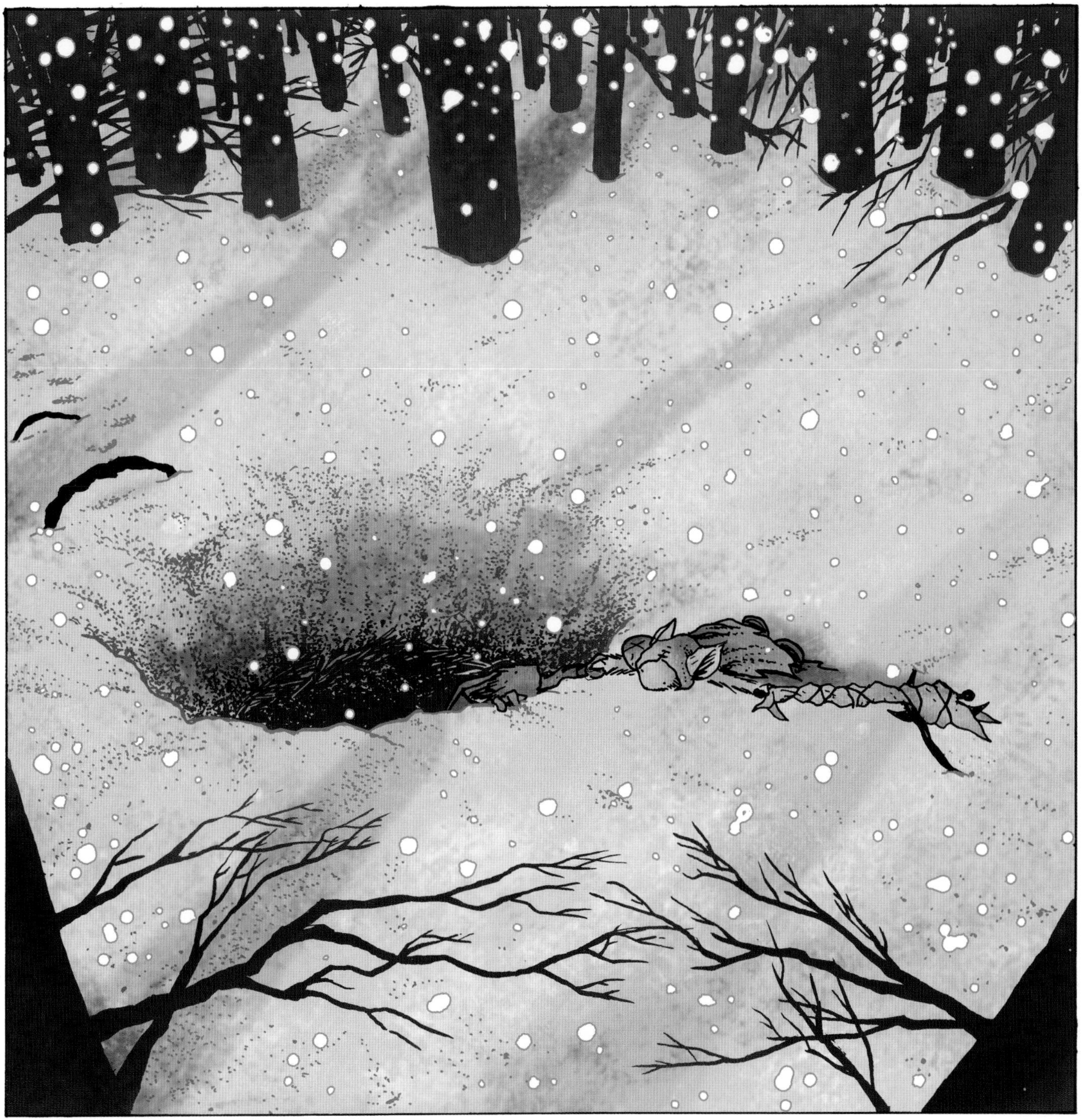

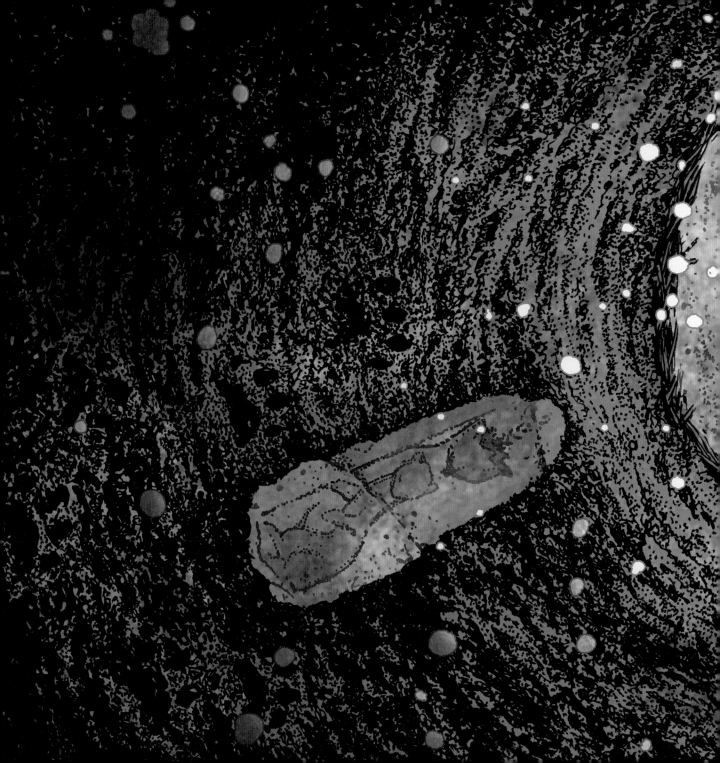

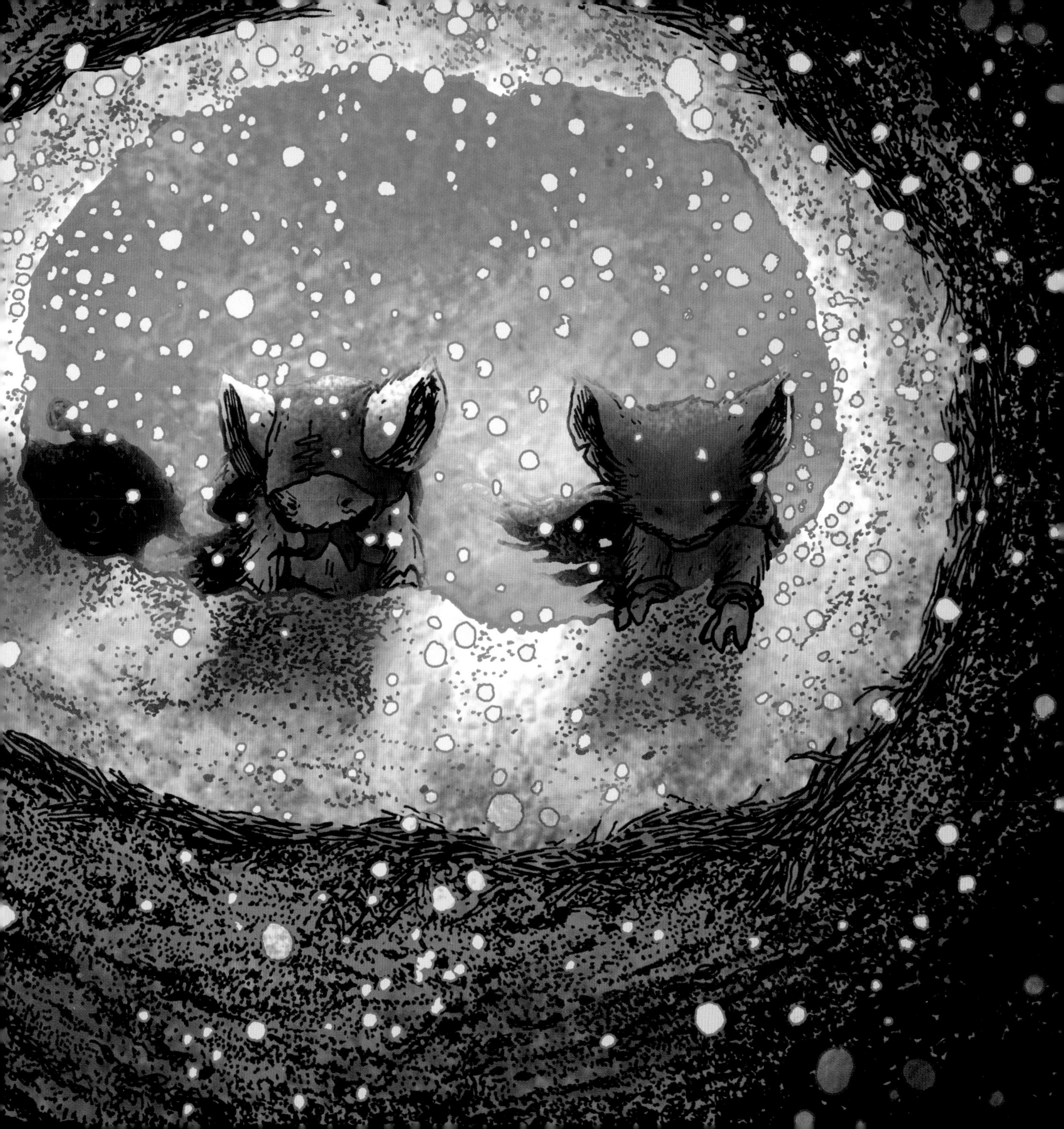

CHAPTER TWO

Three parties of Guardmice left Lockhaven in hopes of gathering supplies and medicine from surrounding villages and to deliver invitations to a summit for the heads of state.

After the party led by Kenzie was attacked by a great horned owl, they suffered more hardships when the ground itself opened into a great hole swallowing the mice, preventing their timely return with supplies to Lockhaven.

"Heroes fall, heroes break, heroes bleed.
They shed bitter tears, pull themselves up, not to concede.
Often are they waylaid and frequent they mourn.
Heroes are rarely made and even more seldom born.
Not till after they die, do mice sing of their tale.
A job, a duty, a thankless obligation not to fail.
Still many a mouse think only the name is required
What becomes of them? They either quit or expire."

-"A Heroes Warning" Poem by the Scribe Roibin

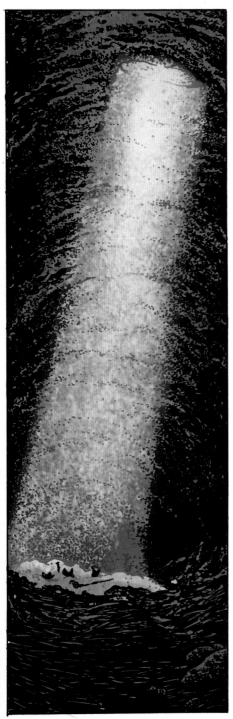
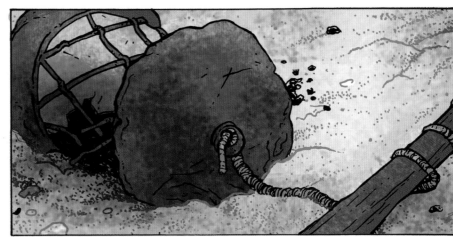

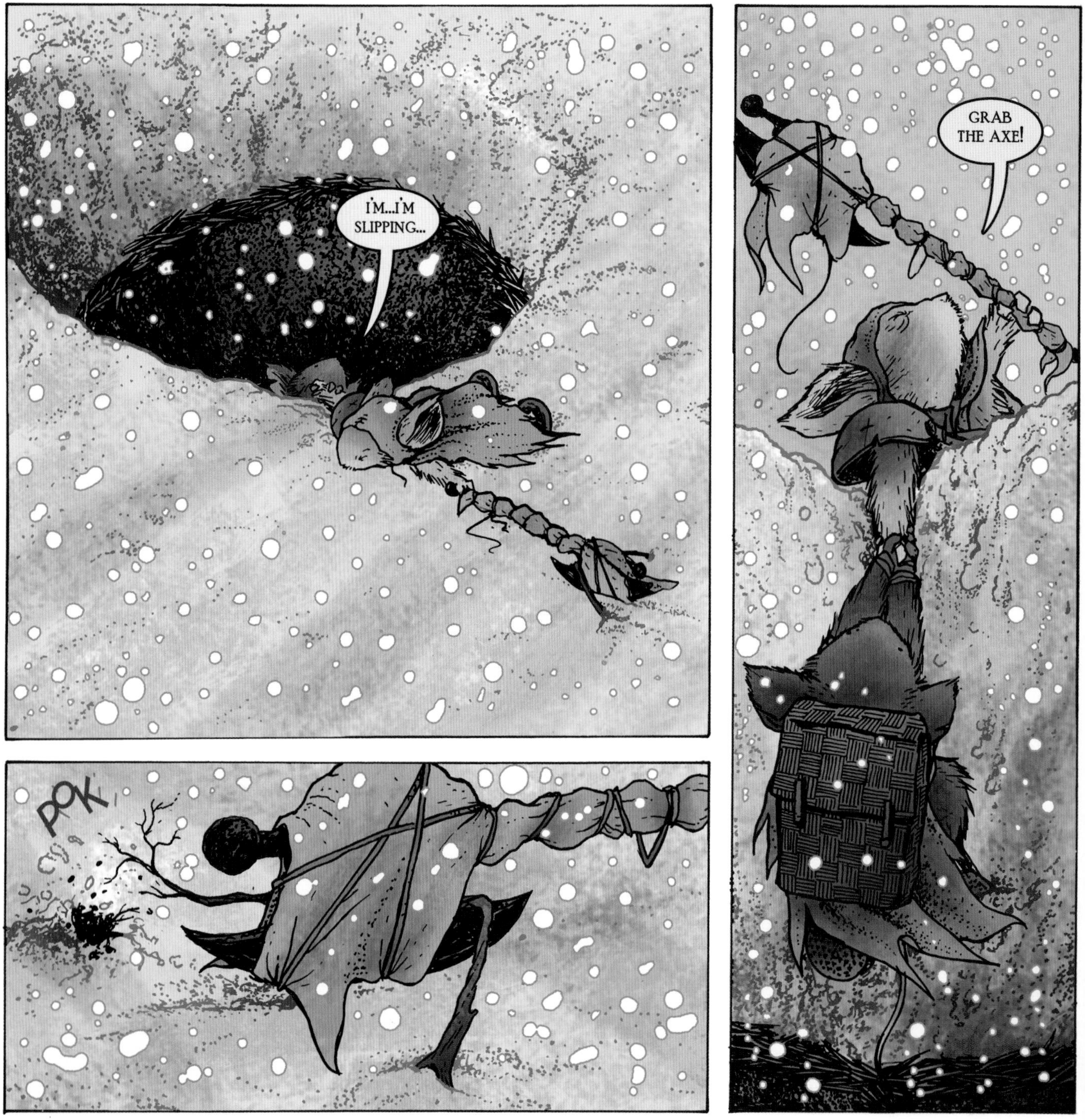
I'M...I'M SLIPPING...
GRAB THE AXE!
POK

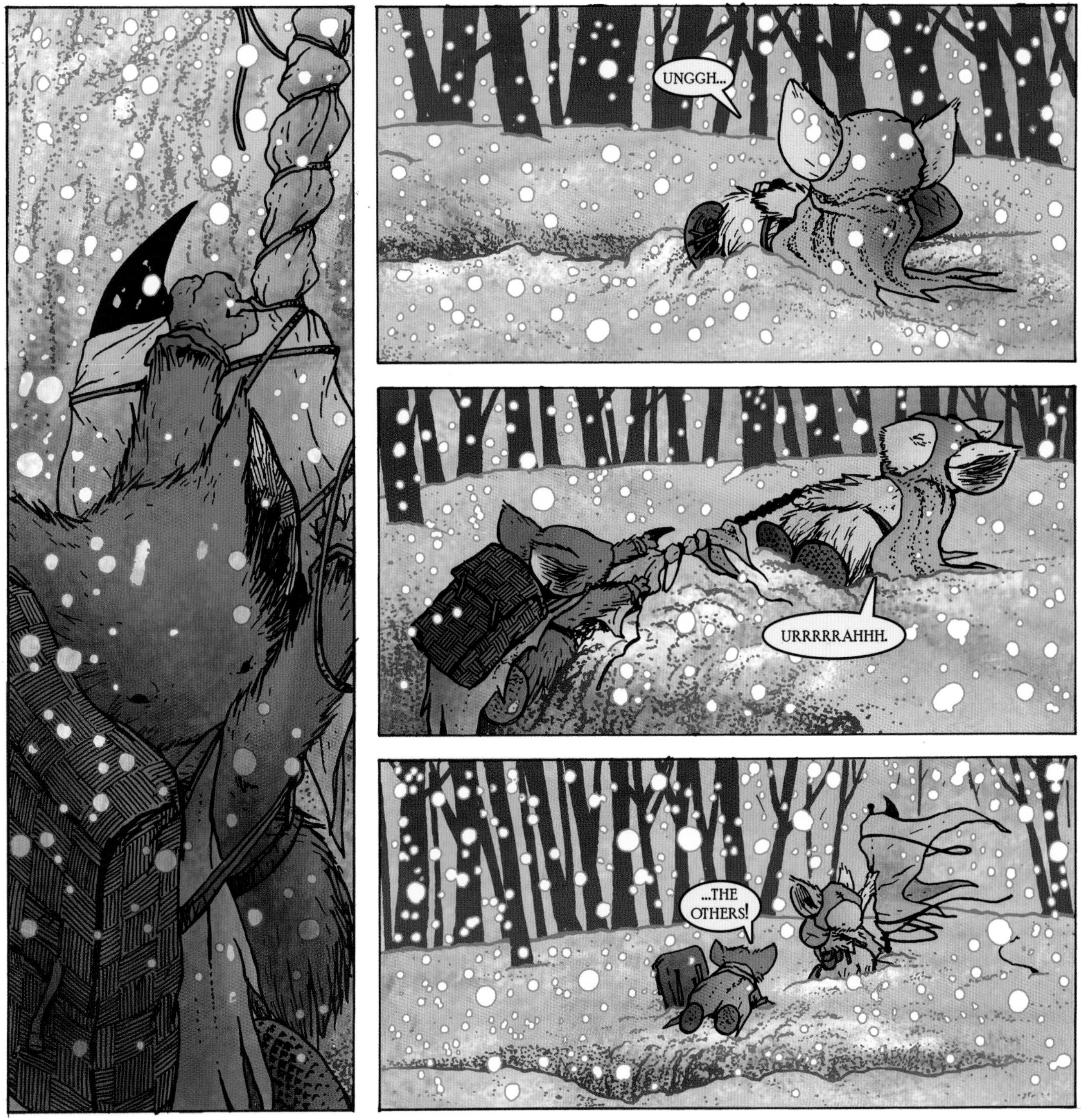
UNGGH...
URRRRRAHHH.
...THE OTHERS!

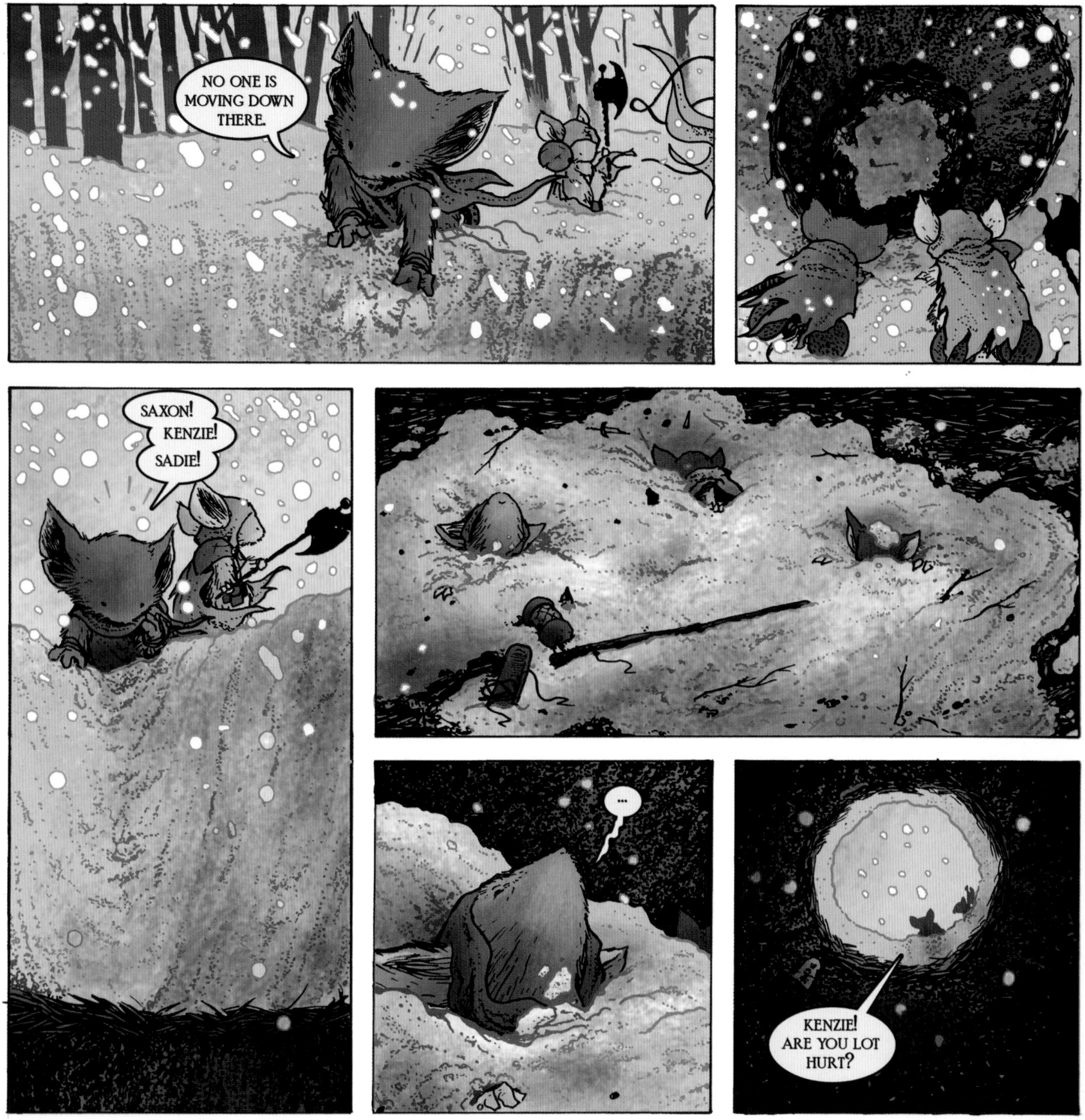
NO ONE IS MOVING DOWN THERE.
SAXON!
KENZIE!
SADIE!
...
KENZIE! ARE YOU LOT HURT?

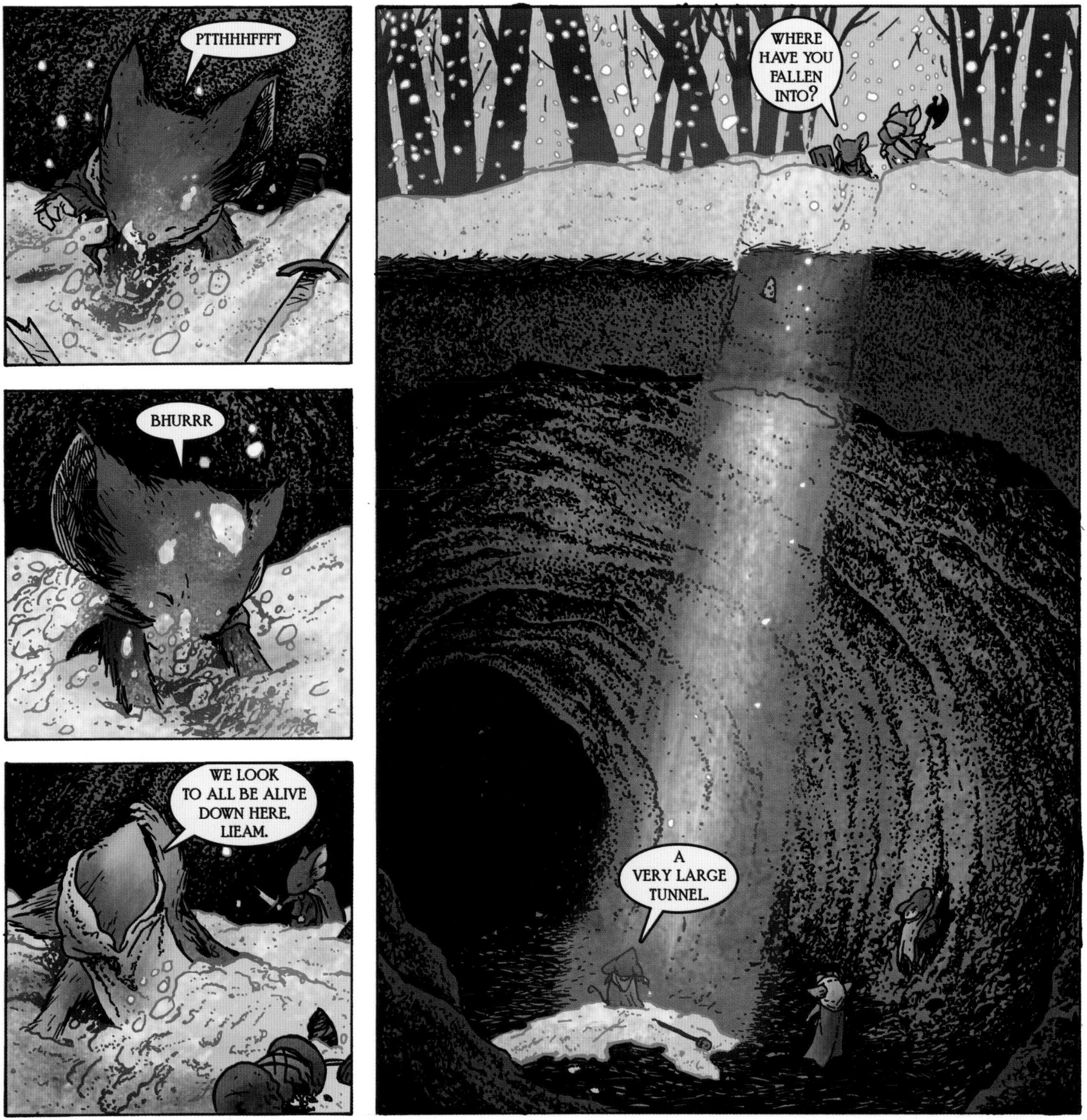
PTTHHHFFFT
BHURRR
WE LOOK TO ALL BE ALIVE DOWN HERE. LIEAM.
WHERE HAVE YOU FALLEN INTO?
A VERY LARGE TUNNEL.

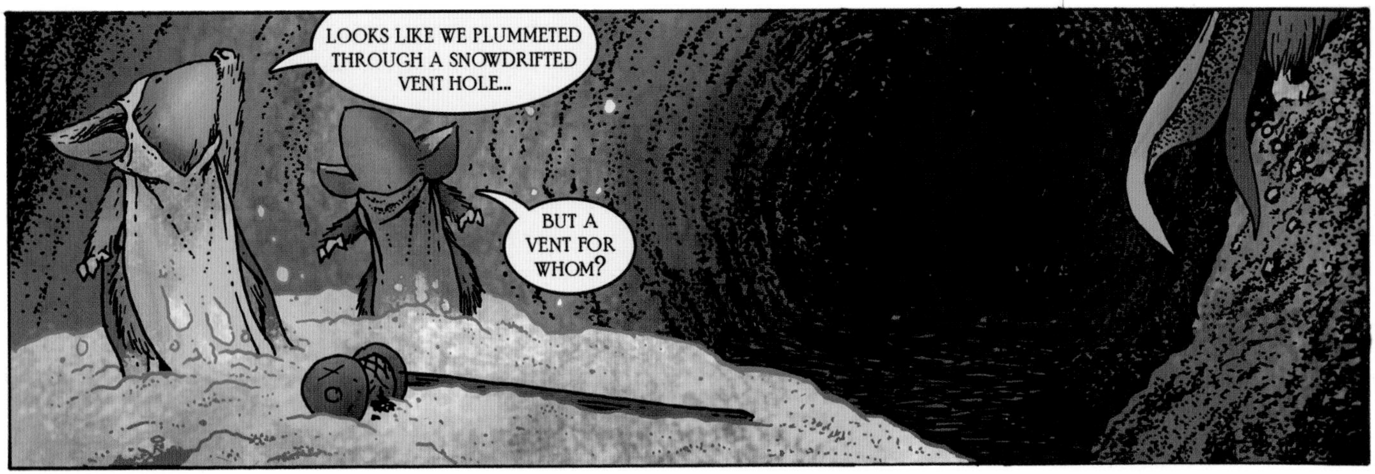
LOOKS LIKE WE PLUMMETED THROUGH A SNOWDRIFTED VENT HOLE...
BUT A VENT FOR WHOM?

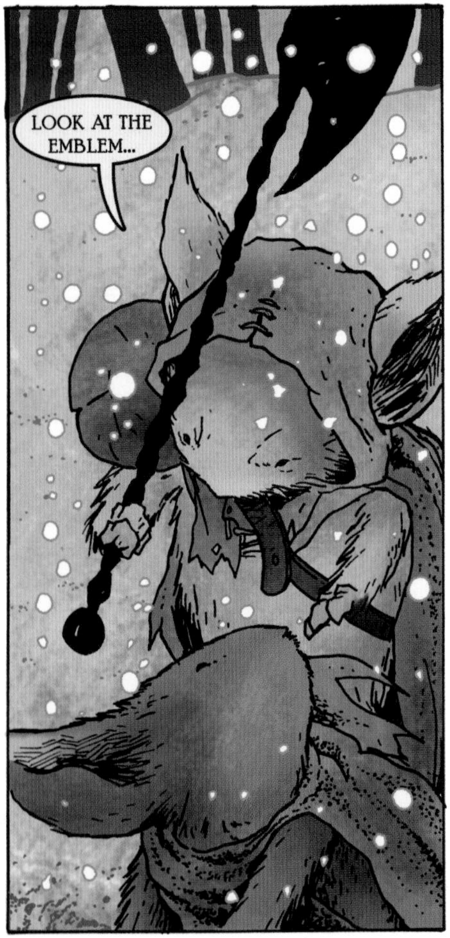
LOOK AT THE EMBLEM...

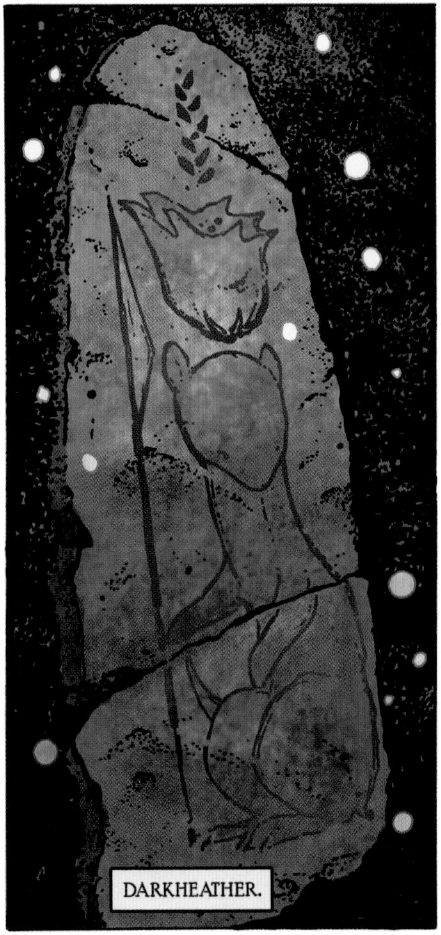
DARKHEATHER.

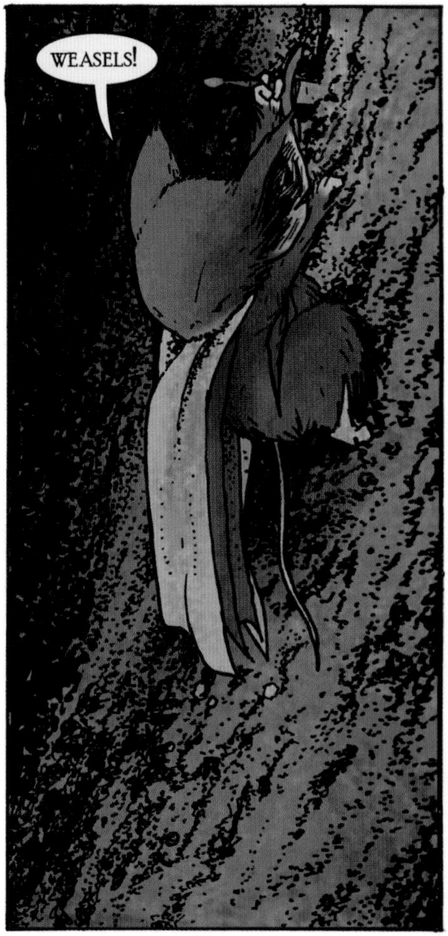
WEASELS!

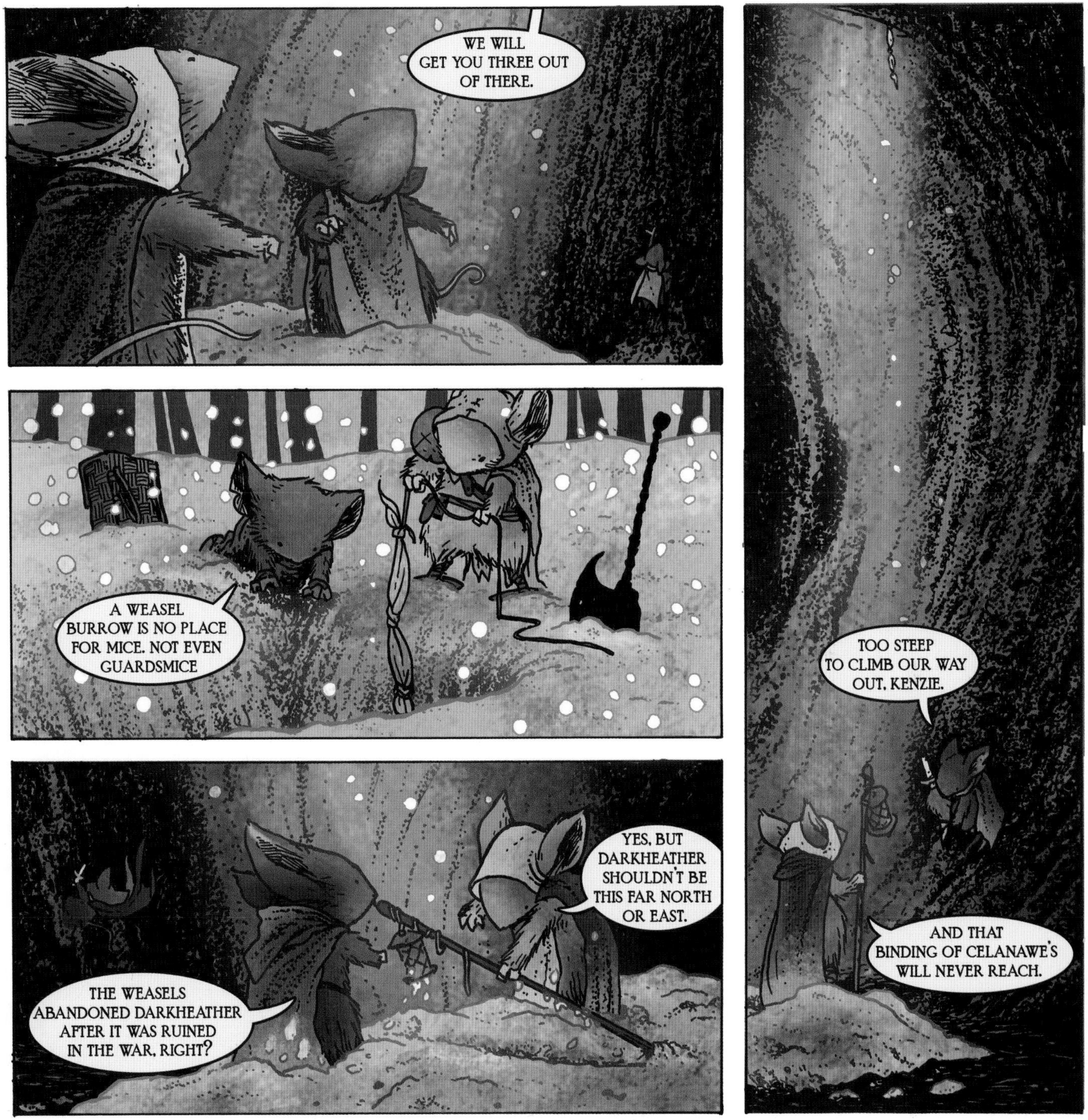
WE WILL GET YOU THREE OUT OF THERE.
A WEASEL BURROW IS NO PLACE FOR MICE. NOT EVEN GUARDSMICE
YES, BUT DARKHEATHER SHOULDN'T BE THIS FAR NORTH OR EAST.
THE WEASELS ABANDONED DARKHEATHER AFTER IT WAS RUINED IN THE WAR, RIGHT?
TOO STEEP TO CLIMB OUR WAY OUT, KENZIE.
AND THAT BINDING OF CELANAWE'S WILL NEVER REACH.

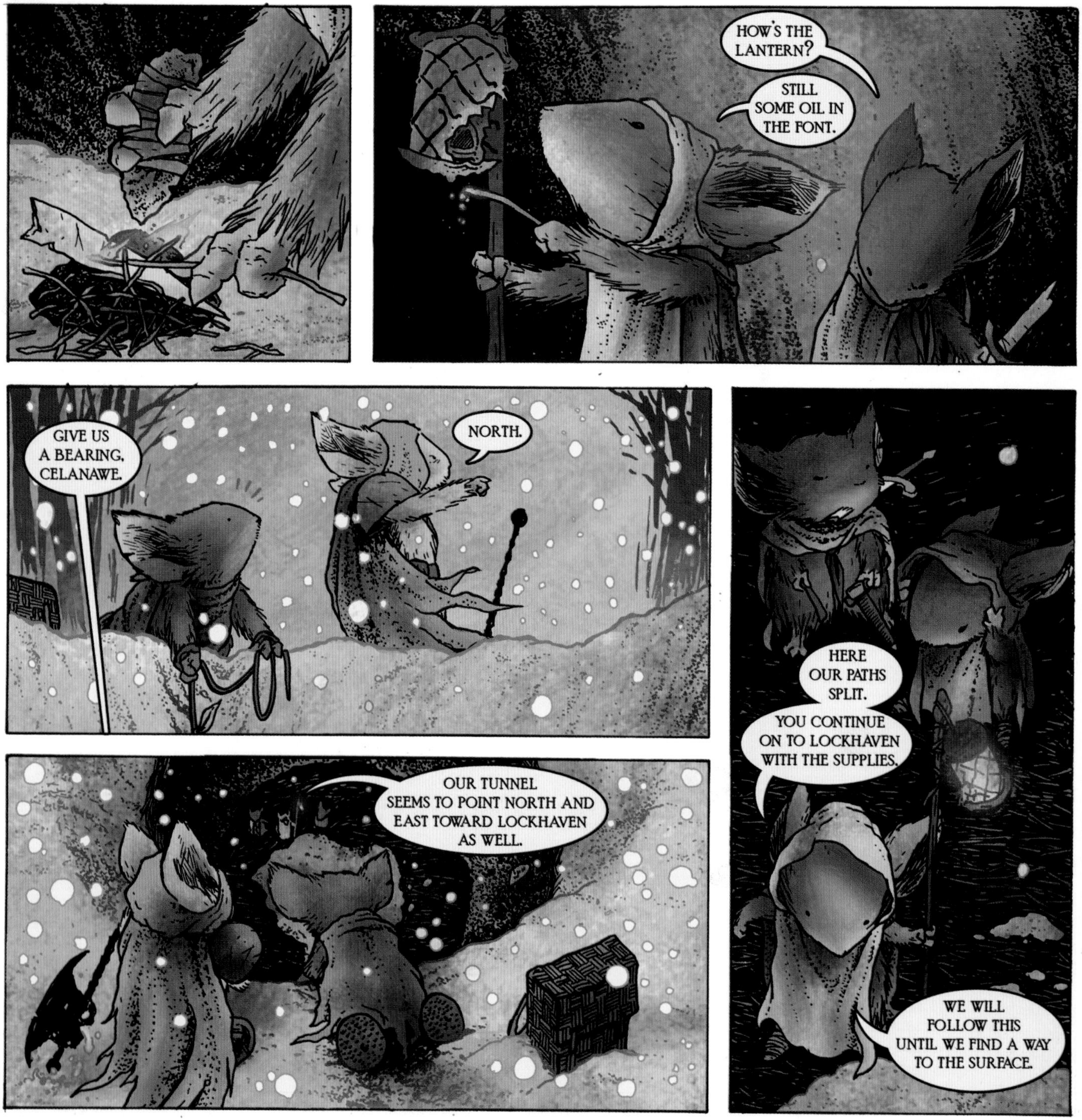
HOW'S THE LANTERN?
STILL SOME OIL IN THE FONT.
GIVE US A BEARING, CELANAWE.
NORTH.
OUR TUNNEL SEEMS TO POINT NORTH AND EAST TOWARD LOCKHAVEN AS WELL.
HERE OUR PATHS SPLIT.
YOU CONTINUE ON TO LOCKHAVEN WITH THE SUPPLIES.
WE WILL FOLLOW THIS UNTIL WE FIND A WAY TO THE SURFACE.

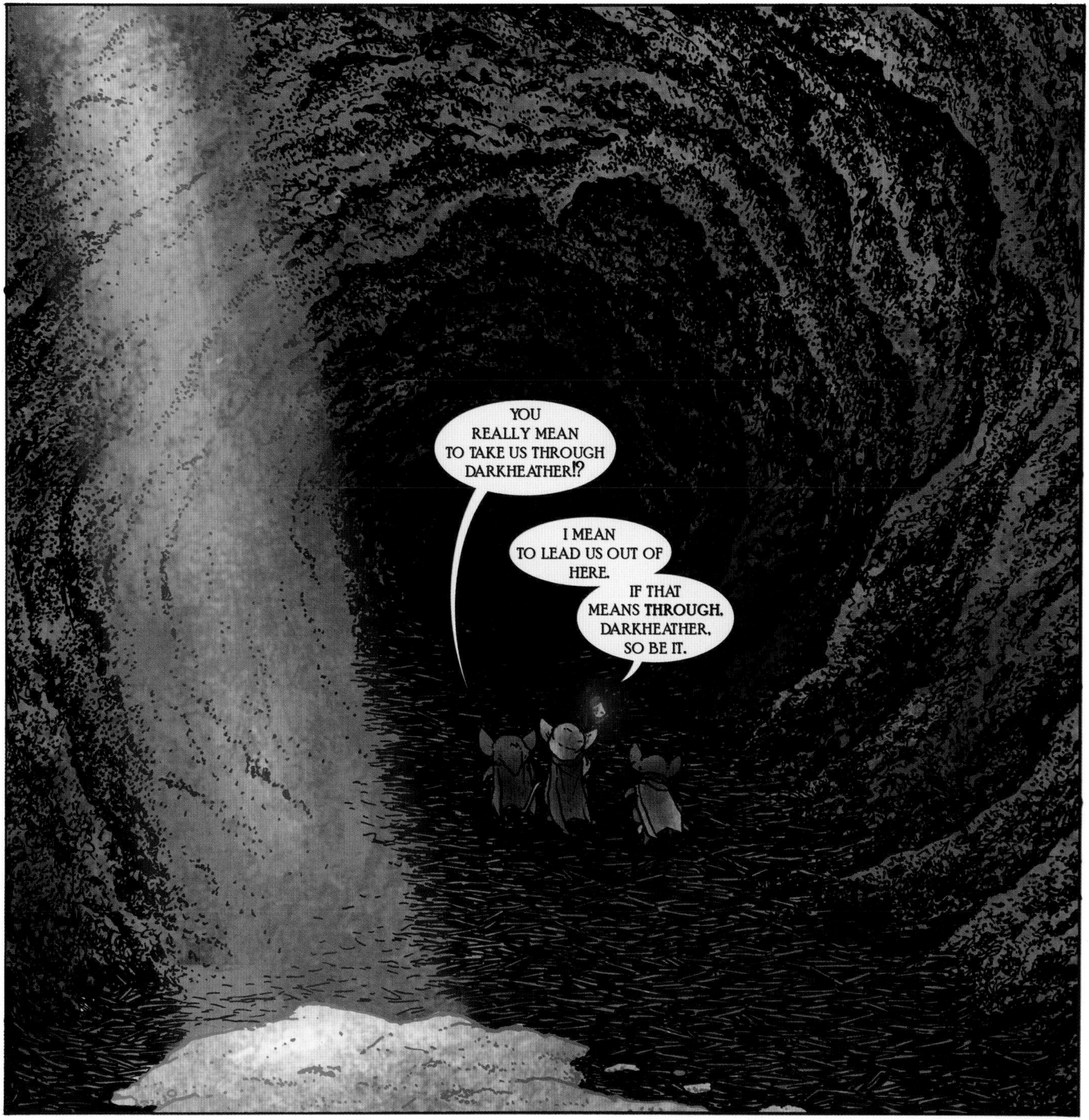
YOU REALLY MEAN TO TAKE US THROUGH DARKHEATHER!?
I MEAN TO LEAD US OUT OF HERE.
IF THAT MEANS THROUGH DARKHEATHER, SO BE IT.

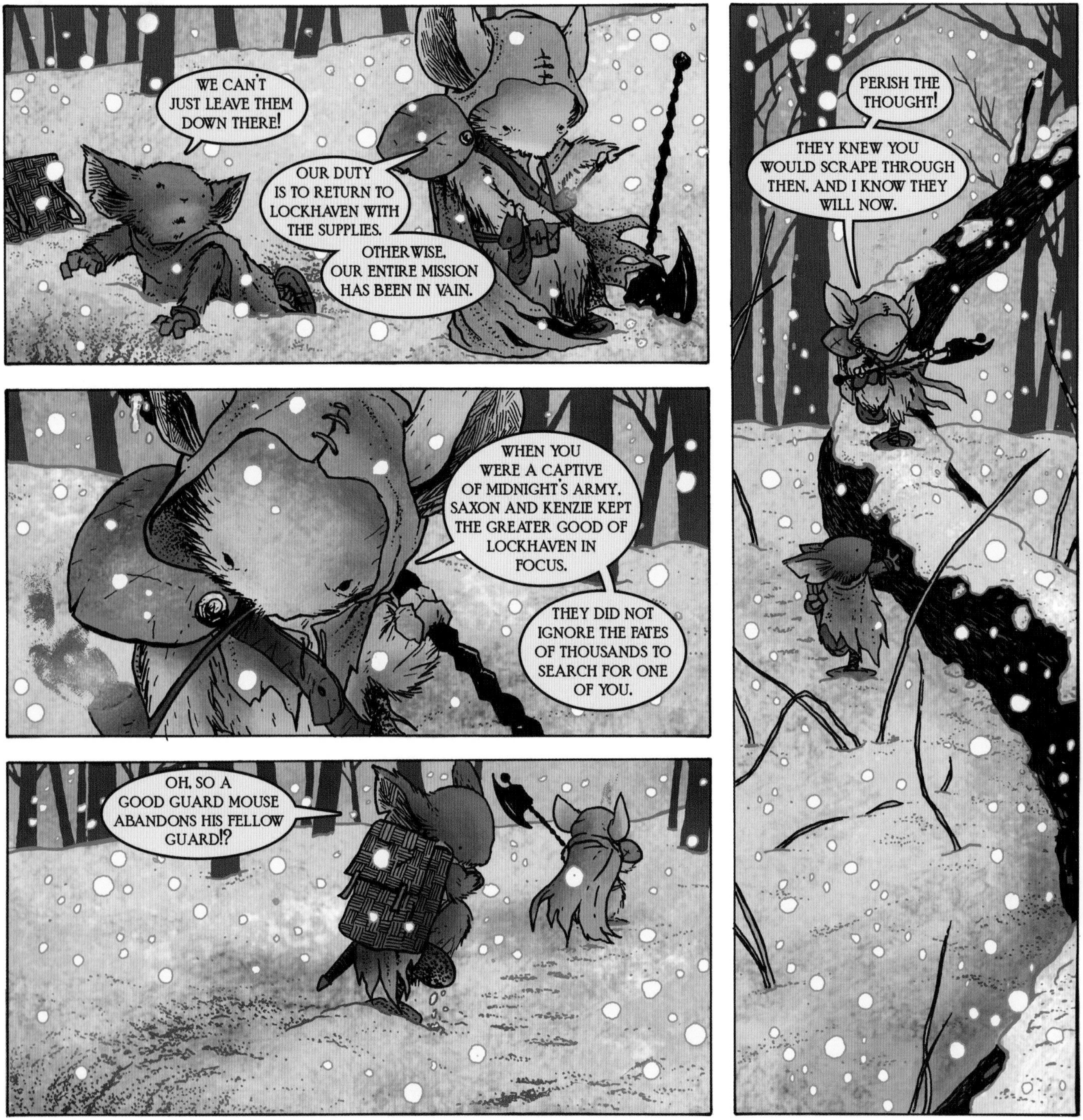
WE CAN'T JUST LEAVE THEM DOWN THERE!
OUR DUTY IS TO RETURN TO LOCKHAVEN WITH THE SUPPLIES.
OTHERWISE, OUR ENTIRE MISSION HAS BEEN IN VAIN.
WHEN YOU WERE A CAPTIVE OF MIDNIGHT'S ARMY, SAXON AND KENZIE KEPT THE GREATER GOOD OF LOCKHAVEN IN FOCUS.
THEY DID NOT IGNORE THE FATES OF THOUSANDS TO SEARCH FOR ONE OF YOU.
OH, SO A GOOD GUARD MOUSE ABANDONS HIS FELLOW GUARD!?
PERISH THE THOUGHT!
THEY KNEW YOU WOULD SCRAPE THROUGH THEN, AND I KNOW THEY WILL NOW.

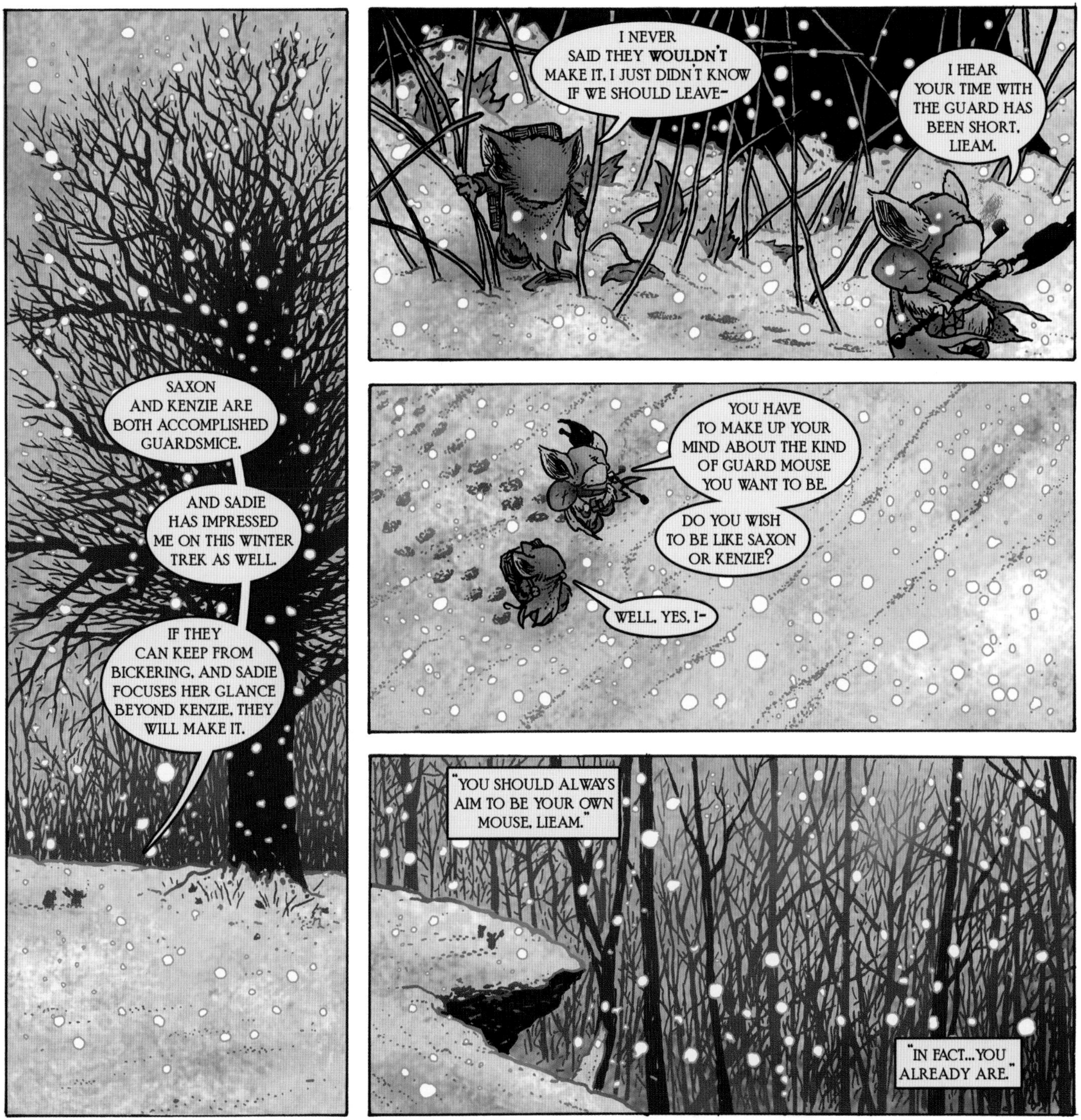
SAXON AND KENZIE ARE BOTH ACCOMPLISHED GUARDSMICE.
AND SADIE HAS IMPRESSED ME ON THIS WINTER TREK AS WELL.
IF THEY CAN KEEP FROM BICKERING, AND SADIE FOCUSES HER GLANCE BEYOND KENZIE, THEY WILL MAKE IT.
I NEVER SAID THEY WOULDN'T MAKE IT, I JUST DIDN'T KNOW IF WE SHOULD LEAVE-
I HEAR YOUR TIME WITH THE GUARD HAS BEEN SHORT, LIEAM.
YOU HAVE TO MAKE UP YOUR MIND ABOUT THE KIND OF GUARD MOUSE YOU WANT TO BE.
DO YOU WISH TO BE LIKE SAXON OR KENZIE?
WELL, YES, I-
"YOU SHOULD ALWAYS AIM TO BE YOUR OWN MOUSE, LIEAM."
"IN FACT...YOU ALREADY ARE."

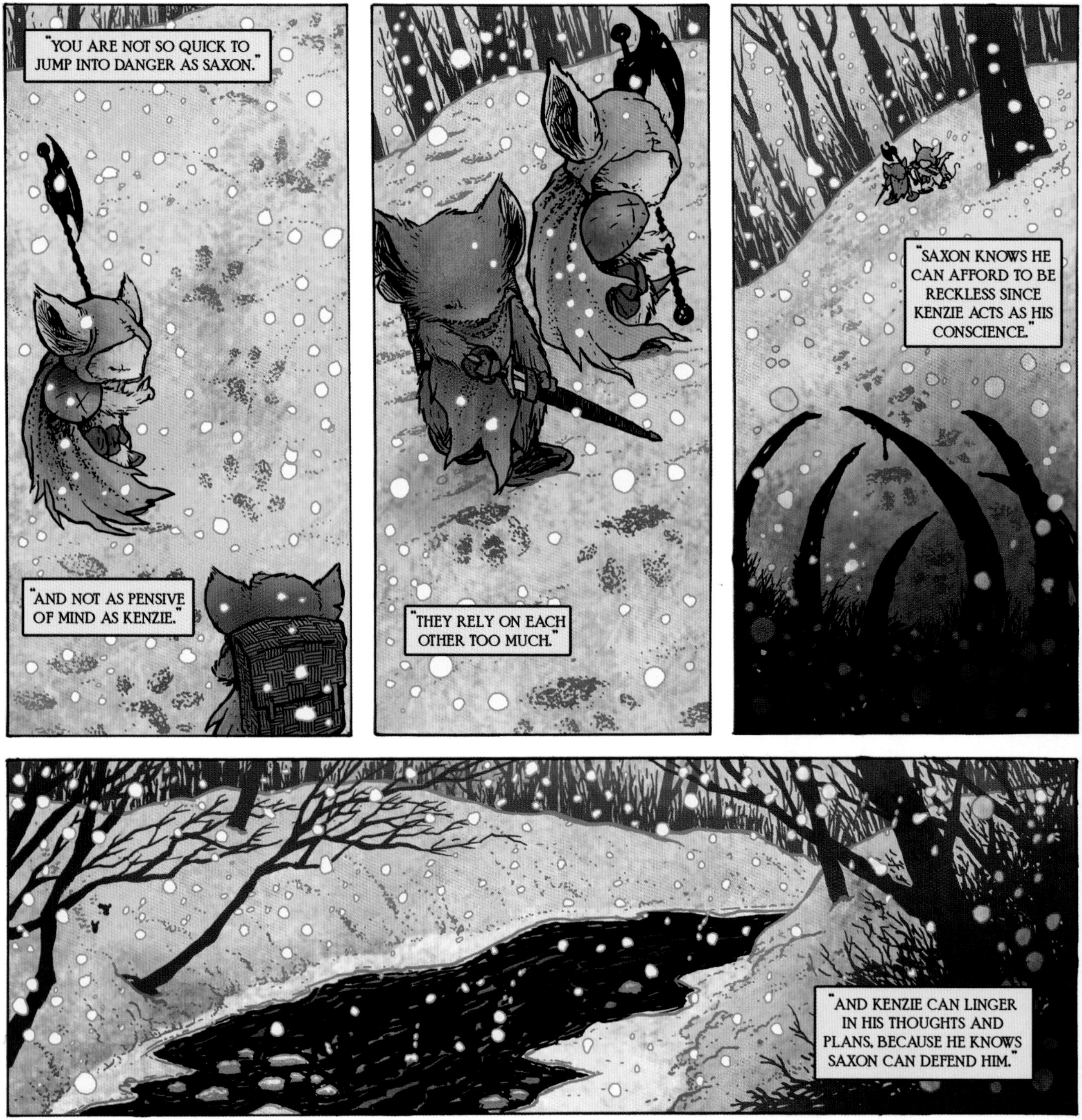
"YOU ARE NOT SO QUICK TO JUMP INTO DANGER AS SAXON."
"AND NOT AS PENSIVE OF MIND AS KENZIE."
"THEY RELY ON EACH OTHER TOO MUCH."
"SAXON KNOWS HE CAN AFFORD TO BE RECKLESS SINCE KENZIE ACTS AS HIS CONSCIENCE."
"AND KENZIE CAN LINGER IN HIS THOUGHTS AND PLANS, BECAUSE HE KNOWS SAXON CAN DEFEND HIM."

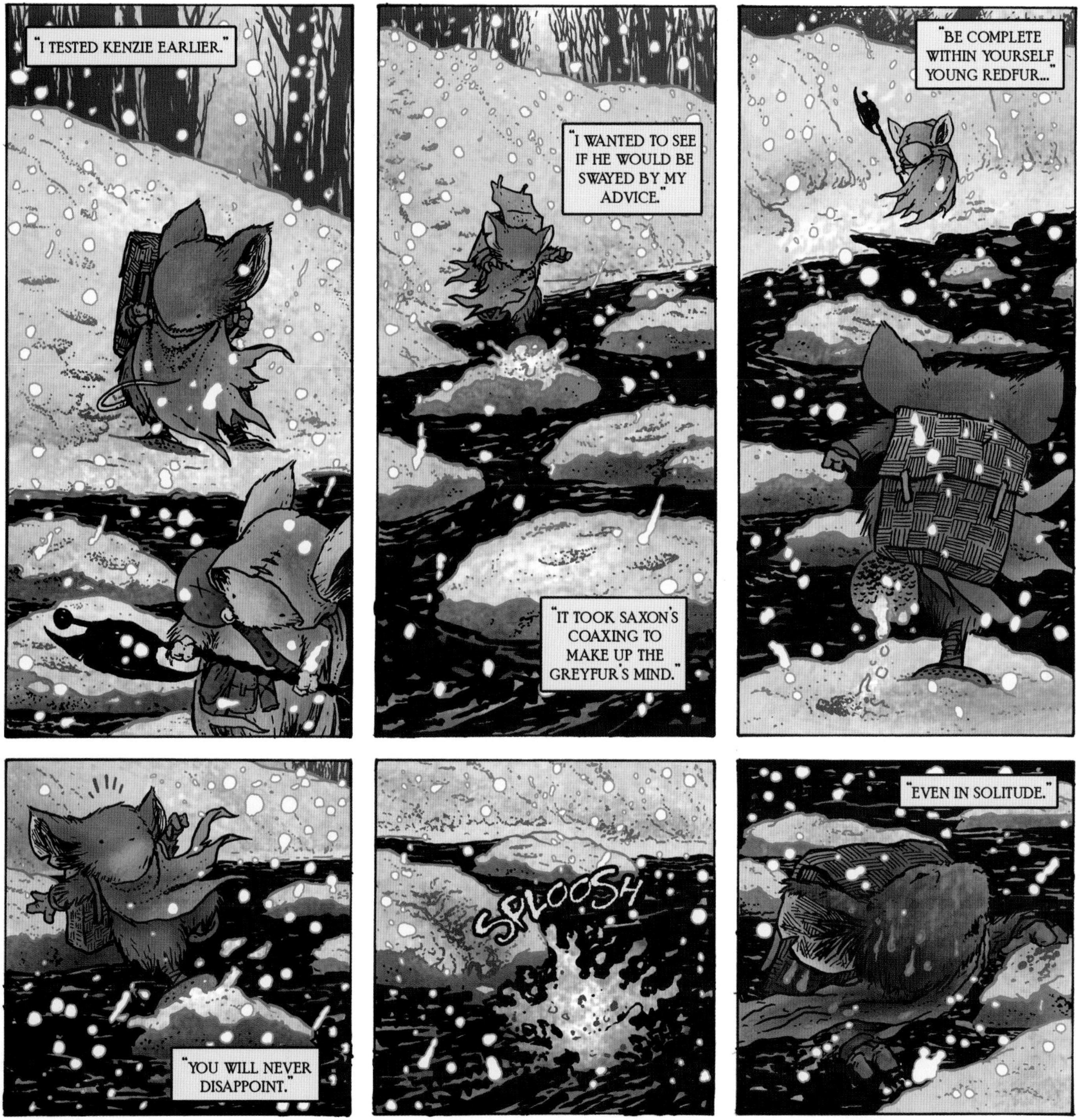
"I TESTED KENZIE EARLIER."
"I WANTED TO SEE IF HE WOULD BE SWAYED BY MY ADVICE."
"IT TOOK SAXON'S COAXING TO MAKE UP THE GREYFUR'S MIND."
"BE COMPLETE WITHIN YOURSELF YOUNG REDFUR..."
"YOU WILL NEVER DISAPPOINT."
SPLOOSH
"EVEN IN SOLITUDE."

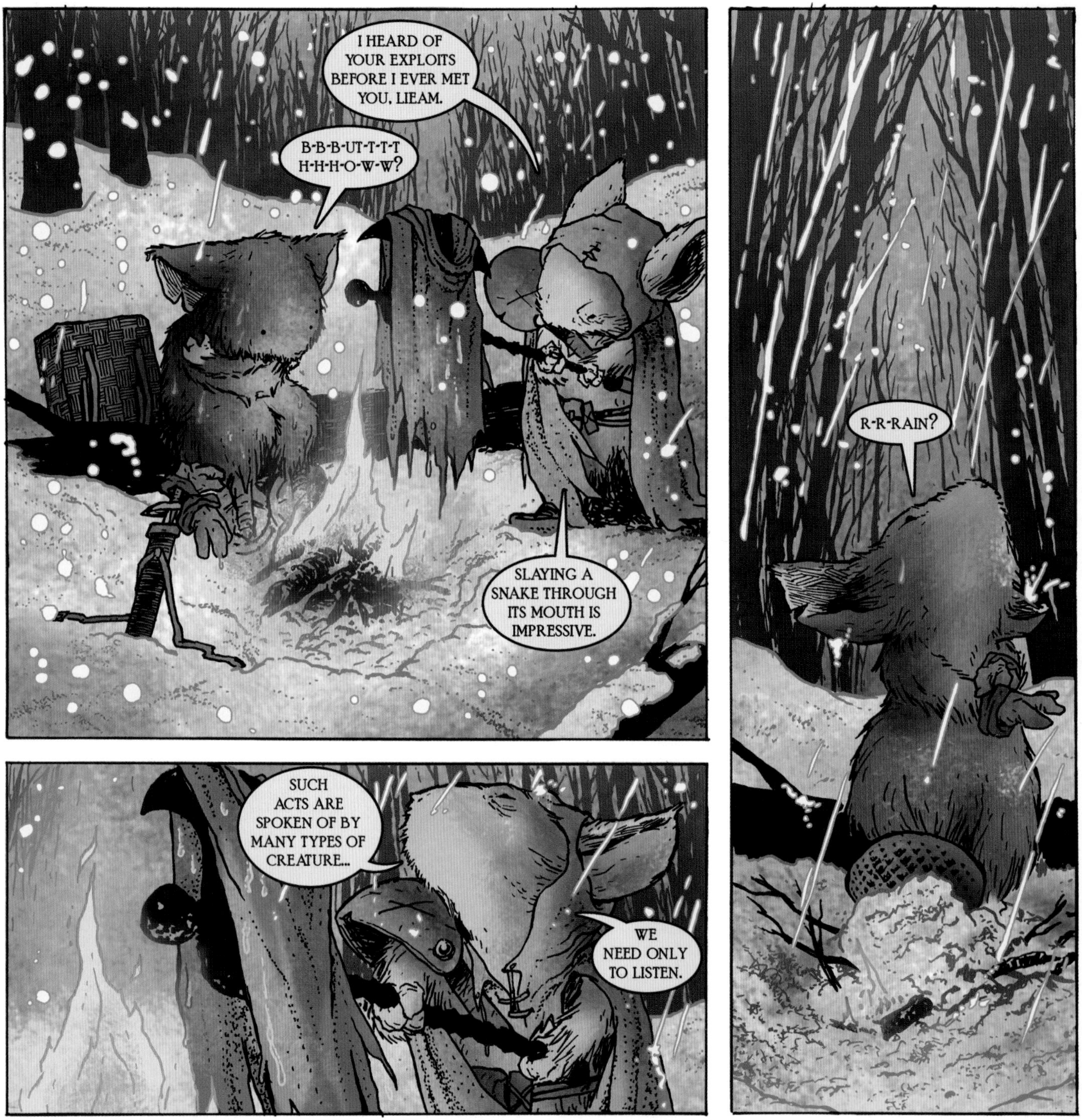
I HEARD OF YOUR EXPLOITS BEFORE I EVER MET YOU, LIEAM.
B-B-B-UT-T-T-T H-H-H-O-W-W?
SLAYING A SNAKE THROUGH ITS MOUTH IS IMPRESSIVE.
SUCH ACTS ARE SPOKEN OF BY MANY TYPES OF CREATURE...
WE NEED ONLY TO LISTEN.
R-R-RAIN?

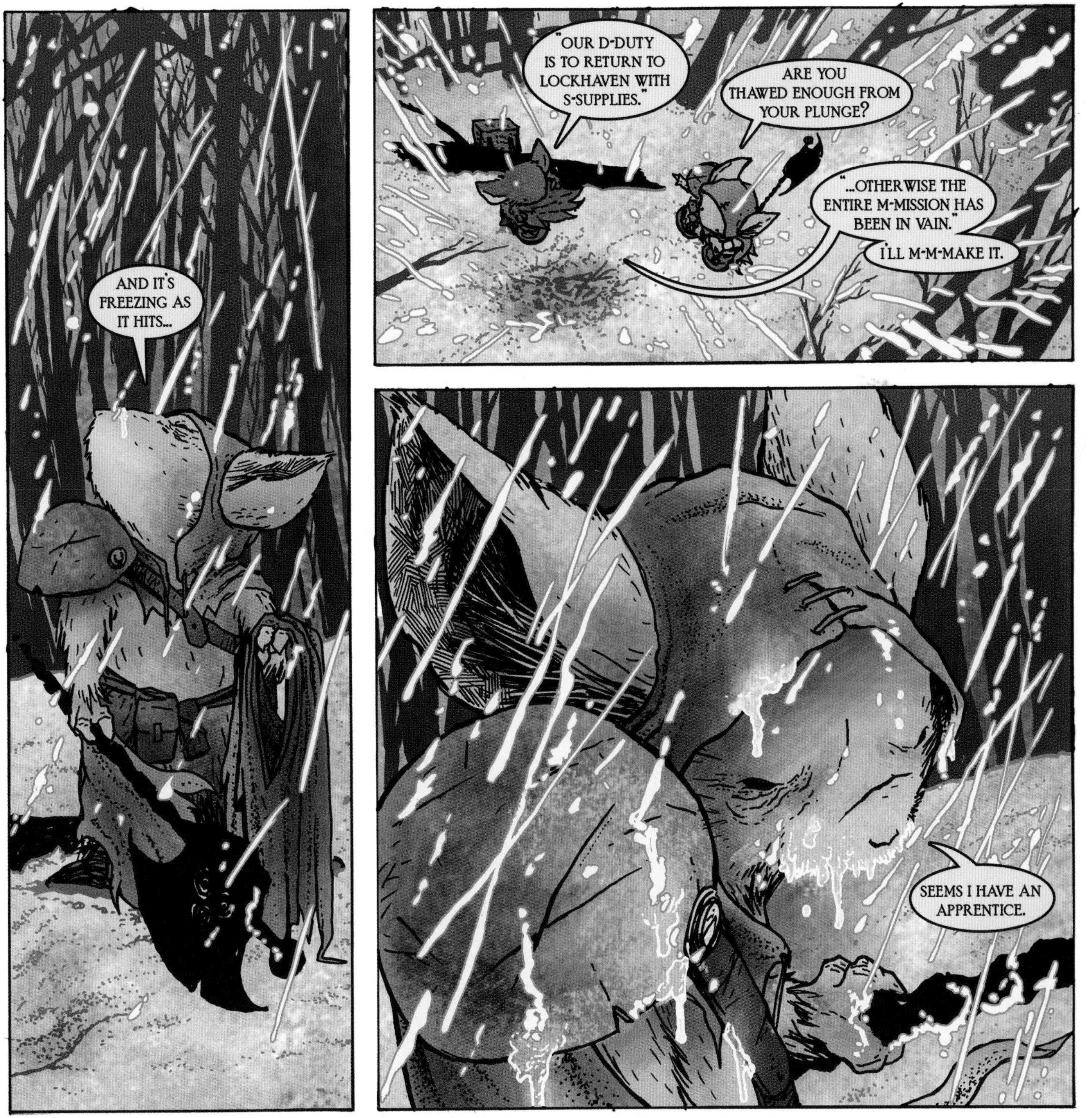
AND IT'S FREEZING AS IT HITS...
"OUR D-DUTY IS TO RETURN TO LOCKHAVEN WITH S-SUPPLIES."
ARE YOU THAWED ENOUGH FROM YOUR PLUNGE?
"...OTHERWISE THE ENTIRE M-MISSION HAS BEEN IN VAIN."
I'LL M-M-MAKE IT.
SEEMS I HAVE AN APPRENTICE.

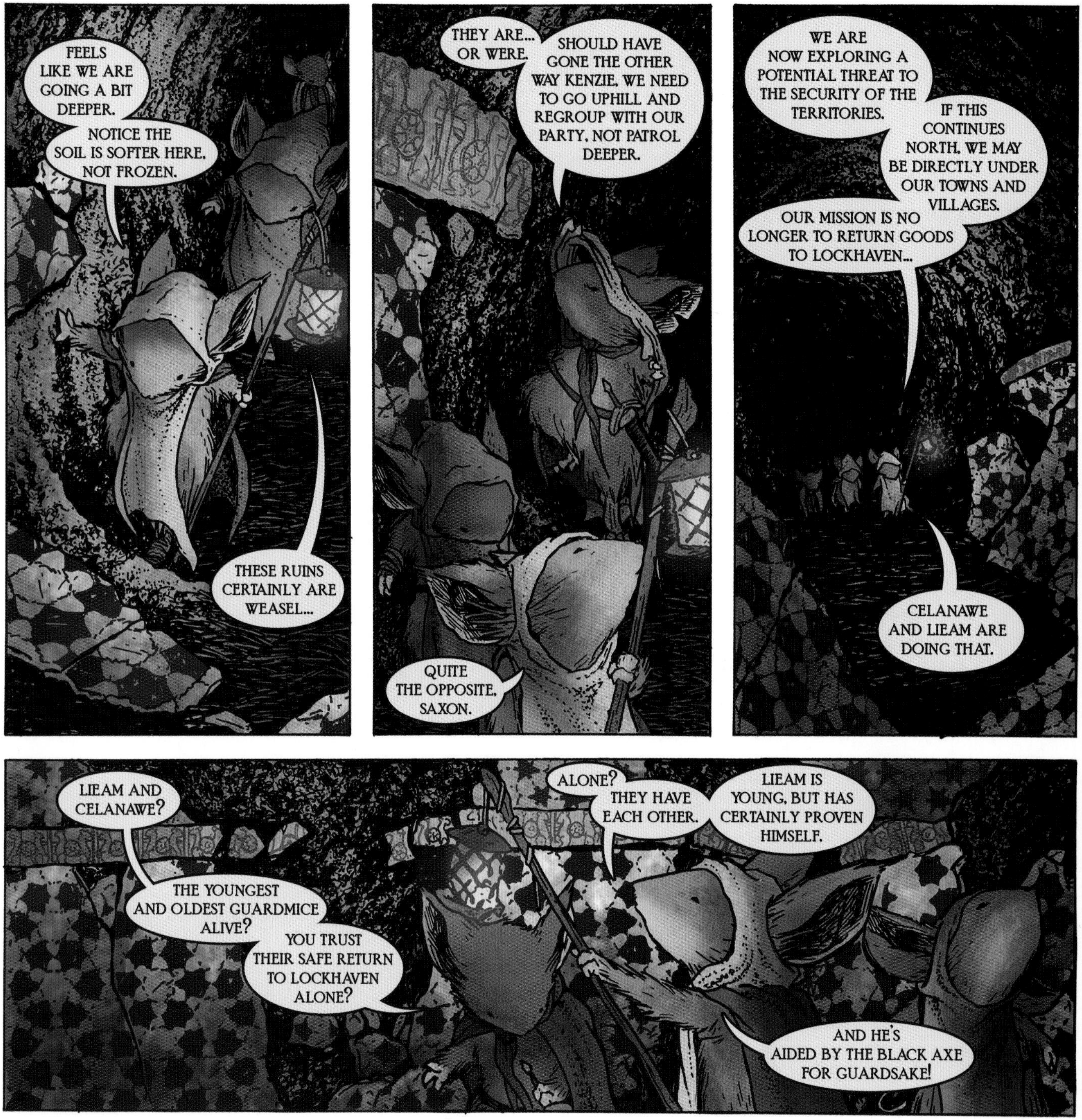
FEELS LIKE WE ARE GOING A BIT DEEPER.
NOTICE THE SOIL IS SOFTER HERE, NOT FROZEN.
THESE RUINS CERTAINLY ARE WEASEL...
THEY ARE... OR WERE.
SHOULD HAVE GONE THE OTHER WAY KENZIE, WE NEED TO GO UPHILL AND REGROUP WITH OUR PARTY, NOT PATROL DEEPER.
QUITE THE OPPOSITE, SAXON.
WE ARE NOW EXPLORING A POTENTIAL THREAT TO THE SECURITY OF THE TERRITORIES.
IF THIS CONTINUES NORTH, WE MAY BE DIRECTLY UNDER OUR TOWNS AND VILLAGES.
OUR MISSION IS NO LONGER TO RETURN GOODS TO LOCKHAVEN...
CELANAWE AND LIEAM ARE DOING THAT.
LIEAM AND CELANAWE?
THE YOUNGEST AND OLDEST GUARDMICE ALIVE?
YOU TRUST THEIR SAFE RETURN TO LOCKHAVEN ALONE?
ALONE? THEY HAVE EACH OTHER.
LIEAM IS YOUNG, BUT HAS CERTAINLY PROVEN HIMSELF.
AND HE'S AIDED BY THE BLACK AXE FOR GUARDSAKE!

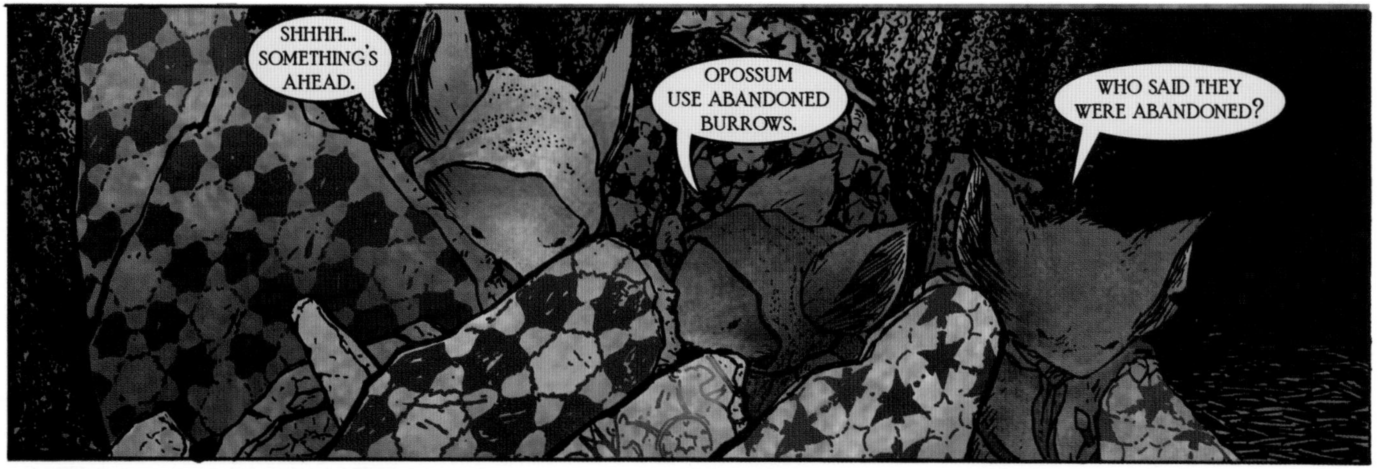
SHHHH... SOMETHING'S AHEAD.
OPOSSUM USE ABANDONED BURROWS.
WHO SAID THEY WERE ABANDONED?

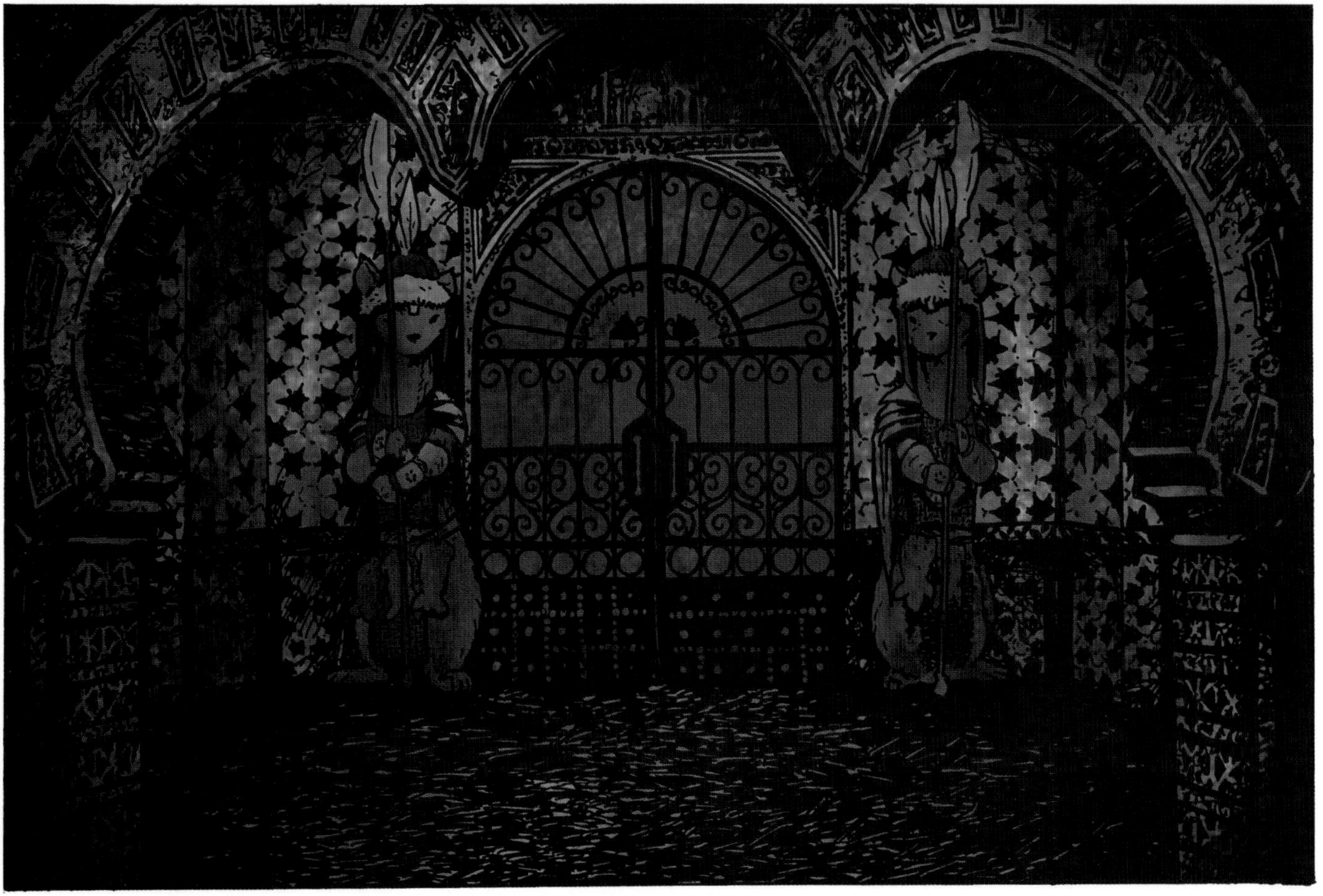

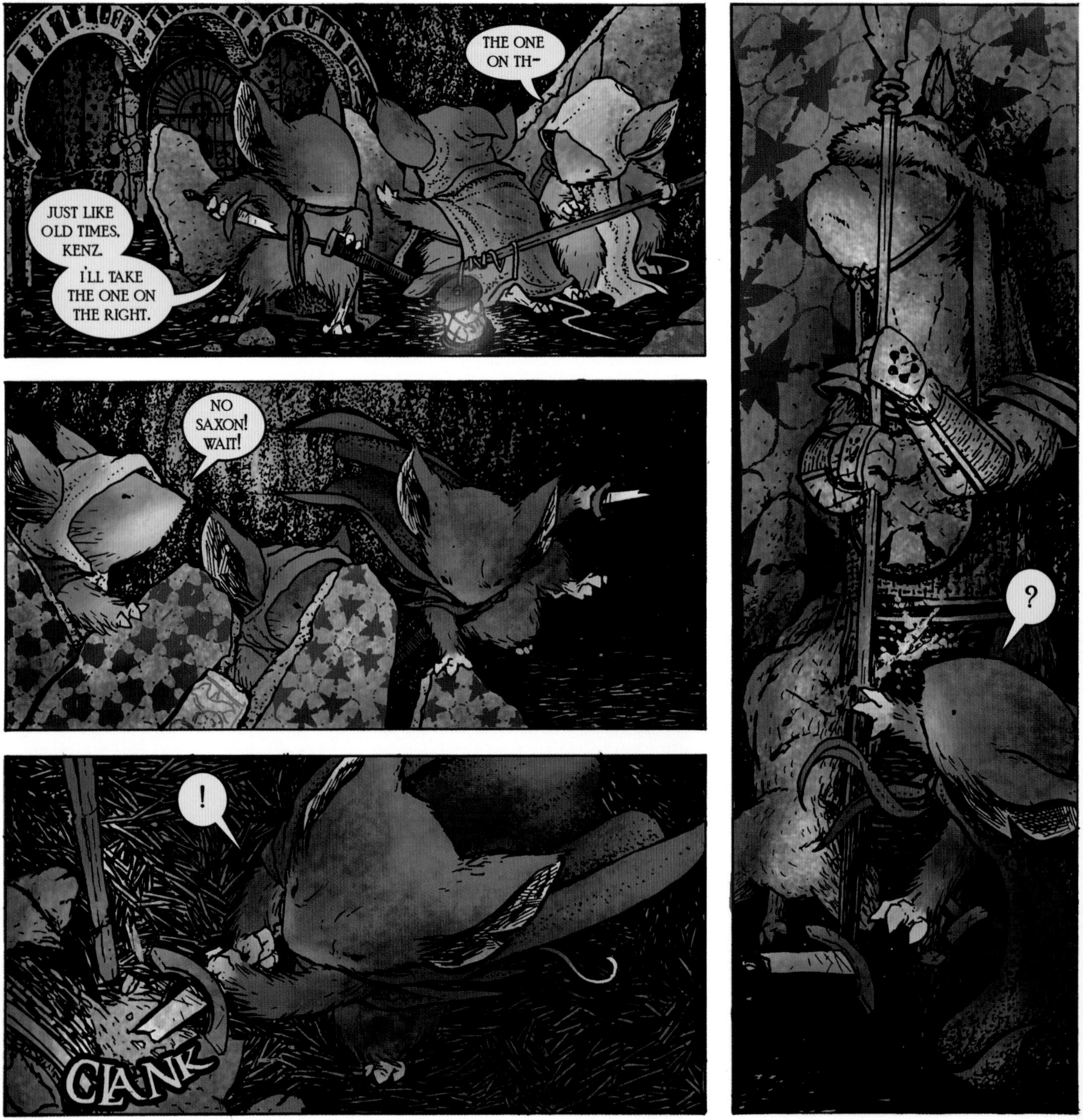
JUST LIKE OLD TIMES, KENZ.
I'LL TAKE THE ONE ON THE RIGHT.
THE ONE ON TH–
NO SAXON! WAIT!
!
CLANK
?

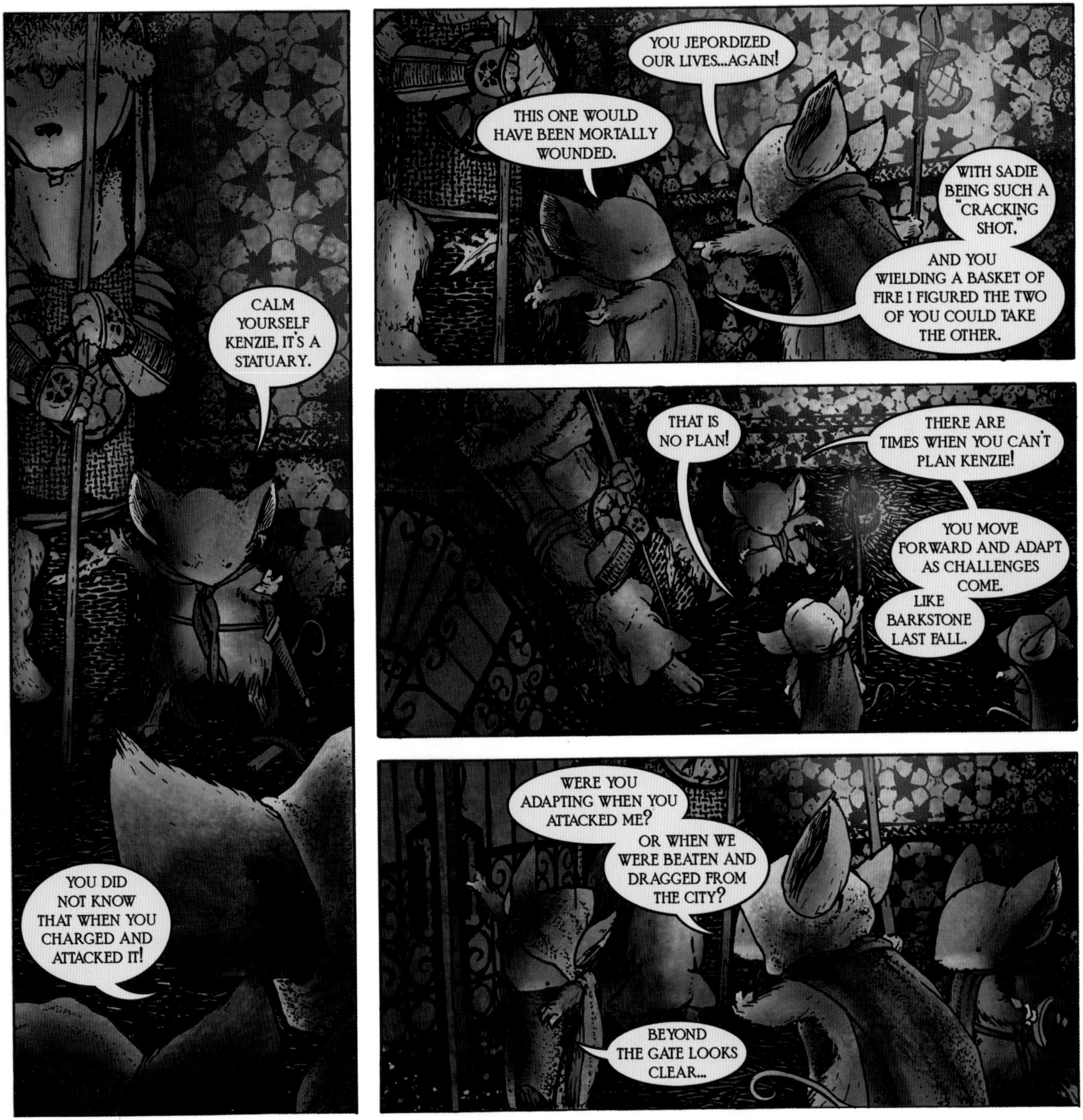
CALM YOURSELF KENZIE, IT'S A STATUARY.
YOU DID NOT KNOW THAT WHEN YOU CHARGED AND ATTACKED IT!
YOU JEPORDIZED OUR LIVES...AGAIN!
THIS ONE WOULD HAVE BEEN MORTALLY WOUNDED.
WITH SADIE BEING SUCH A "CRACKING SHOT,"
AND YOU WIELDING A BASKET OF FIRE I FIGURED THE TWO OF YOU COULD TAKE THE OTHER.
THAT IS NO PLAN!
THERE ARE TIMES WHEN YOU CAN'T PLAN KENZIE!
YOU MOVE FORWARD AND ADAPT AS CHALLENGES COME.
LIKE BARKSTONE LAST FALL.
WERE YOU ADAPTING WHEN YOU ATTACKED ME?
OR WHEN WE WERE BEATEN AND DRAGGED FROM THE CITY?
BEYOND THE GATE LOOKS CLEAR...

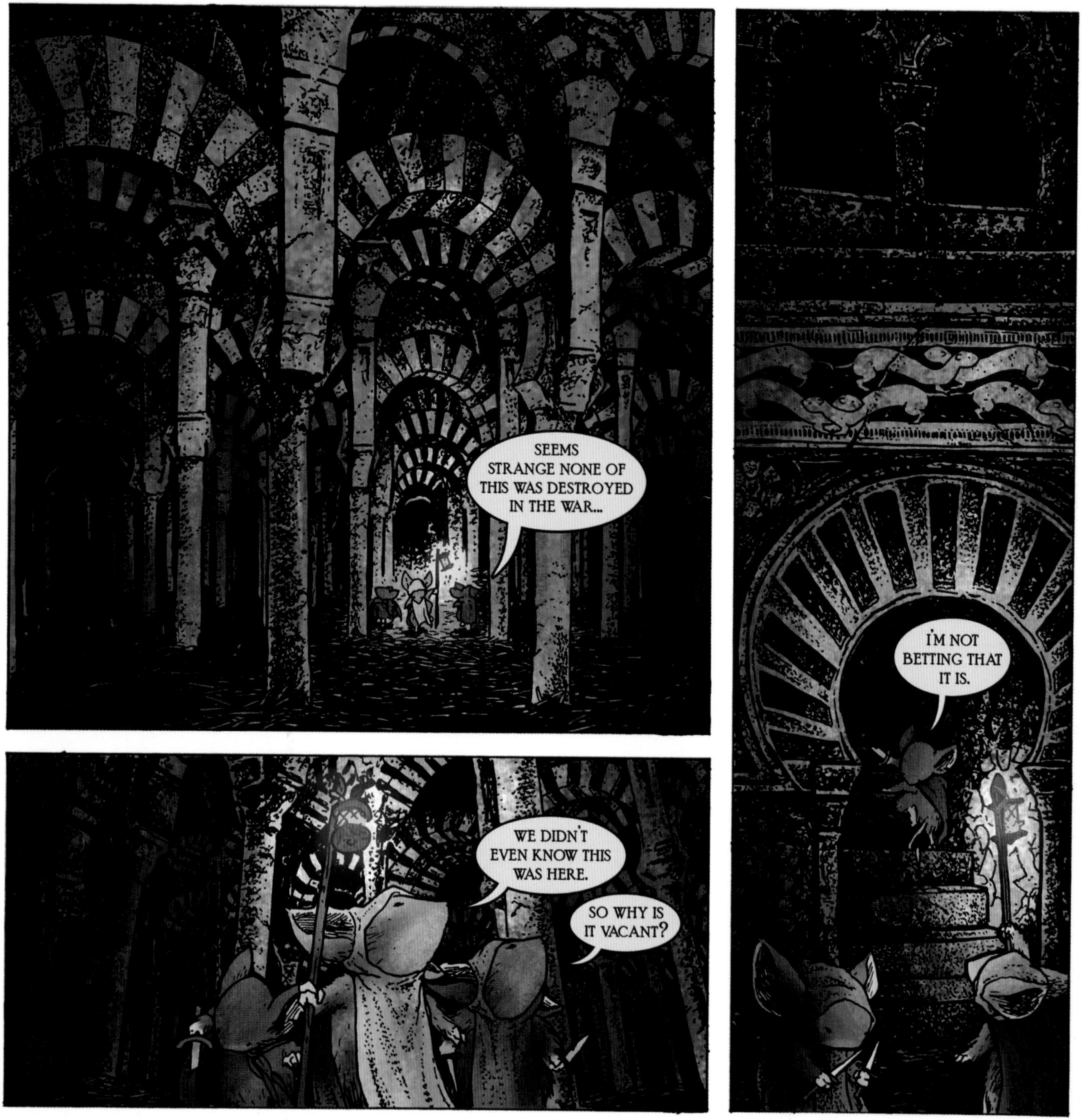
SEEMS STRANGE NONE OF THIS WAS DESTROYED IN THE WAR...
WE DIDN'T EVEN KNOW THIS WAS HERE.
SO WHY IS IT VACANT?
I'M NOT BETTING THAT IT IS.

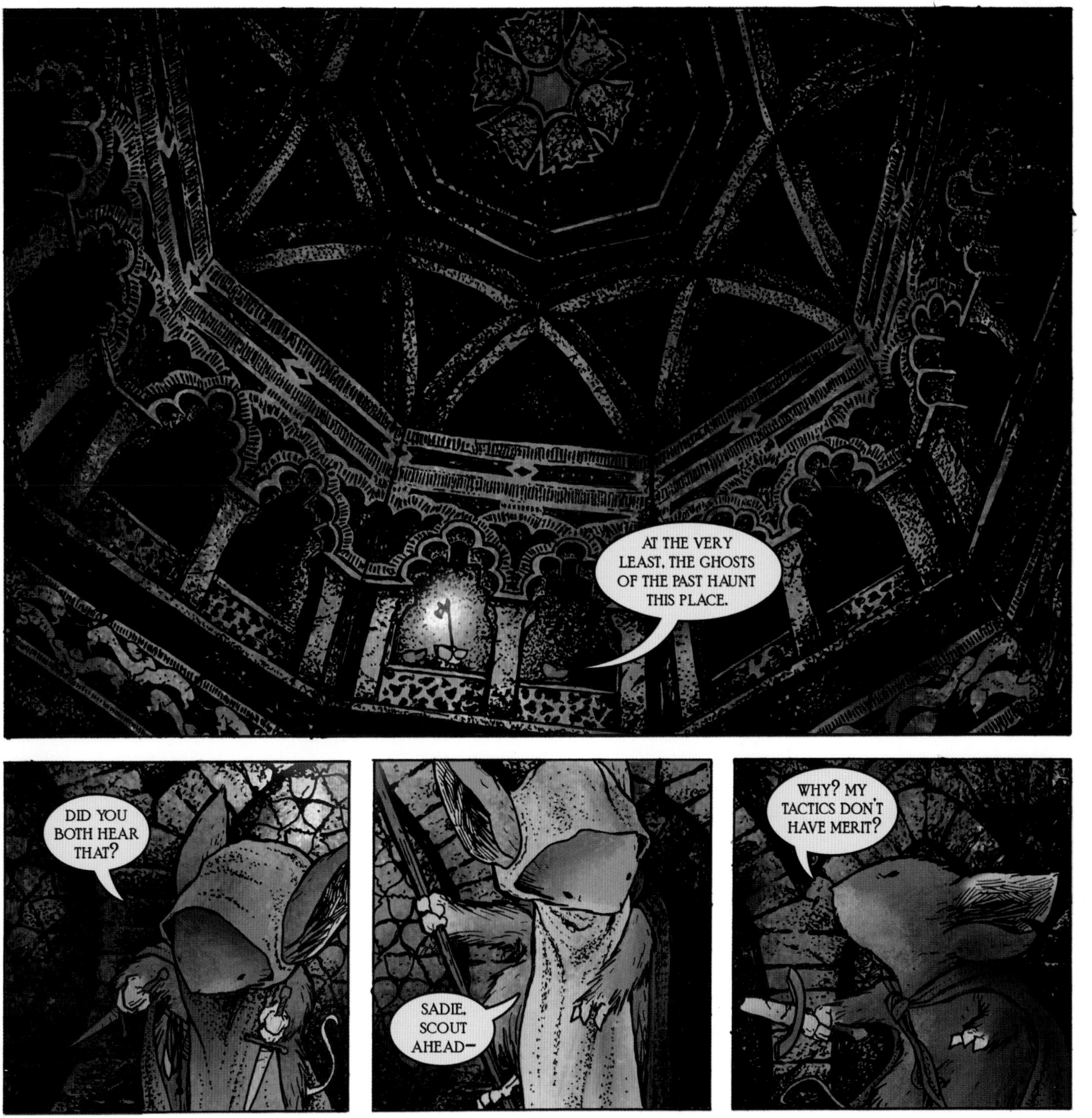
AT THE VERY LEAST, THE GHOSTS OF THE PAST HAUNT THIS PLACE.
DID YOU BOTH HEAR THAT?
SADIE, SCOUT AHEAD–
WHY? MY TACTICS DON'T HAVE MERIT?

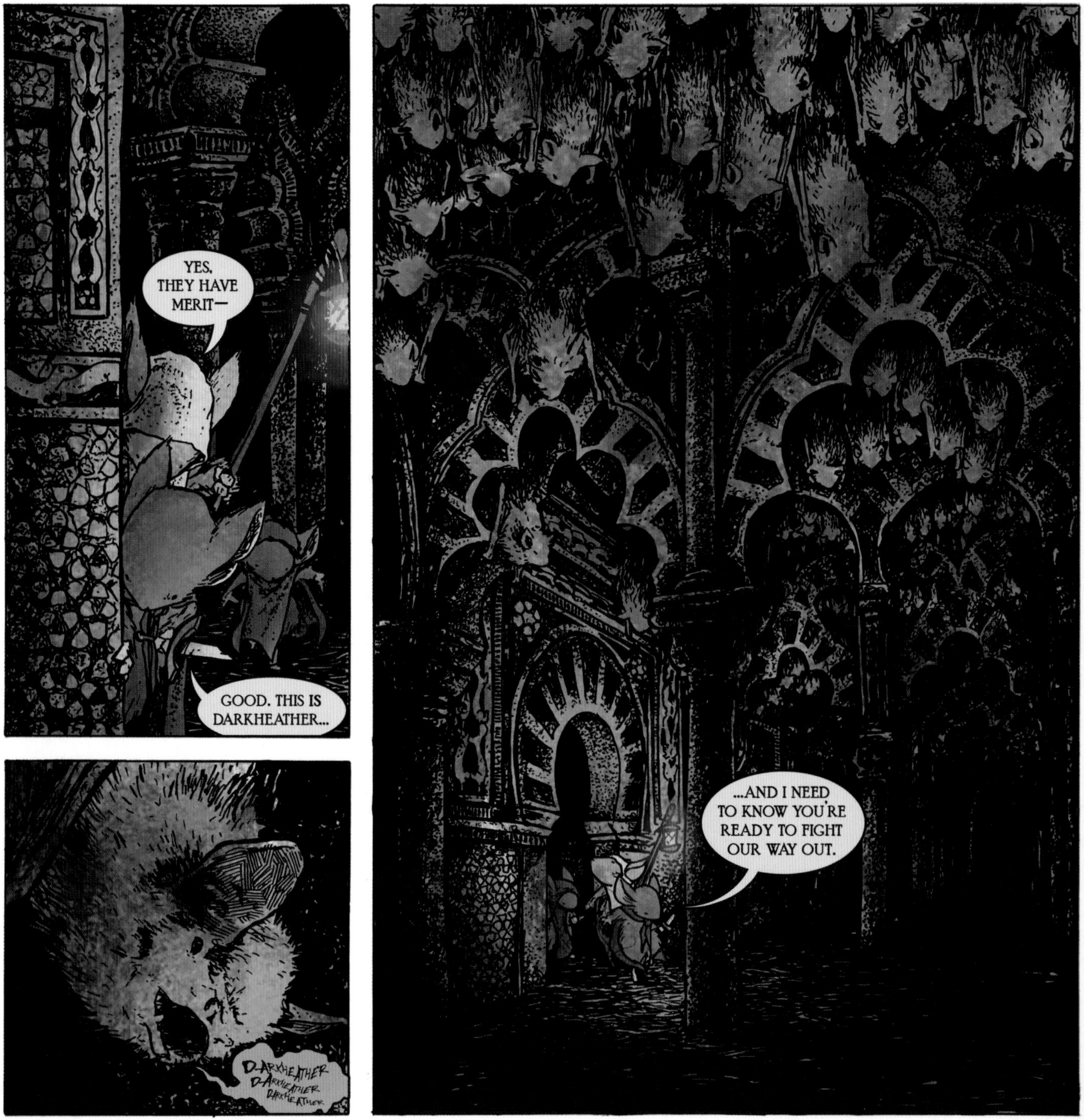
YES, THEY HAVE MERIT—
GOOD. THIS IS DARKHEATHER...
DARKHEATHER DARKHEATHER DARKHEATHER
...AND I NEED TO KNOW YOU'RE READY TO FIGHT OUR WAY OUT.

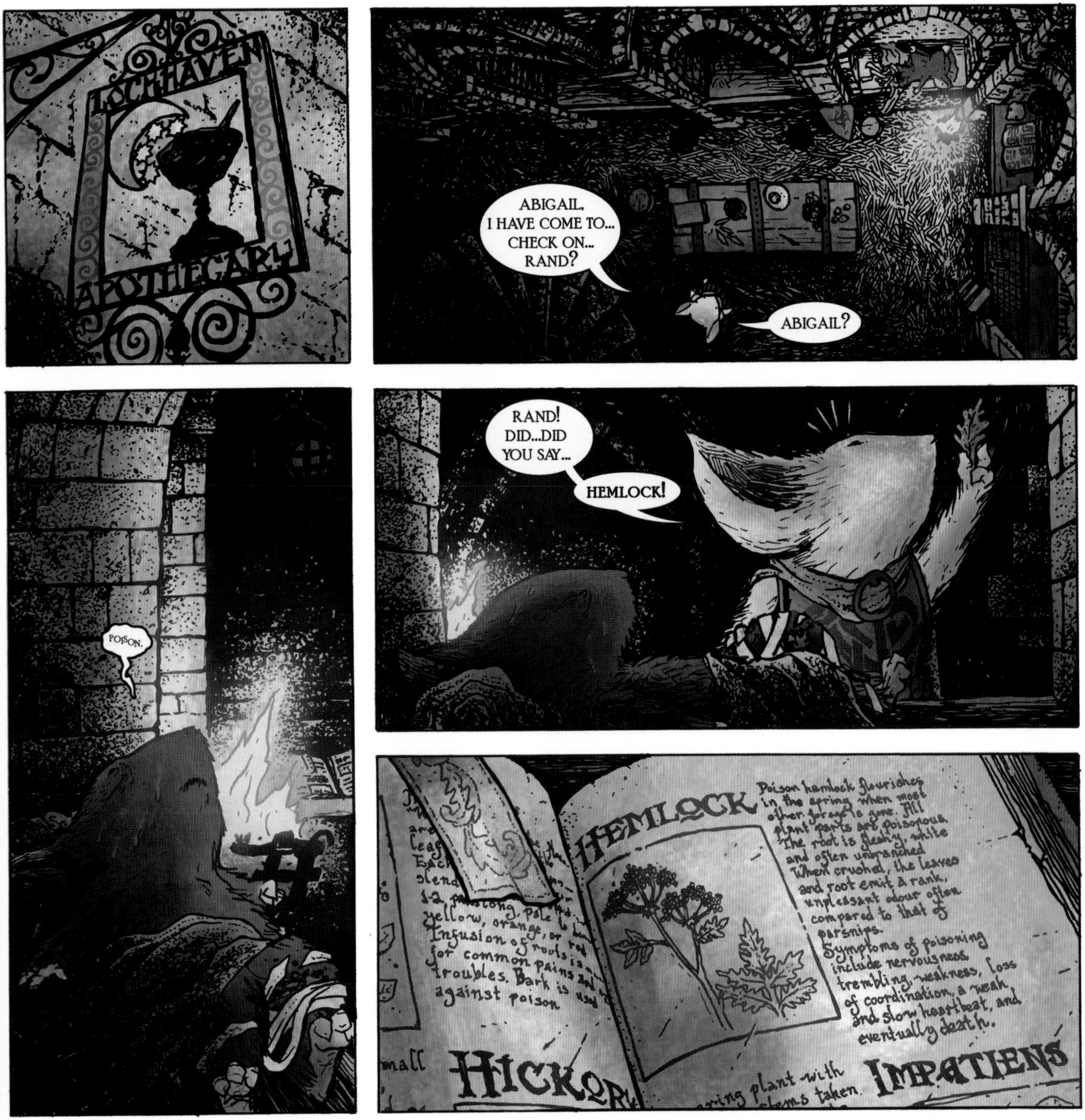
LOCKHAVEN
APOTHECARY
ABIGAIL, I HAVE COME TO... CHECK ON... RAND?
ABIGAIL?
POISON.
RAND! DID...DID YOU SAY...
HEMLOCK!
yellow, orange, or
Infusion of roots
for common pains
troubles. Bark is
against poison
HICKORY
HEMLOCK
Poison hemlock flourishes in the spring when most other forage is gone. All plant parts are poisonous. The root is fleshy, white and often unbranched. When crushed, the leaves and root emit a rank, unpleasant odour often compared to that of parsnips.
Symptoms of poisoning include nervousness, trembling, weakness, loss of coordination, a weak and slow heartbeat, and eventually death.
IMPATIENS

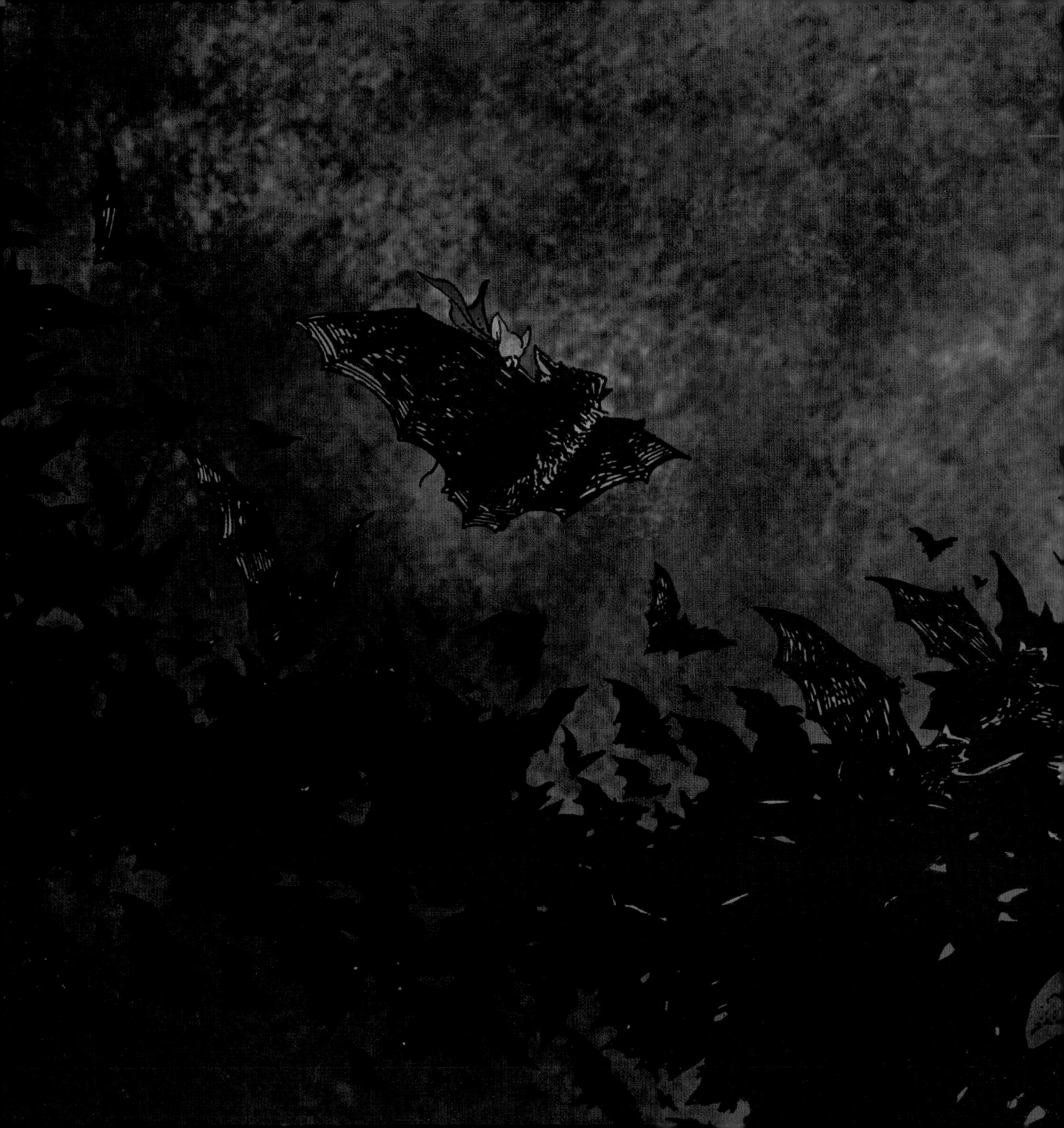

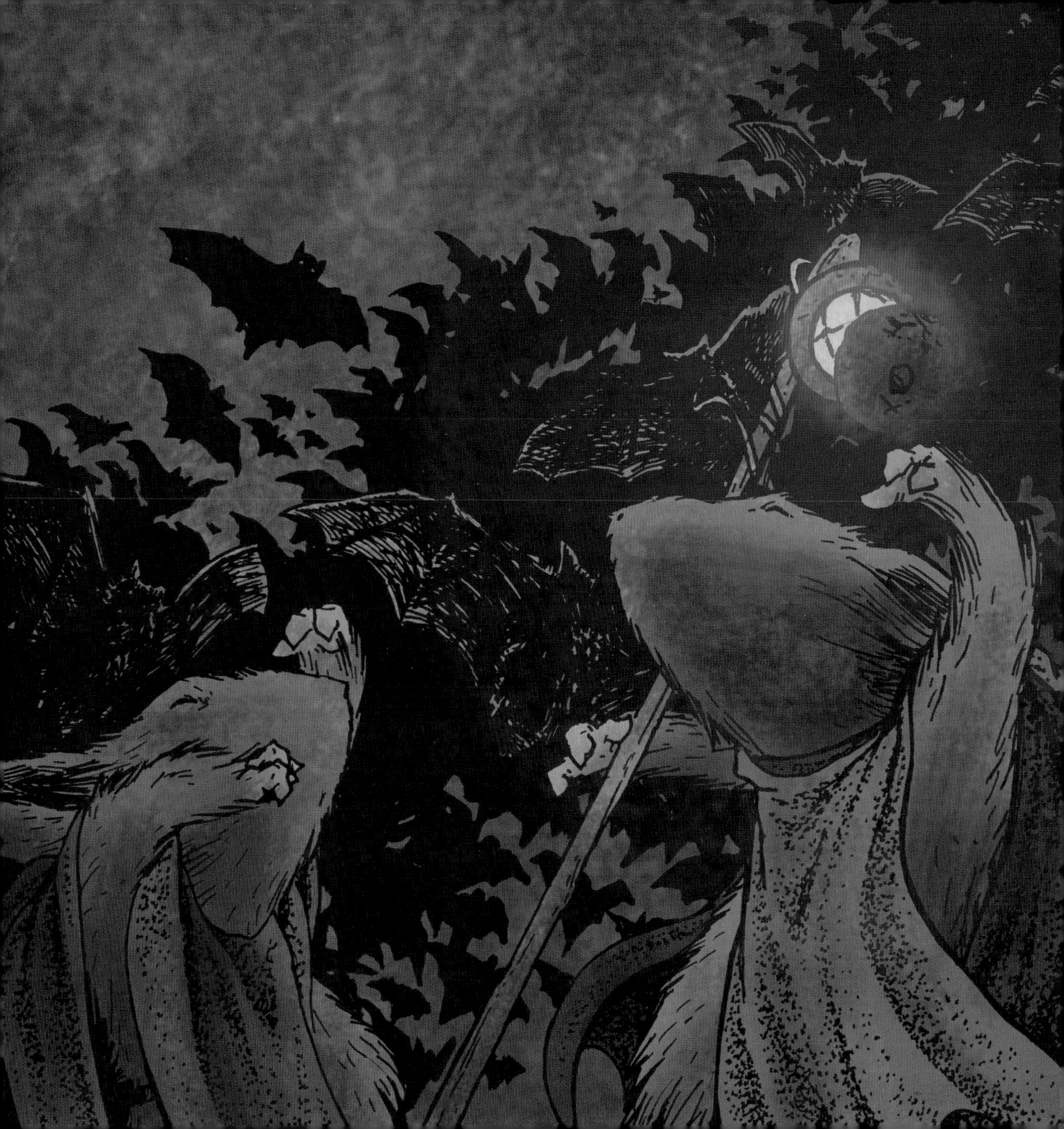

CHAPTER THREE

As Gwendolyn finds Lockhaven's shield bearer to
have been poisoned, the party led by Kenzie has
been forced apart. Kenzie, Saxon, and Sadie travel
though the seemingly abandoned weasel kingdom of
Darkheather.

Above ground, Celanawe counsels Lieam as they
trod through an icy winter storm with the medicine
retrieved from Sprucetuck.

"Secrets are a burden to those who swallow them whole.
They sit like a seed in the heart, each beat an aching toll.
Rooting and reaching they grow to want out.
The will of the keeper determines which wins that bout.
Is the fact so bitter and foul it shouldn't be heard?
One can effect a great deal with few chosen words.
Begging its owner often pushes the morsel deeper.
But who is truly being kept, the secret or the keeper?"

-An excerpt from "The Ballad of Em of Appleloft"
by Roibin the Scribe of Lockhaven

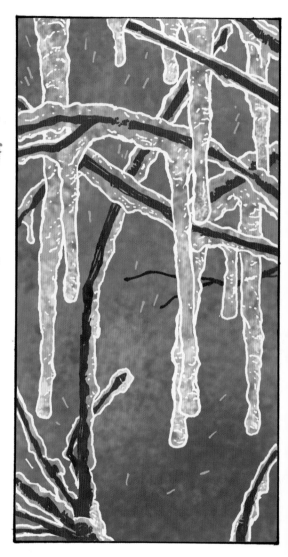

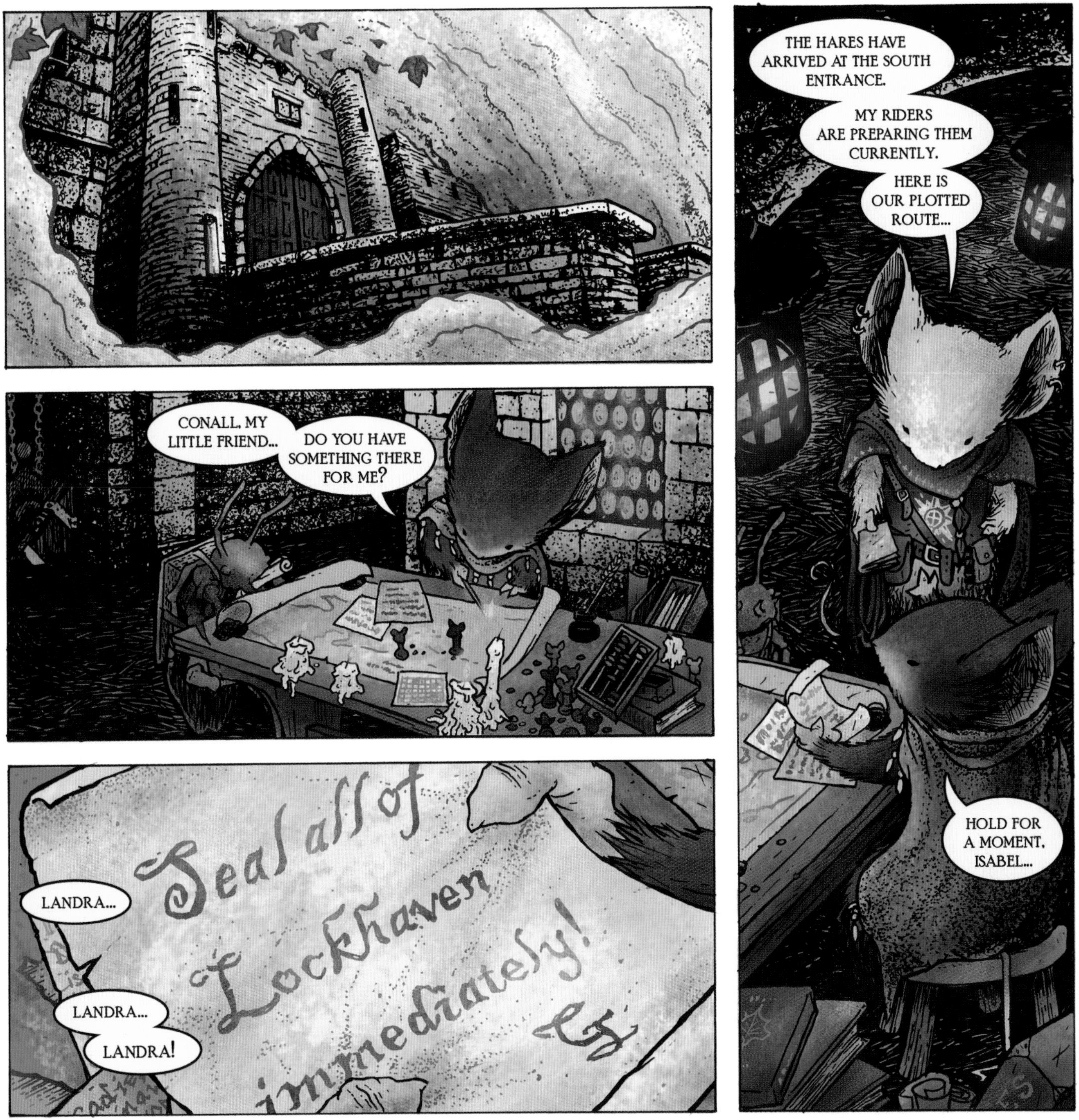

CONALL, MY LITTLE FRIEND...
DO YOU HAVE SOMETHING THERE FOR ME?
Seal all of Lockhaven immediately!
LANDRA...
LANDRA...
LANDRA!
THE HARES HAVE ARRIVED AT THE SOUTH ENTRANCE.
MY RIDERS ARE PREPARING THEM CURRENTLY.
HERE IS OUR PLOTTED ROUTE...
HOLD FOR A MOMENT, ISABEL...

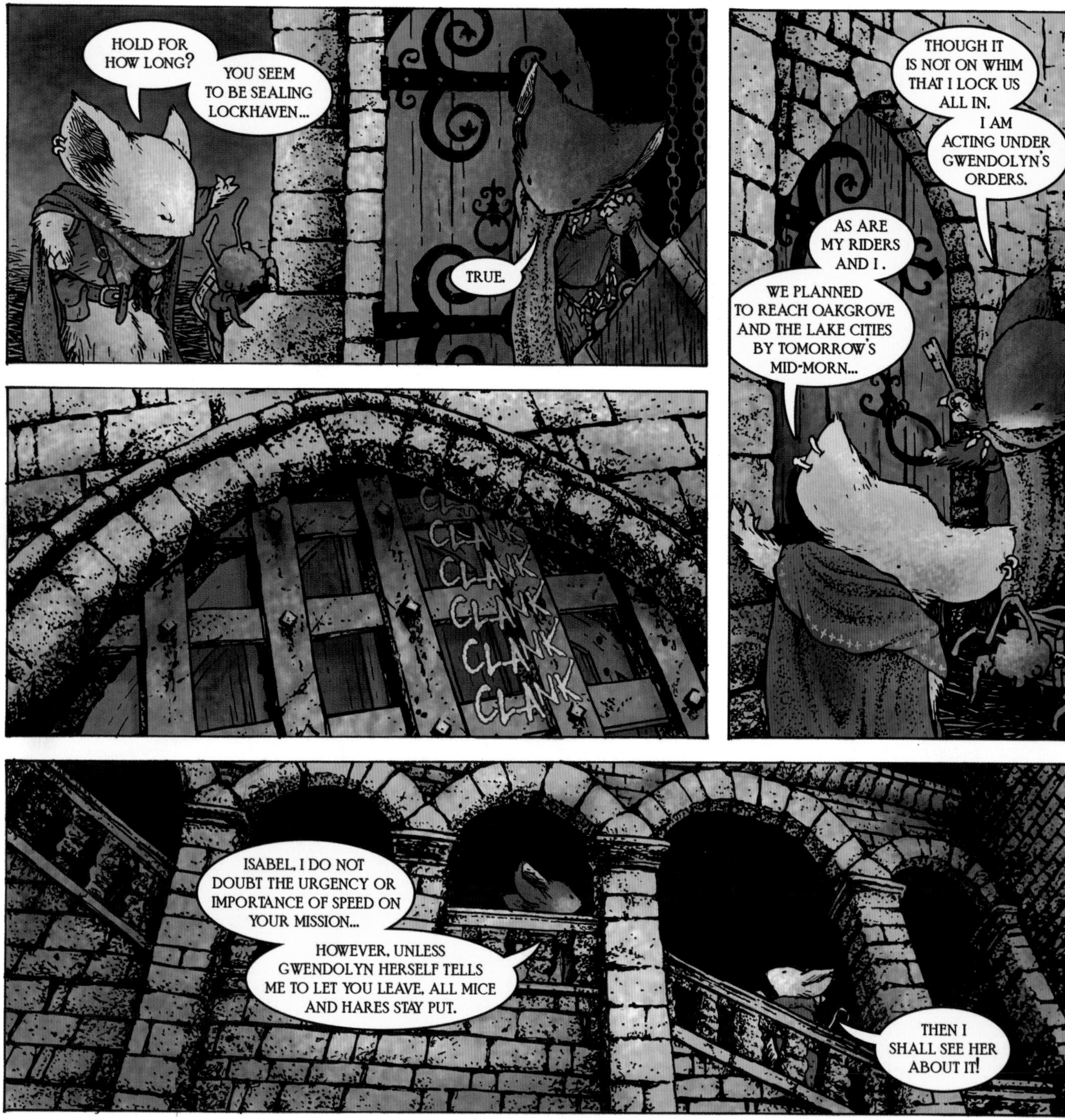
HOLD FOR HOW LONG?
YOU SEEM TO BE SEALING LOCKHAVEN...
TRUE.
THOUGH IT IS NOT ON WHIM THAT I LOCK US ALL IN.
I AM ACTING UNDER GWENDOLYN'S ORDERS.
AS ARE MY RIDERS AND I.
WE PLANNED TO REACH OAKGROVE AND THE LAKE CITIES BY TOMORROW'S MID-MORN...
CLANK
CLANK
CLANK
CLANK
CLANK
CLANK
ISABEL, I DO NOT DOUBT THE URGENCY OR IMPORTANCE OF SPEED ON YOUR MISSION...
HOWEVER, UNLESS GWENDOLYN HERSELF TELLS ME TO LET YOU LEAVE, ALL MICE AND HARES STAY PUT.
THEN I SHALL SEE HER ABOUT IT!

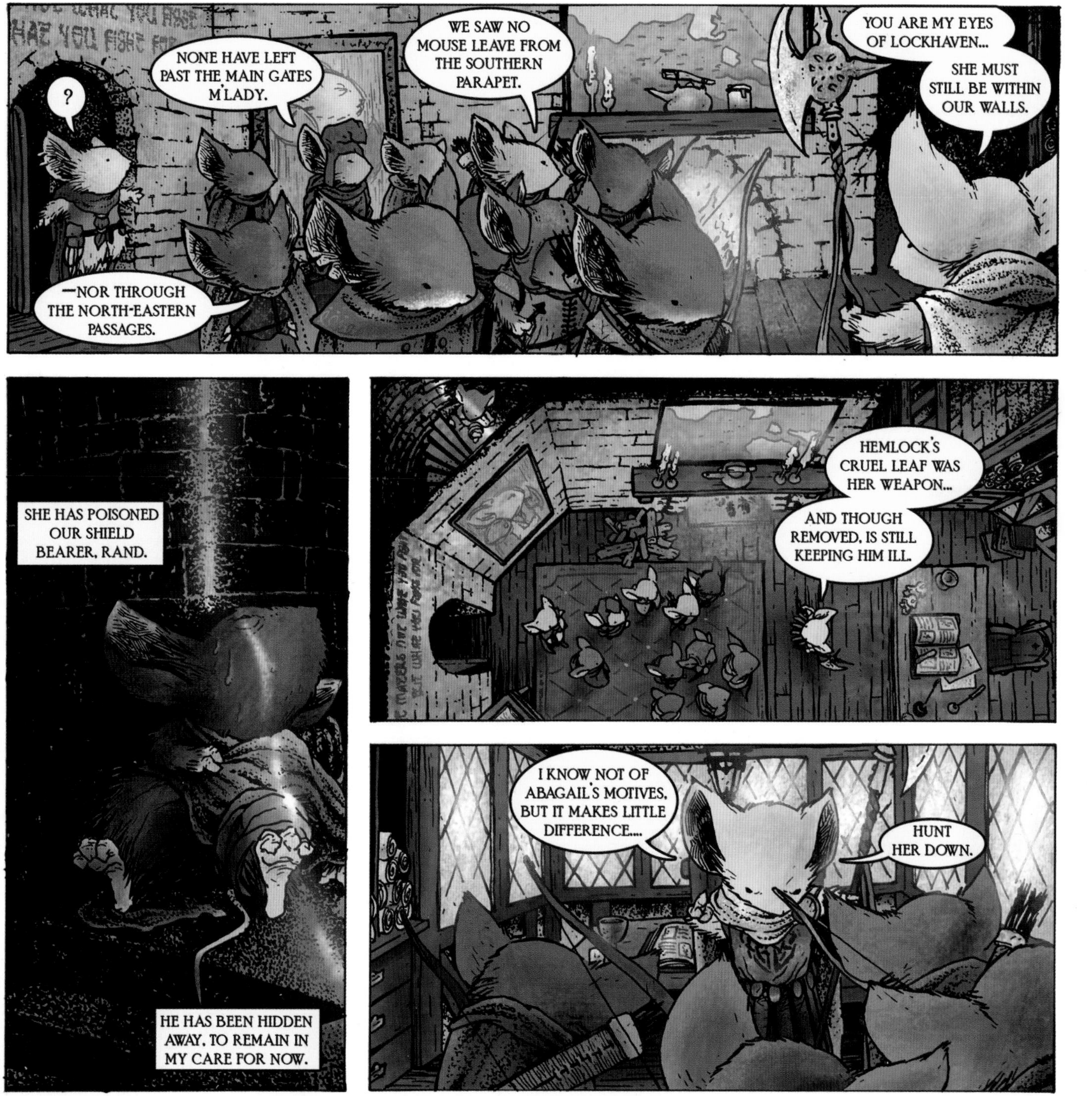

?
NONE HAVE LEFT PAST THE MAIN GATES M'LADY.
WE SAW NO MOUSE LEAVE FROM THE SOUTHERN PARAPET.
—NOR THROUGH THE NORTH-EASTERN PASSAGES.
YOU ARE MY EYES OF LOCKHAVEN...
SHE MUST STILL BE WITHIN OUR WALLS.
SHE HAS POISONED OUR SHIELD BEARER, RAND.
HE HAS BEEN HIDDEN AWAY, TO REMAIN IN MY CARE FOR NOW.
HEMLOCK'S CRUEL LEAF WAS HER WEAPON...
AND THOUGH REMOVED, IS STILL KEEPING HIM ILL.
I KNOW NOT OF ABAGAIL'S MOTIVES, BUT IT MAKES LITTLE DIFFERENCE....
HUNT HER DOWN.

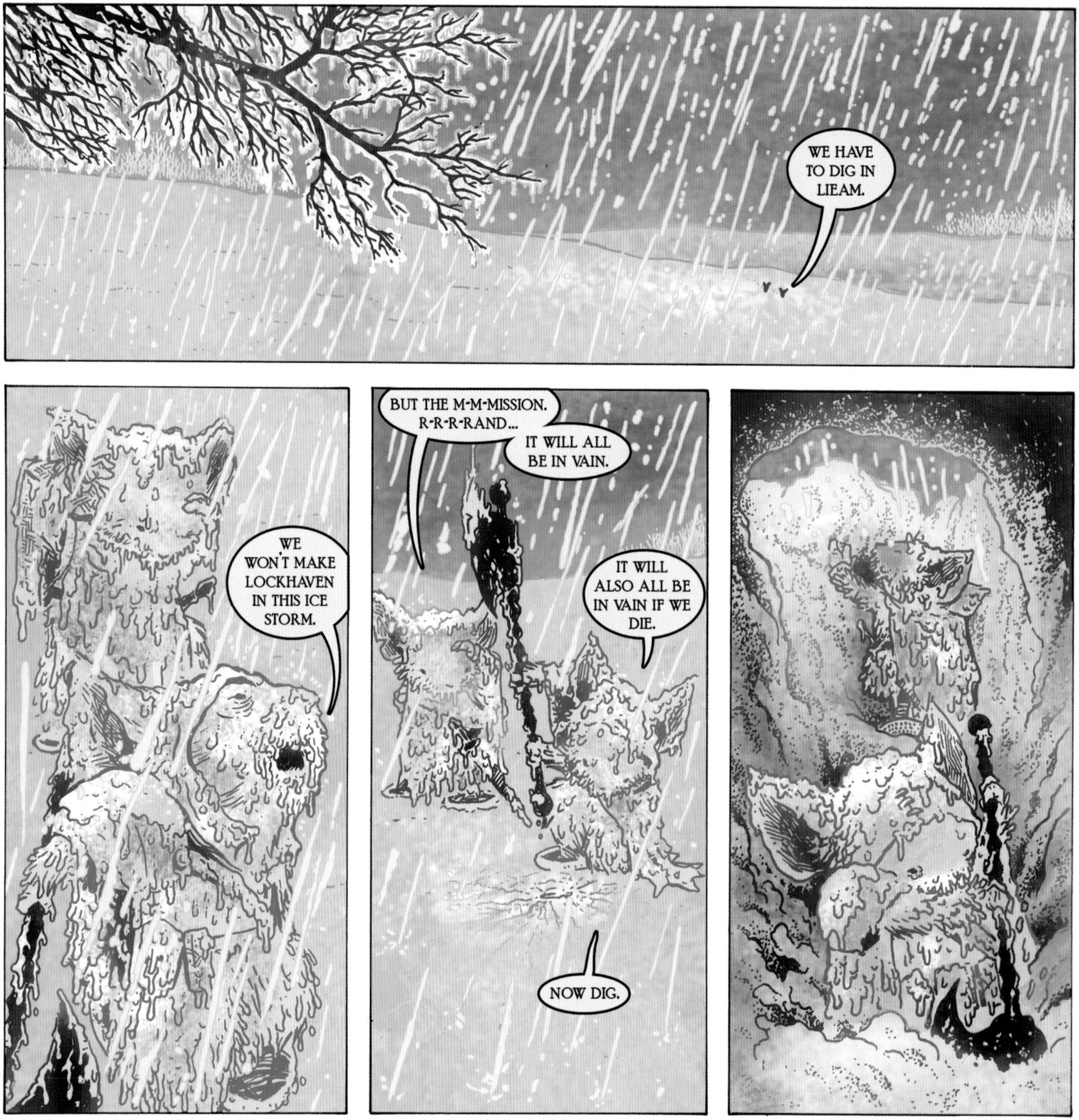
WE HAVE TO DIG IN LIEAM.
WE WON'T MAKE LOCKHAVEN IN THIS ICE STORM.
BUT THE M-M-MISSION. R-R-R-RAND...
IT WILL ALL BE IN VAIN.
IT WILL ALSO ALL BE IN VAIN IF WE DIE.
NOW DIG.

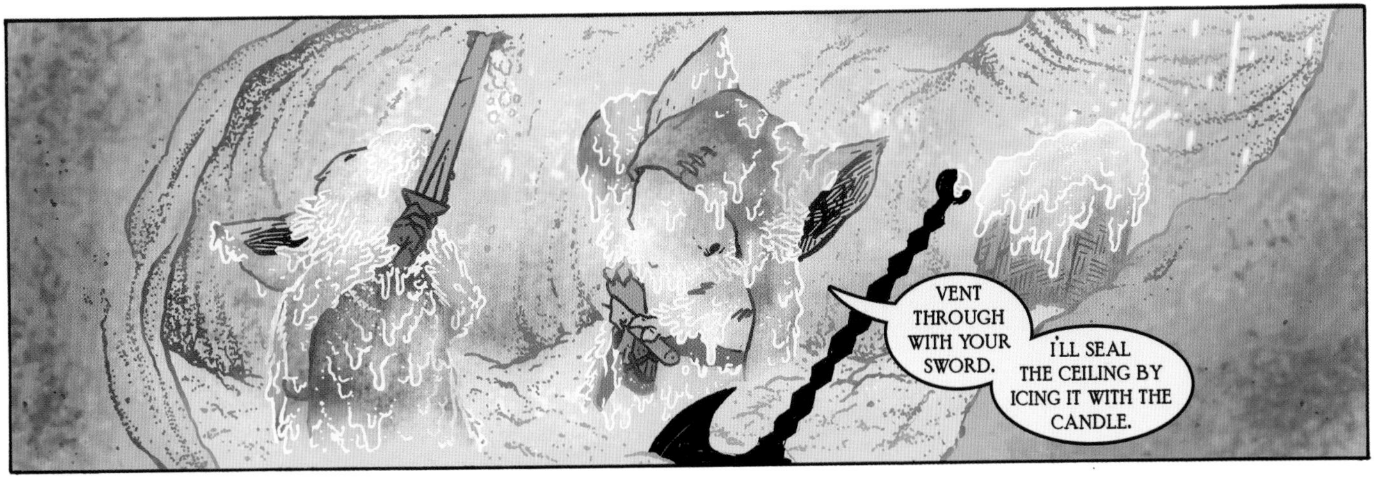
VENT THROUGH WITH YOUR SWORD.
I'LL SEAL THE CEILING BY ICING IT WITH THE CANDLE.

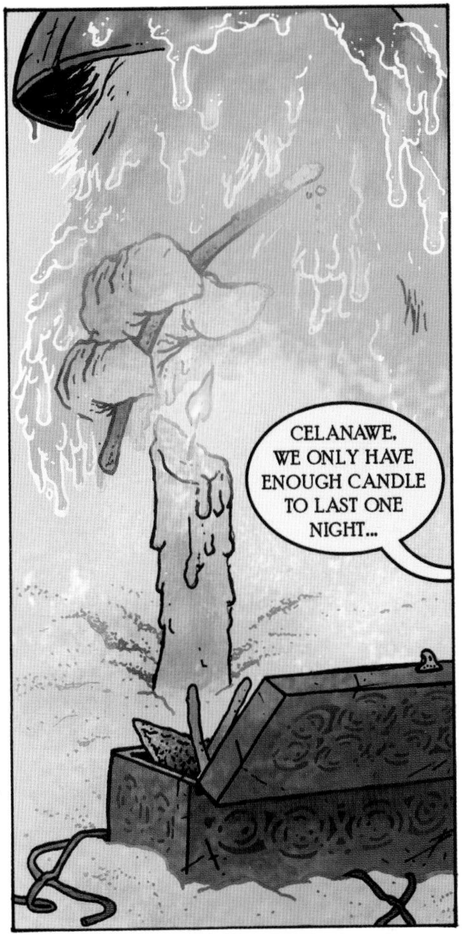
CELANAWE, WE ONLY HAVE ENOUGH CANDLE TO LAST ONE NIGHT...

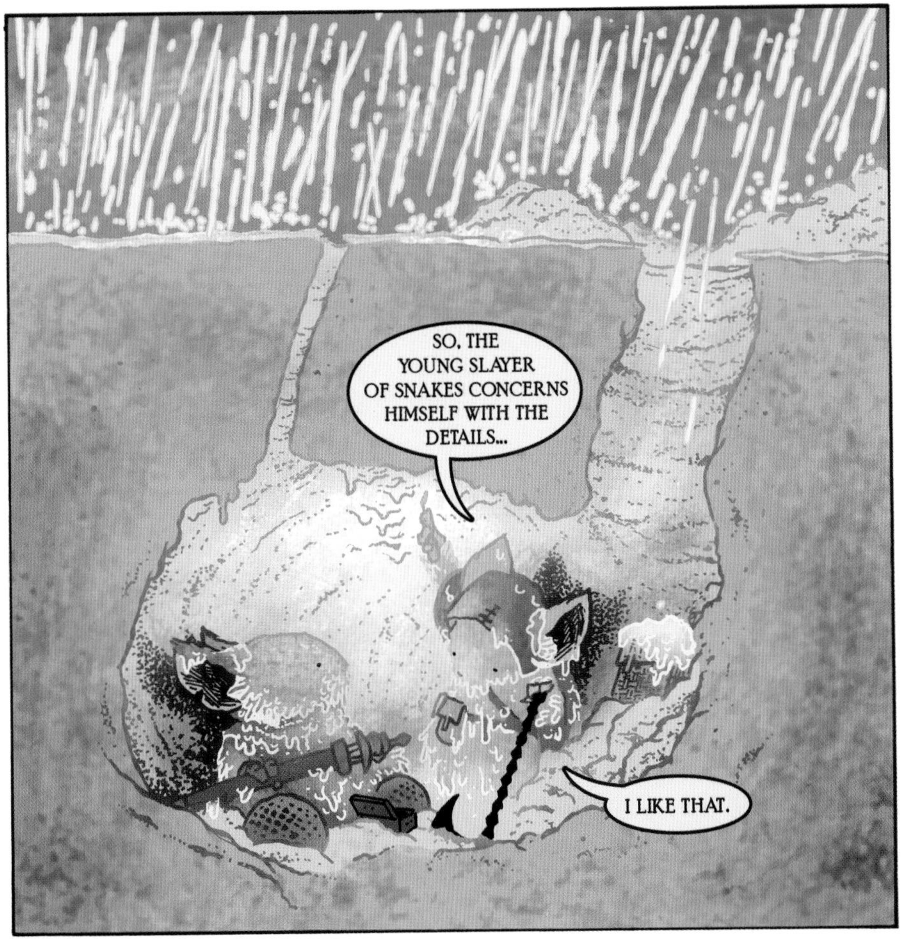
SO, THE YOUNG SLAYER OF SNAKES CONCERNS HIMSELF WITH THE DETAILS...
I LIKE THAT.

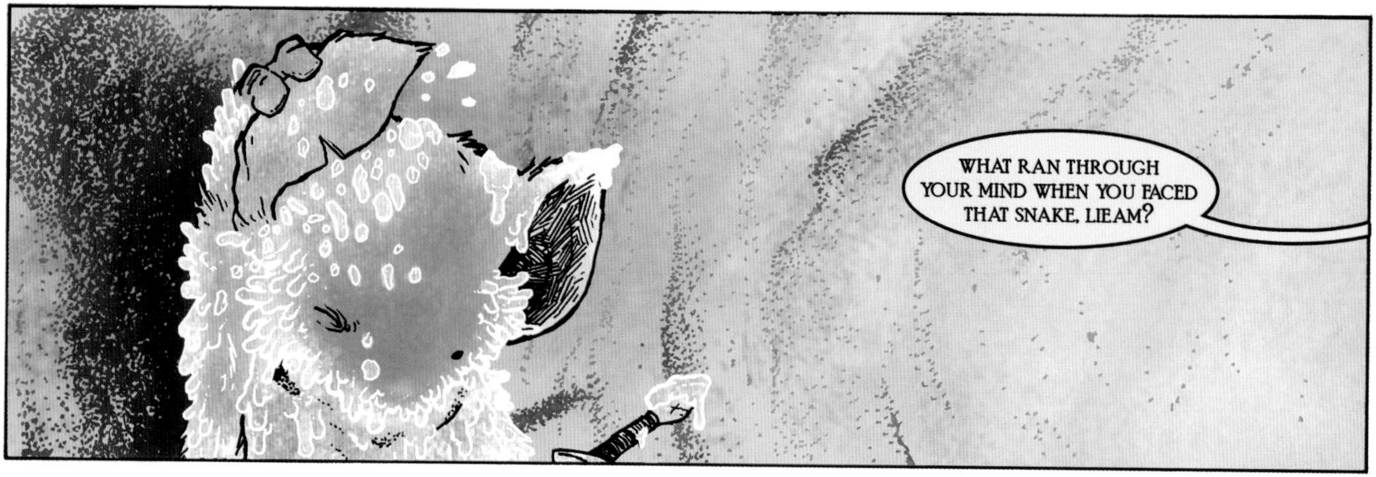
WHAT RAN THROUGH YOUR MIND WHEN YOU FACED THAT SNAKE, LIEAM?

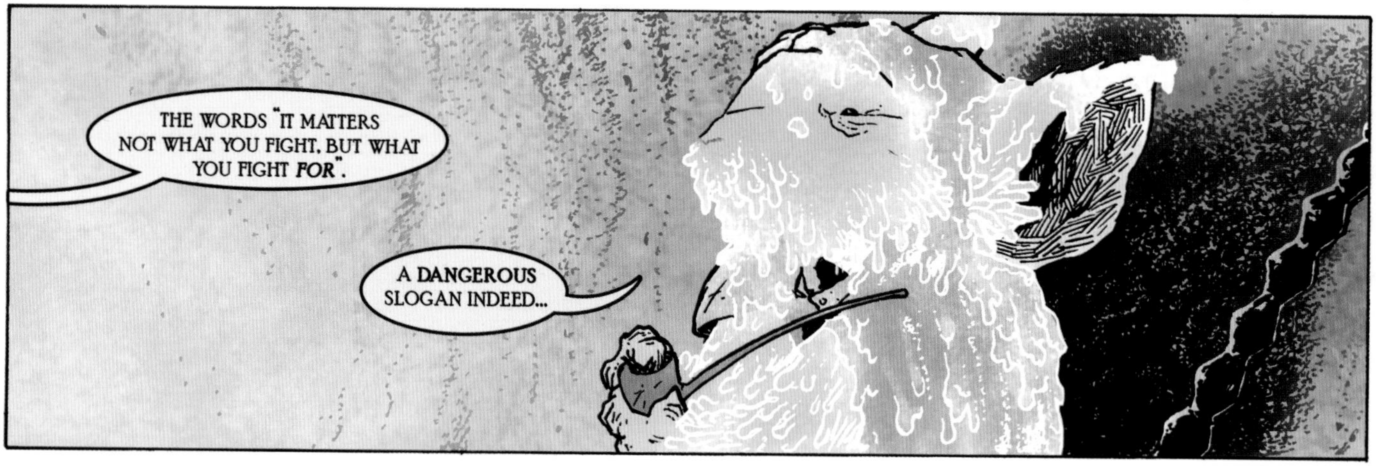
THE WORDS "IT MATTERS NOT WHAT YOU FIGHT, BUT WHAT YOU FIGHT ***FOR***".
A **DANGEROUS** SLOGAN INDEED...

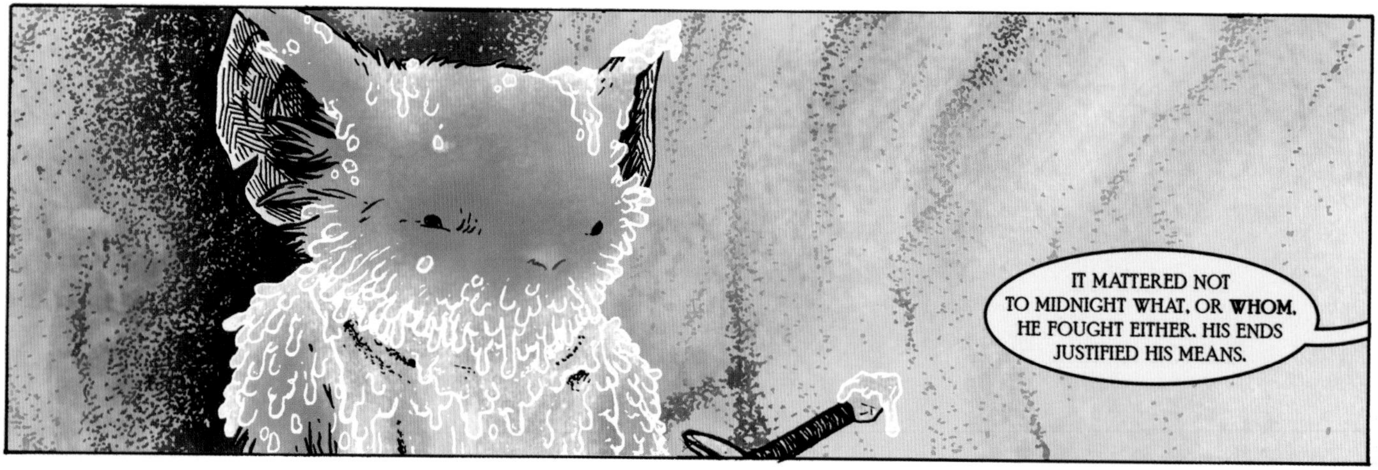
IT MATTERED NOT TO MIDNIGHT WHAT, OR **WHOM**, HE FOUGHT EITHER. HIS ENDS JUSTIFIED HIS MEANS.

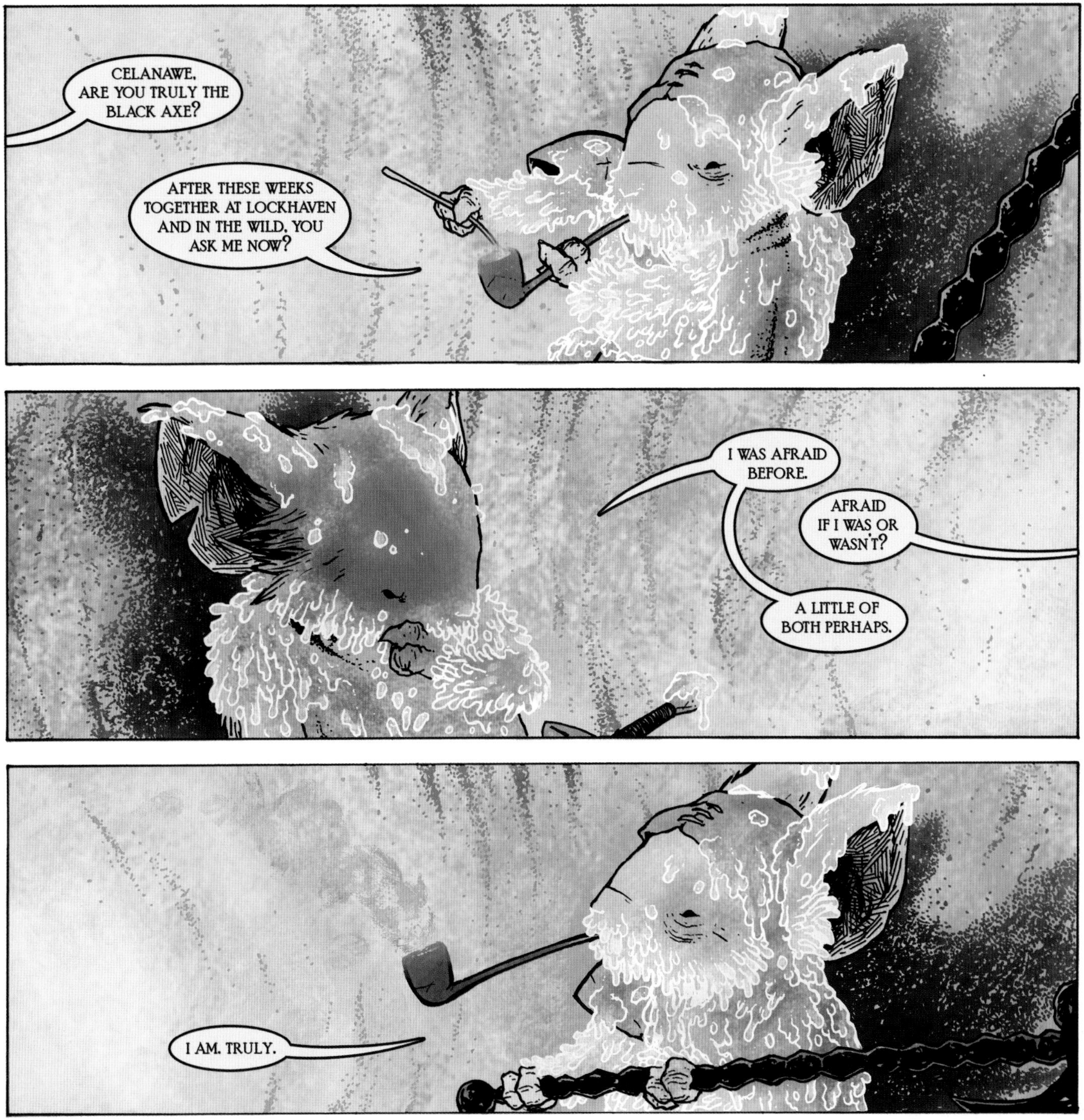
CELANAWE, ARE YOU TRULY THE BLACK AXE?
AFTER THESE WEEKS TOGETHER AT LOCKHAVEN AND IN THE WILD, YOU ASK ME NOW?
I WAS AFRAID BEFORE.
AFRAID IF I WAS OR WASN'T?
A LITTLE OF BOTH PERHAPS.
I AM. TRULY.

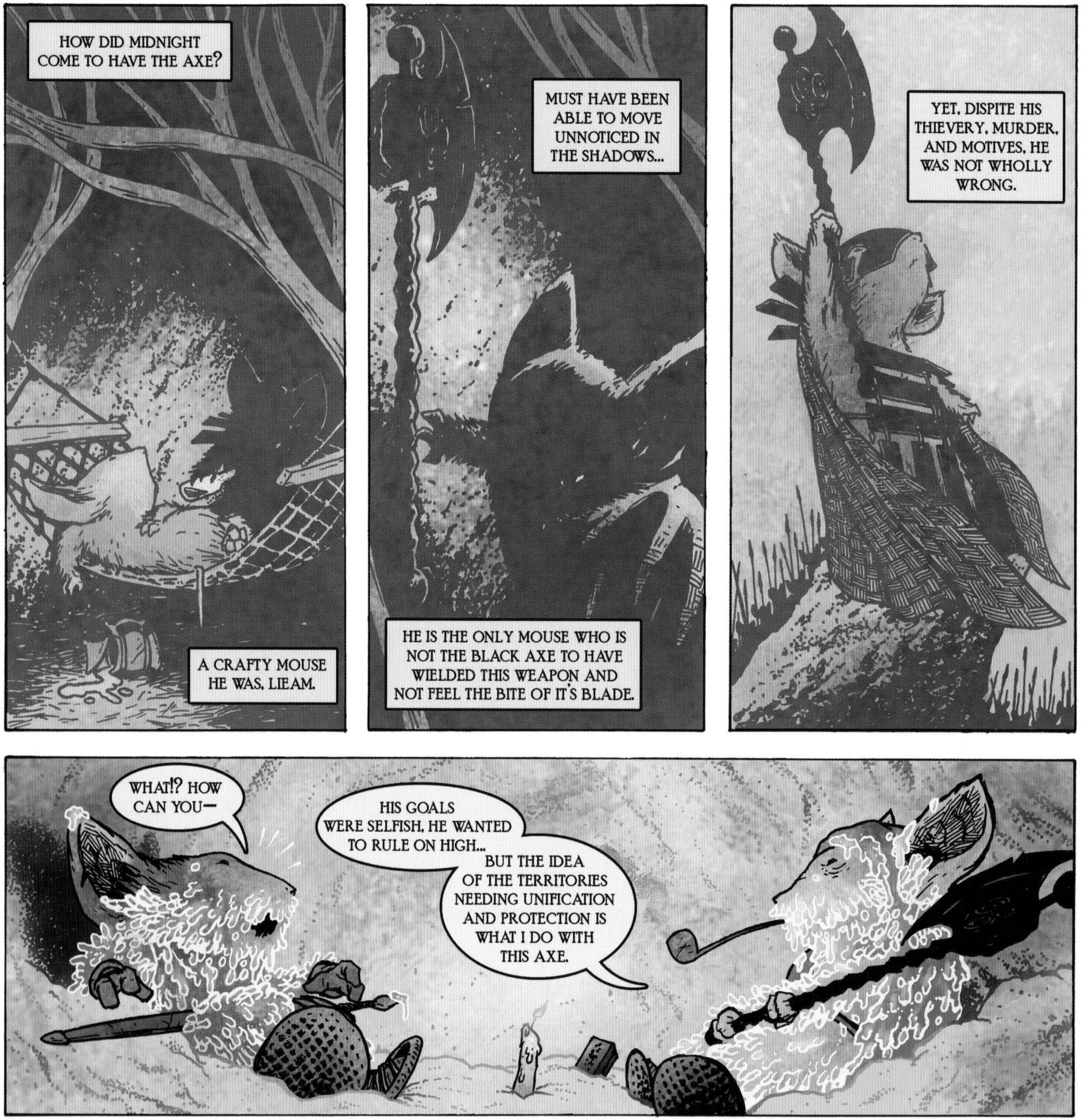
HOW DID MIDNIGHT COME TO HAVE THE AXE?
A CRAFTY MOUSE HE WAS, LIEAM.
MUST HAVE BEEN ABLE TO MOVE UNNOTICED IN THE SHADOWS...
HE IS THE ONLY MOUSE WHO IS NOT THE BLACK AXE TO HAVE WIELDED THIS WEAPON AND NOT FEEL THE BITE OF IT'S BLADE.
YET, DISPITE HIS THIEVERY, MURDER, AND MOTIVES, HE WAS NOT WHOLLY WRONG.
WHAT!? HOW CAN YOU—
HIS GOALS WERE SELFISH, HE WANTED TO RULE ON HIGH...
BUT THE IDEA OF THE TERRITORIES NEEDING UNIFICATION AND PROTECTION IS WHAT I DO WITH THIS AXE.

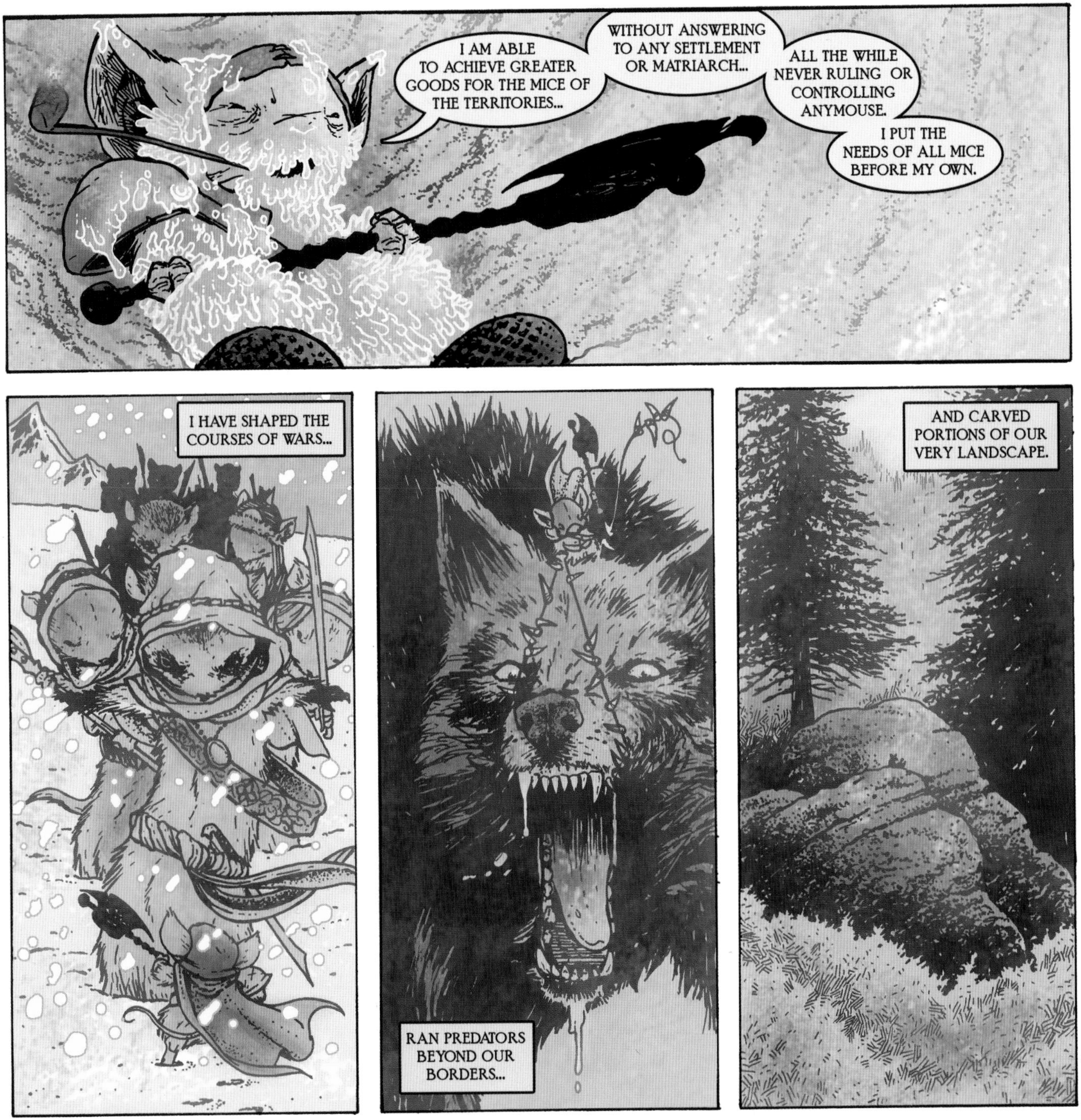
I AM ABLE TO ACHIEVE GREATER GOODS FOR THE MICE OF THE TERRITORIES...
WITHOUT ANSWERING TO ANY SETTLEMENT OR MATRIARCH...
ALL THE WHILE NEVER RULING OR CONTROLLING ANYMOUSE.
I PUT THE NEEDS OF ALL MICE BEFORE MY OWN.
I HAVE SHAPED THE COURSES OF WARS...
RAN PREDATORS BEYOND OUR BORDERS...
AND CARVED PORTIONS OF OUR VERY LANDSCAPE.

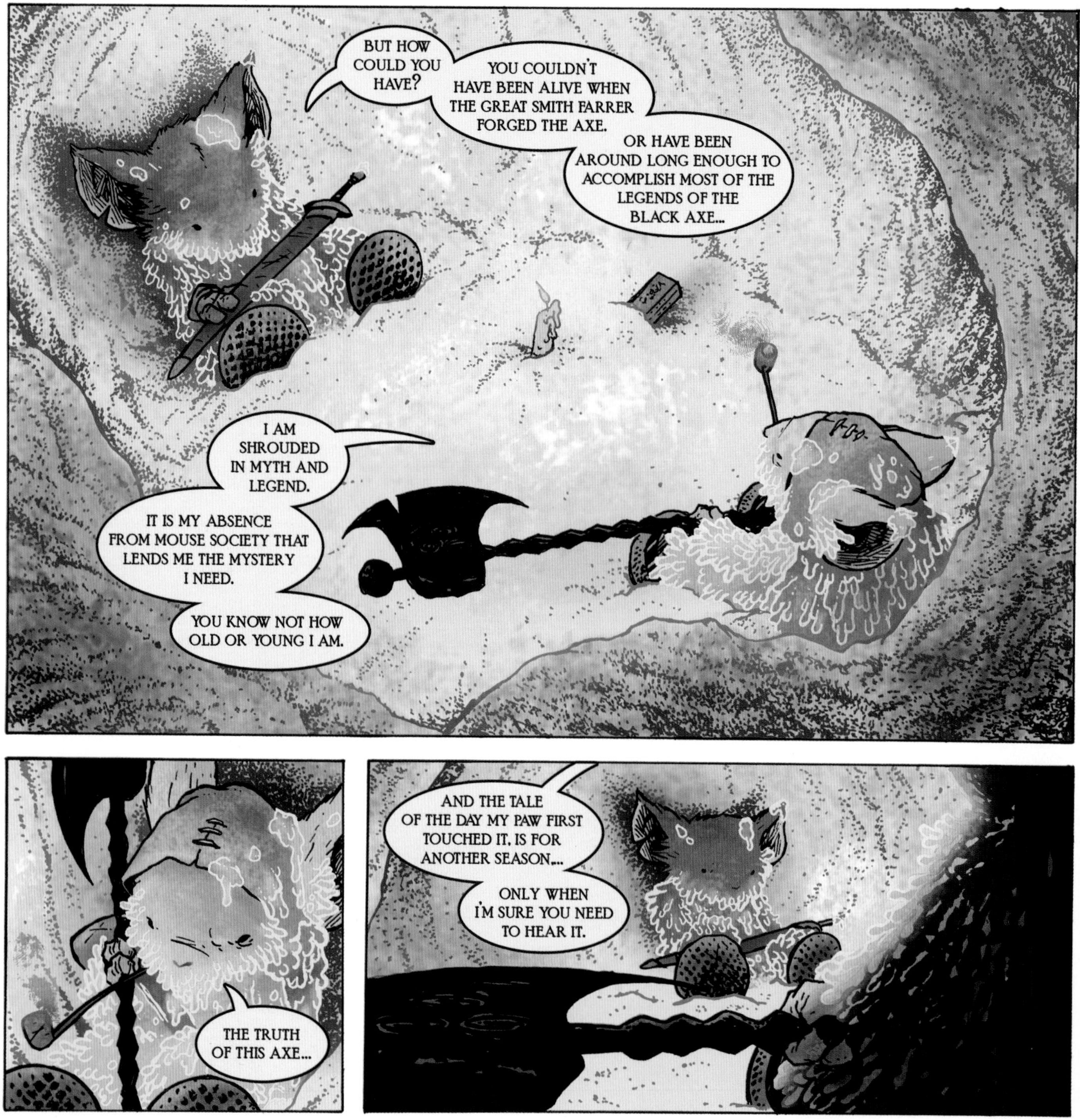
BUT HOW COULD YOU HAVE?
YOU COULDN'T HAVE BEEN ALIVE WHEN THE GREAT SMITH FARRER FORGED THE AXE.
OR HAVE BEEN AROUND LONG ENOUGH TO ACCOMPLISH MOST OF THE LEGENDS OF THE BLACK AXE...
I AM SHROUDED IN MYTH AND LEGEND.
IT IS MY ABSENCE FROM MOUSE SOCIETY THAT LENDS ME THE MYSTERY I NEED.
YOU KNOW NOT HOW OLD OR YOUNG I AM.
THE TRUTH OF THIS AXE...
AND THE TALE OF THE DAY MY PAW FIRST TOUCHED IT, IS FOR ANOTHER SEASON...
ONLY WHEN I'M SURE YOU NEED TO HEAR IT.

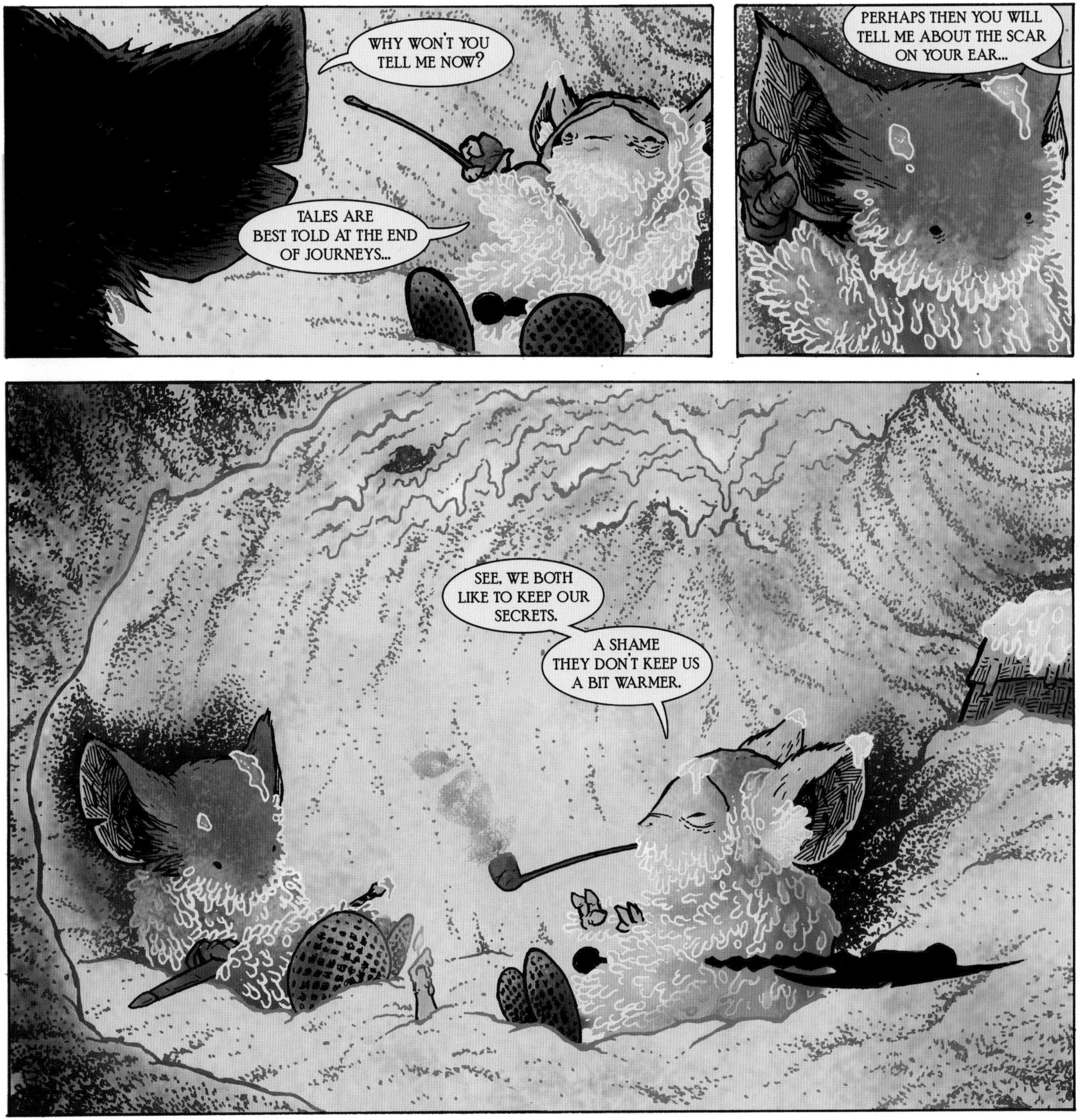

WHY WON'T YOU TELL ME NOW?
TALES ARE BEST TOLD AT THE END OF JOURNEYS...
PERHAPS THEN YOU WILL TELL ME ABOUT THE SCAR ON YOUR EAR...
SEE, WE BOTH LIKE TO KEEP OUR SECRETS.
A SHAME THEY DON'T KEEP US A BIT WARMER.

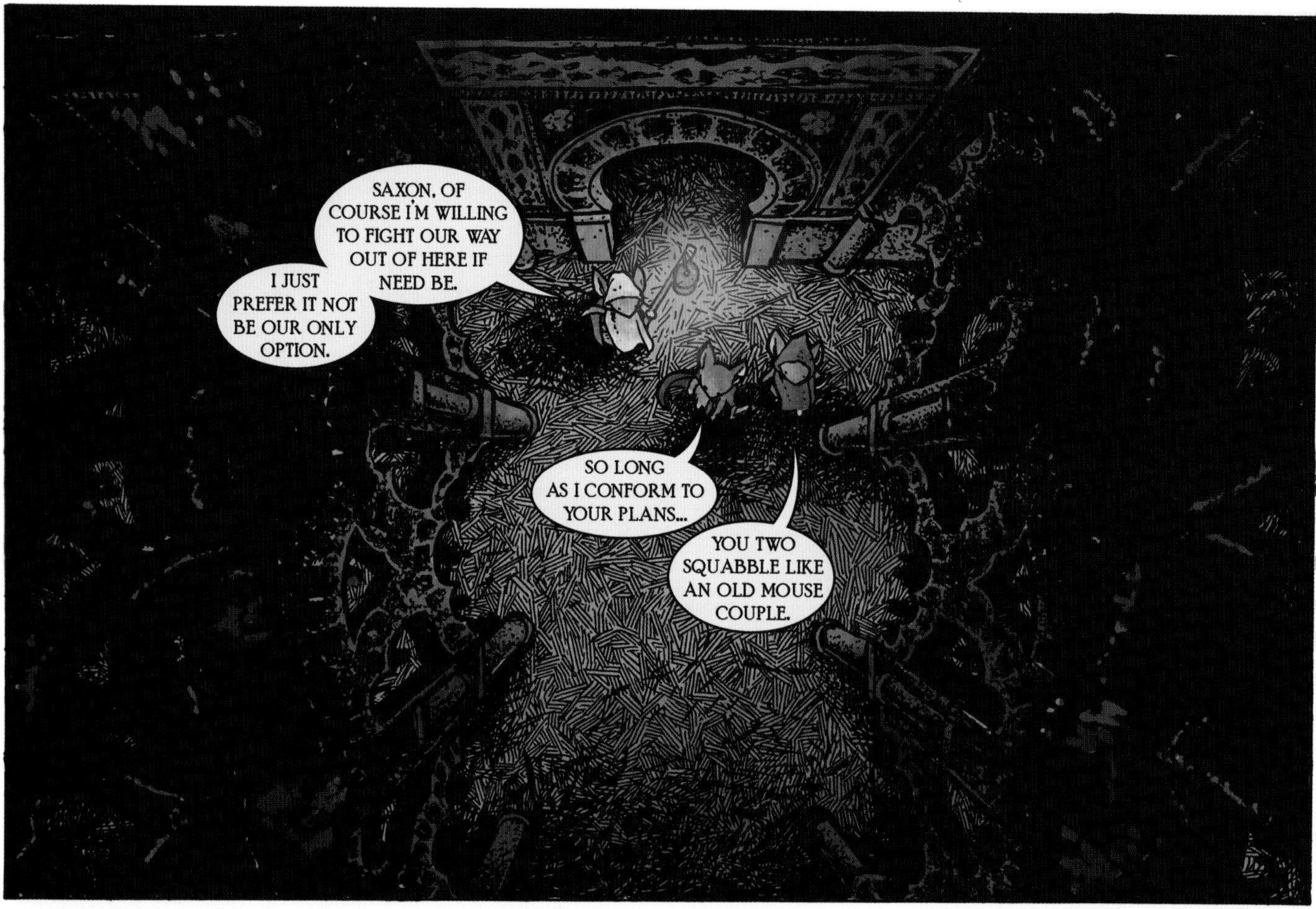
SAXON, OF COURSE I'M WILLING TO FIGHT OUR WAY OUT OF HERE IF NEED BE.
I JUST PREFER IT NOT BE OUR ONLY OPTION.
SO LONG AS I CONFORM TO YOUR PLANS...
YOU TWO SQUABBLE LIKE AN OLD MOUSE COUPLE.

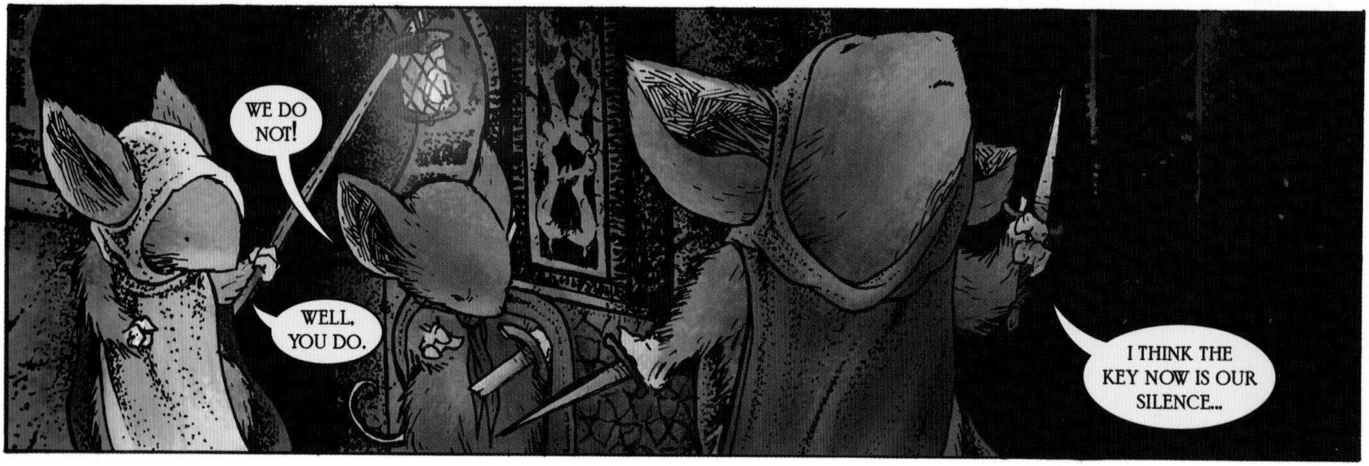
WE DO NOT!
WELL, YOU DO.
I THINK THE KEY NOW IS OUR SILENCE...

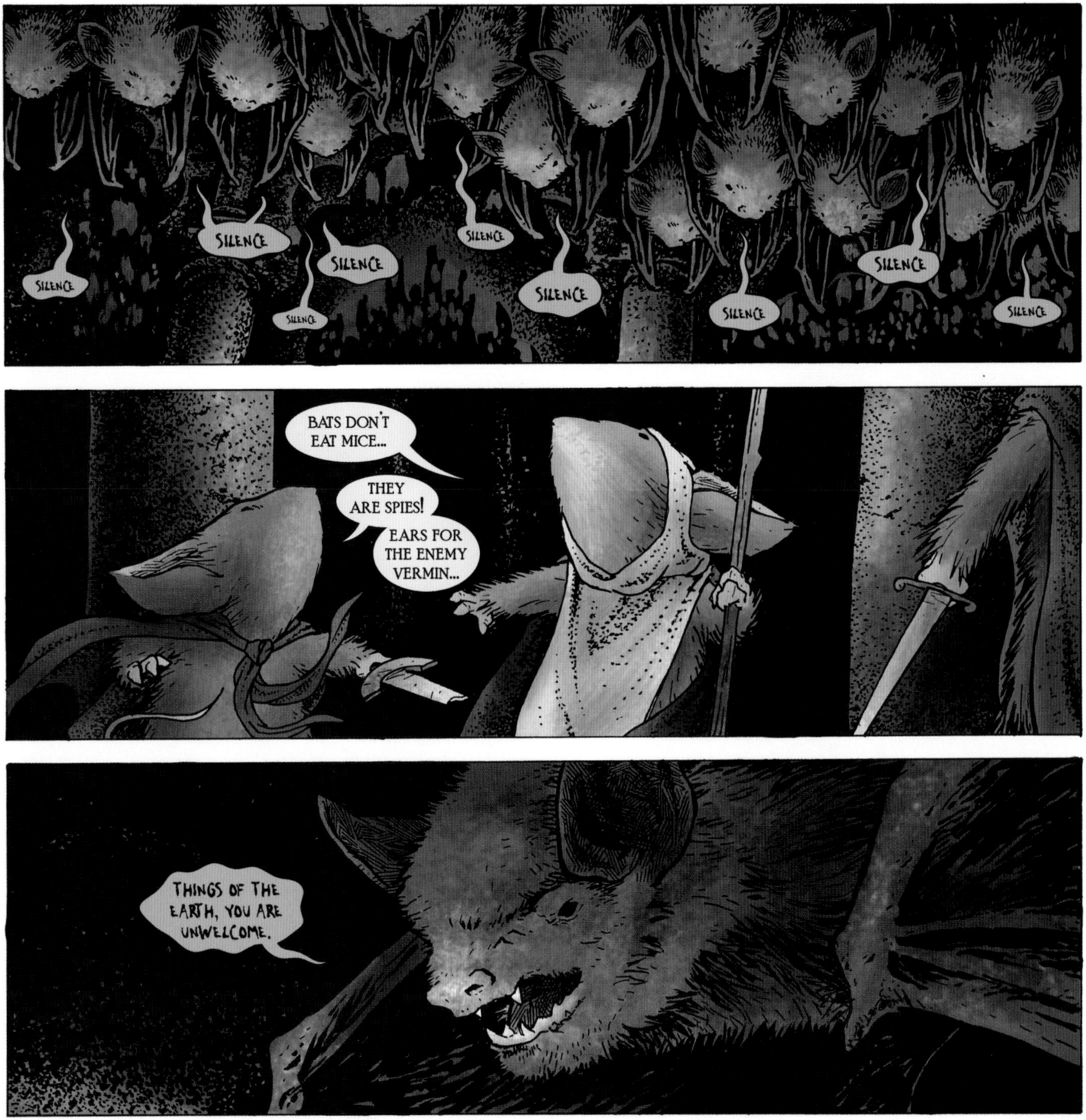
SILENCE
SILENCE
SILENCE
SILENCE
SILENCE
SILENCE
SILENCE
SILENCE
SILENCE
SILENCE
BATS DON'T EAT MICE...
THEY ARE SPIES!
EARS FOR THE ENEMY VERMIN...
THINGS OF THE EARTH, YOU ARE UNWELCOME.

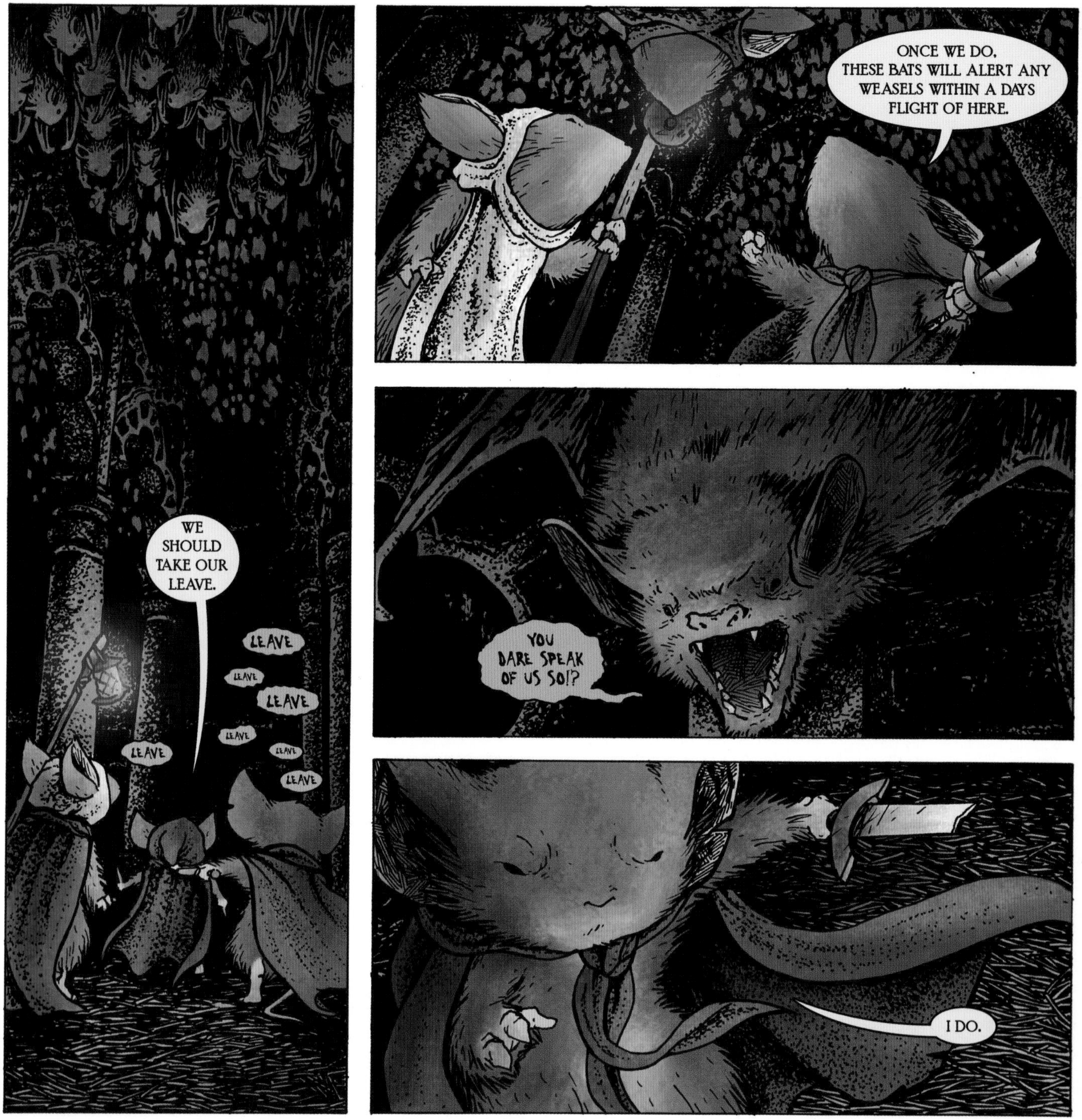
WE SHOULD TAKE OUR LEAVE.
LEAVE
LEAVE
LEAVE
LEAVE
LEAVE
LEAVE
LEAVE
ONCE WE DO, THESE BATS WILL ALERT ANY WEASELS WITHIN A DAYS FLIGHT OF HERE.
YOU DARE SPEAK OF US SO!?
I DO.

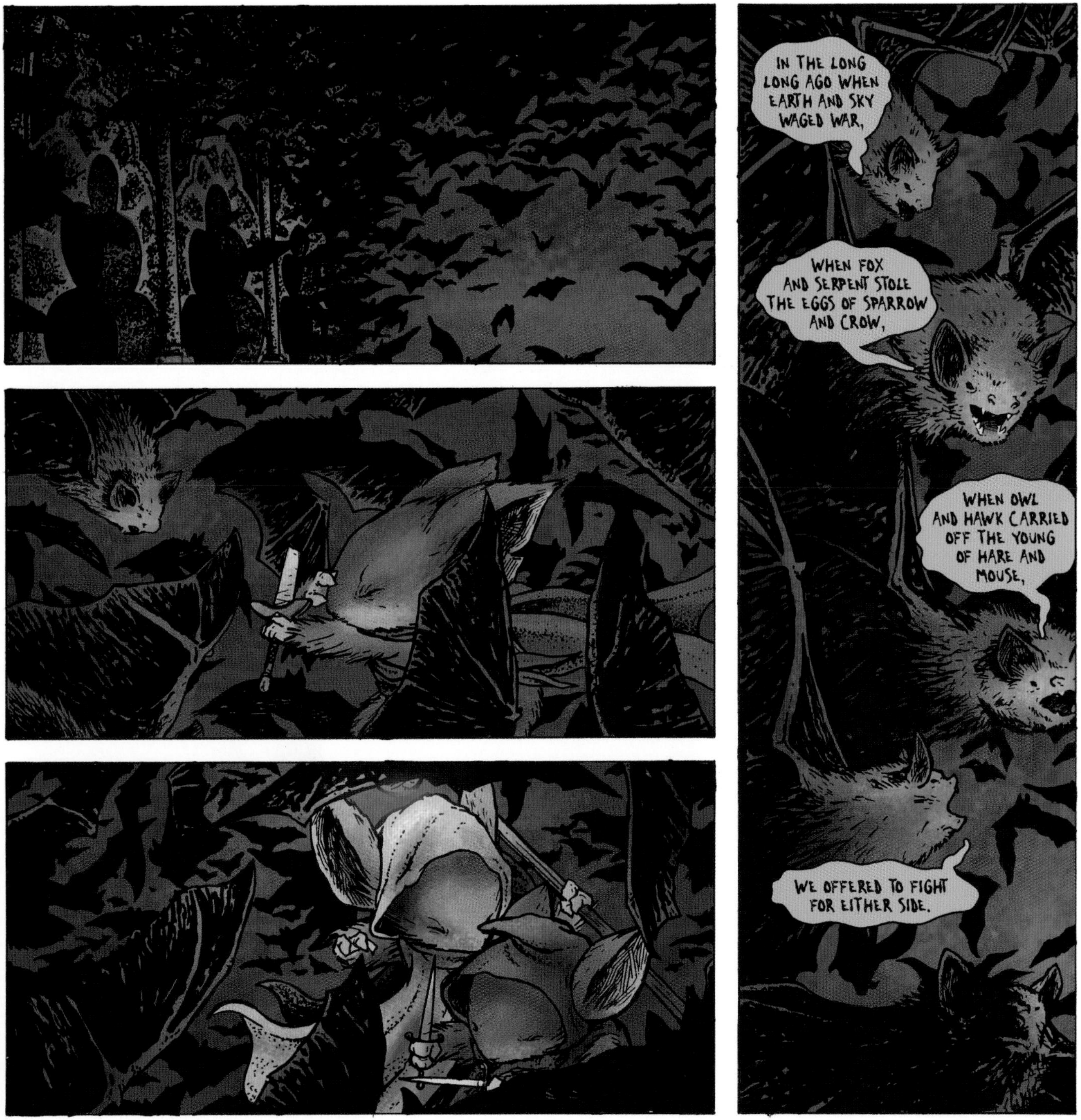
IN THE LONG LONG AGO WHEN EARTH AND SKY WAGED WAR,
WHEN FOX AND SERPENT STOLE THE EGGS OF SPARROW AND CROW,
WHEN OWL AND HAWK CARRIED OFF THE YOUNG OF HARE AND MOUSE,
WE OFFERED TO FIGHT FOR EITHER SIDE.

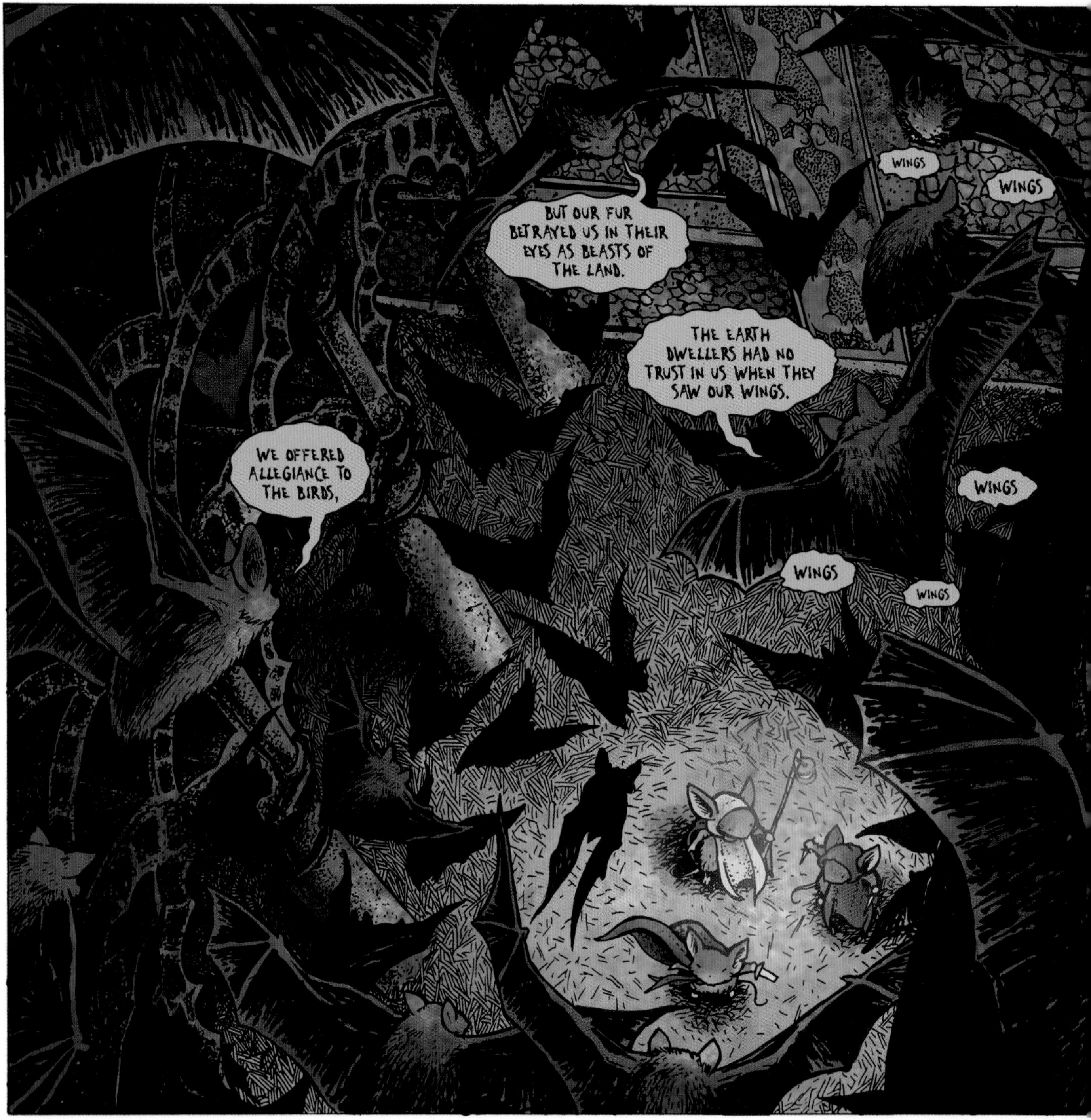
WE OFFERED ALLEGIANCE TO THE BIRDS,
BUT OUR FUR BETRAYED US IN THEIR EYES AS BEASTS OF THE LAND.
THE EARTH DWELLERS HAD NO TRUST IN US WHEN THEY SAW OUR WINGS.
WINGS
WINGS
WINGS
WINGS
WINGS

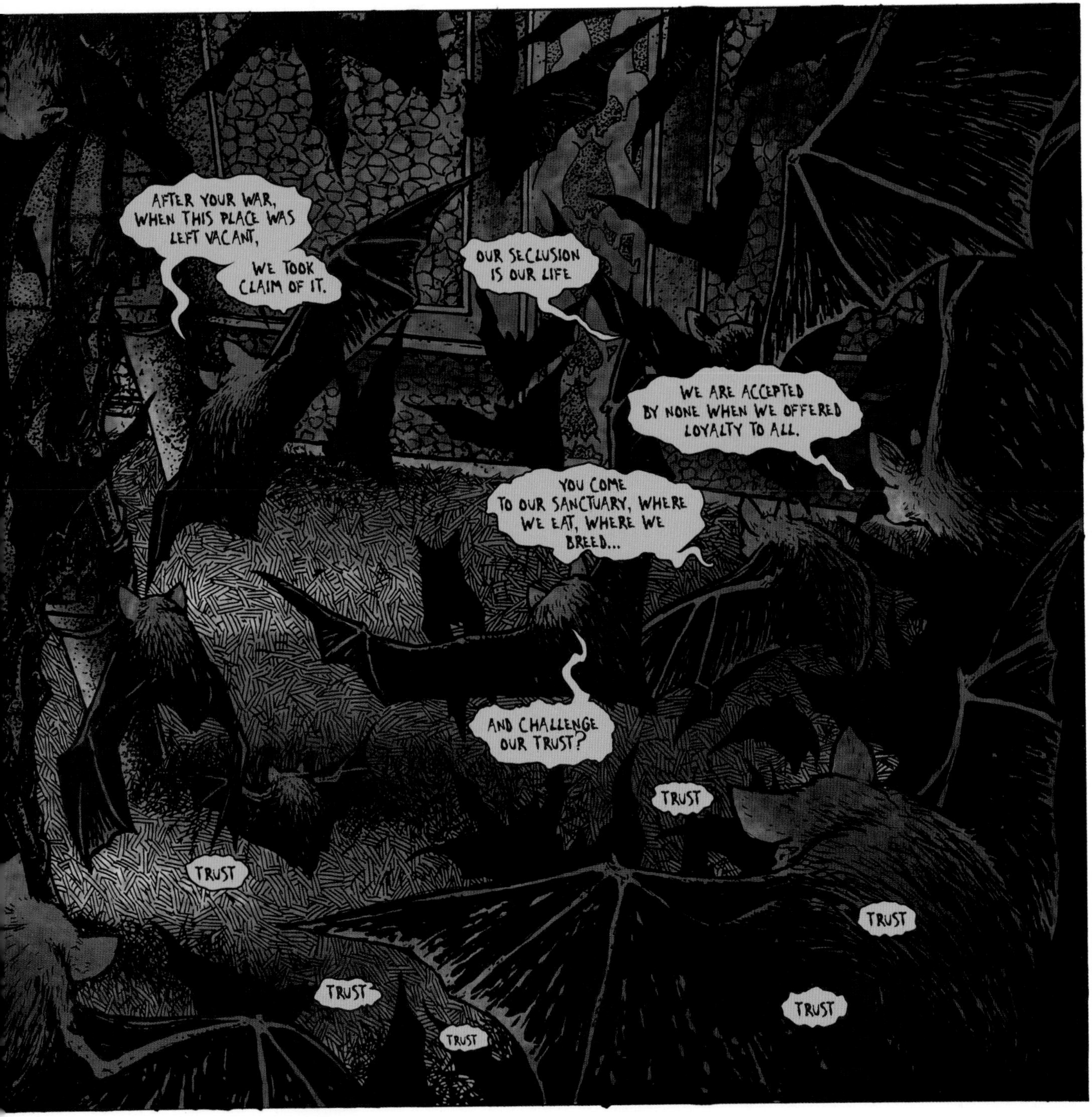
AFTER YOUR WAR, WHEN THIS PLACE WAS LEFT VACANT,
WE TOOK CLAIM OF IT.
OUR SECLUSION IS OUR LIFE
WE ARE ACCEPTED BY NONE WHEN WE OFFERED LOYALTY TO ALL.
YOU COME TO OUR SANCTUARY, WHERE WE EAT, WHERE WE BREED...
AND CHALLENGE OUR TRUST?
TRUST
TRUST
TRUST
TRUST
TRUST
TRUST

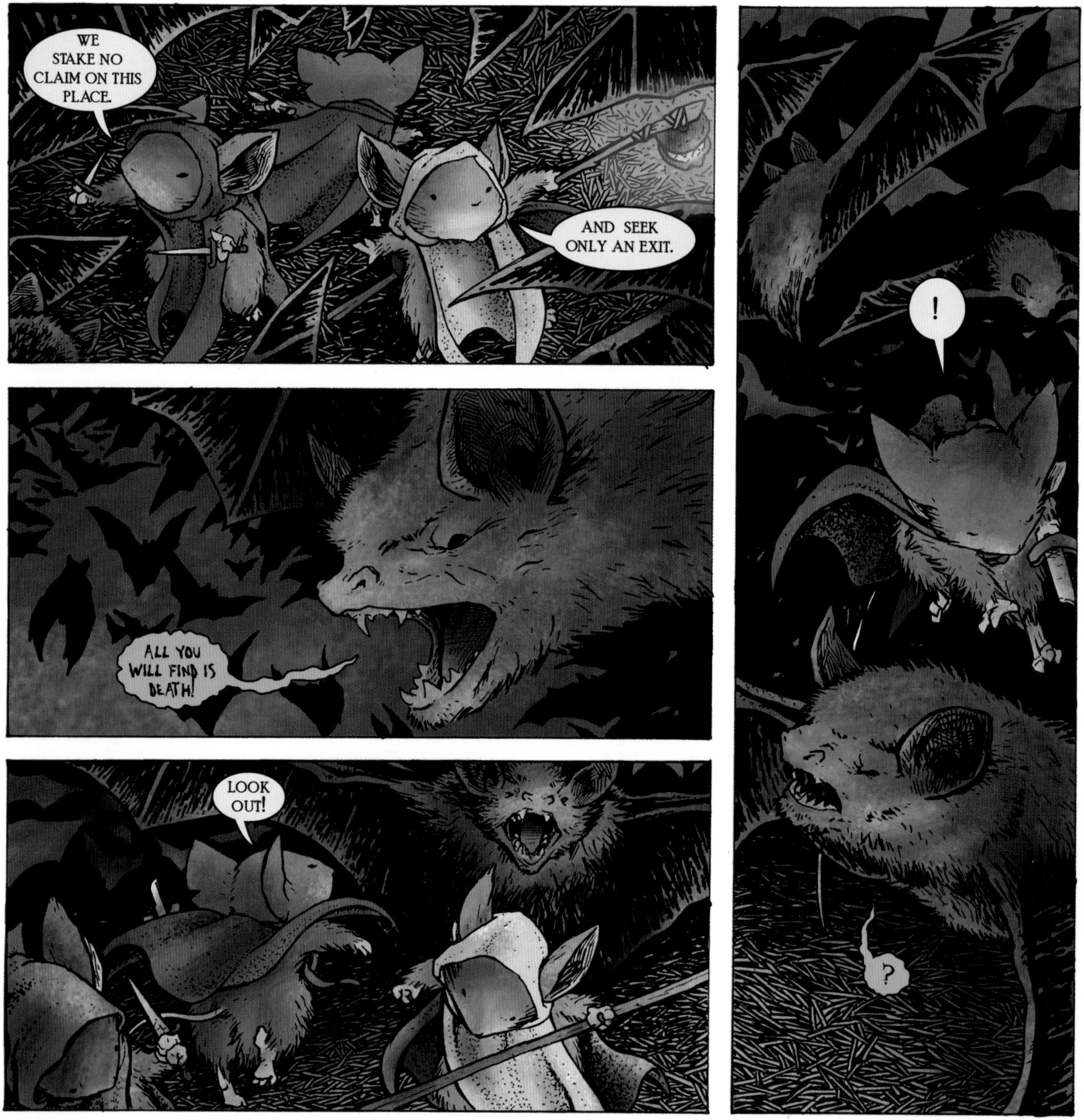
WE STAKE NO CLAIM ON THIS PLACE.
AND SEEK ONLY AN EXIT.
ALL YOU WILL FIND IS DEATH!
LOOK OUT!
!
?

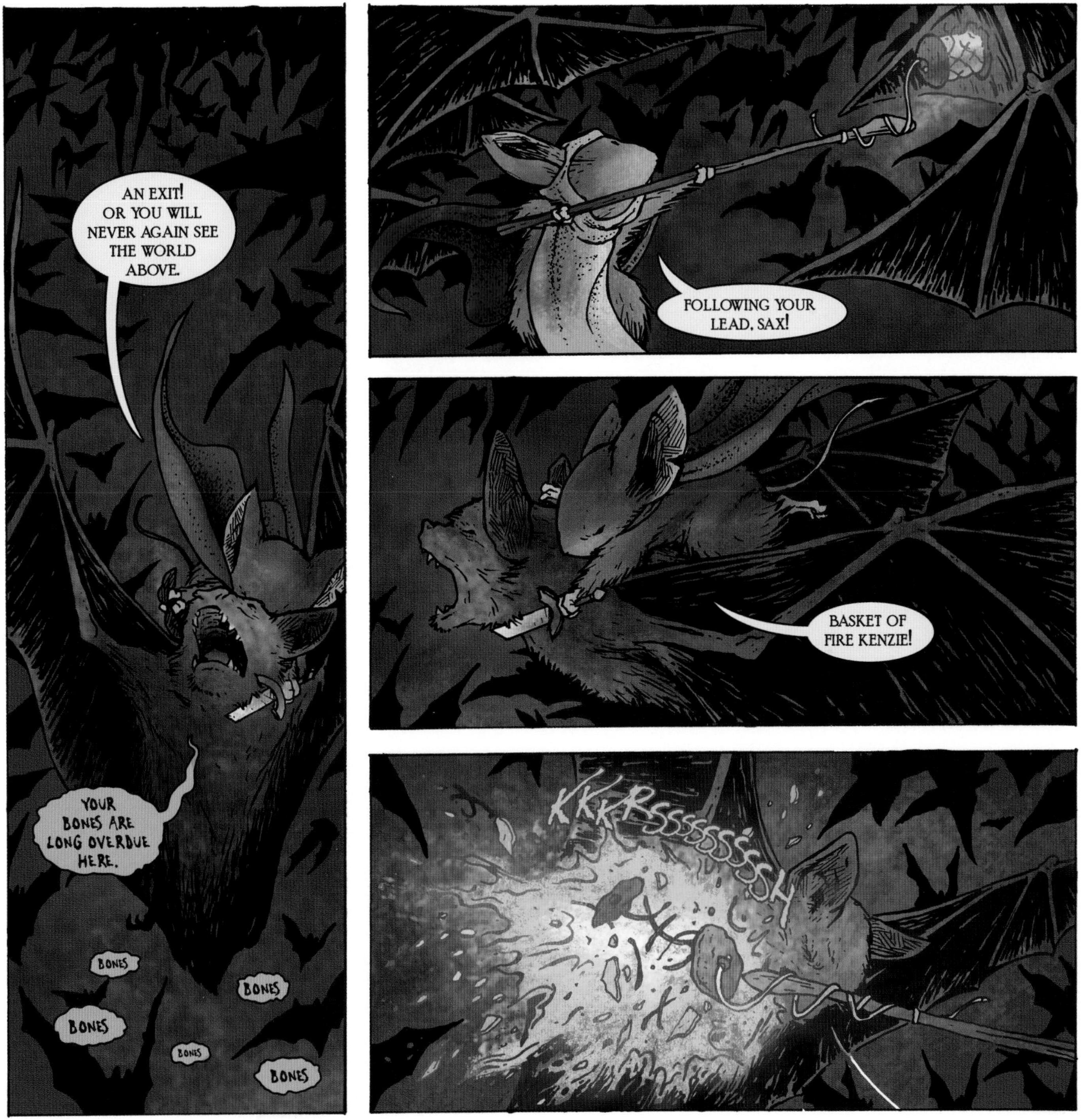
AN EXIT! OR YOU WILL NEVER AGAIN SEE THE WORLD ABOVE.
YOUR BONES ARE LONG OVERDUE HERE.
BONES
BONES
BONES
BONES
BONES
FOLLOWING YOUR LEAD, SAX!
BASKET OF FIRE KENZIE!
KKKRSSSSSSSSSH

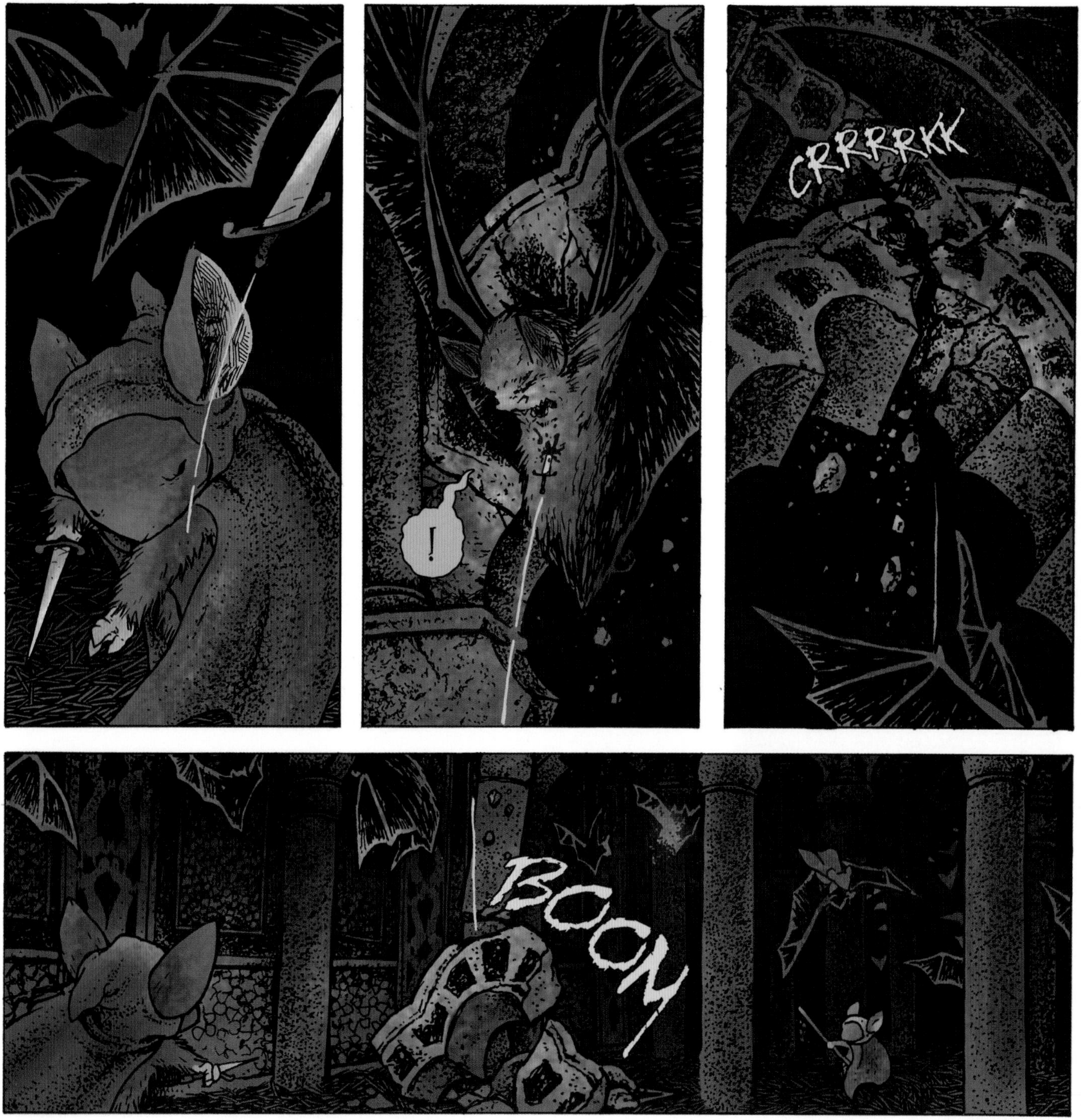
!
CRRRRKK
BOOM

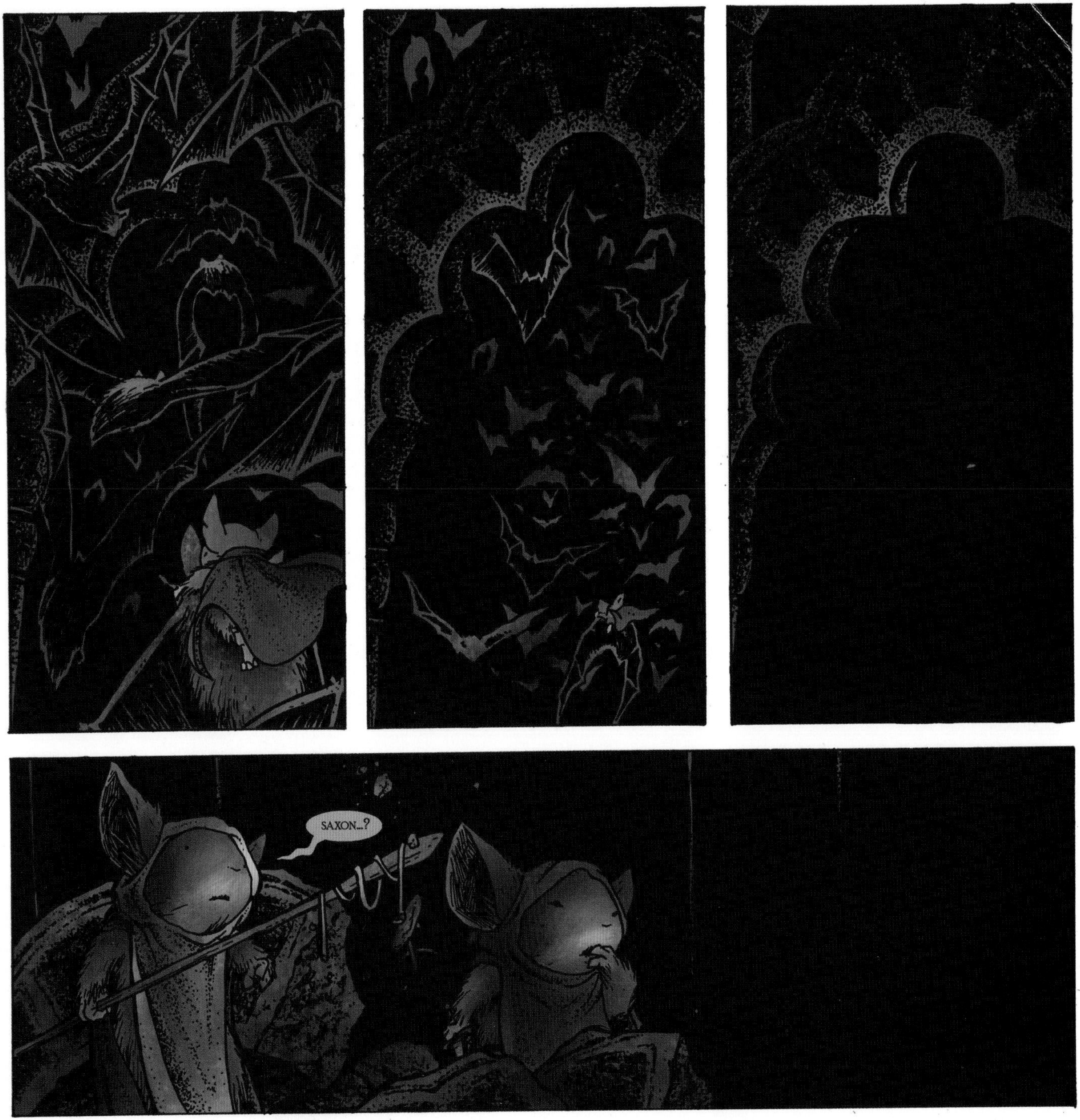
SAXON...?

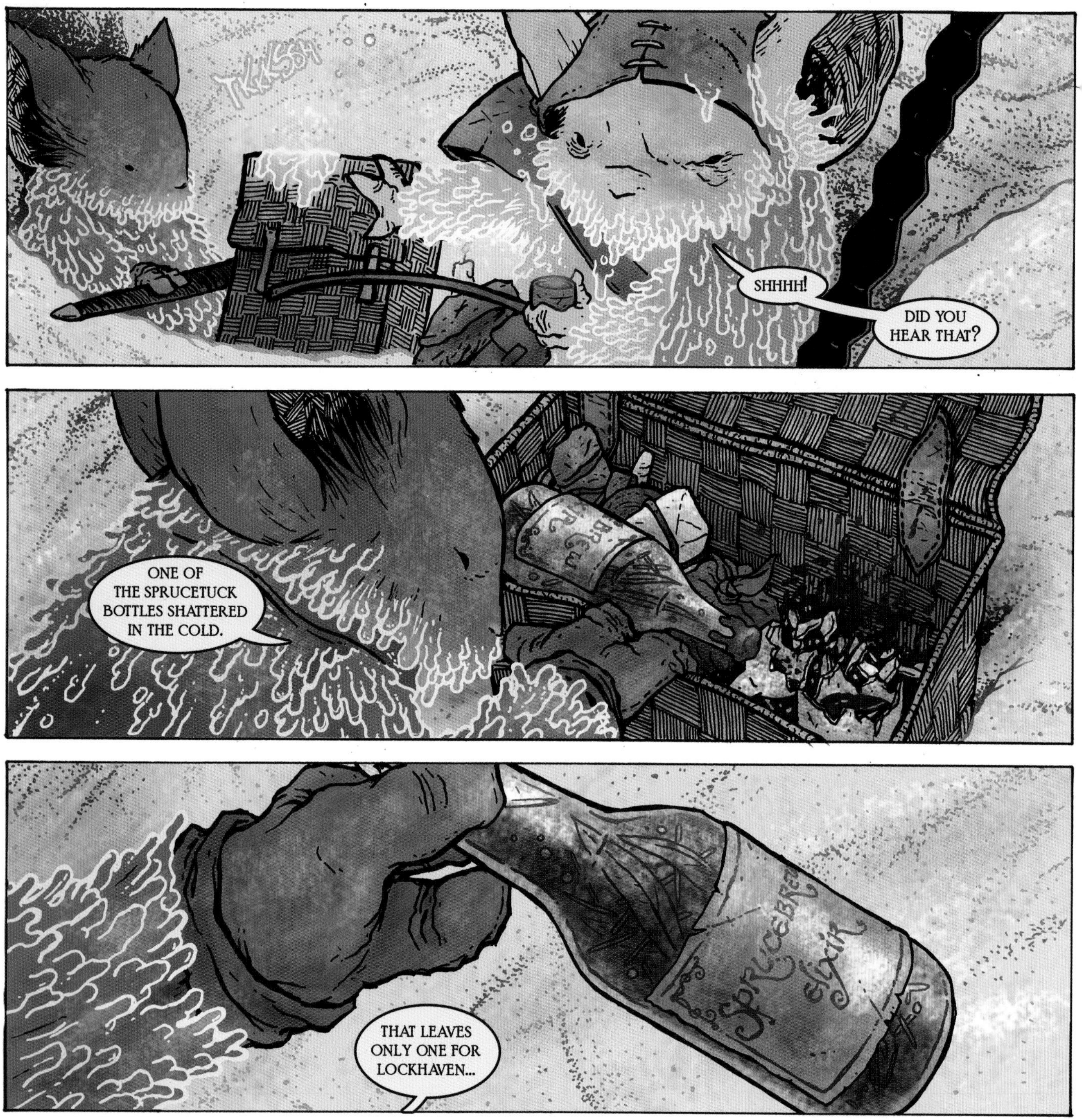
SHHHH!
DID YOU HEAR THAT?
ONE OF THE SPRUCETUCK BOTTLES SHATTERED IN THE COLD.
elixir
THAT LEAVES ONLY ONE FOR LOCKHAVEN...

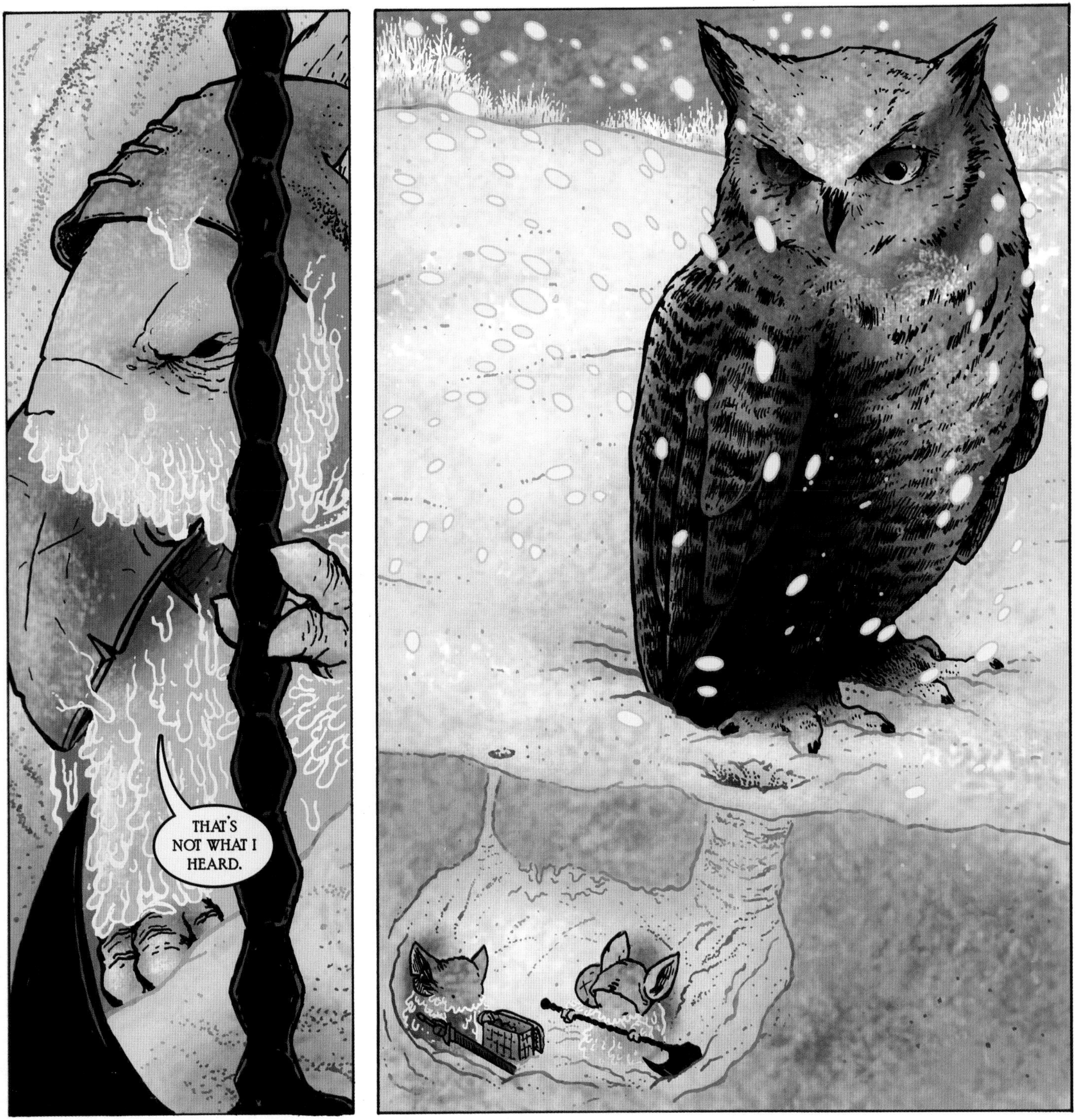
THAT'S NOT WHAT I HEARD.

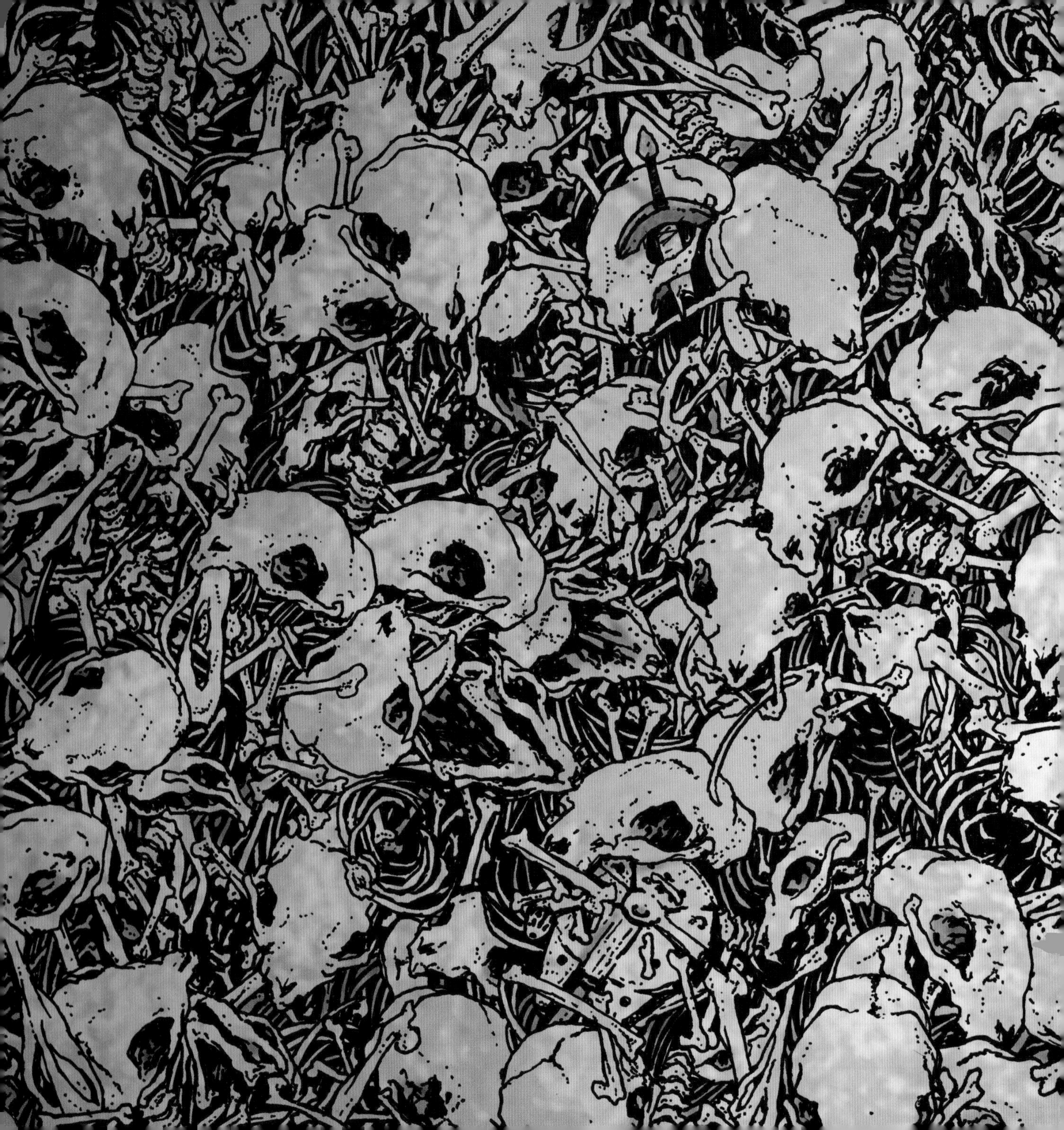

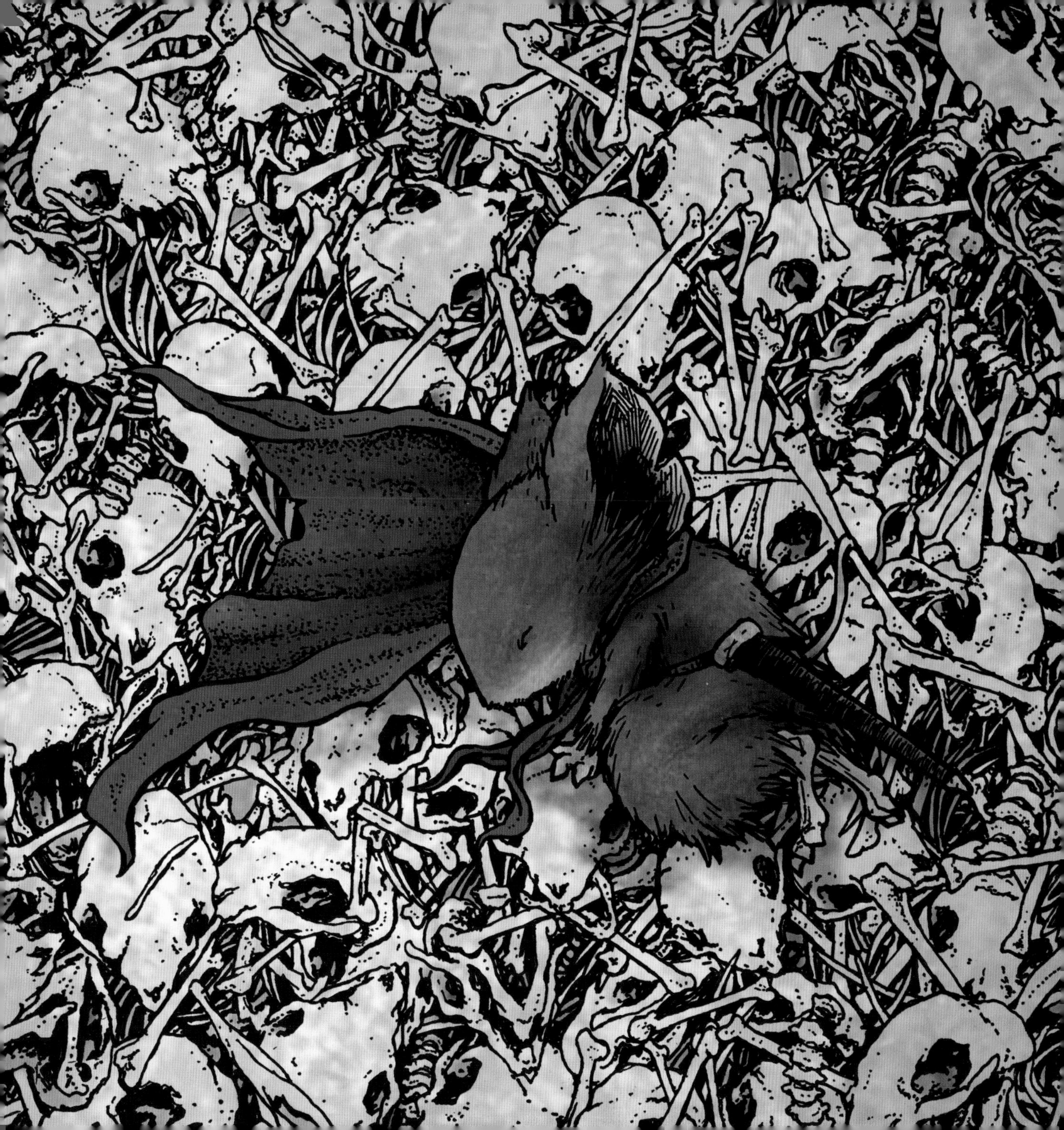

Chapter Four

Bats taking claim of the abandoned weasel kingdom of Darkheather, halted Saxon, Kenzie, and Sadie's progress through the underground nightmare. In a foolishly brave manuver, Saxon raised sword against them and was carried off into darkness.

The remaining bottle of medicine from Sprucetuck is also in danger as an owl has found Celanawe & Lieam's ice shelter.

"Time moves along. Forever will its cycle span.
Unyielding without concern for anymouse's plan.
"All fur becomes grey" is the unstoppable truth.
One that is rarely observed while still in youth.
Collect all of what you can while along a life's route:
Lessons, friends, mentors, loves and truths worthy of pursuit.
They offer no guarantee to be there still if missed once before.
Death can come quickly with no return from its shore."

-"Till it's Gone" Poem by the Scribe Roibin

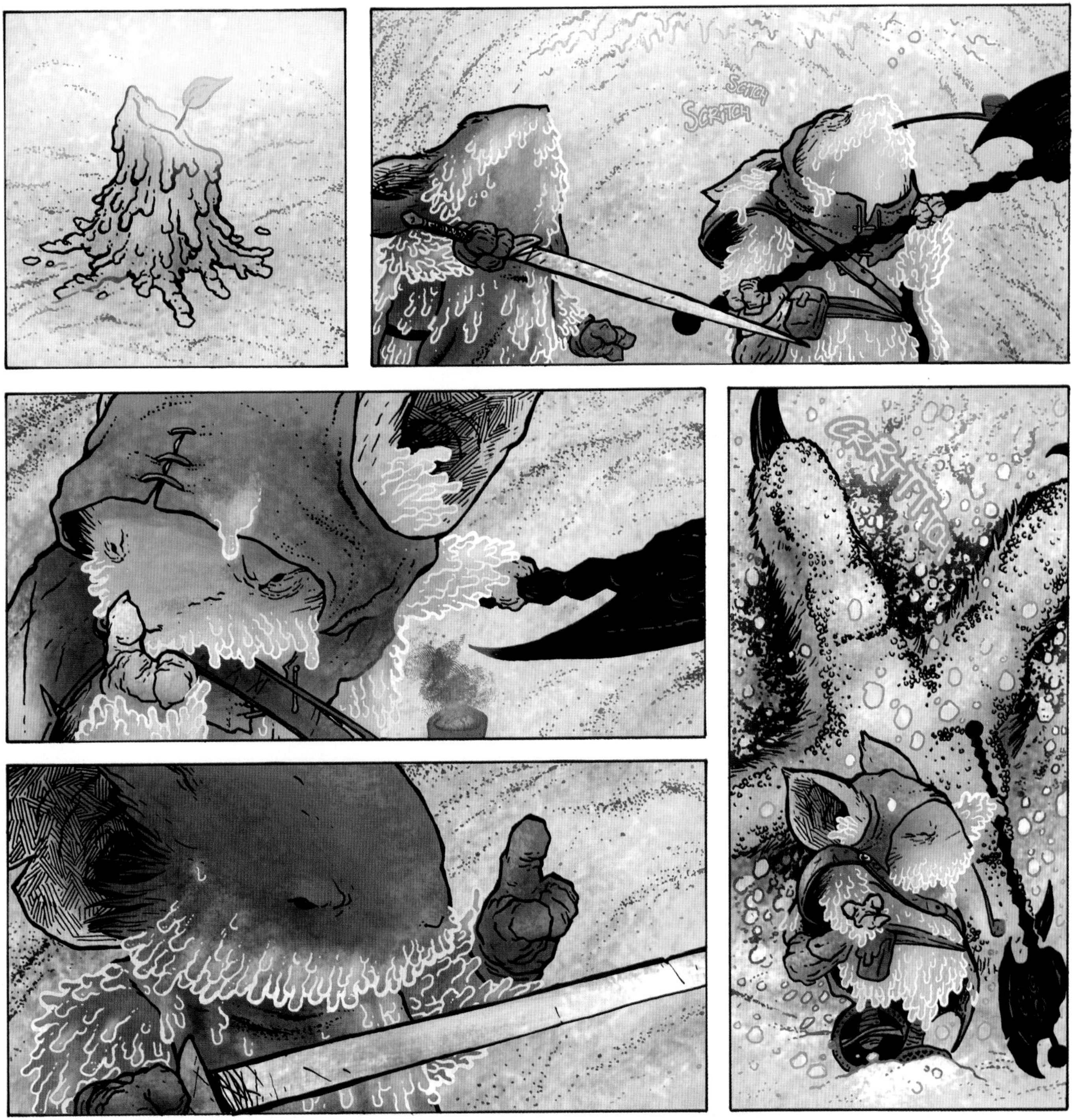
SCRITCH
SCRITCH

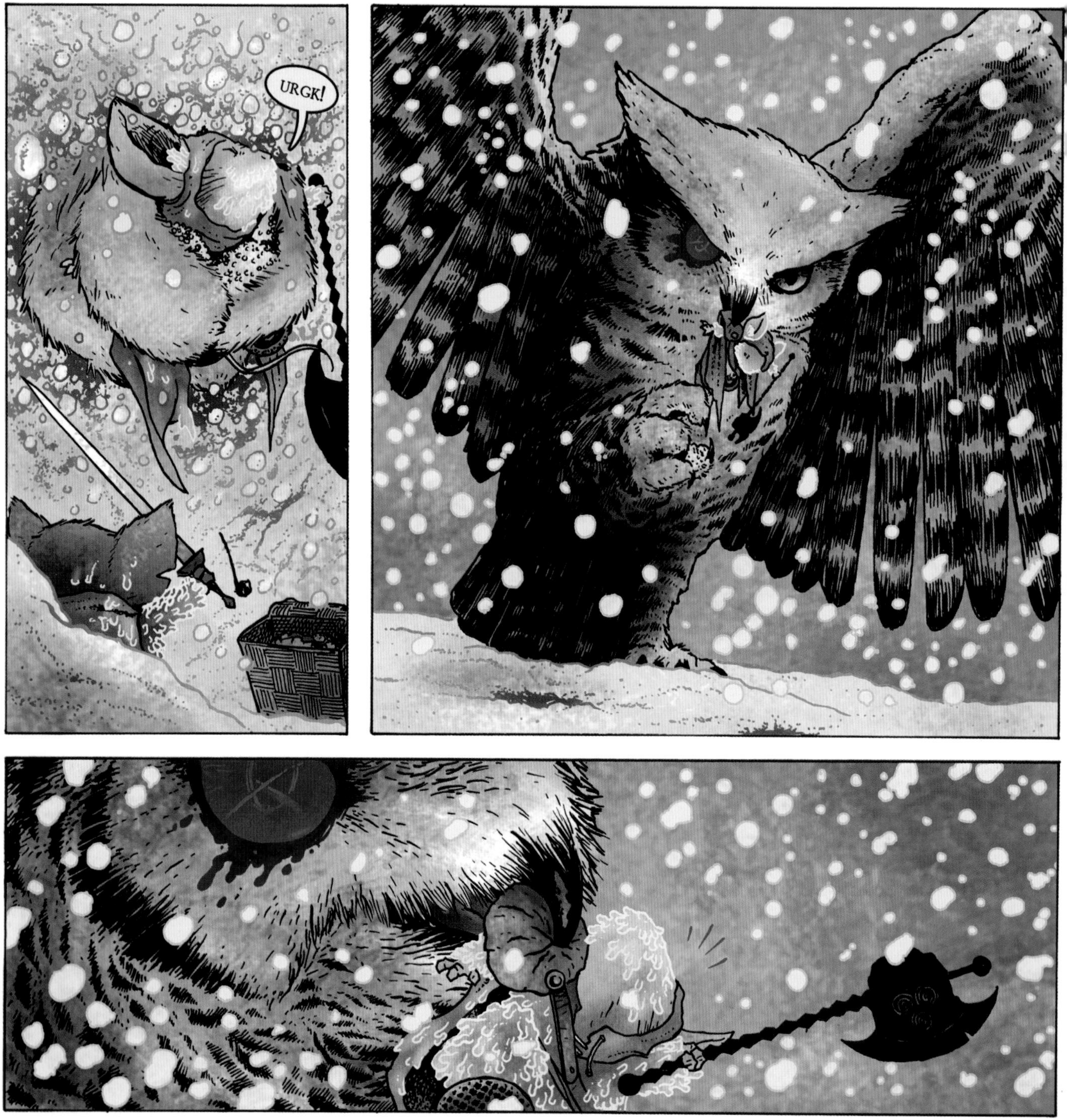
URGK!

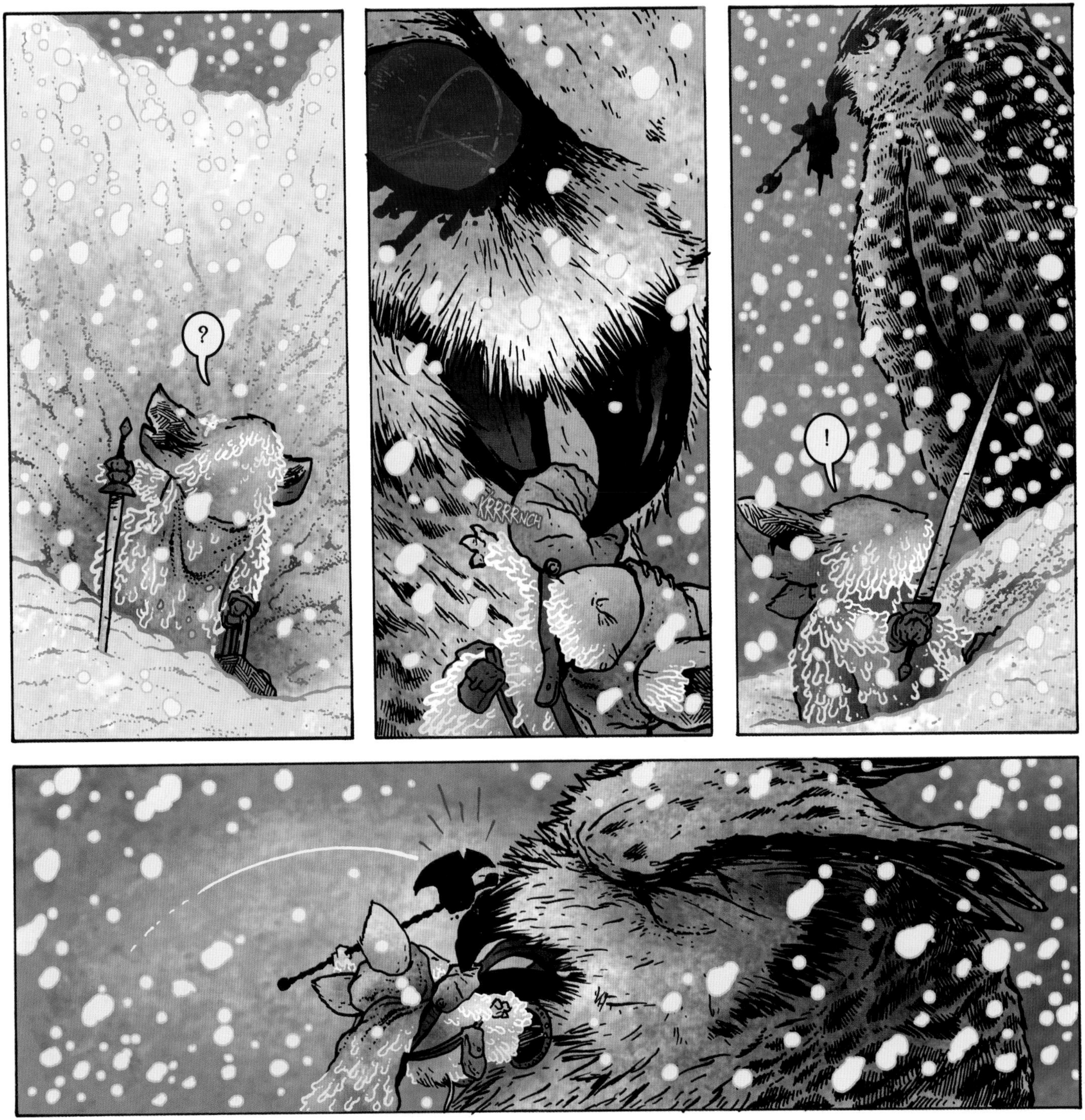
?
KRRRRNCH
!

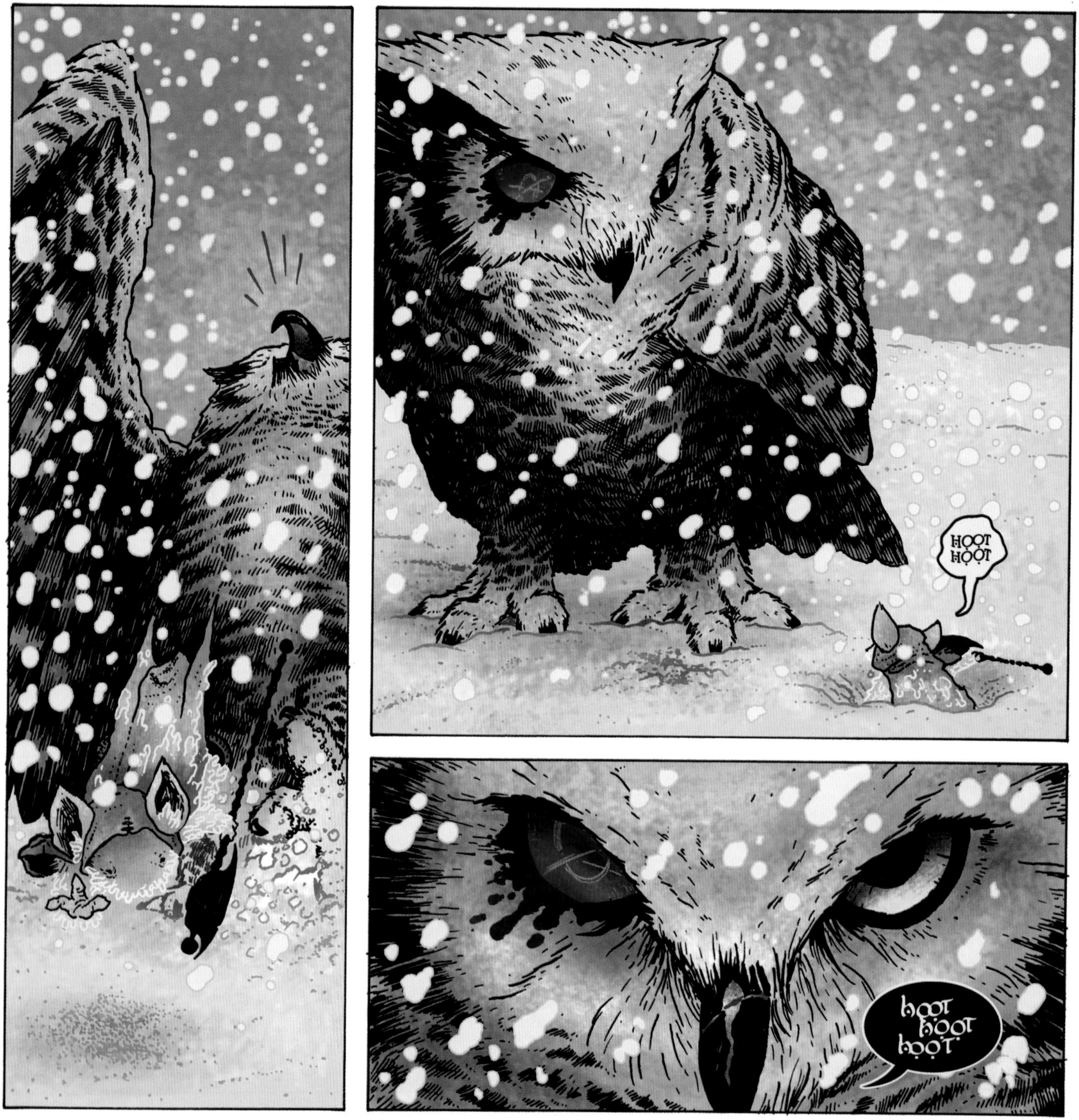
HOOT HOOT
hoot hoot hoot

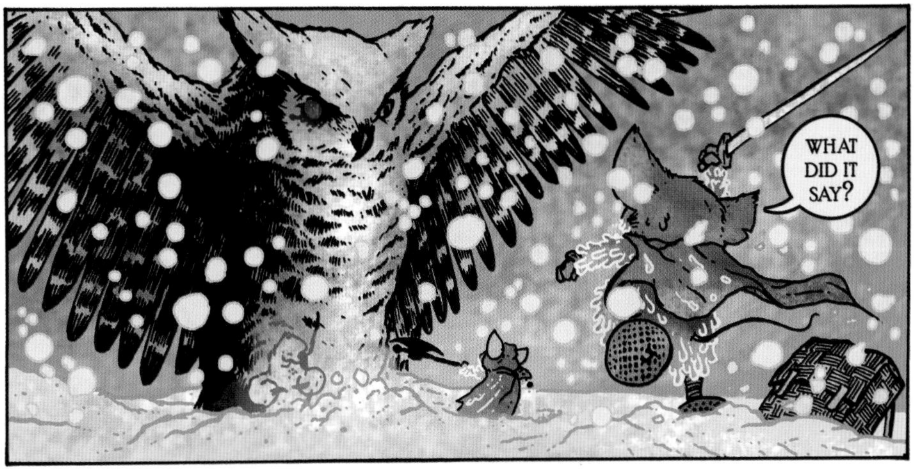
WHAT DID IT SAY?

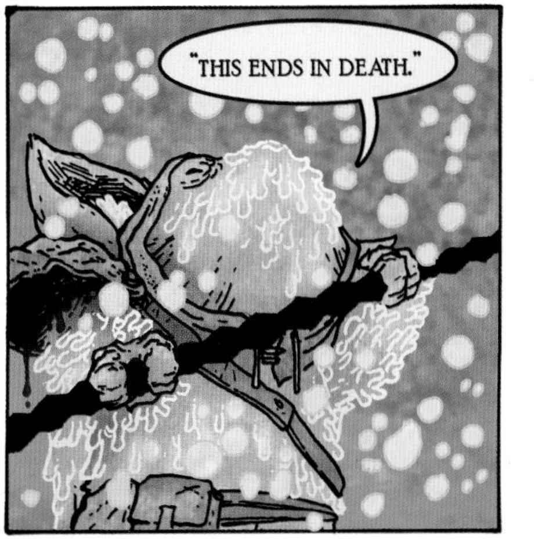
"THIS ENDS IN DEATH."

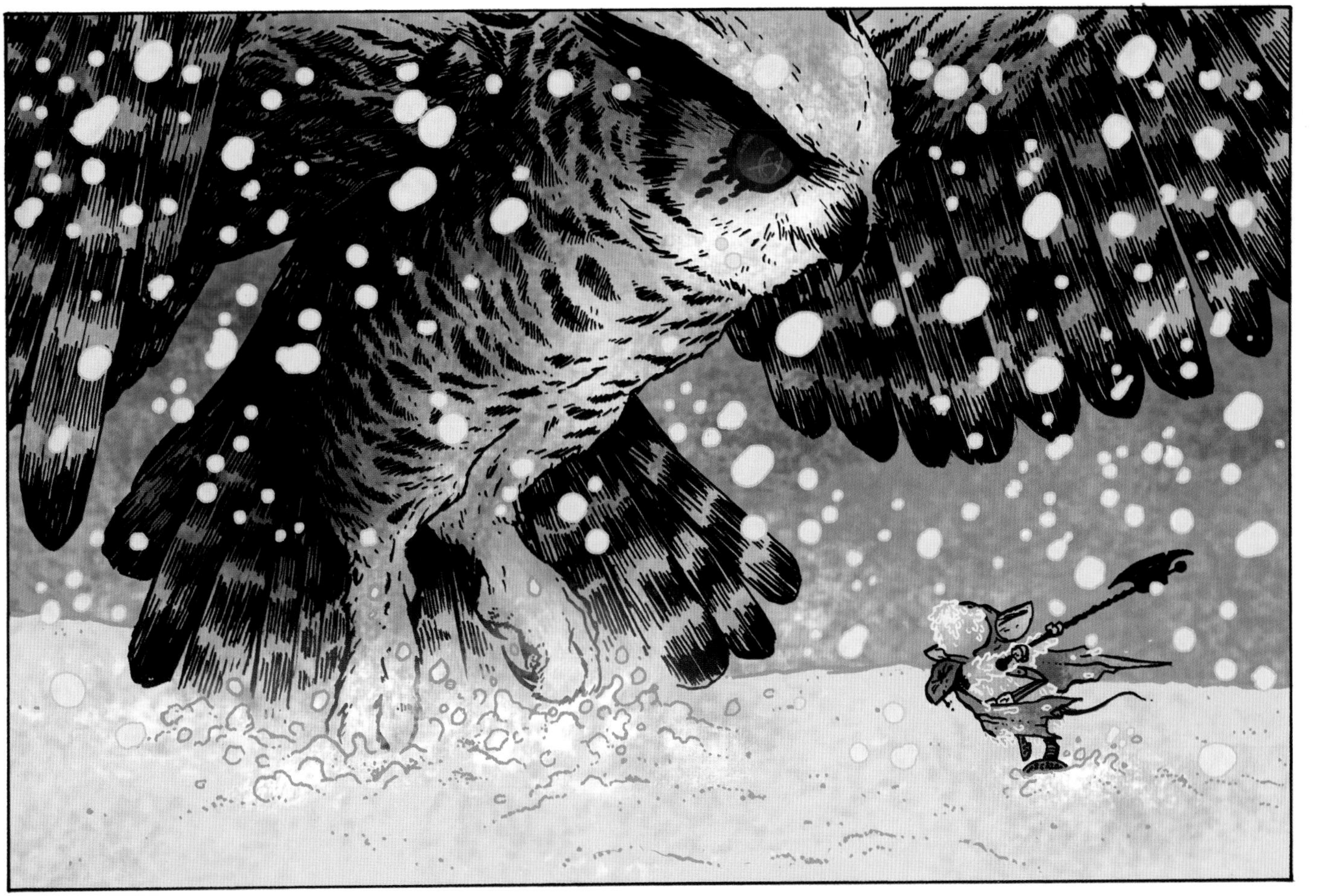

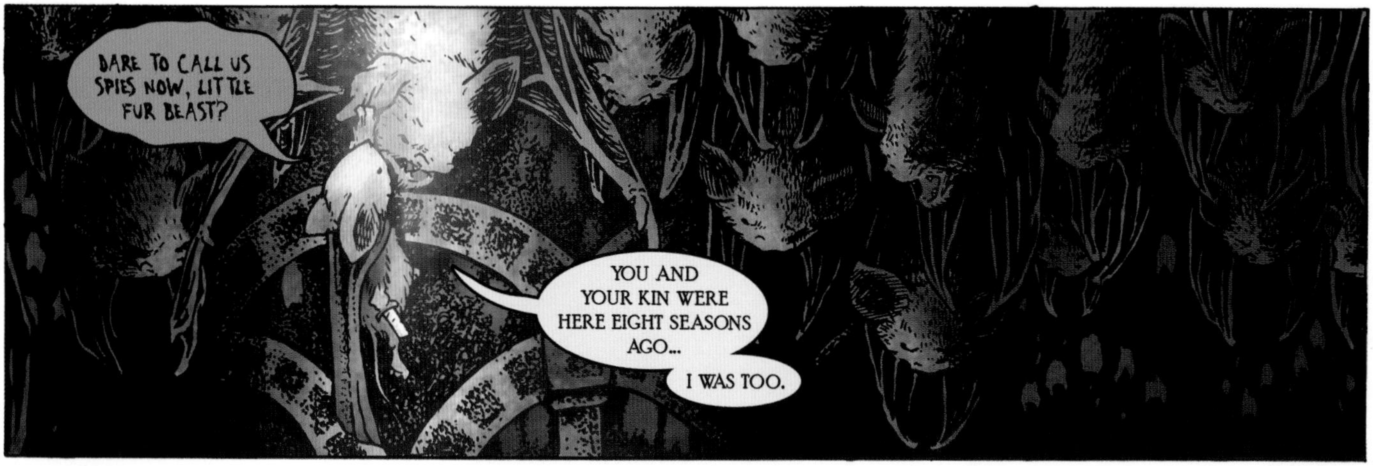
DARE TO CALL US SPIES NOW, LITTLE FUR BEAST?
YOU AND YOUR KIN WERE HERE EIGHT SEASONS AGO...
I WAS TOO.

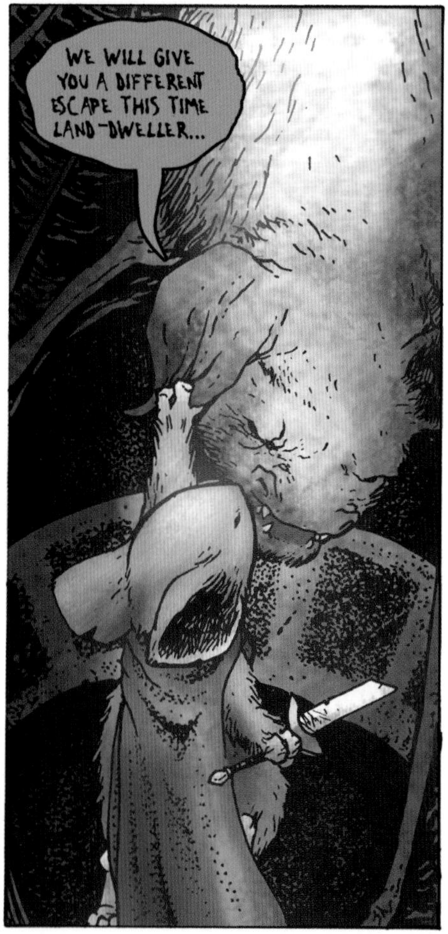
WE WILL GIVE YOU A DIFFERENT ESCAPE THIS TIME LAND-DWELLER...

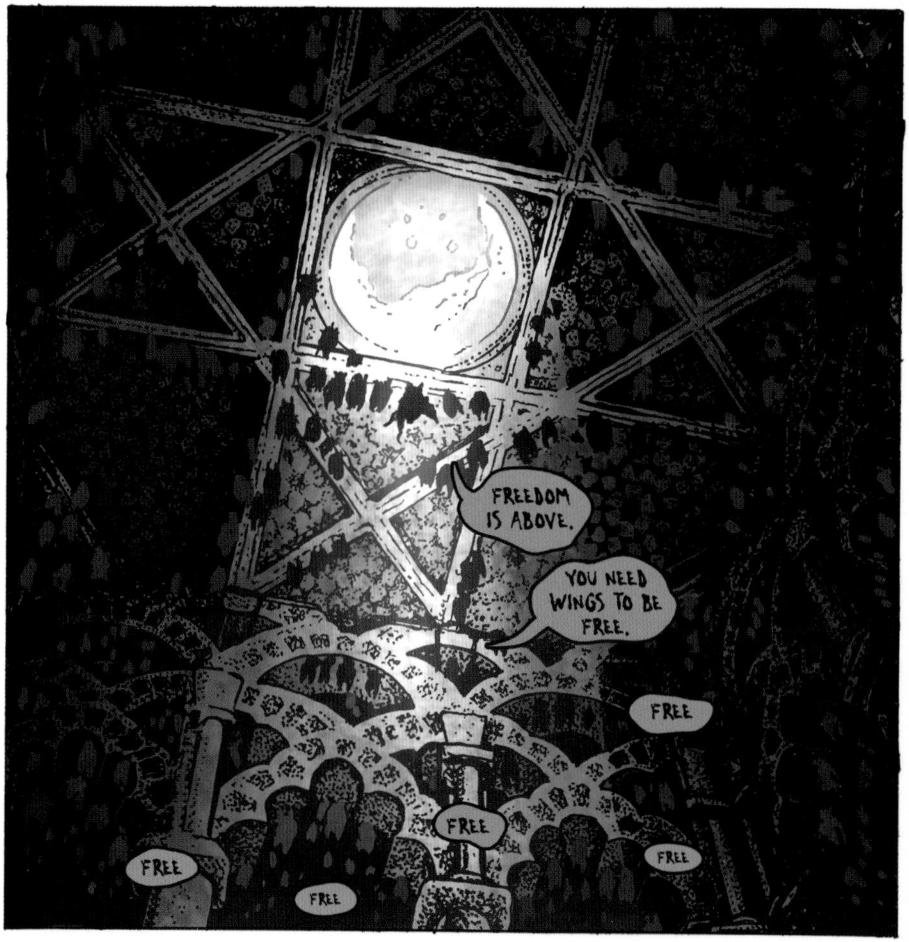
FREEDOM IS ABOVE.
YOU NEED WINGS TO BE FREE.
FREE
FREE
FREE
FREE
FREE

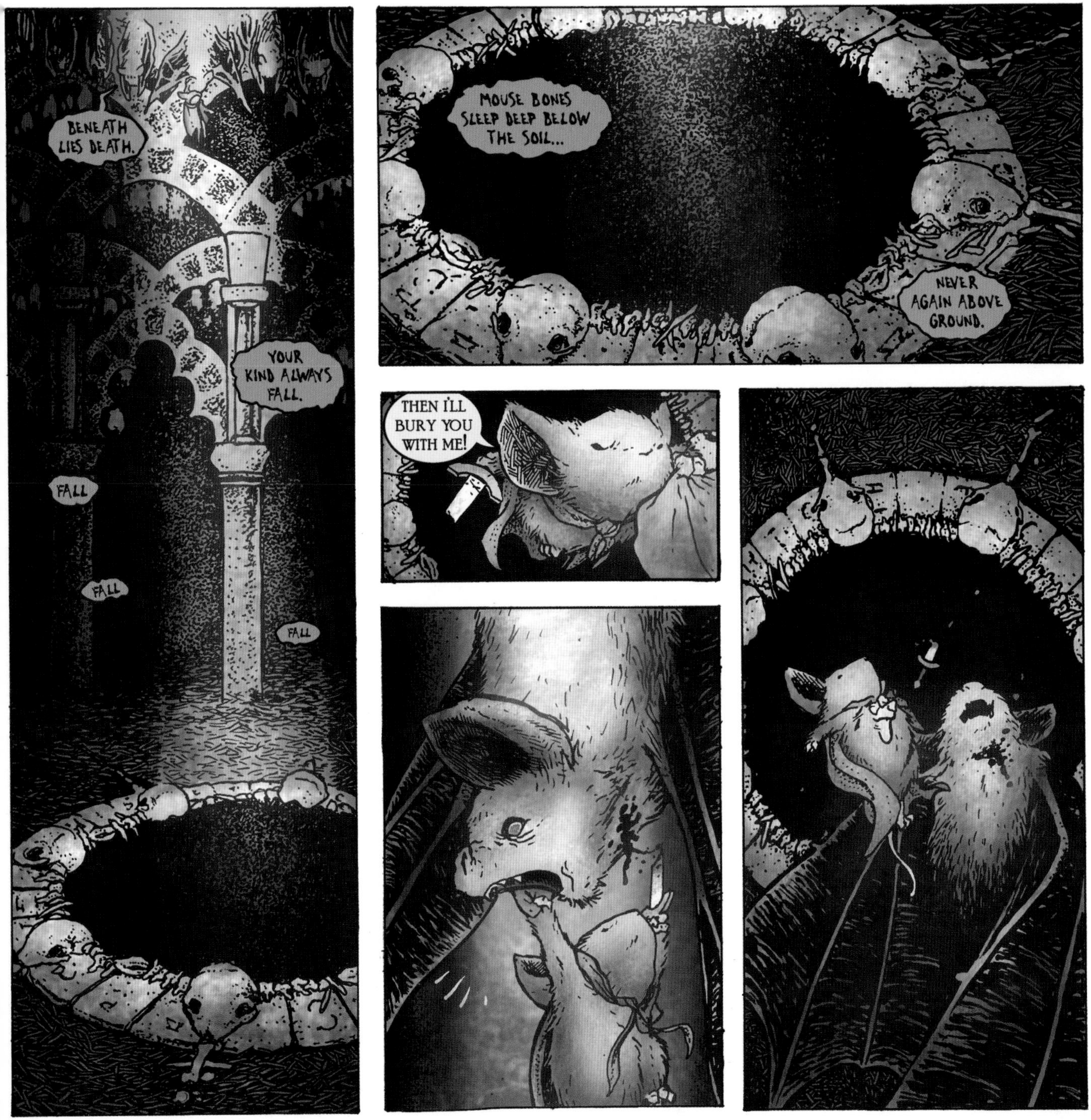
BENEATH LIES DEATH.
YOUR KIND ALWAYS FALL.
FALL
FALL
FALL
MOUSE BONES SLEEP DEEP BELOW THE SOIL...
NEVER AGAIN ABOVE GROUND.
THEN I'LL BURY YOU WITH ME!

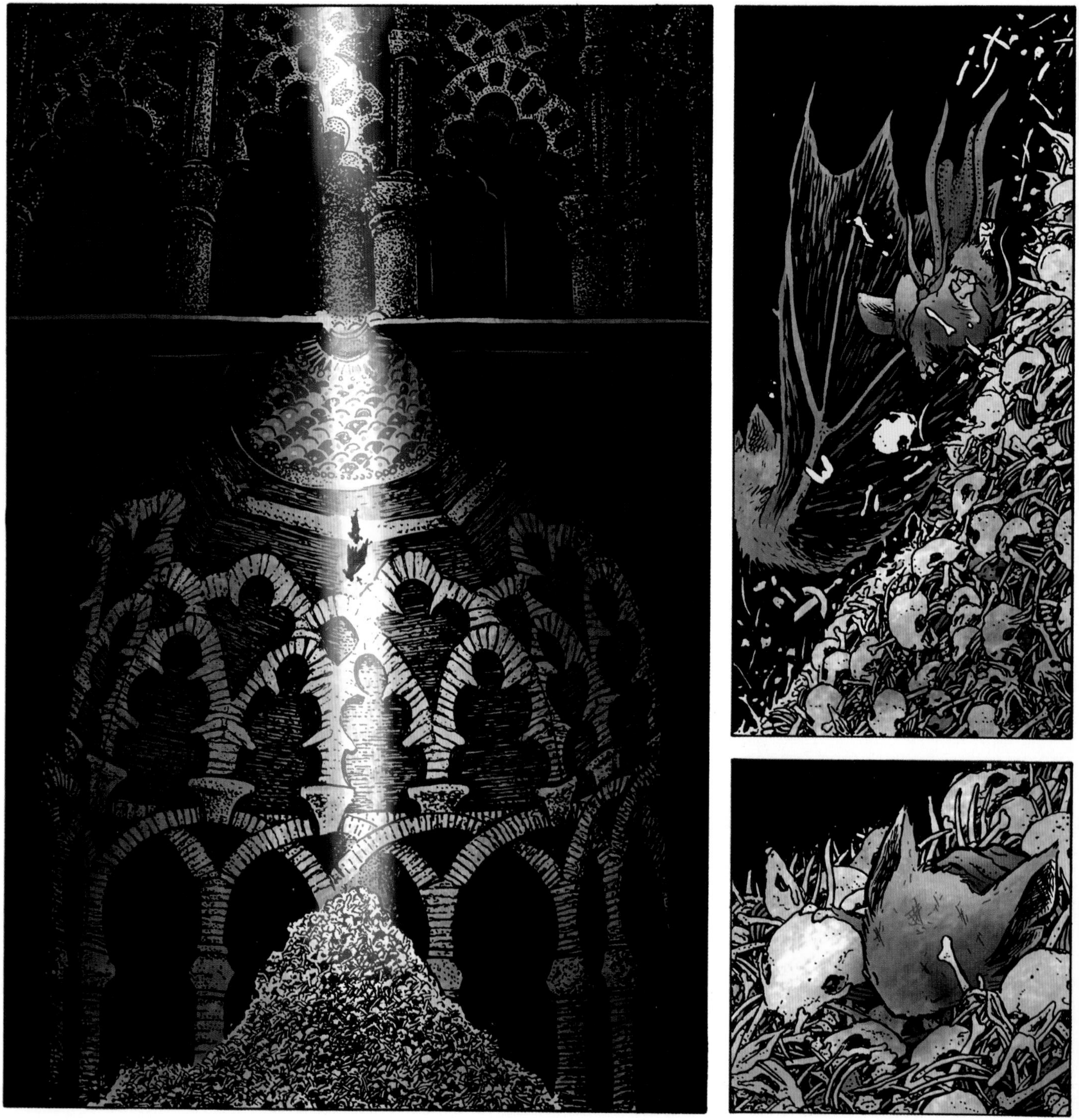

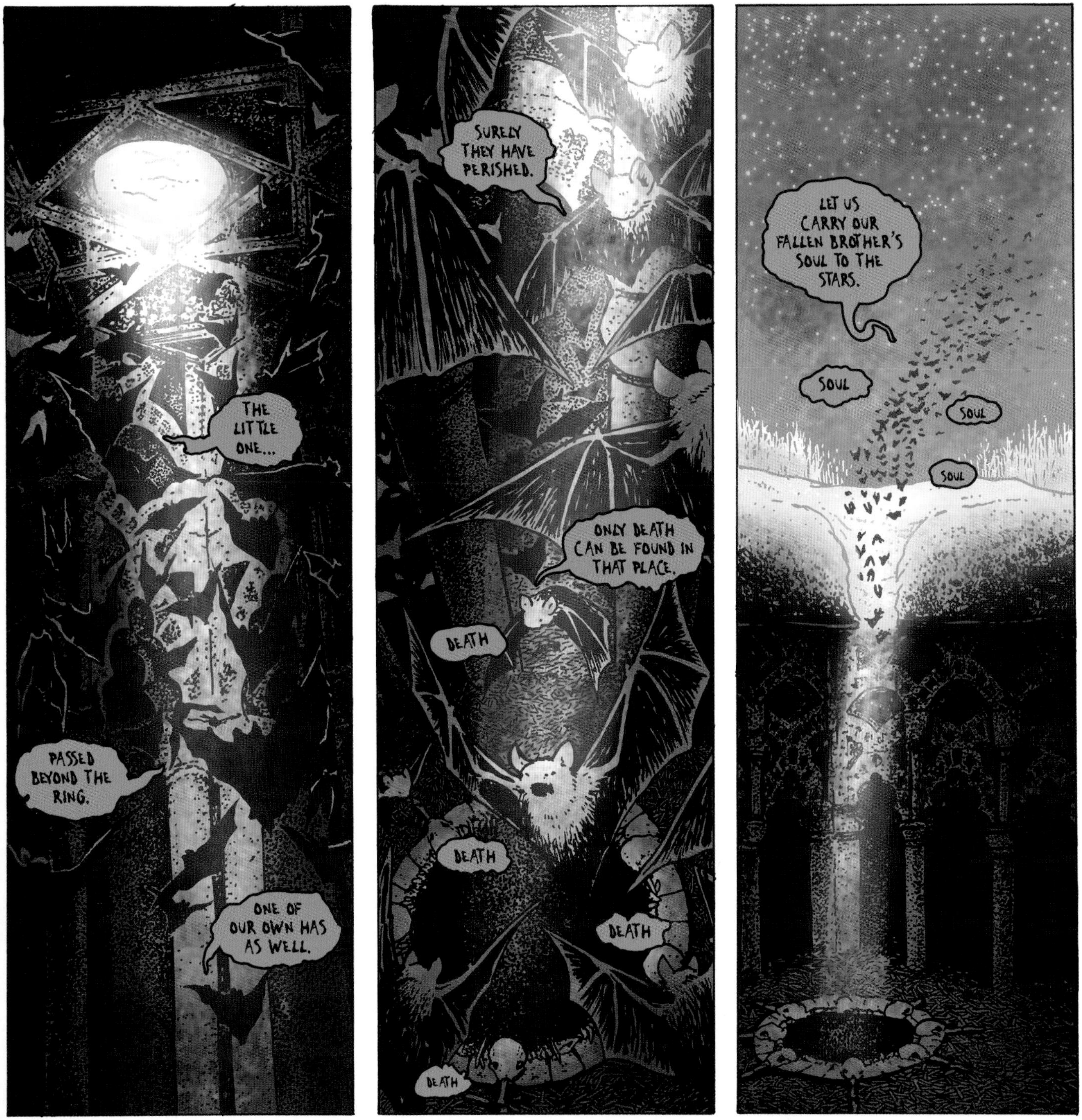
THE LITTLE ONE...
PASSED BEYOND THE RING.
ONE OF OUR OWN HAS AS WELL.
SURELY THEY HAVE PERISHED.
ONLY DEATH CAN BE FOUND IN THAT PLACE.
DEATH
DEATH
DEATH
DEATH
LET US CARRY OUR FALLEN BROTHER'S SOUL TO THE STARS.
SOUL
SOUL
SOUL

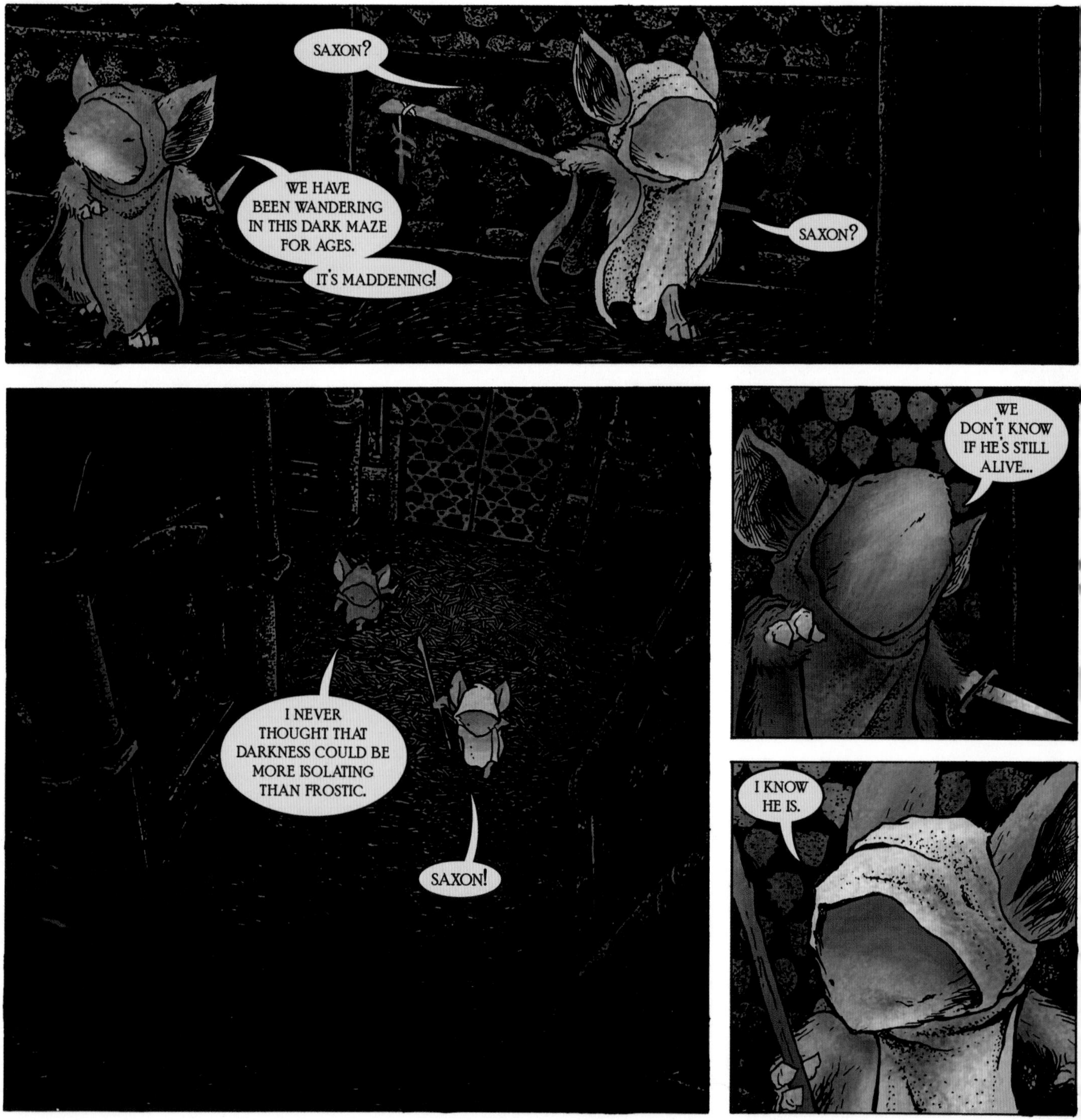
SAXON?
WE HAVE BEEN WANDERING IN THIS DARK MAZE FOR AGES.
IT'S MADDENING!
SAXON?
I NEVER THOUGHT THAT DARKNESS COULD BE MORE ISOLATING THAN FROSTIC.
SAXON!
WE DON'T KNOW IF HE'S STILL ALIVE...
I KNOW HE IS.

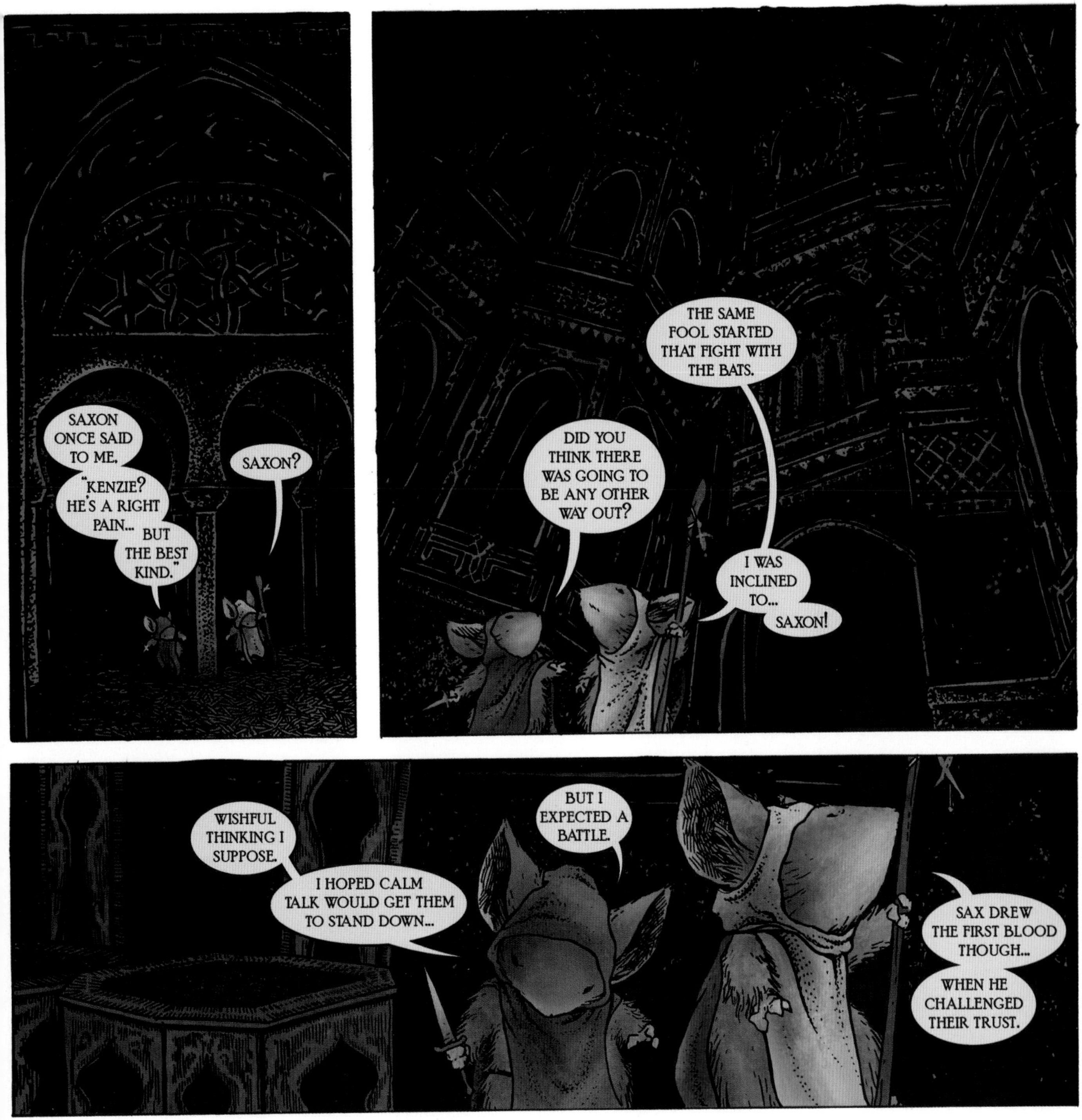
SAXON ONCE SAID TO ME,
"KENZIE? HE'S A RIGHT PAIN...
BUT THE BEST KIND."
SAXON?
THE SAME FOOL STARTED THAT FIGHT WITH THE BATS.
DID YOU THINK THERE WAS GOING TO BE ANY OTHER WAY OUT?
I WAS INCLINED TO...
SAXON!
WISHFUL THINKING I SUPPOSE.
I HOPED CALM TALK WOULD GET THEM TO STAND DOWN...
BUT I EXPECTED A BATTLE.
SAX DREW THE FIRST BLOOD THOUGH...
WHEN HE CHALLENGED THEIR TRUST.

IT'S THE ONLY ACT I'VE KNOWN HIM TO DO IN A SUBTLE FASHION.

AND WHAT ABOUT YOU GOOD KENZIE?

ANY LADYMICE YOU SEE FROM AFAR?

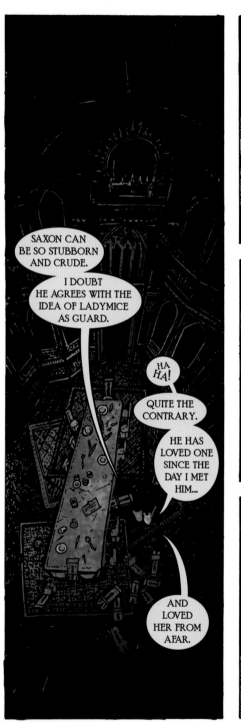

SAXON CAN BE SO STUBBORN AND CRUDE.

I DOUBT HE AGREES WITH THE IDEA OF LADYMICE AS GUARD.

HA HA!

QUITE THE CONTRARY.

HE HAS LOVED ONE SINCE THE DAY I MET HIM...

AND LOVED HER FROM AFAR.

WELL, WITH THE DEMANDS ON THE LIFE OF A GUARD, IT'S DIFFICULT.

I SLEEP ON ROCKY SOIL, HUNT OPOSSUM...

AND SPEND MOST OF MY DAYS OUTSIDE ANY MOUSE DEWLLING...

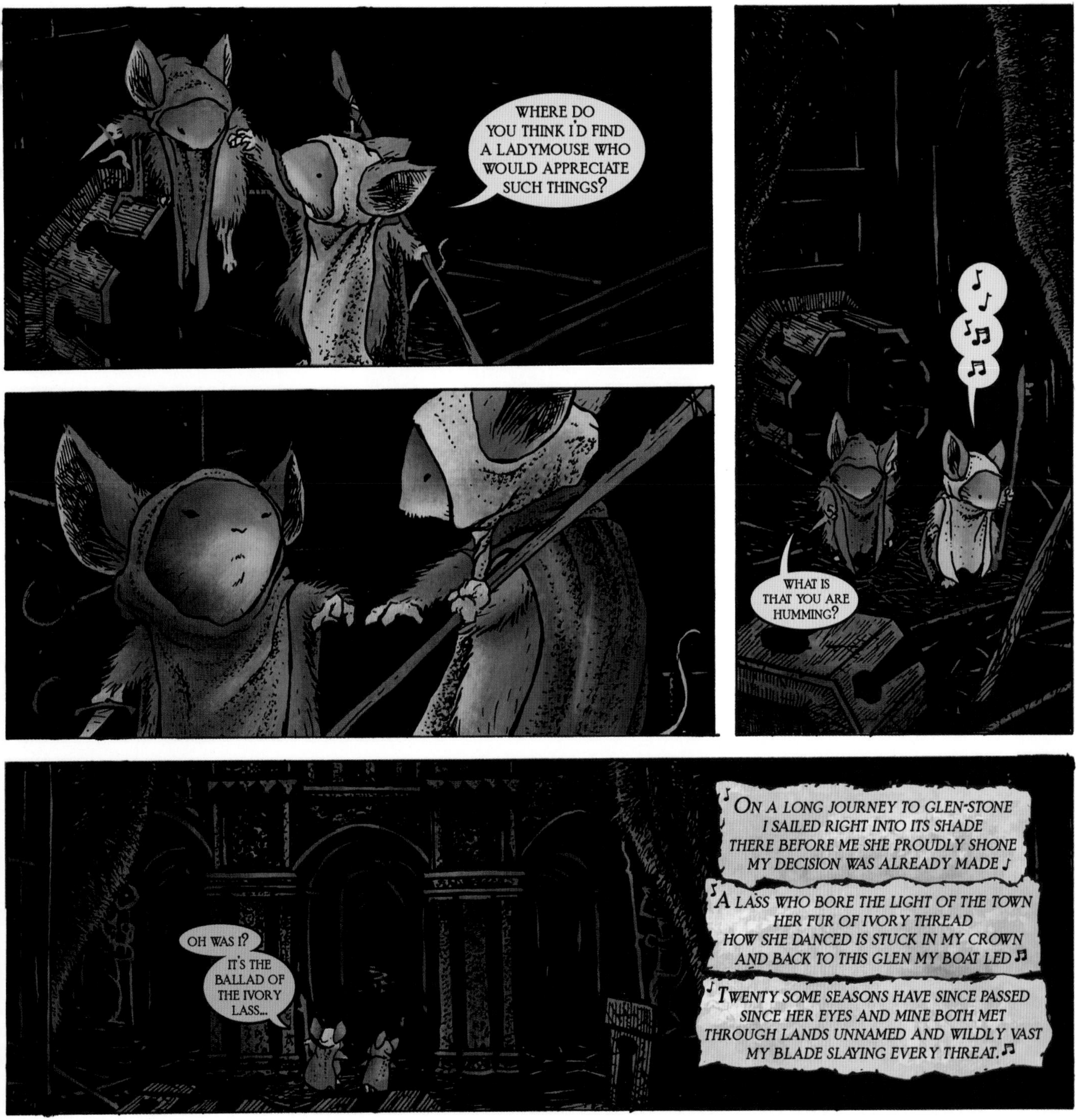
WHERE DO YOU THINK I'D FIND A LADYMOUSE WHO WOULD APPRECIATE SUCH THINGS?
WHAT IS THAT YOU ARE HUMMING?
OH WAS I?
IT'S THE BALLAD OF THE IVORY LASS...
ON A LONG JOURNEY TO GLEN-STONE
I SAILED RIGHT INTO ITS SHADE
THERE BEFORE ME SHE PROUDLY SHONE
MY DECISION WAS ALREADY MADE
A LASS WHO BORE THE LIGHT OF THE TOWN
HER FUR OF IVORY THREAD
HOW SHE DANCED IS STUCK IN MY CROWN
AND BACK TO THIS GLEN MY BOAT LED
TWENTY SOME SEASONS HAVE SINCE PASSED
SINCE HER EYES AND MINE BOTH MET
THROUGH LANDS UNNAMED AND WILDLY VAST
MY BLADE SLAYING EVERY THREAT.

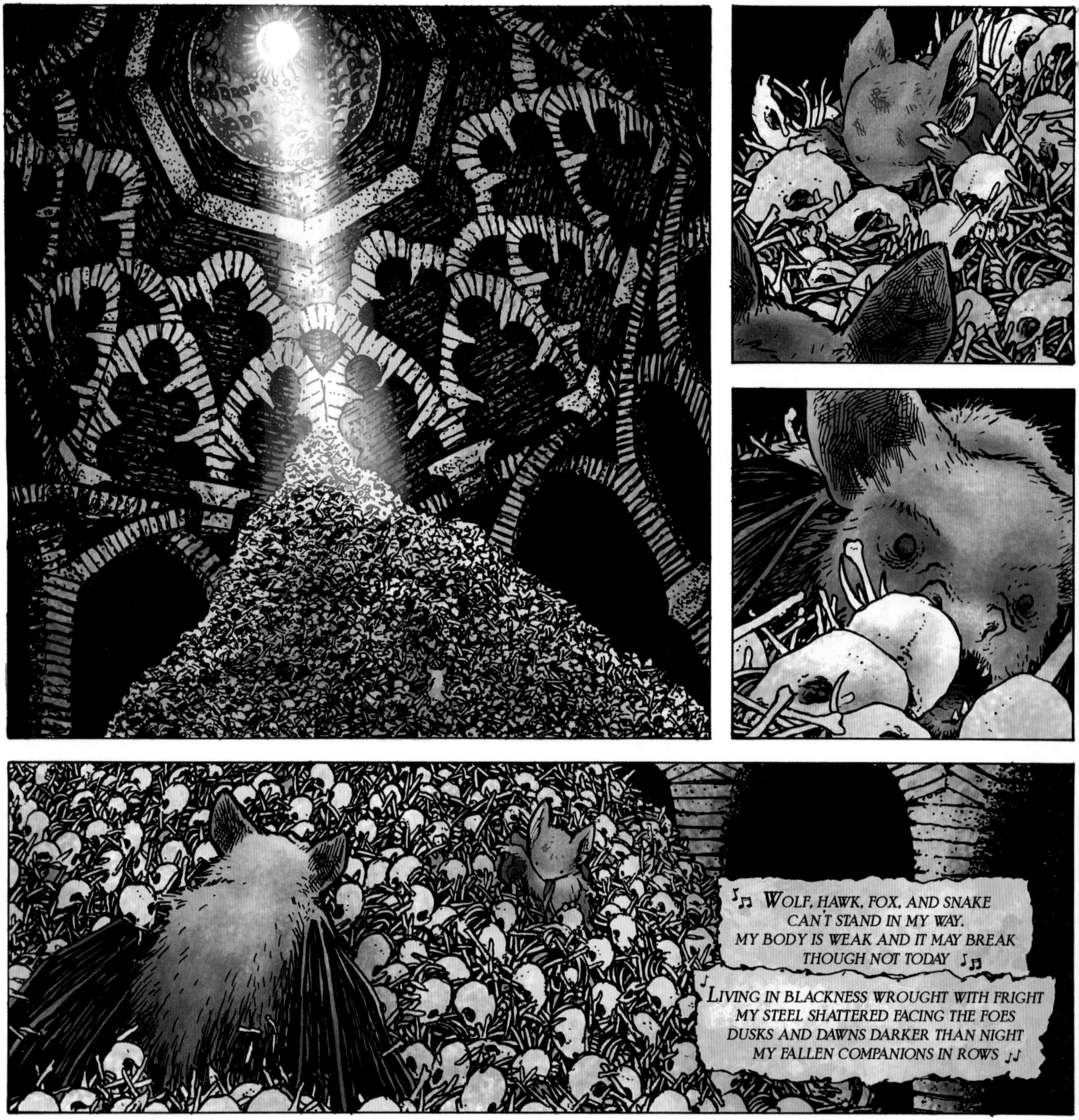
♪♫ WOLF, HAWK, FOX, AND SNAKE
CAN'T STAND IN MY WAY.
MY BODY IS WEAK AND IT MAY BREAK
THOUGH NOT TODAY ♪♫
♪ LIVING IN BLACKNESS WROUGHT WITH FRIGHT
MY STEEL SHATTERED FACING THE FOES
DUSKS AND DAWNS DARKER THAN NIGHT
MY FALLEN COMPANIONS IN ROWS ♪♪

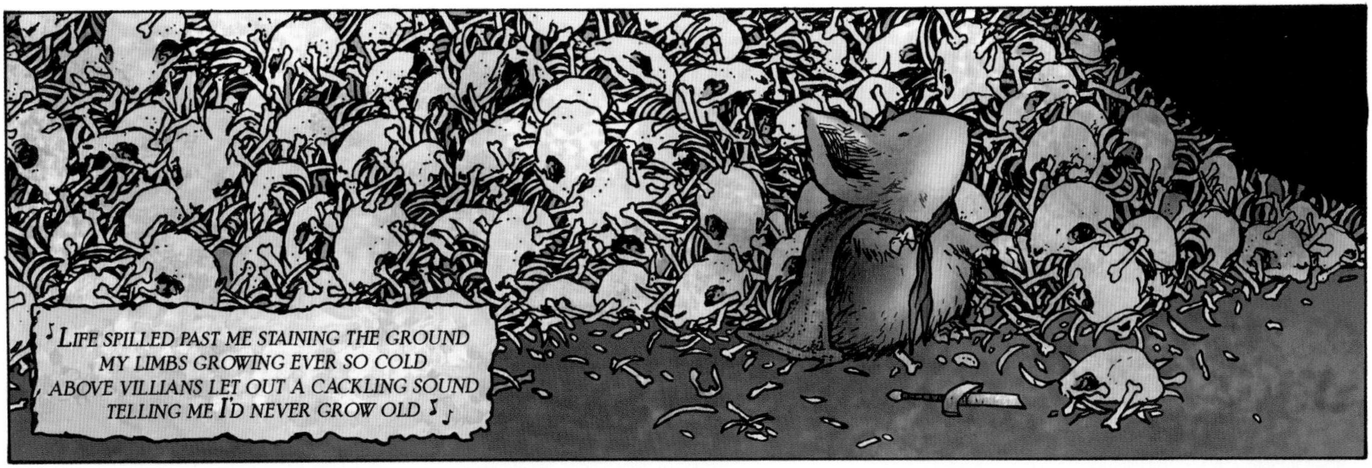
LIFE SPILLED PAST ME STAINING THE GROUND
MY LIMBS GROWING EVER SO COLD
ABOVE VILLIANS LET OUT A CACKLING SOUND
TELLING ME I'D NEVER GROW OLD

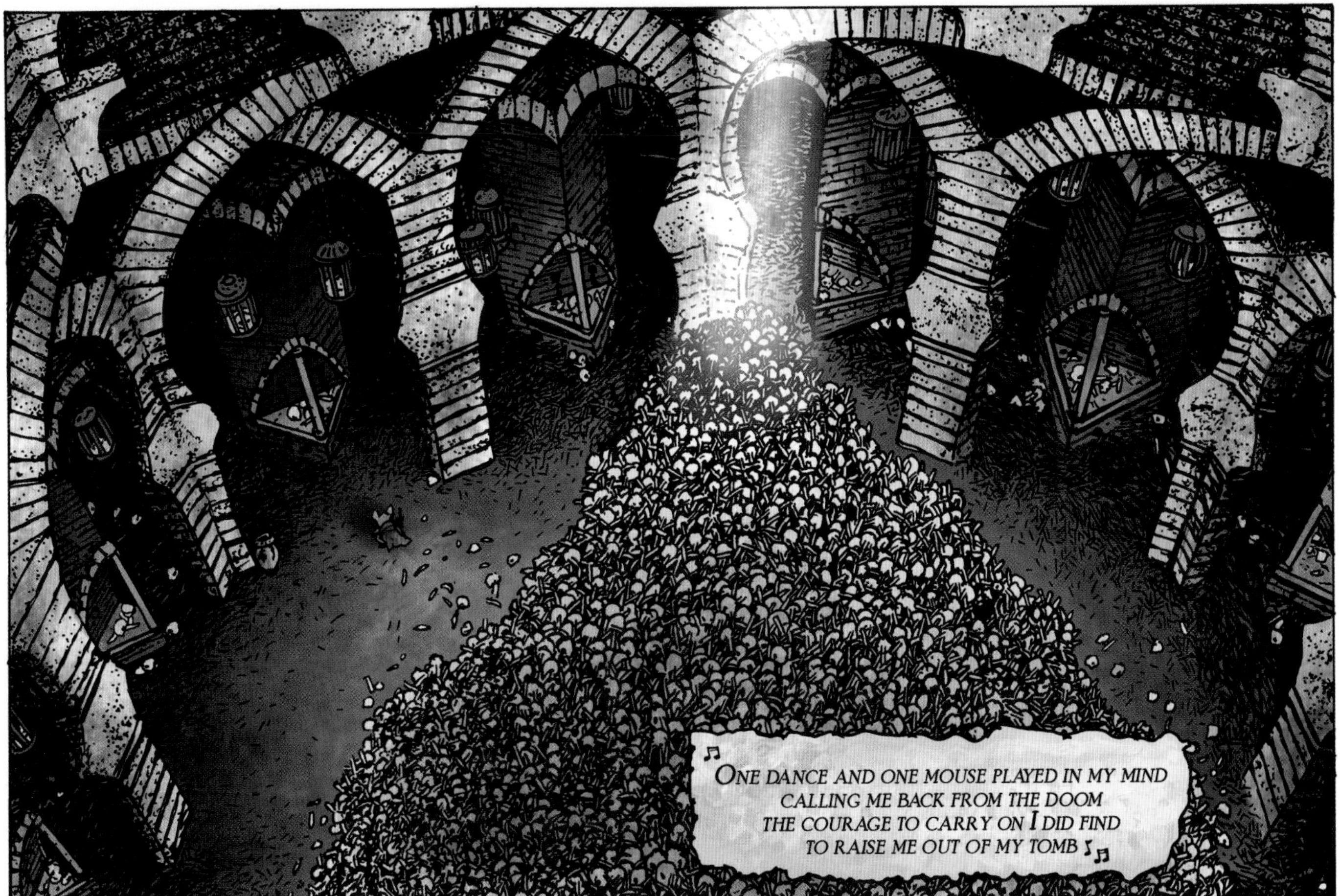
ONE DANCE AND ONE MOUSE PLAYED IN MY MIND
CALLING ME BACK FROM THE DOOM
THE COURAGE TO CARRY ON I DID FIND
TO RAISE ME OUT OF MY TOMB

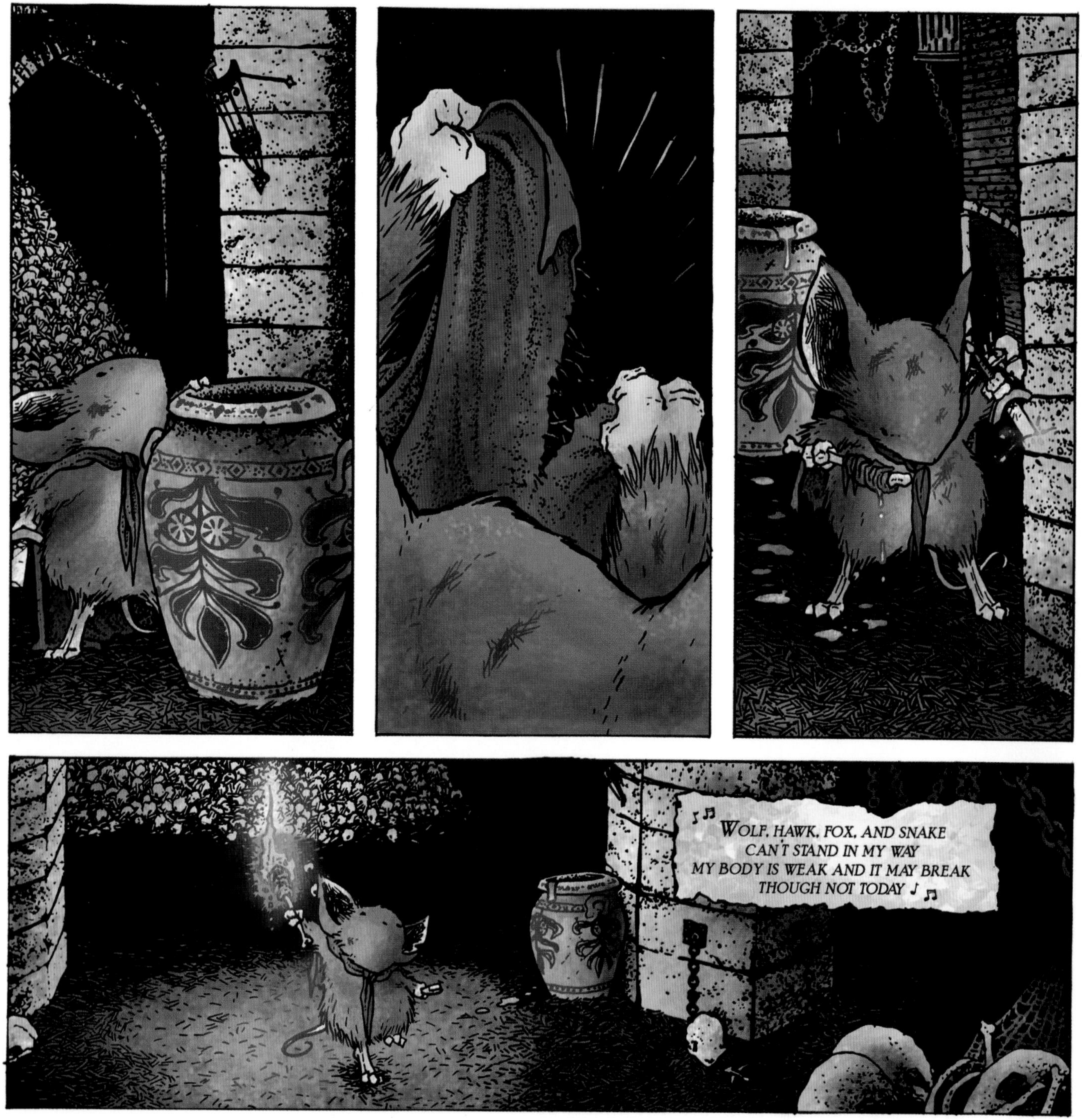
WOLF, HAWK, FOX, AND SNAKE
CAN'T STAND IN MY WAY
MY BODY IS WEAK AND IT MAY BREAK
THOUGH NOT TODAY

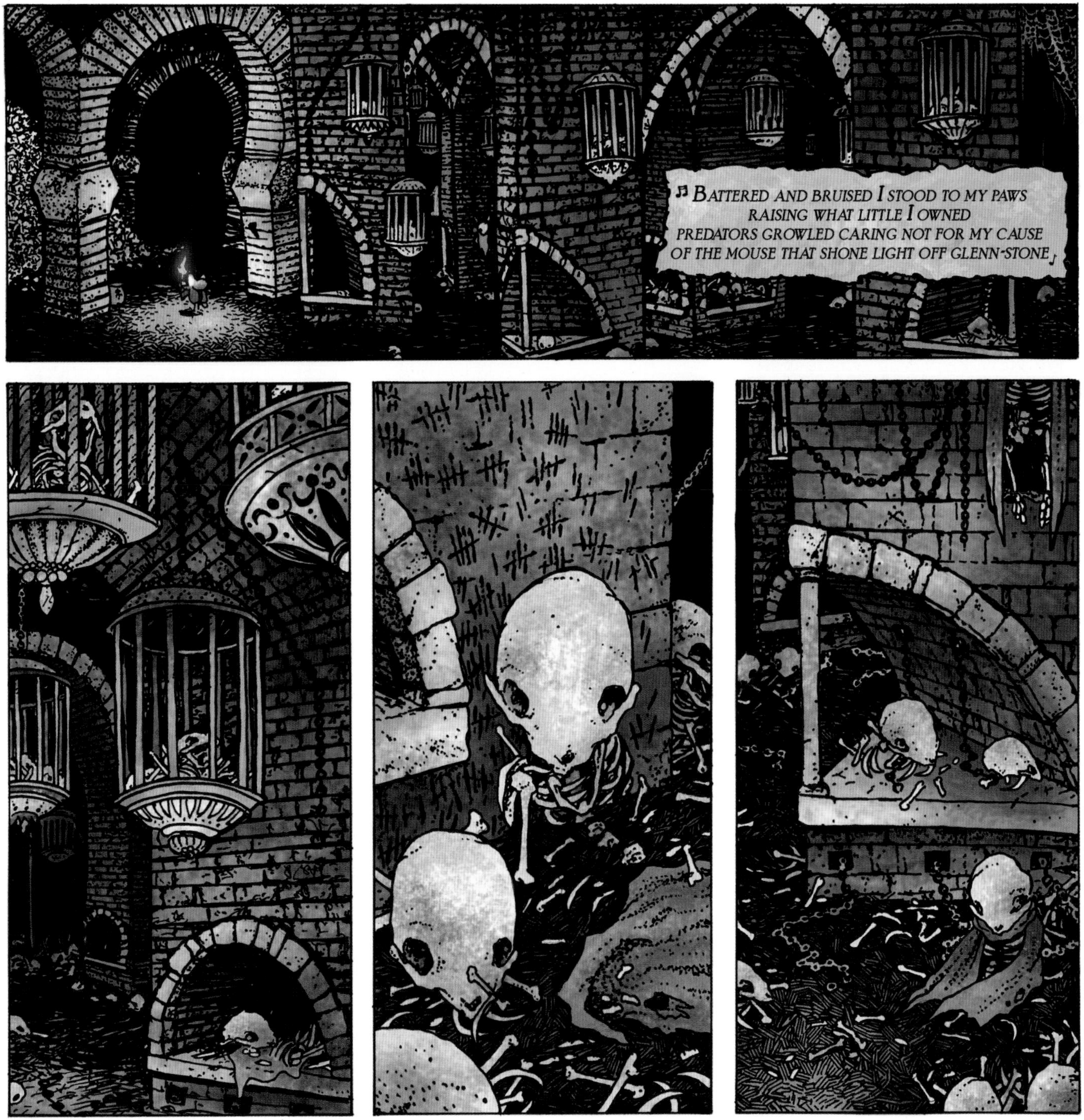
♫ BATTERED AND BRUISED I STOOD TO MY PAWS
RAISING WHAT LITTLE I OWNED
PREDATORS GROWLED CARING NOT FOR MY CAUSE
OF THE MOUSE THAT SHONE LIGHT OFF GLENN-STONE ♪

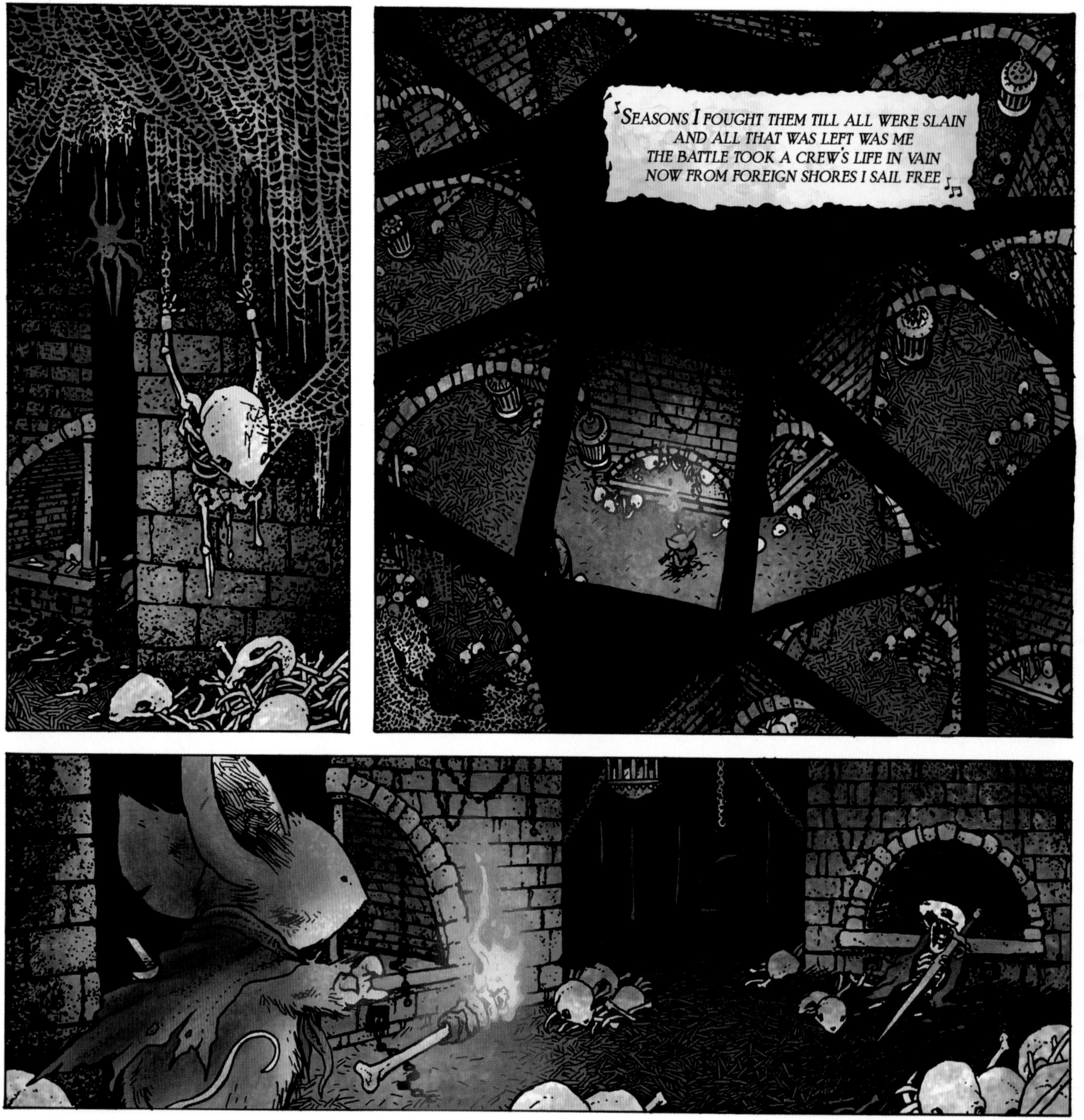
SEASONS I FOUGHT THEM TILL ALL WERE SLAIN
AND ALL THAT WAS LEFT WAS ME
THE BATTLE TOOK A CREW'S LIFE IN VAIN
NOW FROM FOREIGN SHORES I SAIL FREE

♪ AMIDST THE LOSS AND SORROW I'VE SPENT
'TWAS IT ALL WORTH THE COST?
BACK INTO GLENN-STONE MY SHIP I SENT
FOR AN IVORY LASS THAT I LOST ♫♪

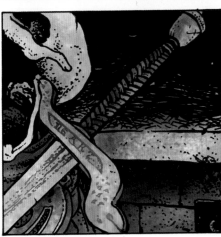

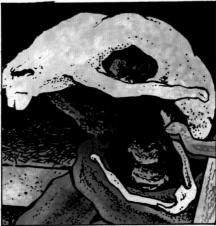

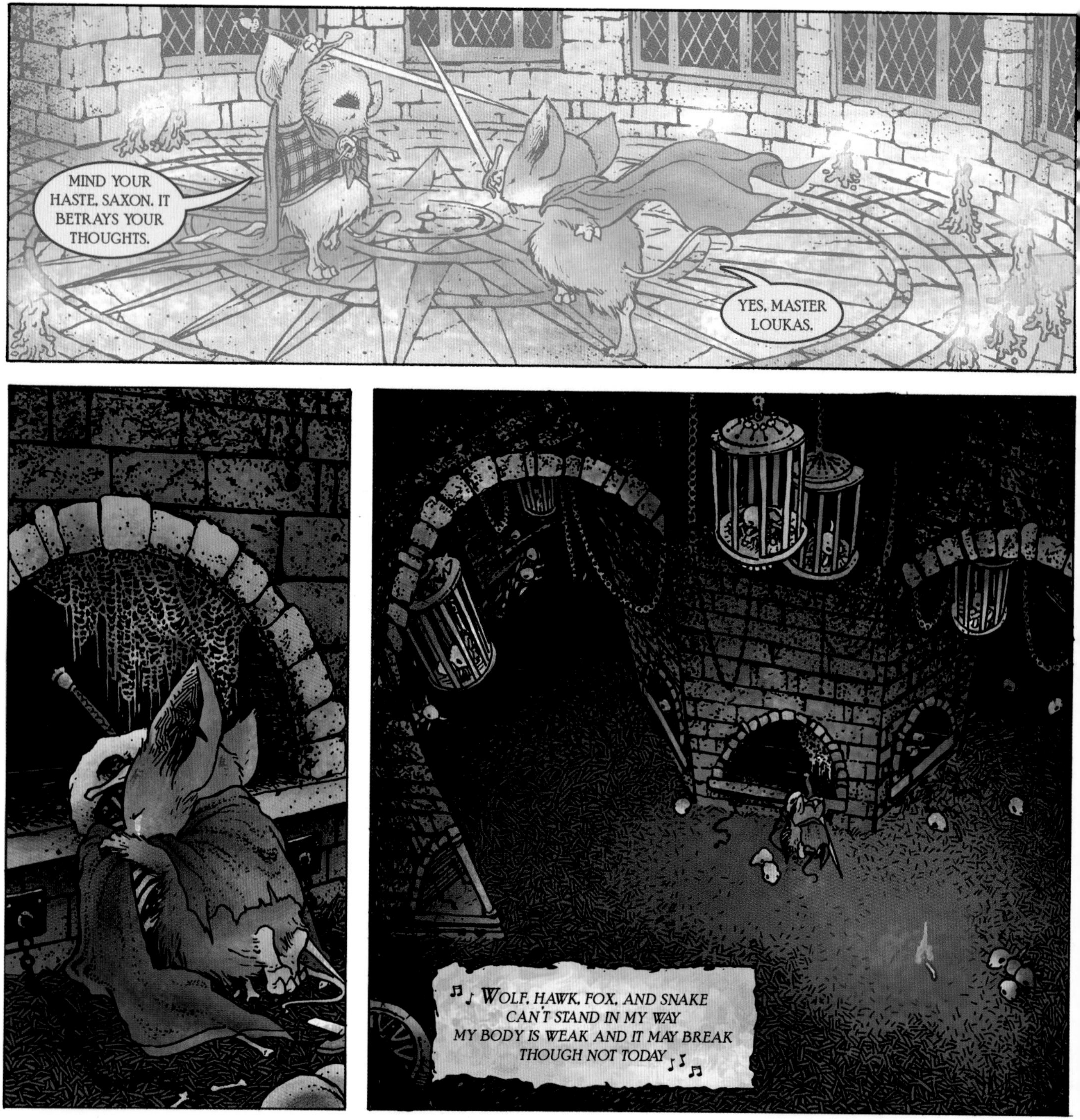
MIND YOUR HASTE, SAXON. IT BETRAYS YOUR THOUGHTS.
YES, MASTER LOUKAS.
WOLF, HAWK, FOX, AND SNAKE
CAN'T STAND IN MY WAY
MY BODY IS WEAK AND IT MAY BREAK
THOUGH NOT TODAY

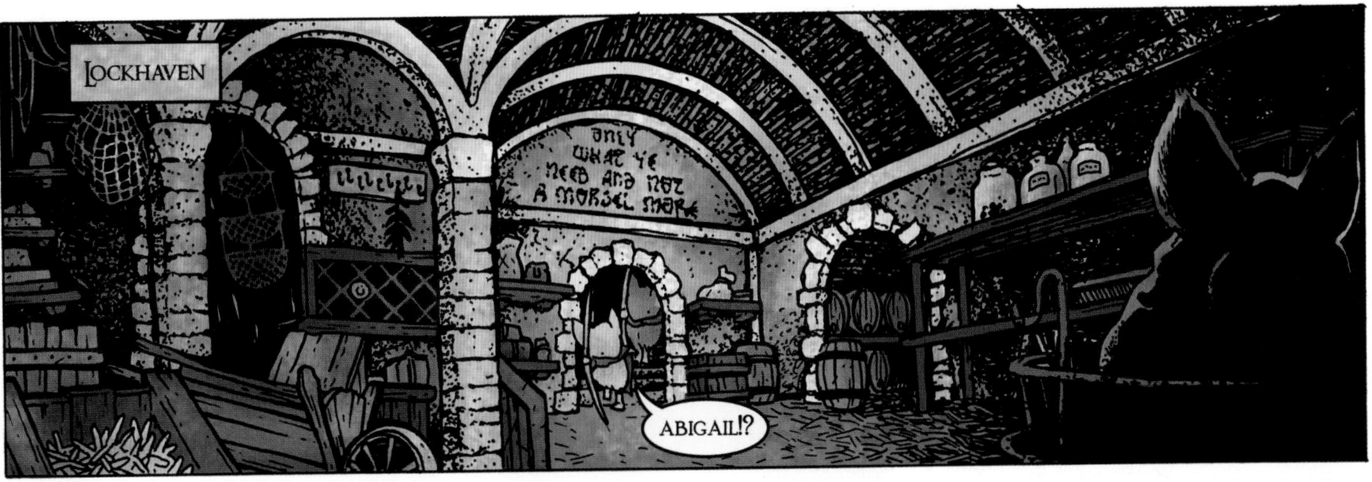
LOCKHAVEN
ONLY WHAT YE NEED AND NOT A MORSEL MORE
ABIGAIL!?

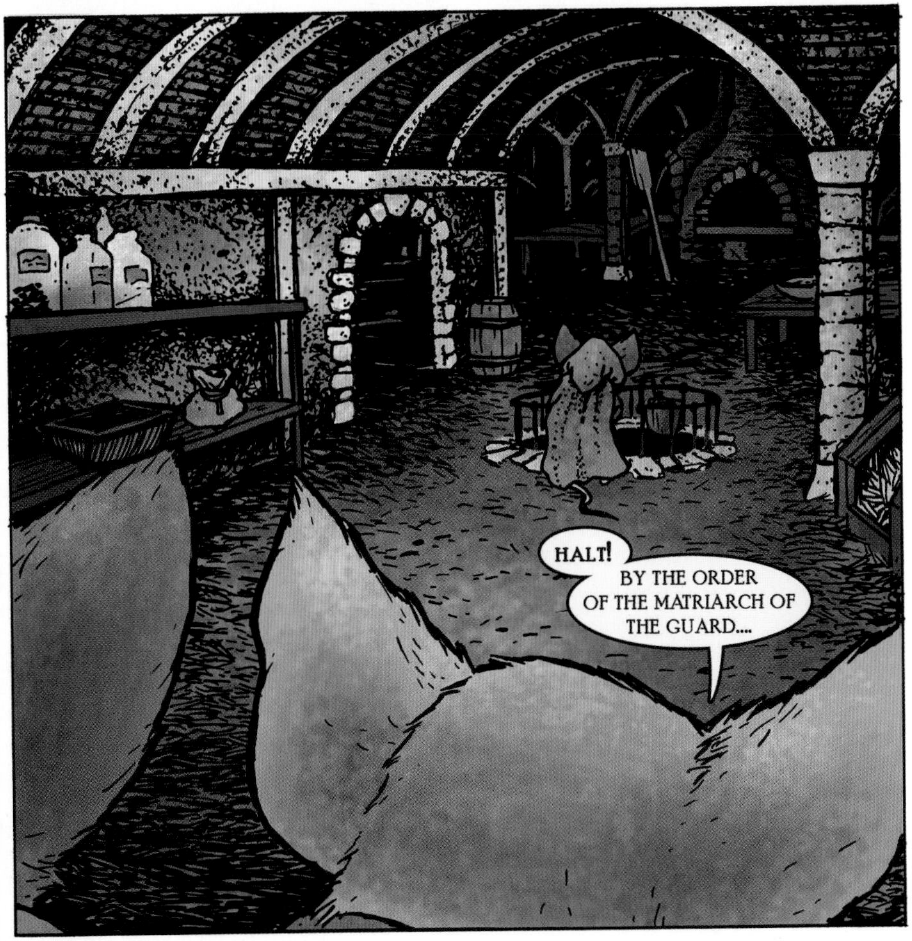
HALT!
BY THE ORDER OF THE MATRIARCH OF THE GUARD....

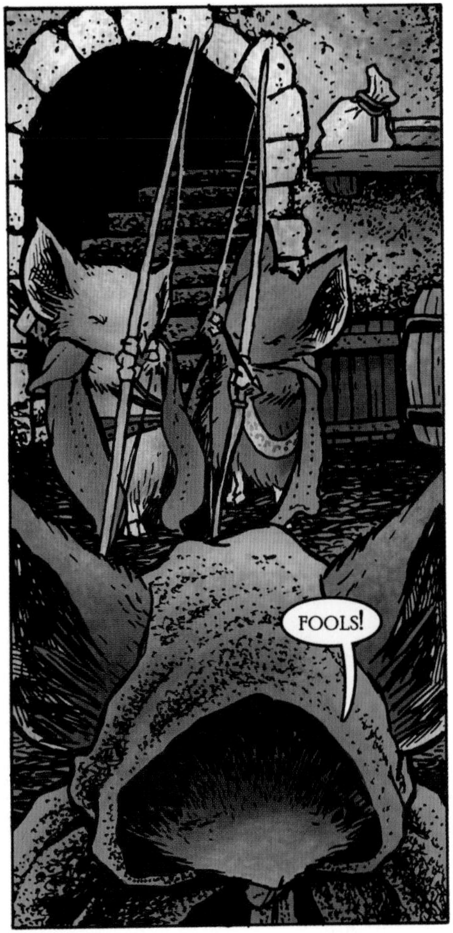
FOOLS!

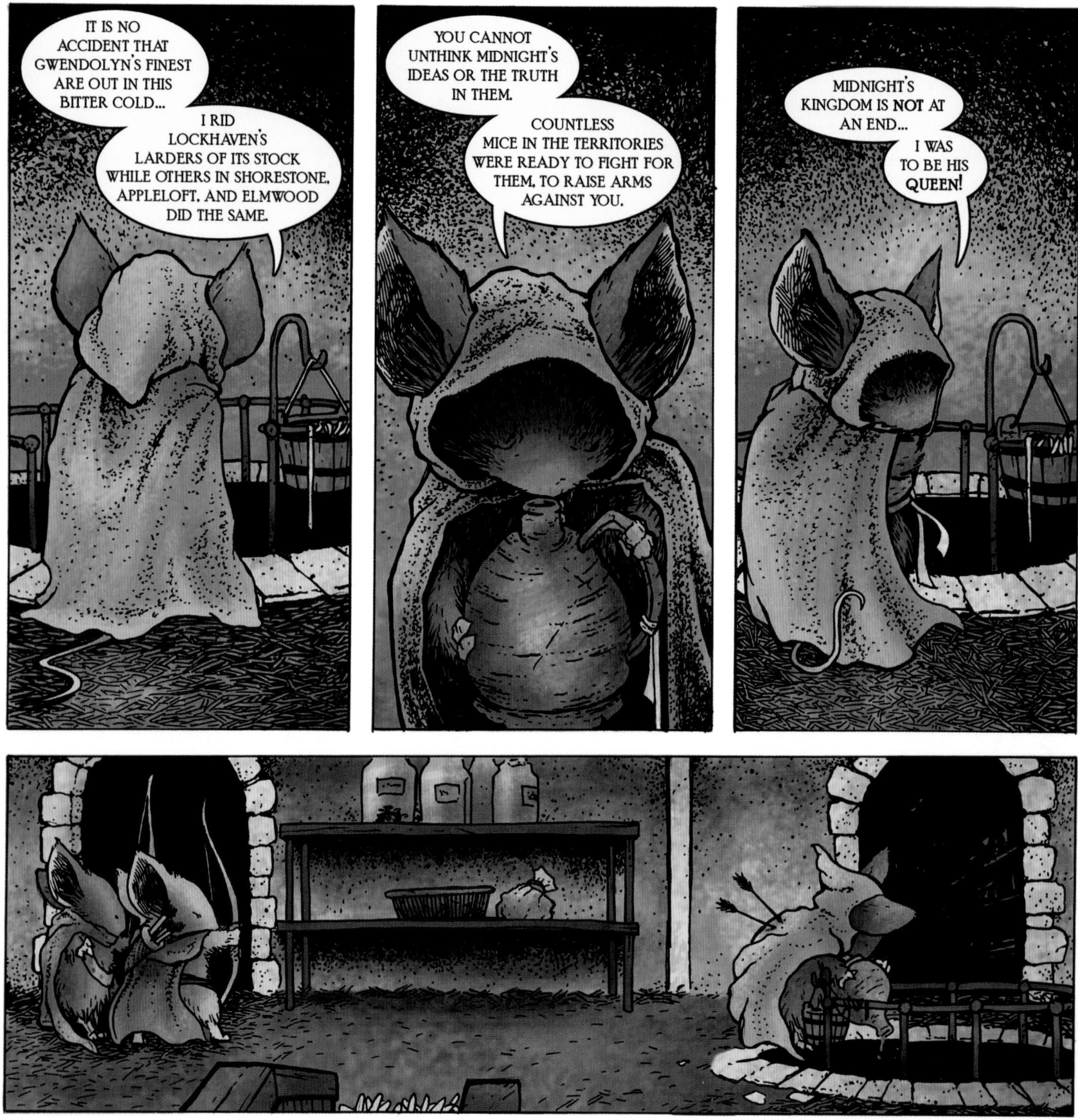
IT IS NO ACCIDENT THAT GWENDOLYN'S FINEST ARE OUT IN THIS BITTER COLD...
I RID LOCKHAVEN'S LARDERS OF ITS STOCK WHILE OTHERS IN SHORESTONE, APPLELOFT, AND ELMWOOD DID THE SAME.
YOU CANNOT UNTHINK MIDNIGHT'S IDEAS OR THE TRUTH IN THEM.
COUNTLESS MICE IN THE TERRITORIES WERE READY TO FIGHT FOR THEM, TO RAISE ARMS AGAINST YOU.
MIDNIGHT'S KINGDOM IS **NOT** AT AN END...
I WAS TO BE HIS **QUEEN!**

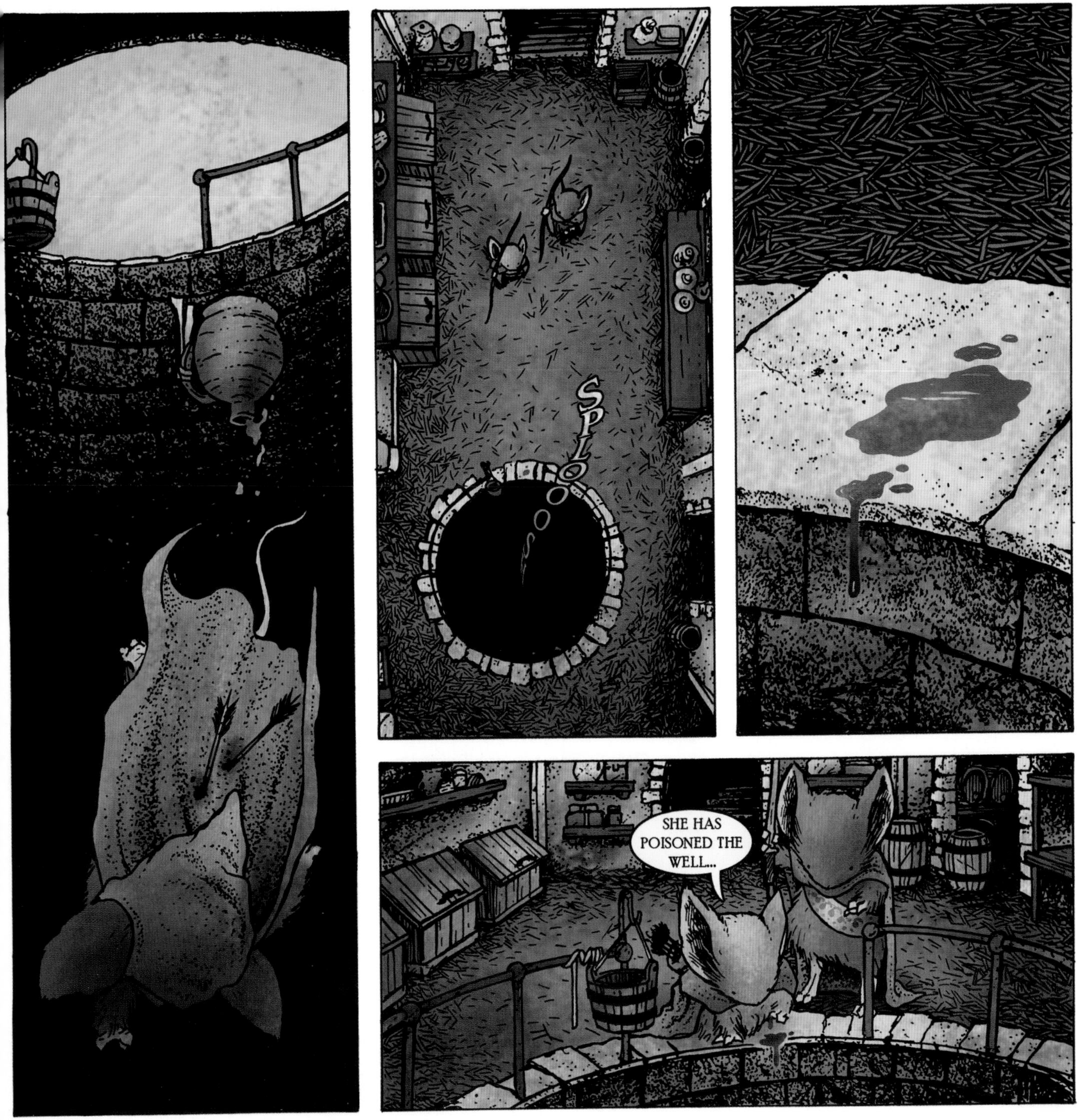
SPLOOOOSH
SHE HAS POISONED THE WELL...

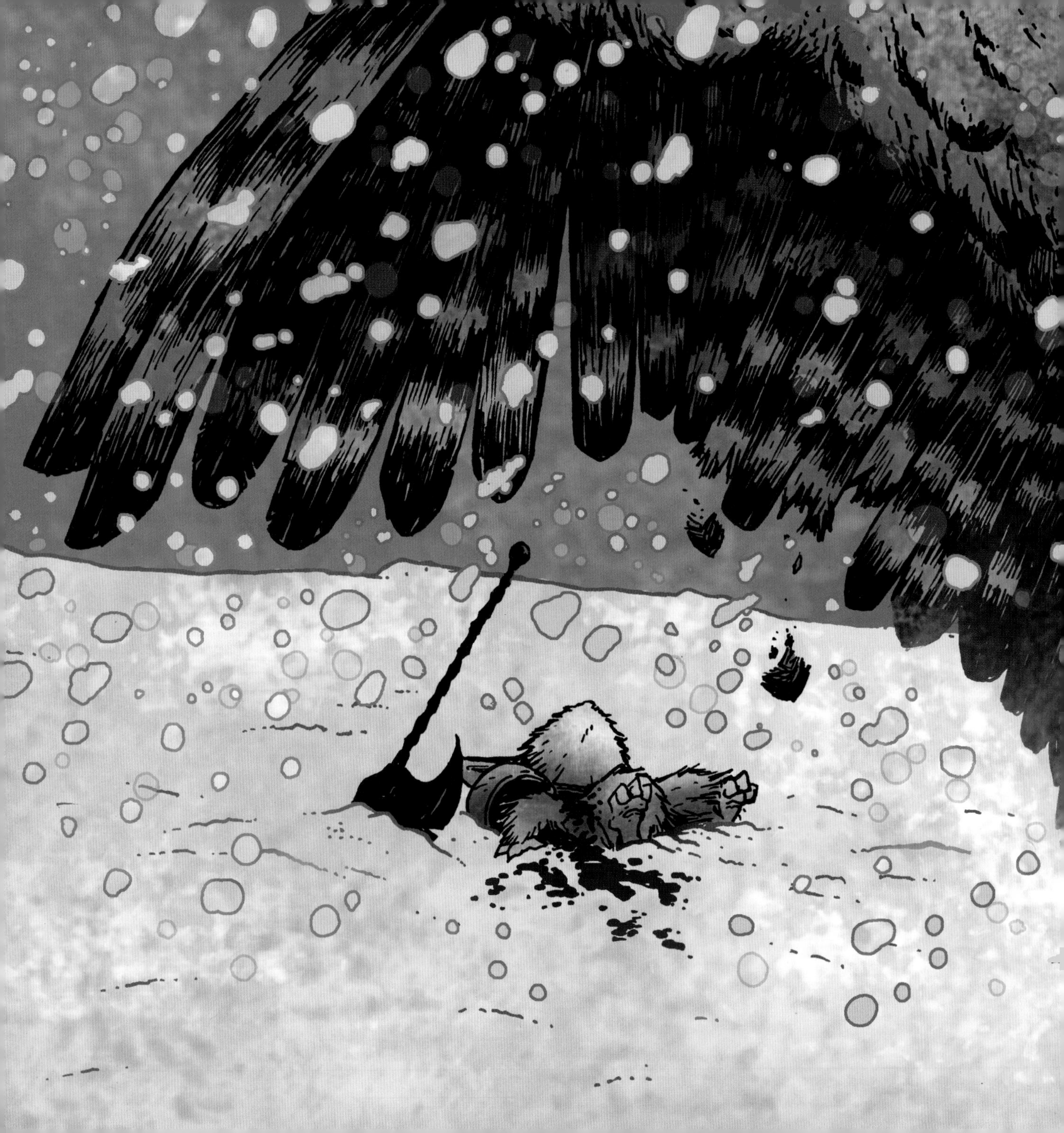

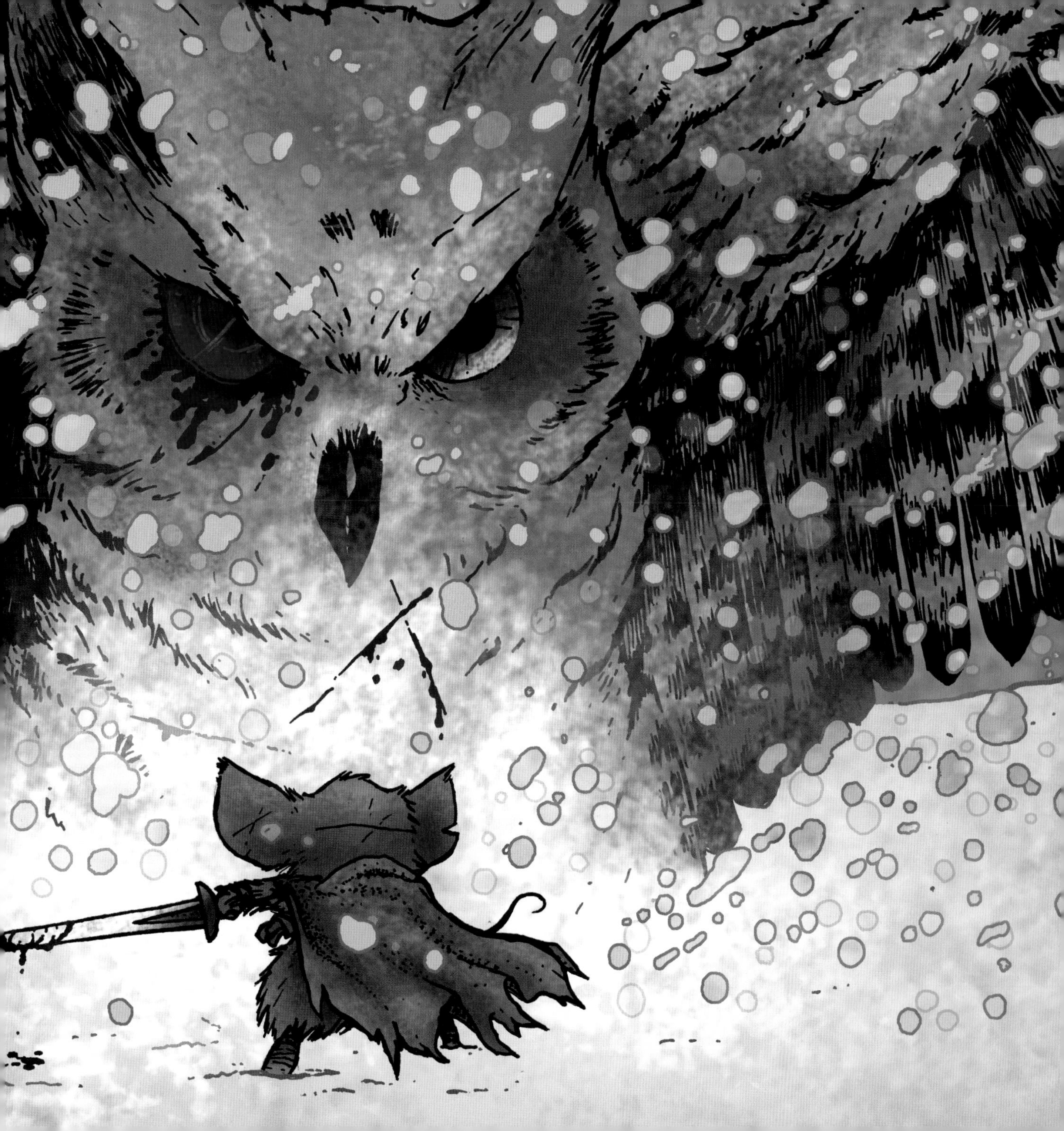

CHAPTER FIVE

In the depths of the prisons of Darkheather, the underground weasel kingdom, Saxon finds the remains of his master Loukas. Sadie and Kenzie seached for the red cloaked mouse, but surrendered to sleep after their efforts were fruitless.

Having found the ice shelter of Lieam and Celanawe, a one-eyed owl seeks its revenge. These of the Guard's finest are far from the poison running through Lockhaven's veins.

> The world beats heavily on us, the smallest of beast
> If not the rain or ice or cold, it's a predator's feast.
> Yet we do not let our determination be plowed;
> Rays of hope can penetrate the thickest of cloud.
> Allow spirit to break and you find the downfall of mice.
> For even if our bodies break, others offer to pay the price.
> It's when we give in and fail and allow doubt to take control
> That the culture of mice will cease to exist in whole.'

- 'A Mouse's Eulogy for life' by Roibin the Scribe

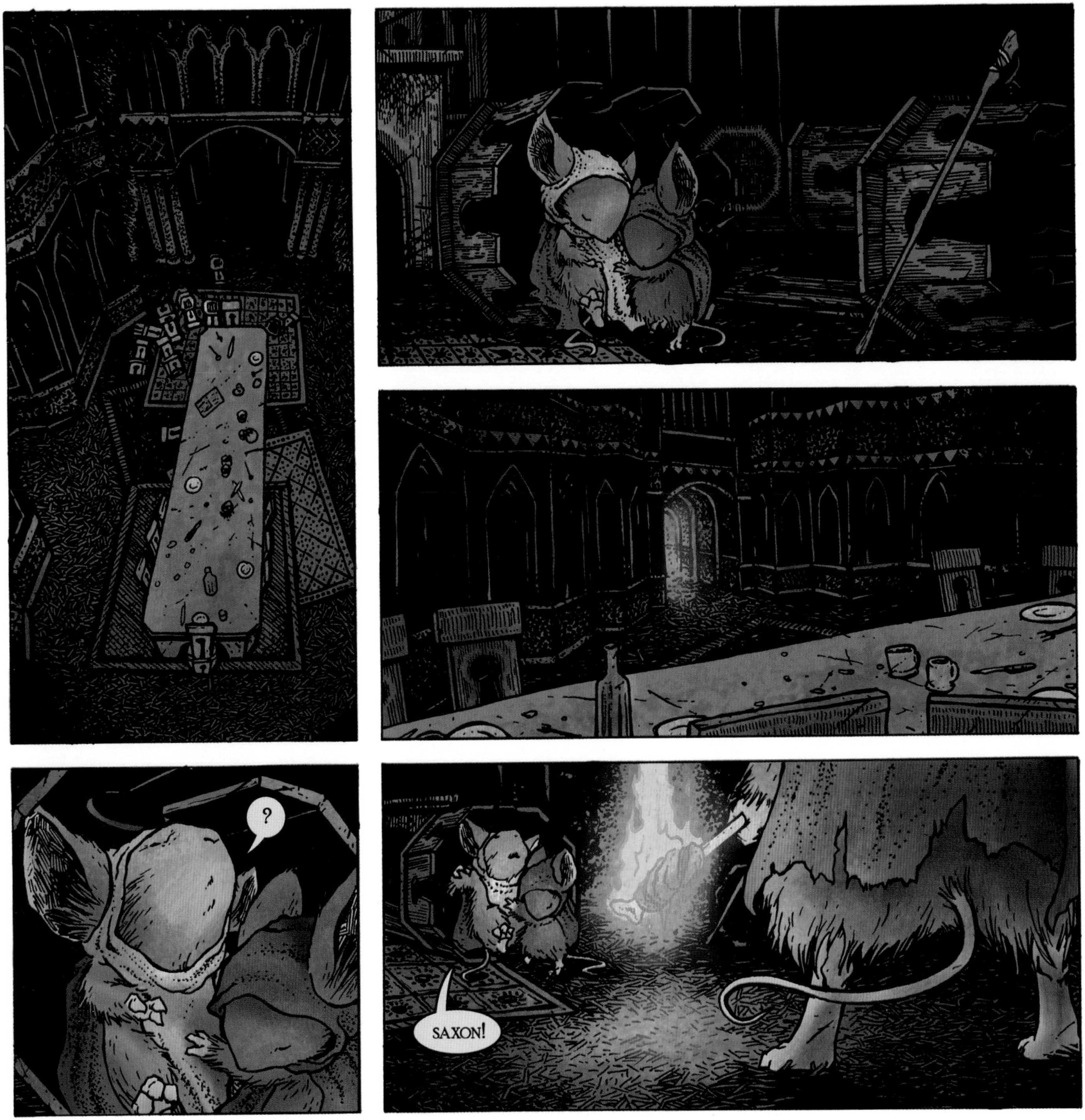
?
SAXON!

I GO MISSING AND I FIND YOU SNUGGLING WITH YOUR NEW LADY?

IT'S NOT LIKE THAT SAXON...

YOU DIDN'T EVEN BOTHER TO FIND ME!

THAT'S NOT TRUE, IT WAS YOU WHO FLEW OFF INTO THIS MAZE!

BATS DON'T LEAVE MUCH TO TRACK THE PATH OF.

WHERE DID YOU END UP?

NEVER YOU MIND... CERTAINLY NOT DREAMING NEXT TO A LADY.

IF YOU ARE UPSET WITH ME, LET'S HAVE IT,

BUT IF YOU ARE UPSET BECAUSE YOU CHOSE TO NOT FOLLOW YOUR HEART

THEN LEAVE SADIE AND I OUT OF IT.

BROTHER, YOUR TRUTHS WOUND ME.

APOLOGY ACCEPT—

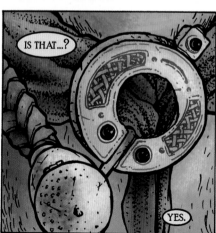

IS THAT...?

YES.

TREAT **THAT** SWORD BETTER THAN YOU EVER HAVE ANY OF YOUR OWN.

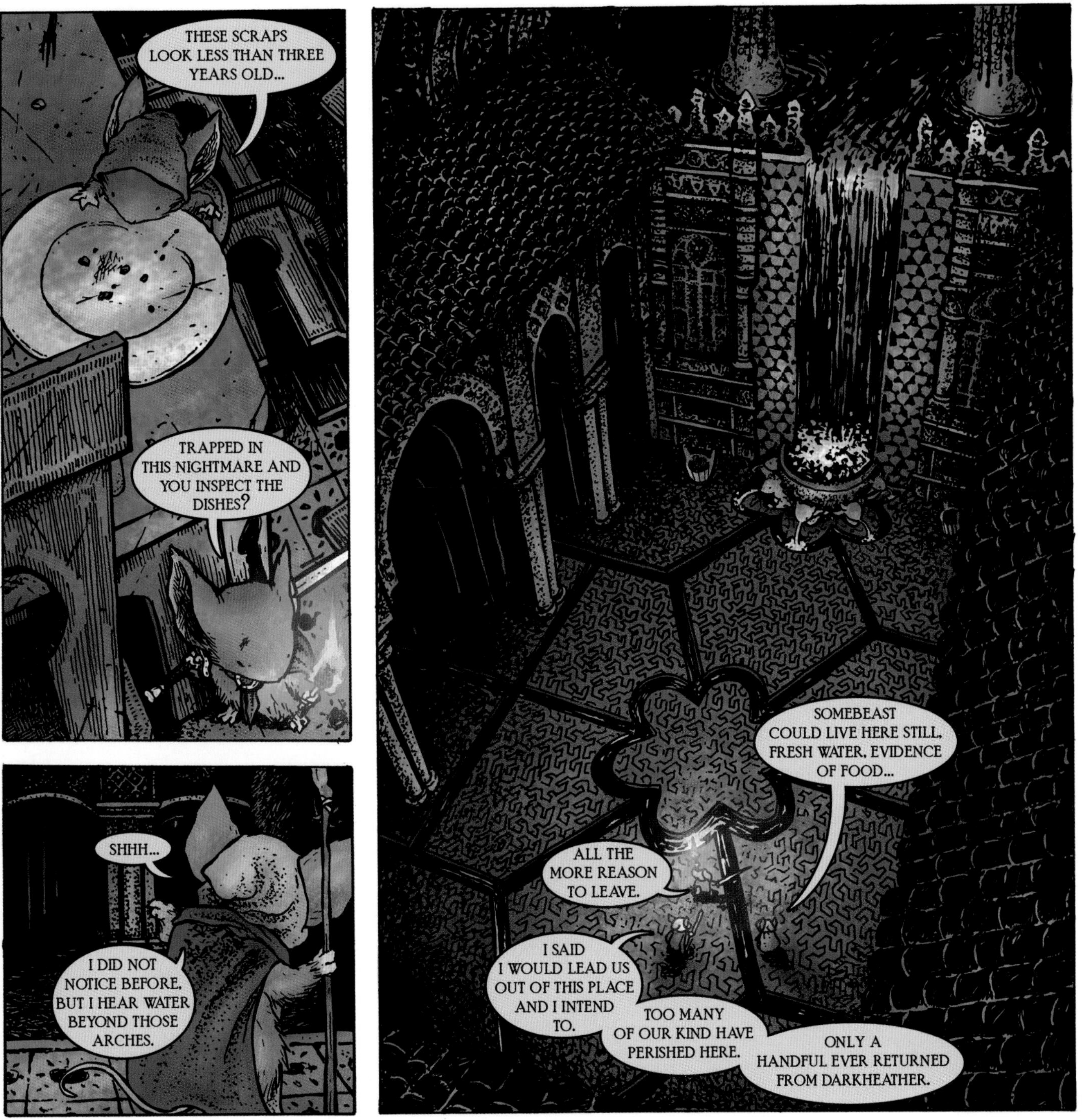
THESE SCRAPS LOOK LESS THAN THREE YEARS OLD...
TRAPPED IN THIS NIGHTMARE AND YOU INSPECT THE DISHES?
SHHH...
I DID NOT NOTICE BEFORE, BUT I HEAR WATER BEYOND THOSE ARCHES.
SOMEBEAST COULD LIVE HERE STILL, FRESH WATER, EVIDENCE OF FOOD...
ALL THE MORE REASON TO LEAVE.
I SAID I WOULD LEAD US OUT OF THIS PLACE AND I INTEND TO.
TOO MANY OF OUR KIND HAVE PERISHED HERE.
ONLY A HANDFUL EVER RETURNED FROM DARKHEATHER.

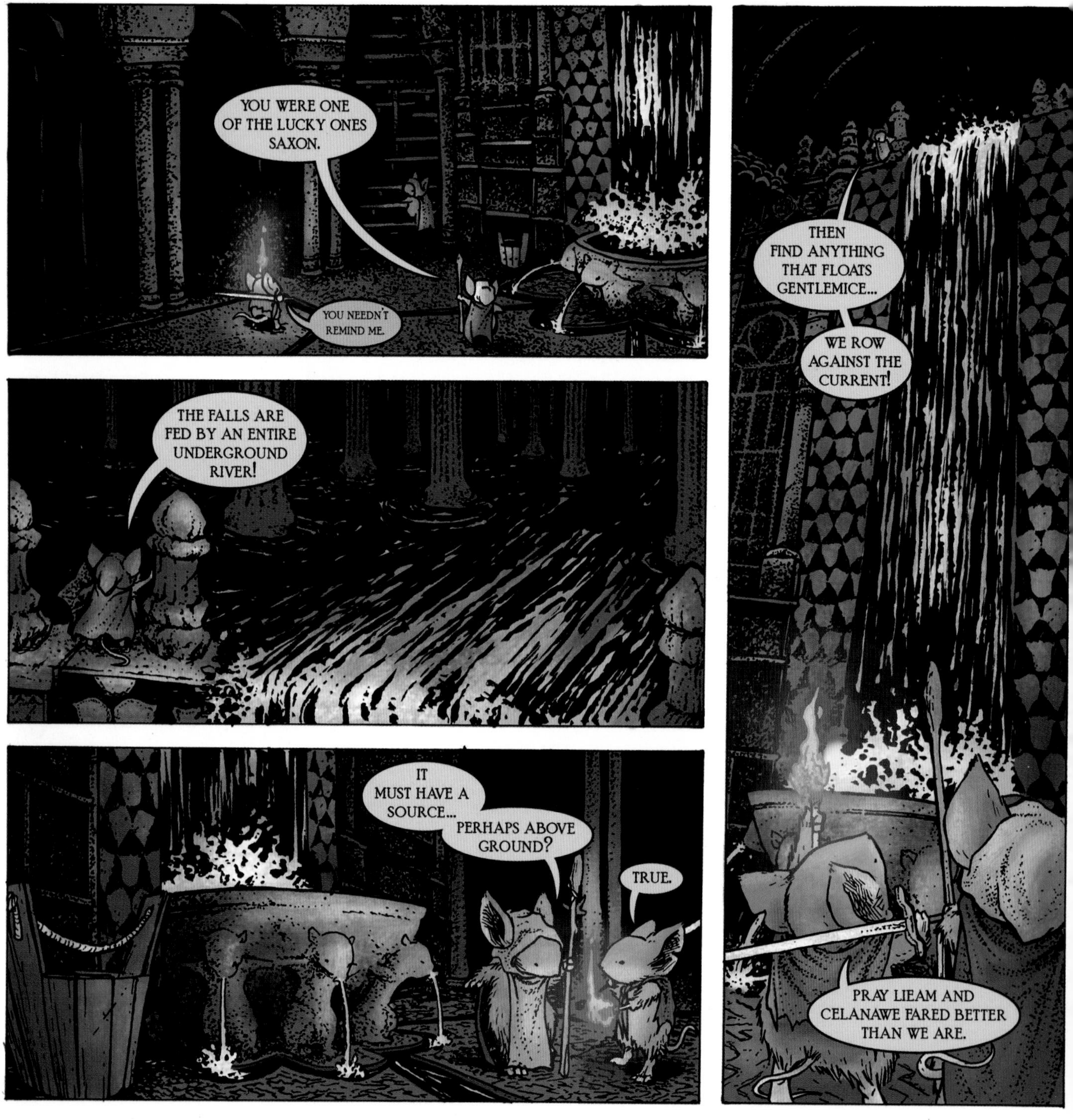
YOU WERE ONE OF THE LUCKY ONES SAXON.
YOU NEEDN'T REMIND ME.
THE FALLS ARE FED BY AN ENTIRE UNDERGROUND RIVER!
IT MUST HAVE A SOURCE...
PERHAPS ABOVE GROUND?
TRUE.
THEN FIND ANYTHING THAT FLOATS GENTLEMICE...
WE ROW AGAINST THE CURRENT!
PRAY LIEAM AND CELANAWE FARED BETTER THAN WE ARE.

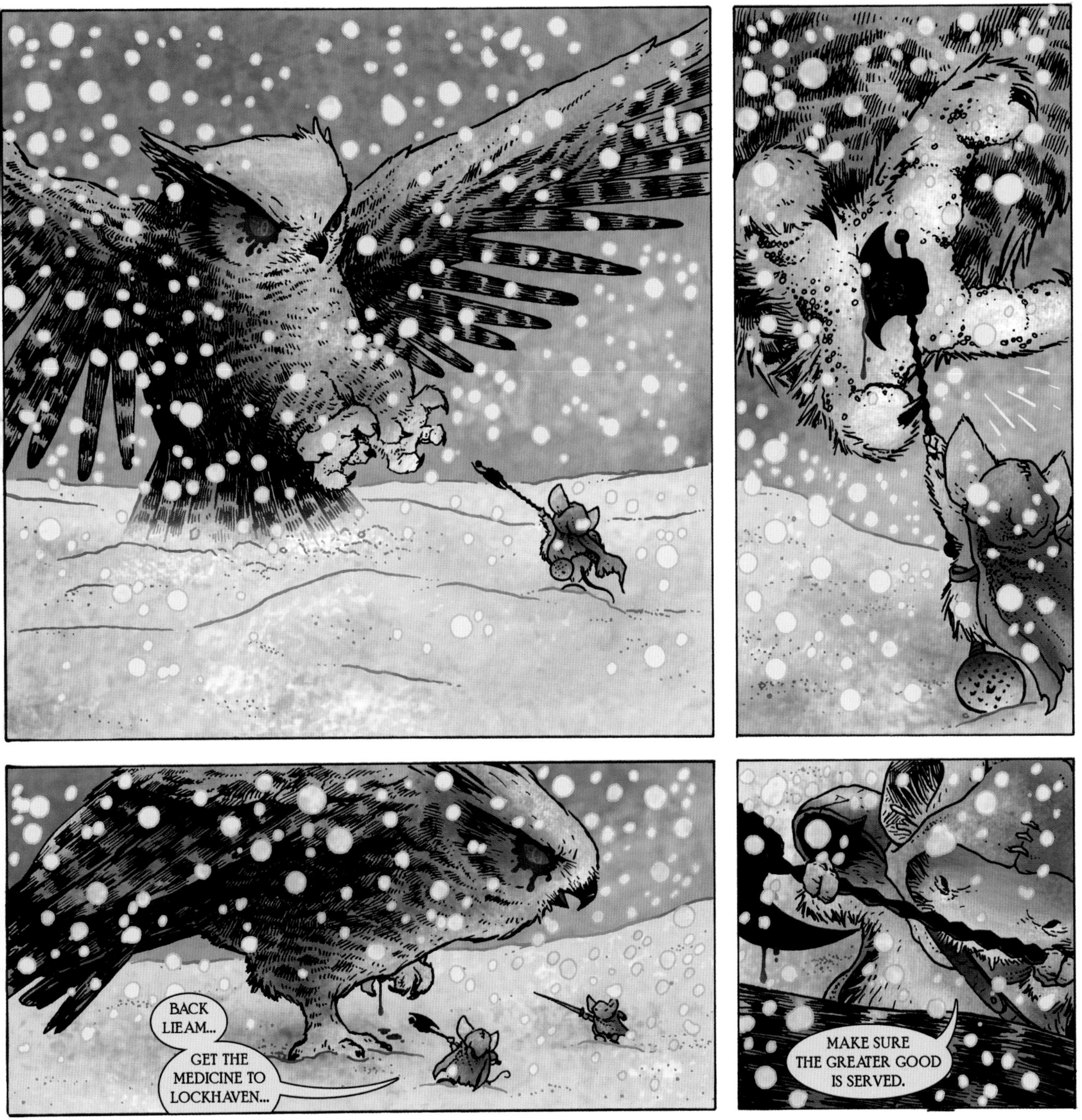
BACK LIEAM...
GET THE MEDICINE TO LOCKHAVEN...
MAKE SURE THE GREATER GOOD IS SERVED.

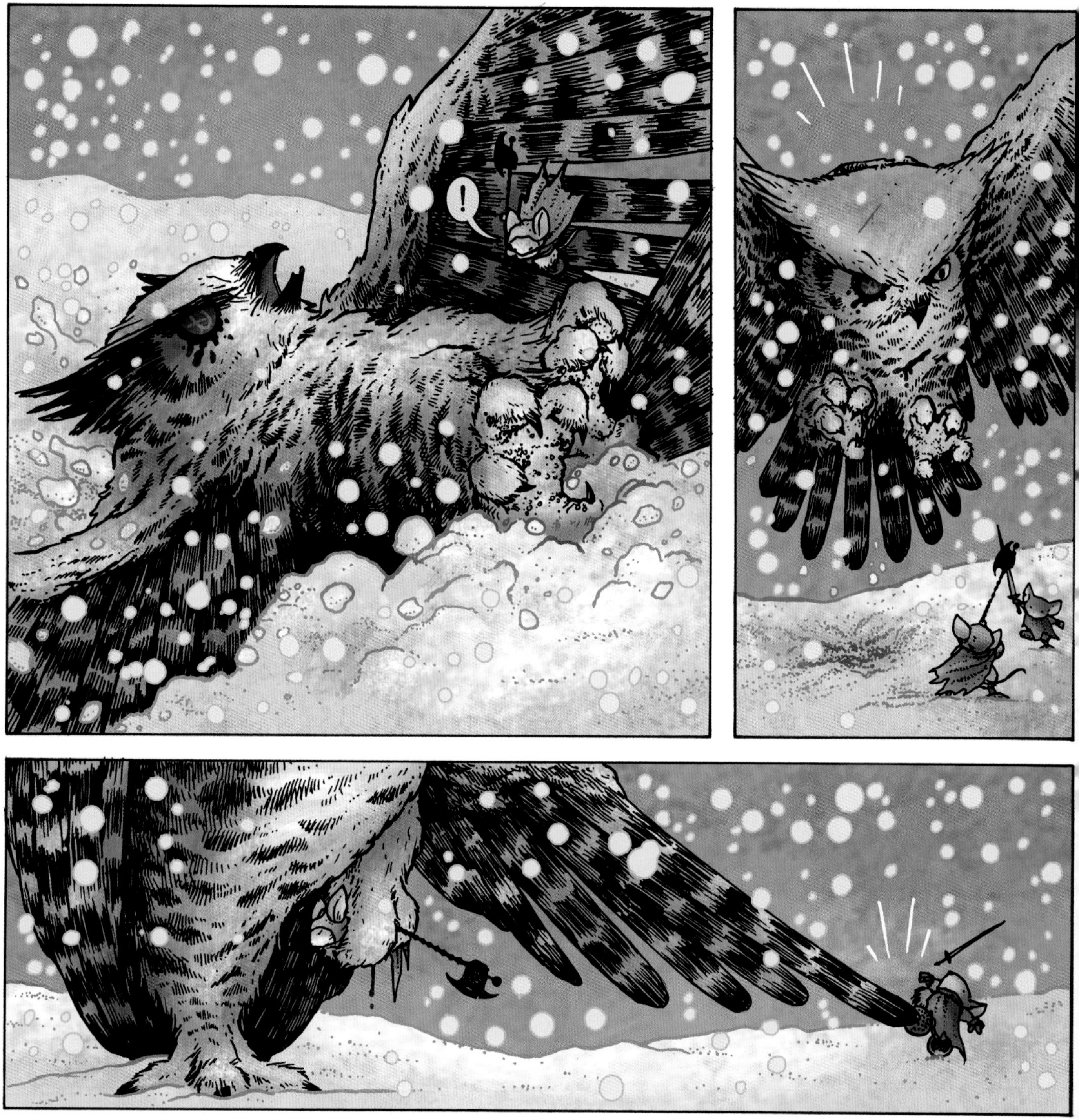
!

CELANAWE...

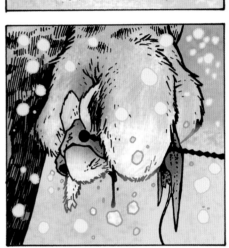

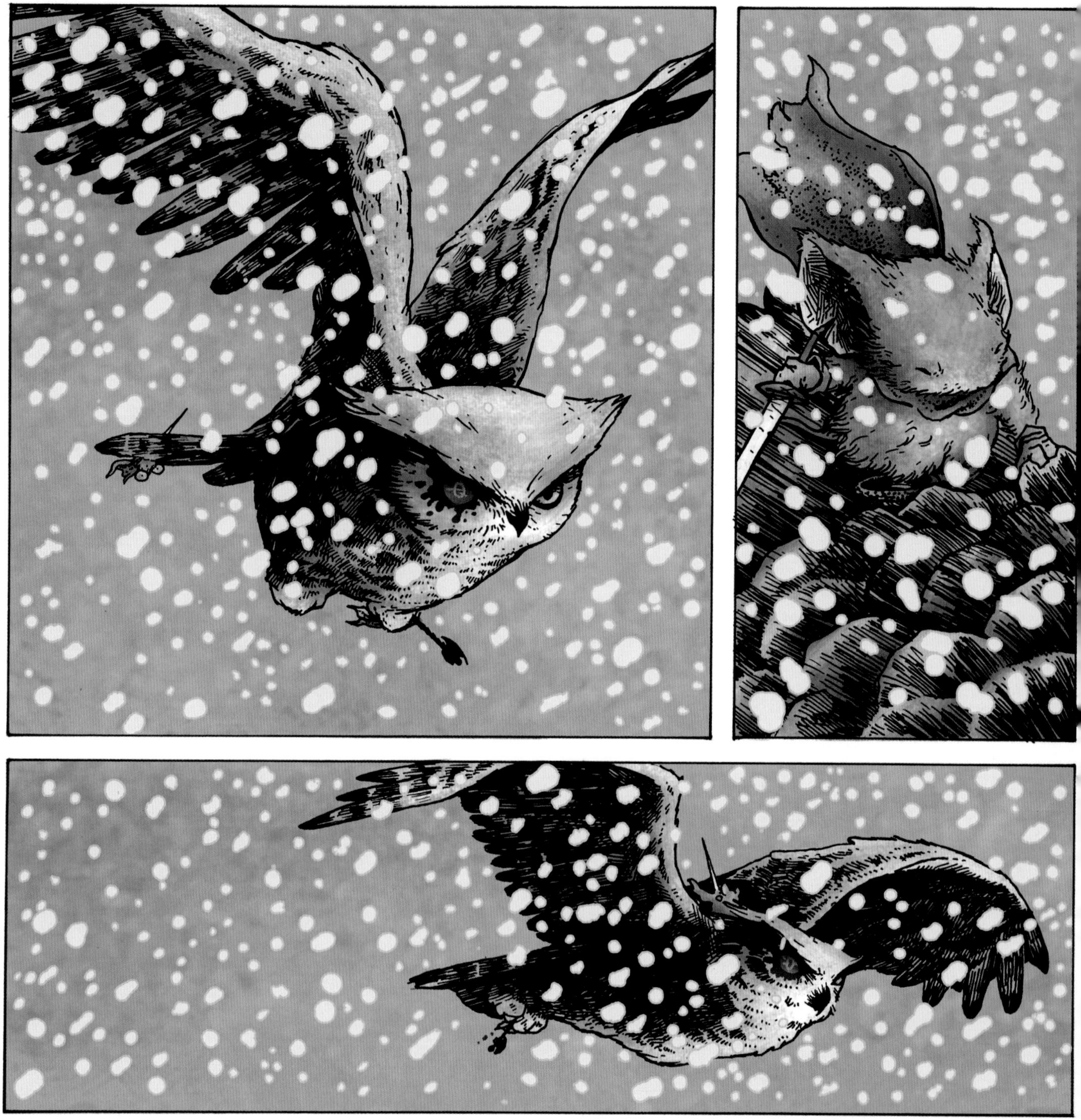

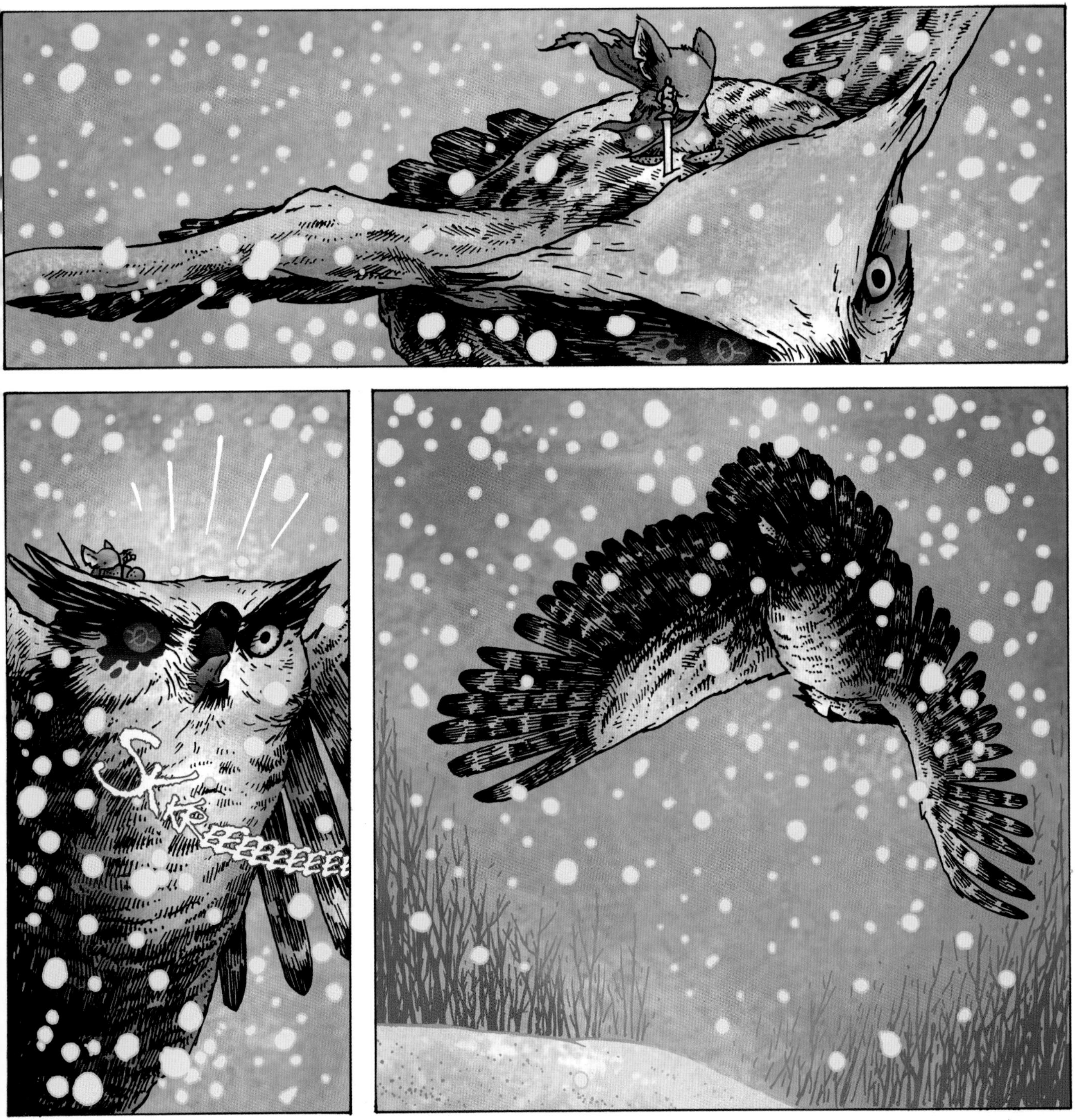
SKREEEEEEEEE

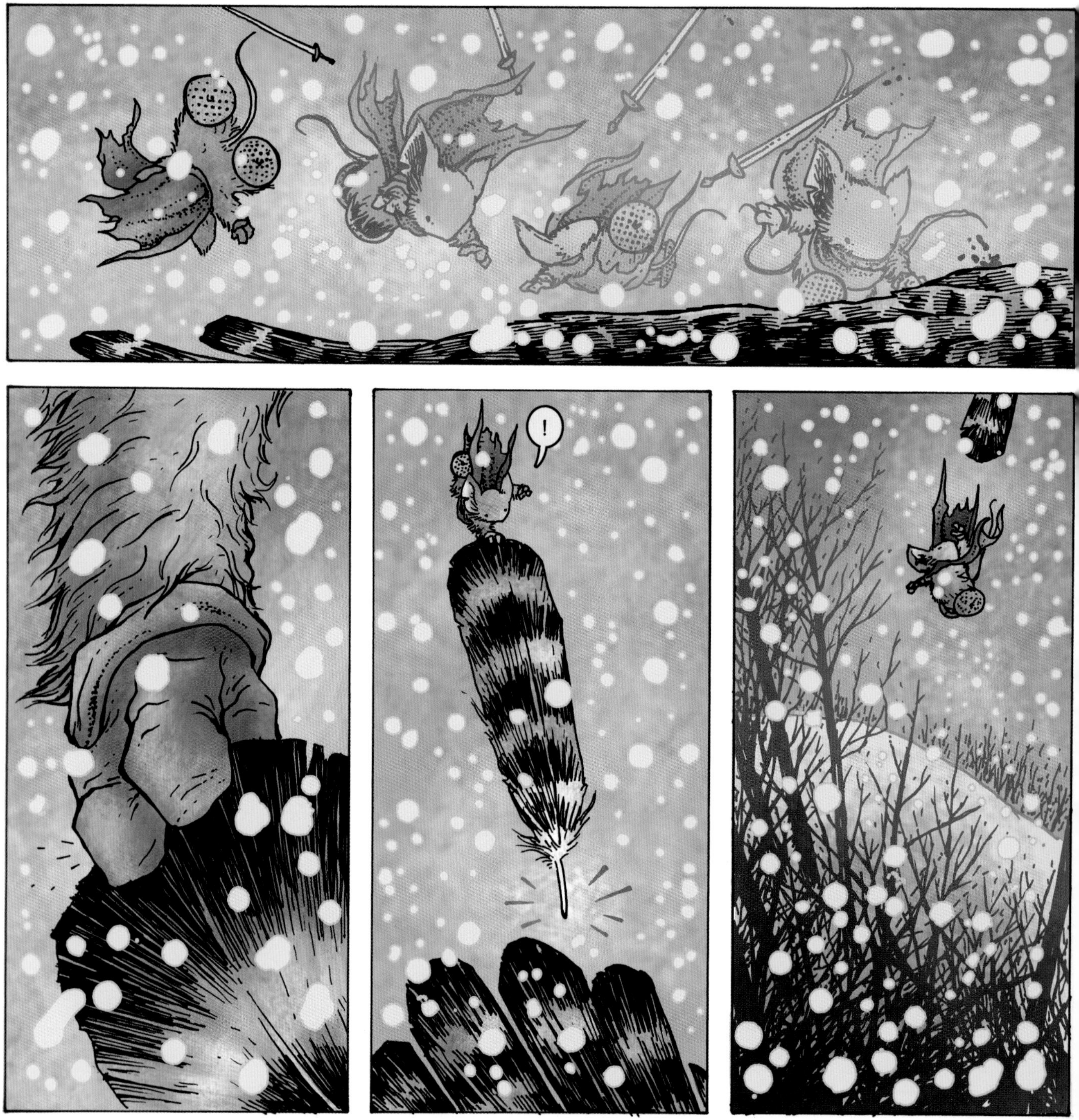
!

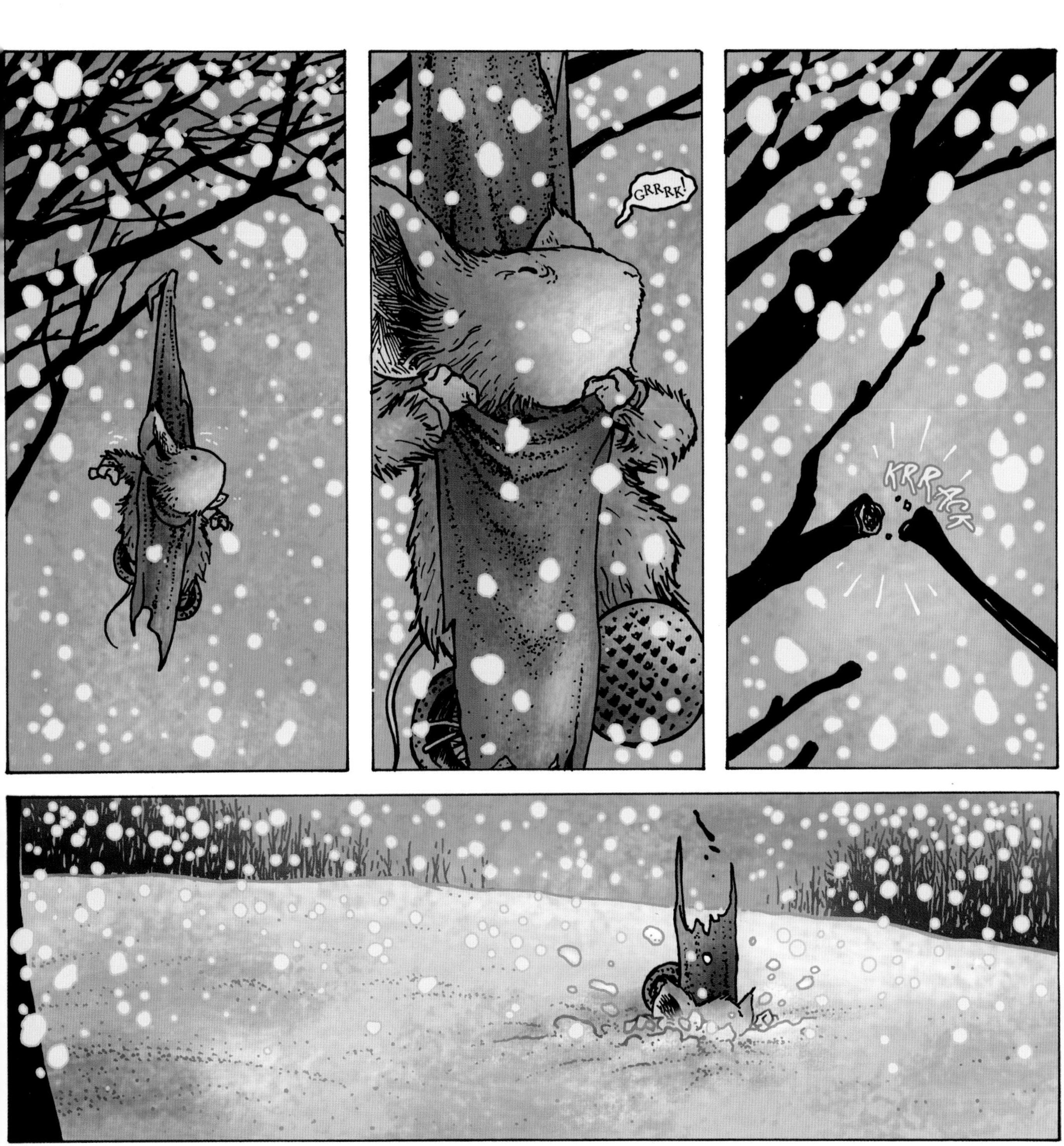
GRRRK!
KRRACK

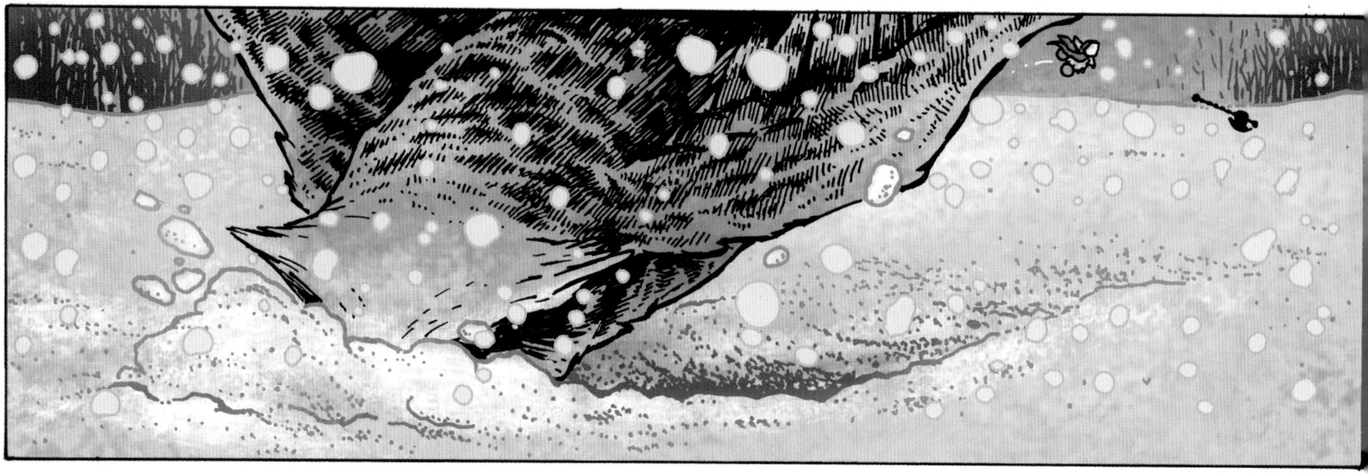
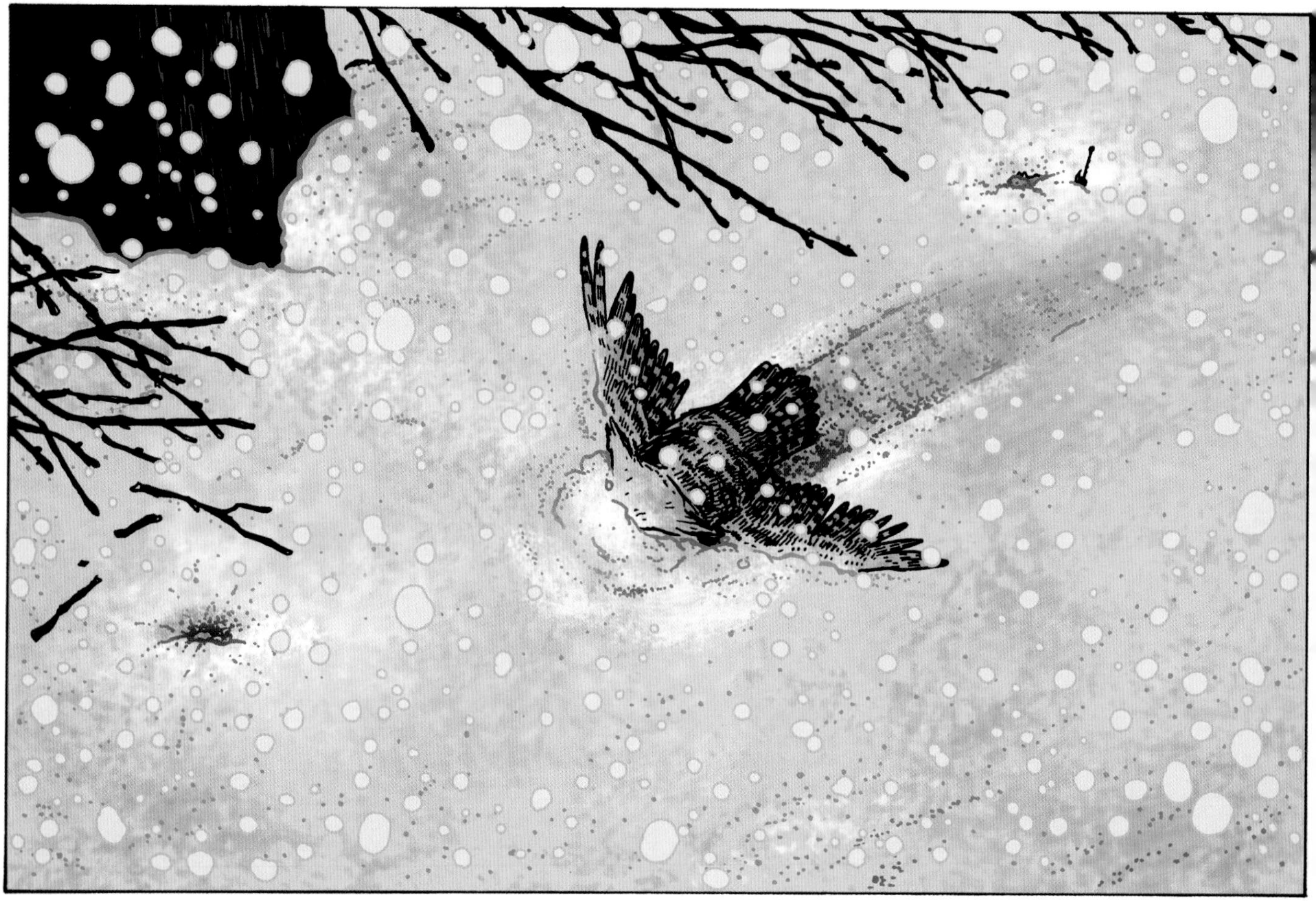

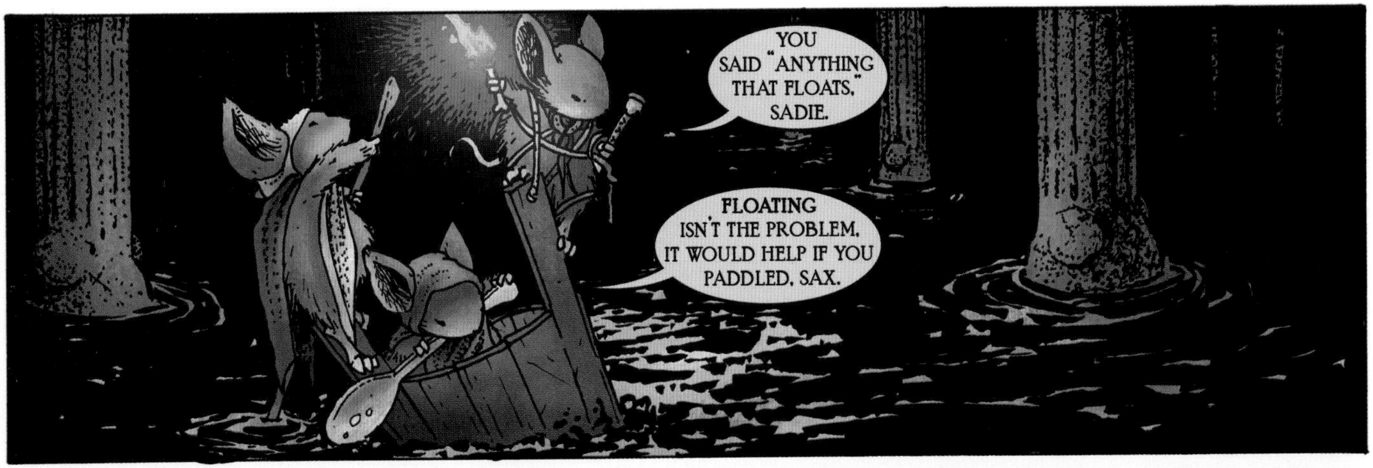
YOU SAID "ANYTHING THAT FLOATS," SADIE.
FLOATING ISN'T THE PROBLEM. IT WOULD HELP IF YOU PADDLED, SAX.

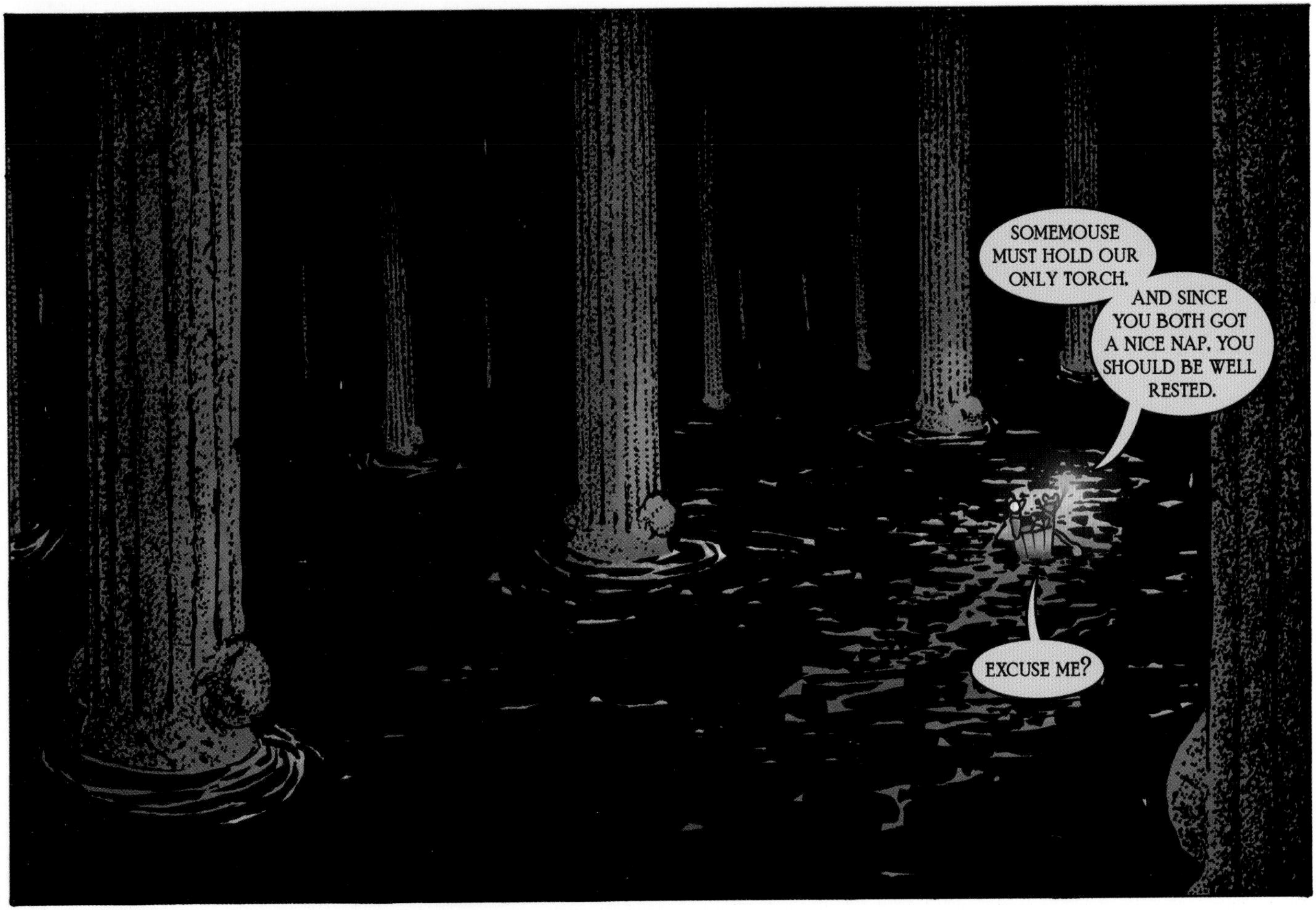
SOMEMOUSE MUST HOLD OUR ONLY TORCH.
AND SINCE YOU BOTH GOT A NICE NAP, YOU SHOULD BE WELL RESTED.
EXCUSE ME?

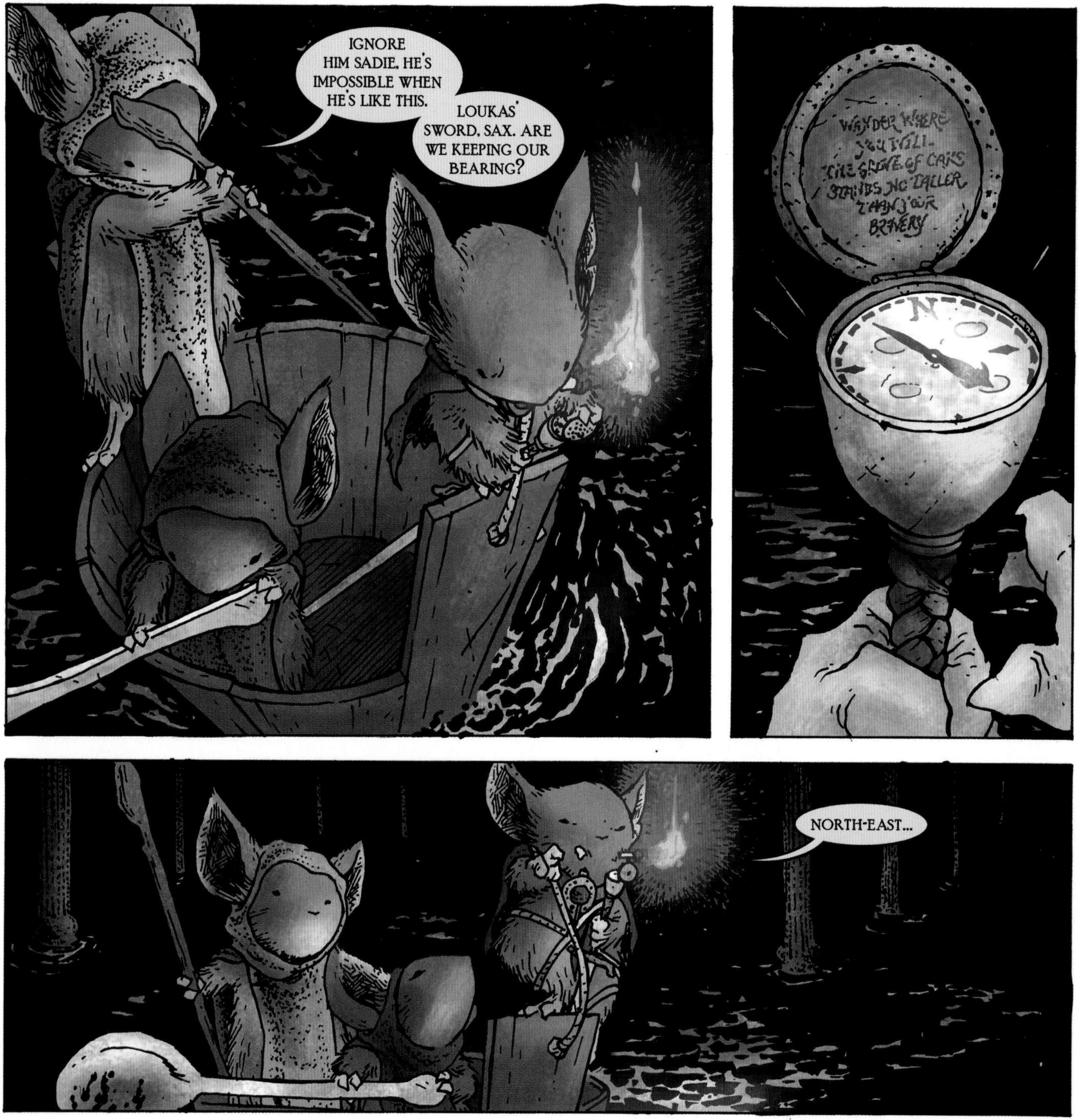
IGNORE HIM SADIE, HE'S IMPOSSIBLE WHEN HE'S LIKE THIS.
LOUKAS' SWORD, SAX. ARE WE KEEPING OUR BEARING?
WANDER WHERE YOU WILL THE GROVE OF OAKS STANDS NO TALLER THAN YOUR BRAVERY
NORTH-EAST...

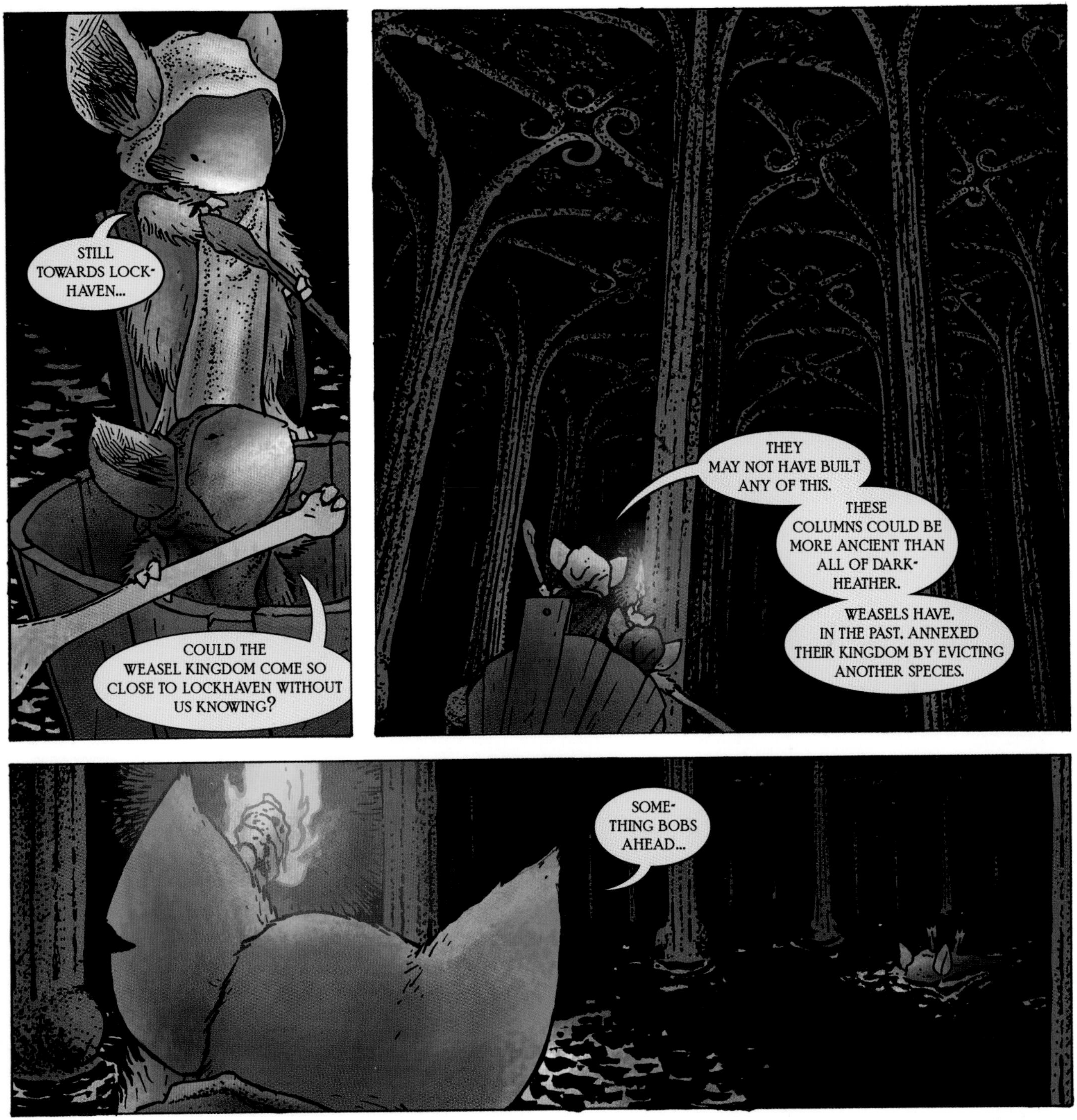
STILL TOWARDS LOCK-HAVEN...
COULD THE WEASEL KINGDOM COME SO CLOSE TO LOCKHAVEN WITHOUT US KNOWING?
THEY MAY NOT HAVE BUILT ANY OF THIS.
THESE COLUMNS COULD BE MORE ANCIENT THAN ALL OF DARK-HEATHER.
WEASELS HAVE, IN THE PAST, ANNEXED THEIR KINGDOM BY EVICTING ANOTHER SPECIES.
SOME-THING BOBS AHEAD...

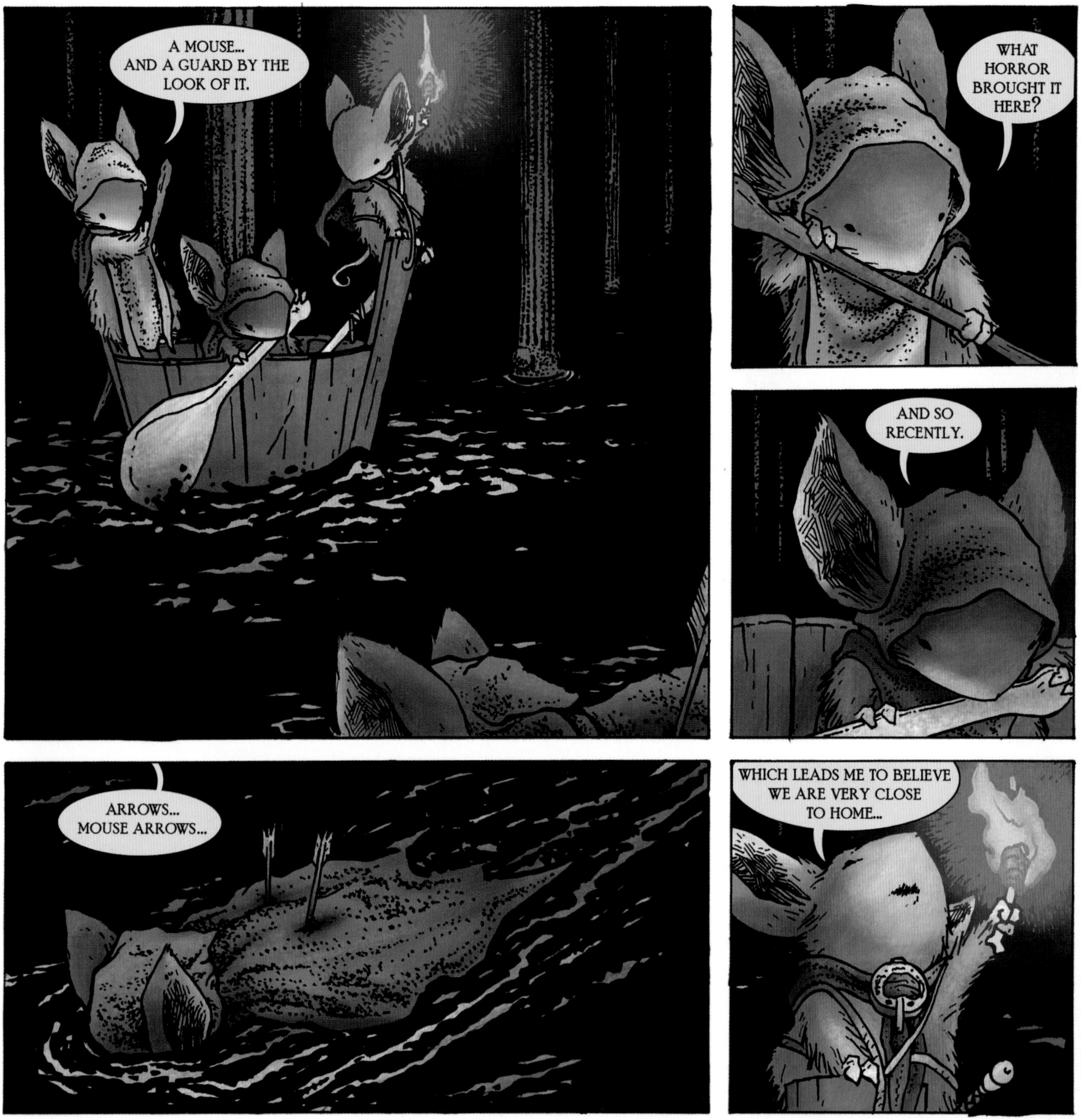
A MOUSE... AND A GUARD BY THE LOOK OF IT.
WHAT HORROR BROUGHT IT HERE?
AND SO RECENTLY.
ARROWS... MOUSE ARROWS...
WHICH LEADS ME TO BELIEVE WE ARE VERY CLOSE TO HOME...

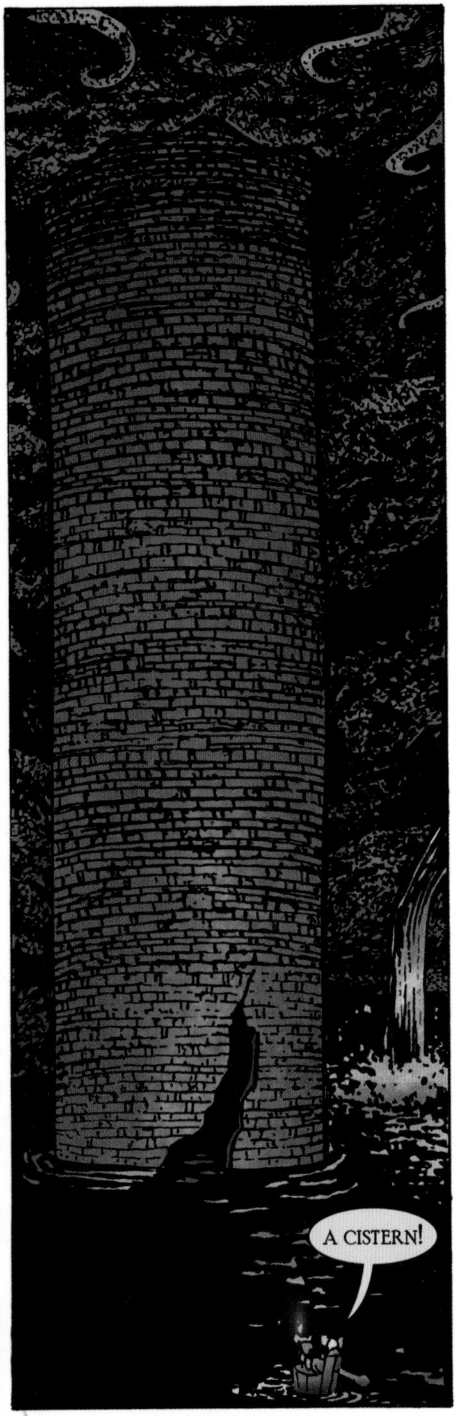
A CISTERN!

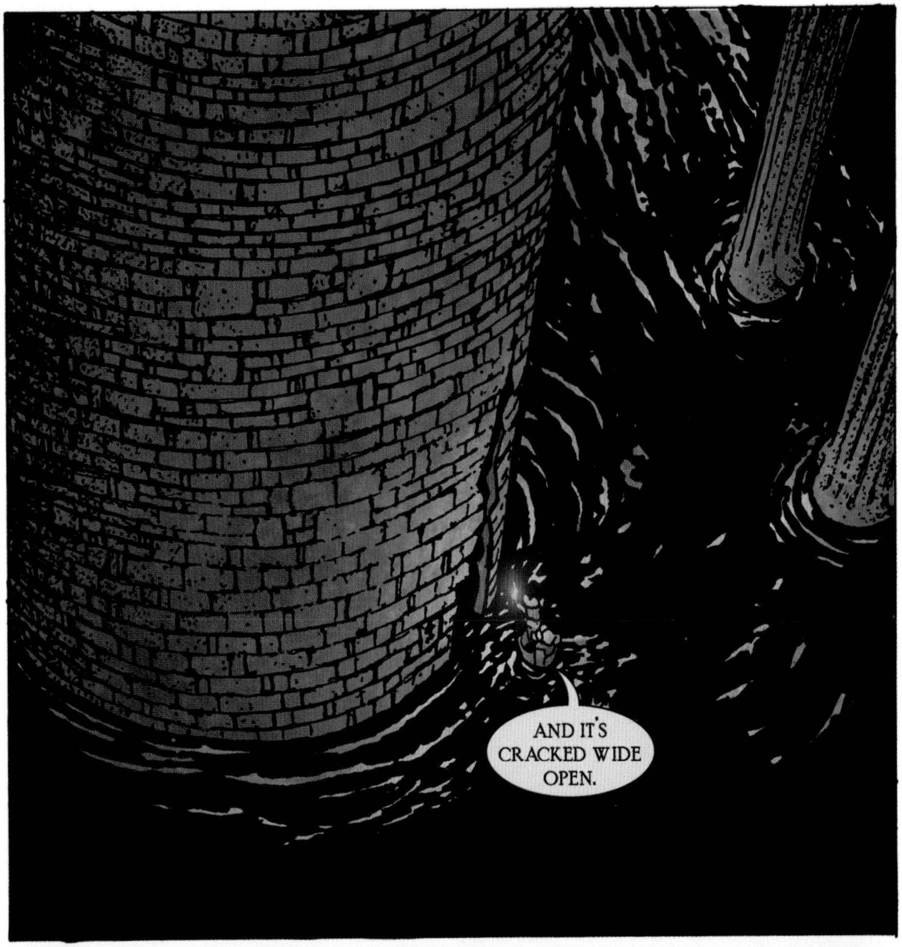
AND IT'S CRACKED WIDE OPEN.

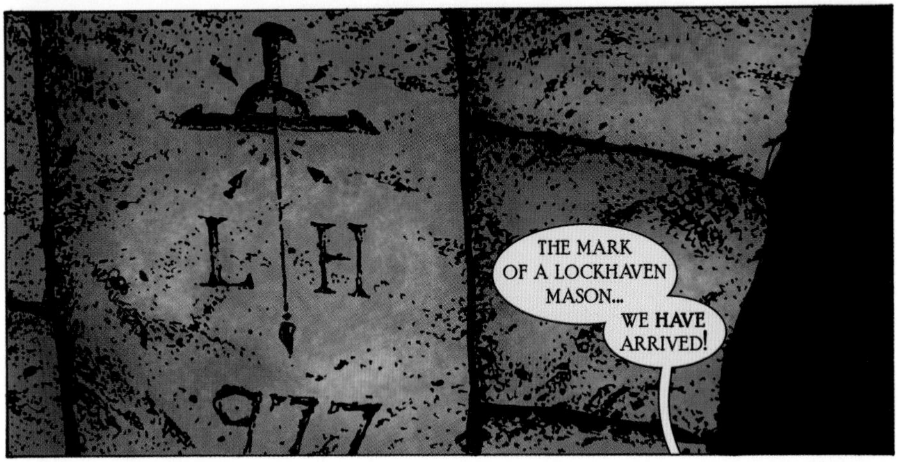
L H
977
THE MARK OF A LOCKHAVEN MASON...
WE HAVE ARRIVED!

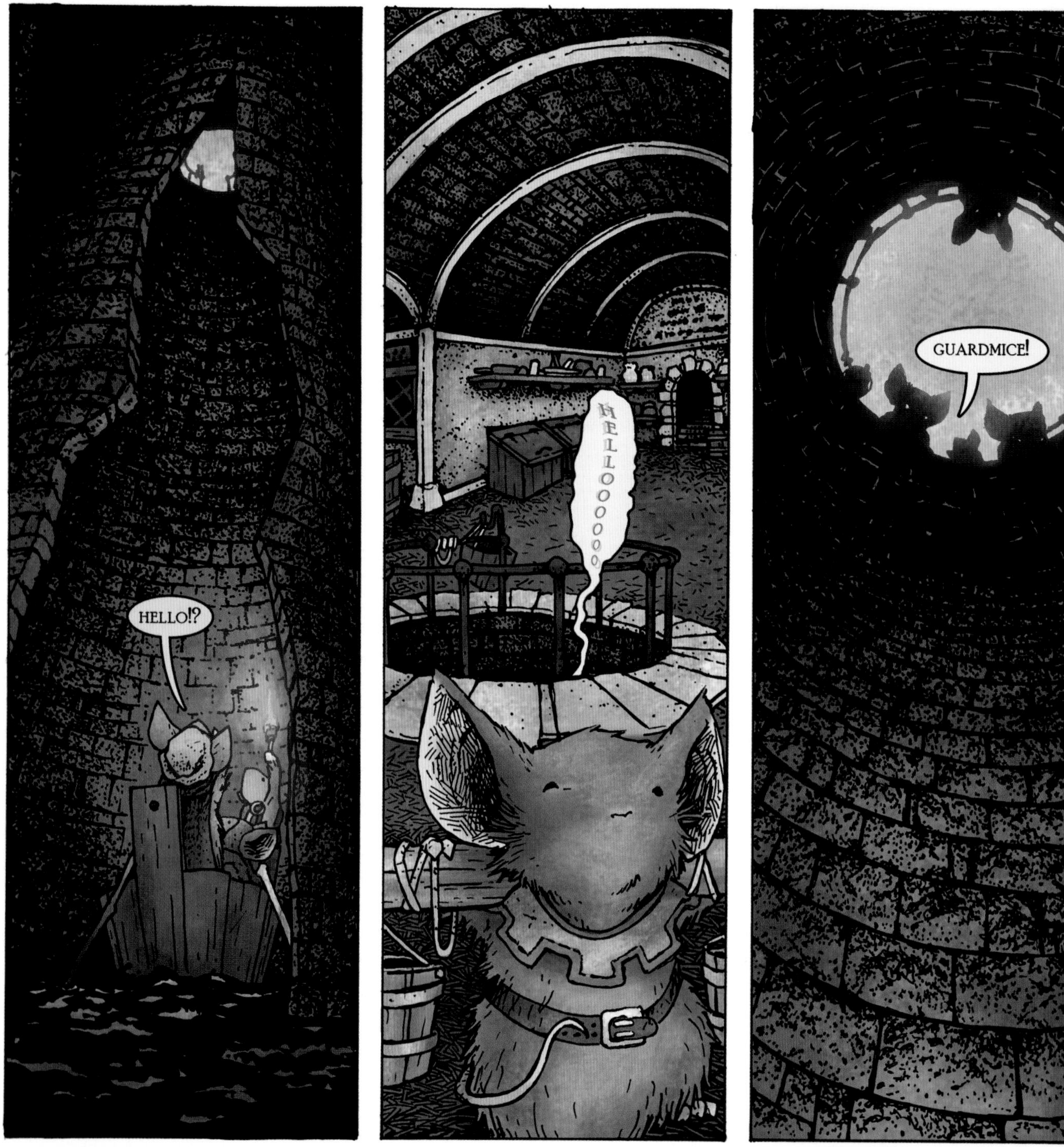
HELLO!?
HELLOOOOOO
GUARDMICE!

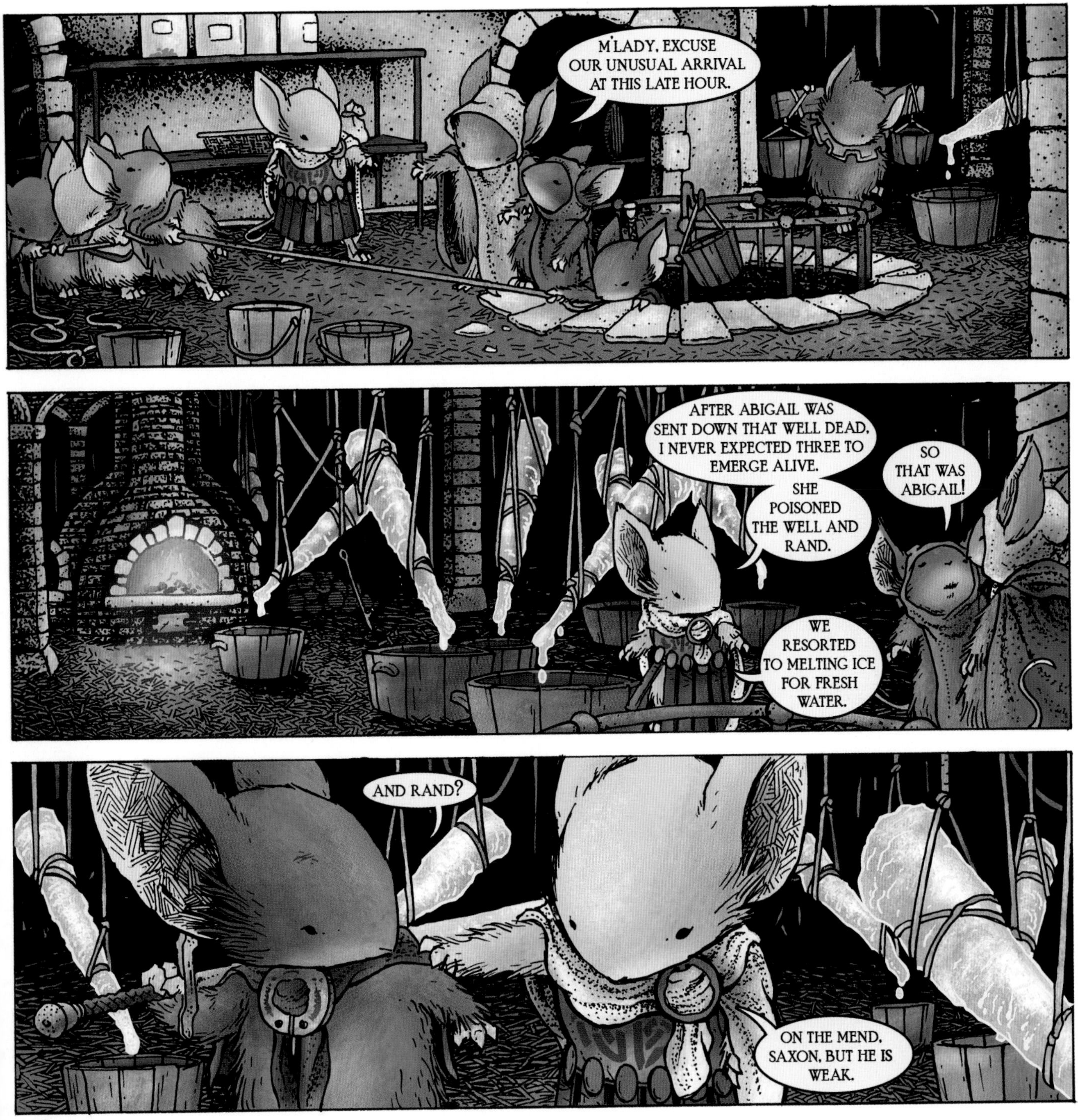
M'LADY, EXCUSE OUR UNUSUAL ARRIVAL AT THIS LATE HOUR.
AFTER ABIGAIL WAS SENT DOWN THAT WELL DEAD, I NEVER EXPECTED THREE TO EMERGE ALIVE.
SHE POISONED THE WELL AND RAND.
SO THAT WAS ABIGAIL!
WE RESORTED TO MELTING ICE FOR FRESH WATER.
AND RAND?
ON THE MEND, SAXON, BUT HE IS WEAK.

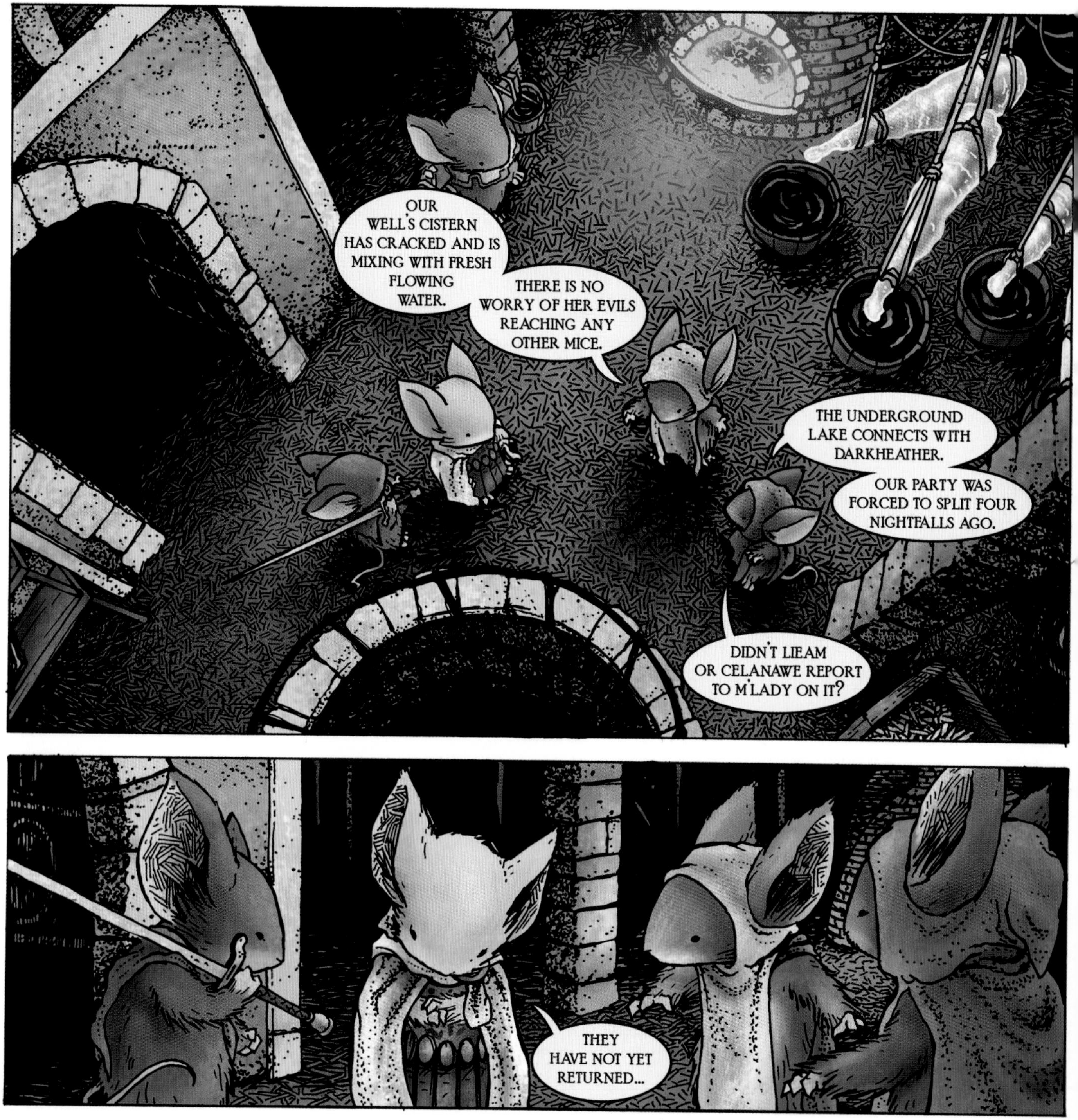
OUR WELL'S CISTERN HAS CRACKED AND IS MIXING WITH FRESH FLOWING WATER.
THERE IS NO WORRY OF HER EVILS REACHING ANY OTHER MICE.
THE UNDERGROUND LAKE CONNECTS WITH DARKHEATHER.
OUR PARTY WAS FORCED TO SPLIT FOUR NIGHTFALLS AGO.
DIDN'T LIEAM OR CELANAWE REPORT TO M'LADY ON IT?
THEY HAVE NOT YET RETURNED...

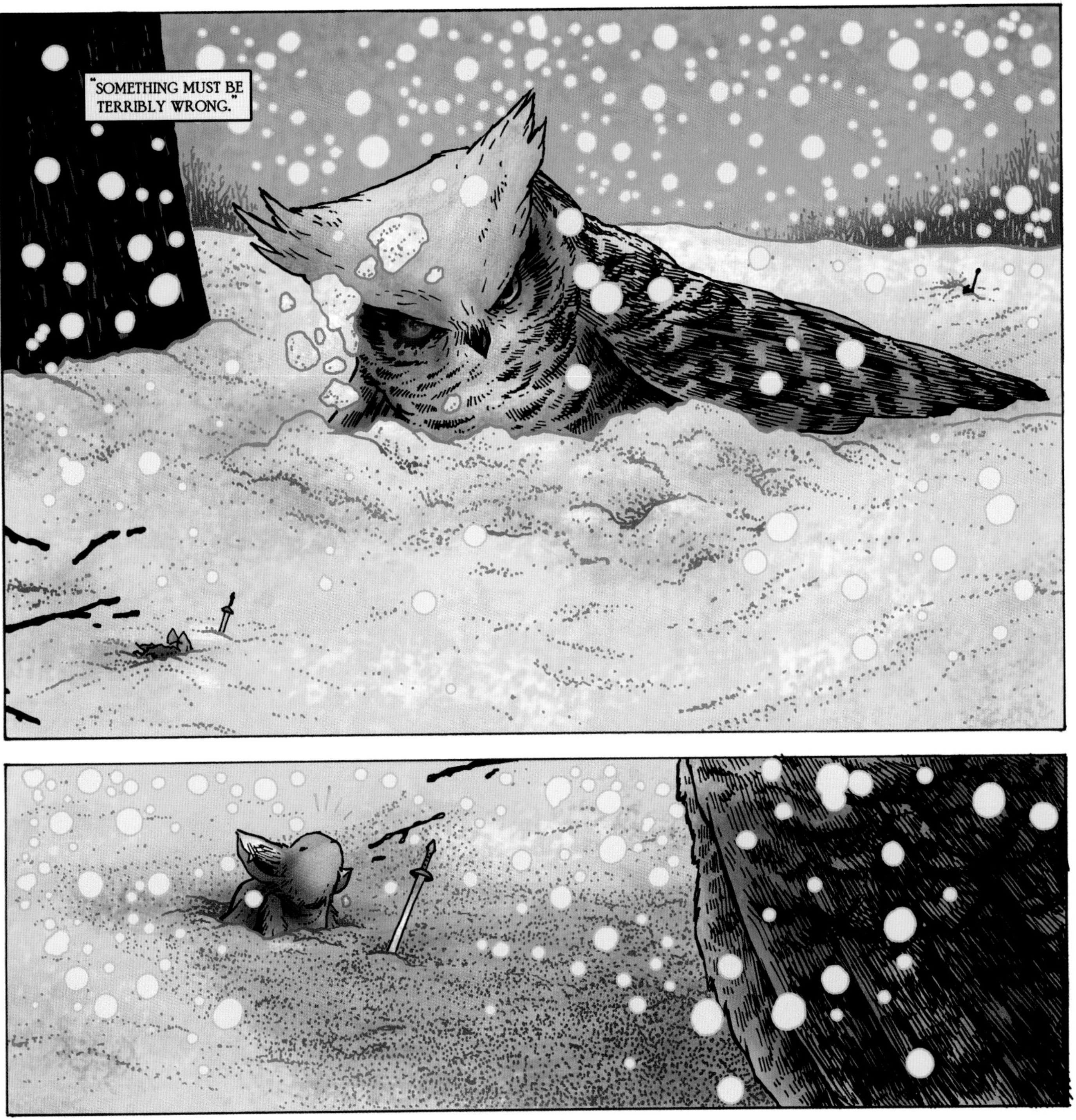
"SOMETHING MUST BE TERRIBLY WRONG."

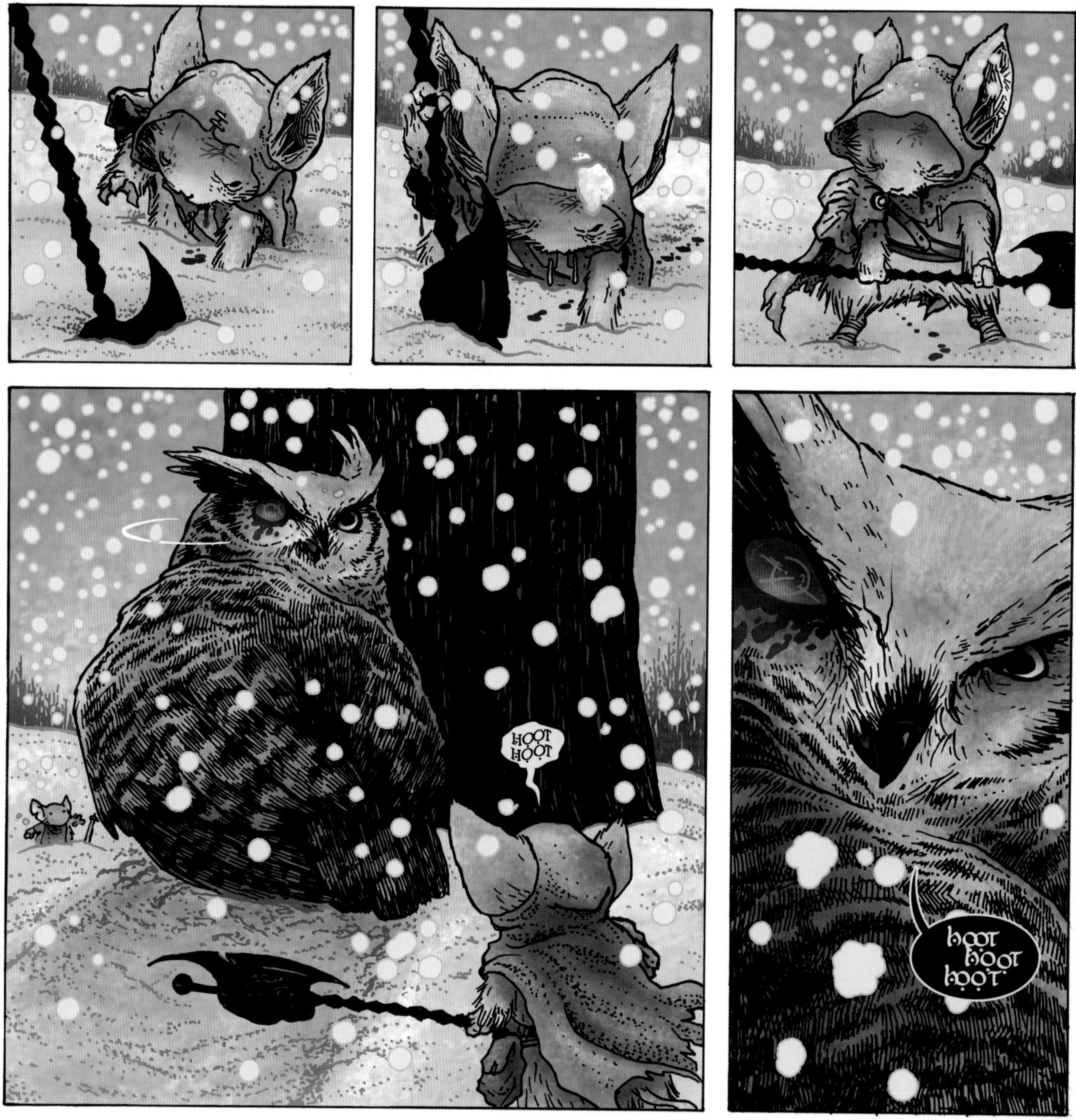
HOOT HOOT
HOOT HOOT HOOT

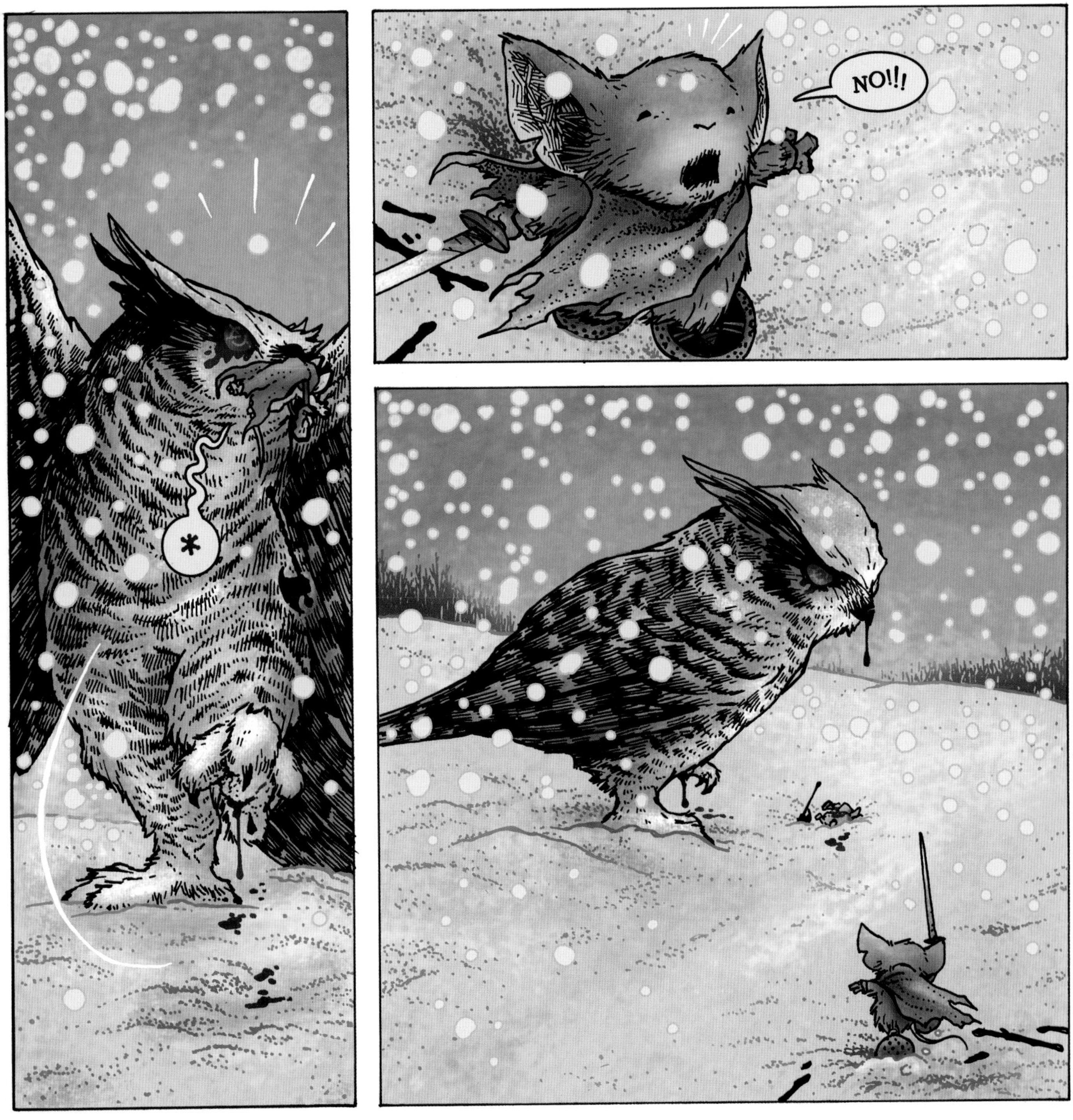
NO!!!

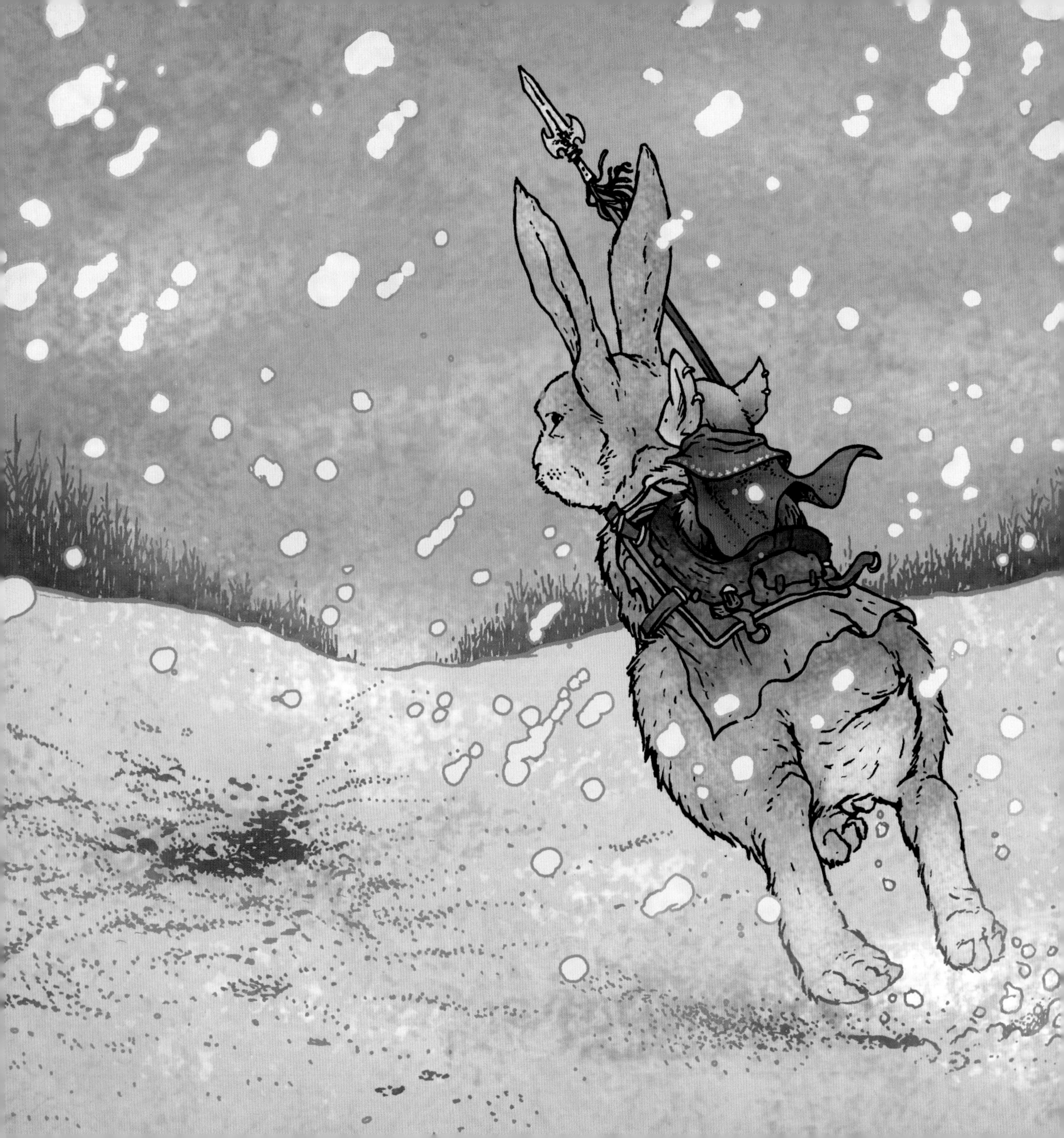

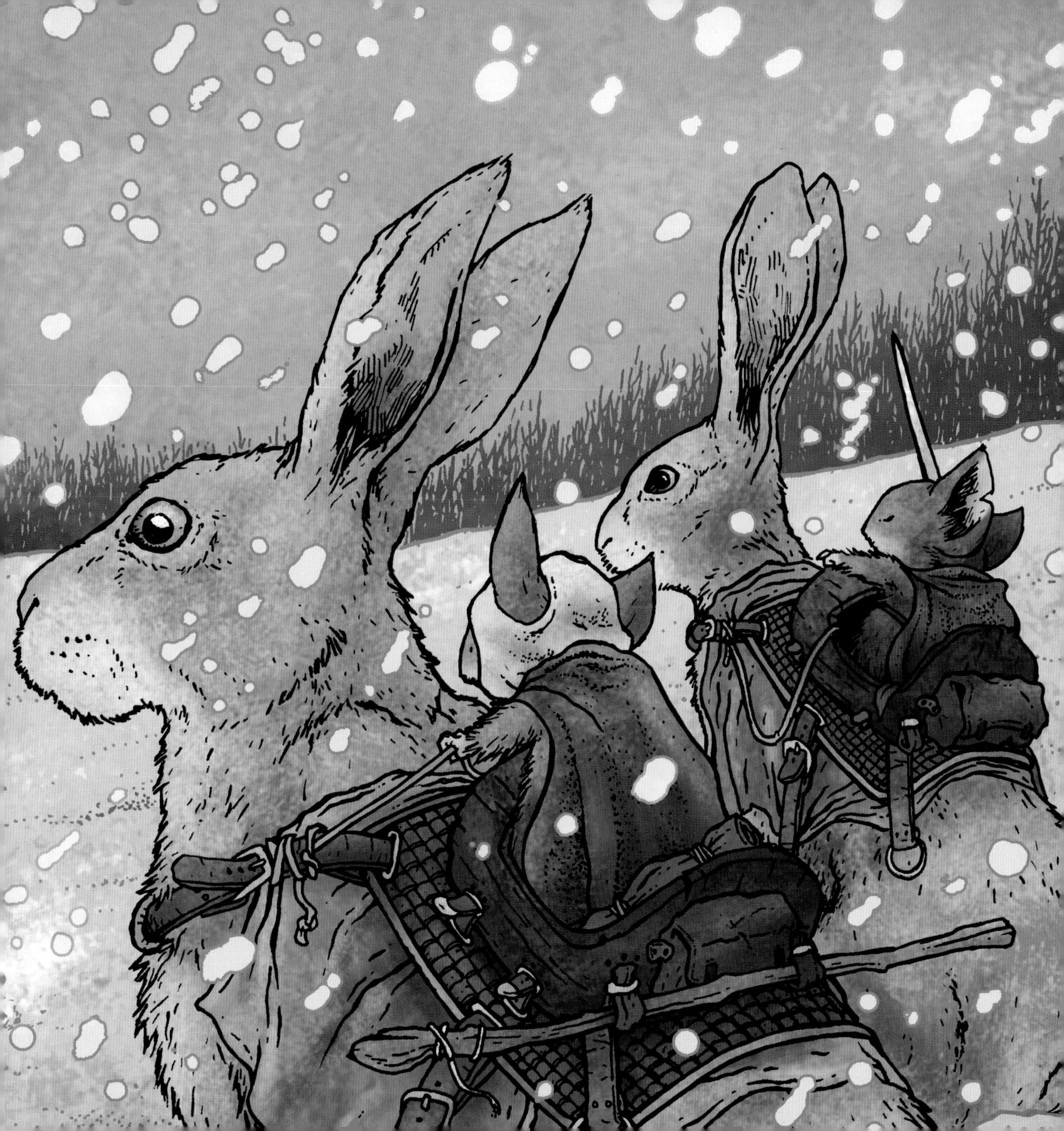

CHAPTER SIX

Saxon, Kenzie, and Sadie escaped from the abandoned weasel kingdom Darkheather, worried to find that Celanawe and Lieam have not arrived back at Lockhaven before them.

Unknown to the rest of the Guard, the redfur and legendary Black Axe are in mortal danger at the talons of the one-eyed owl.

'All manner of beasts dwell in sky and land and sea.
Covered with feather and fur and scale, they never agree.
"Eat to survive and protect your home" all share as a goal.
Livings overlap making some predator and some another role.
No mouse befriends serpents just as no grain loves a mouse.
What are commonalities when on a plate in your enemy's house.
Still we do not unite, those of us wanting seed in our larder.
Can the doubling of our efforts make our tasks any harder?'

-"The Crops of our Burdens" Poem by the Scribe Roibin

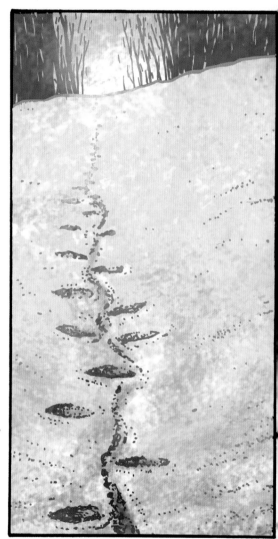

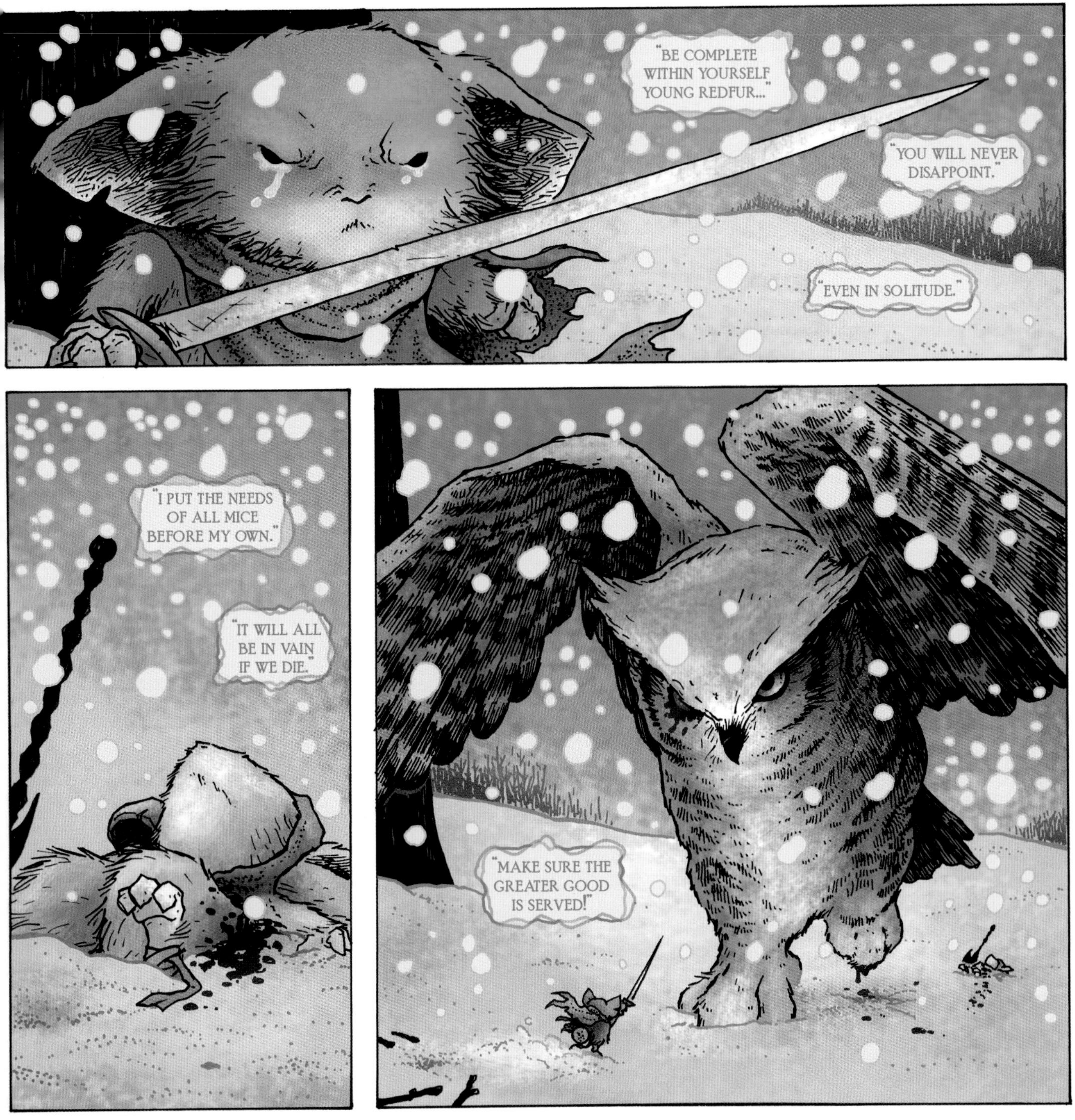
"BE COMPLETE WITHIN YOURSELF YOUNG REDFUR..."
"YOU WILL NEVER DISAPPOINT."
"EVEN IN SOLITUDE."
"I PUT THE NEEDS OF ALL MICE BEFORE MY OWN."
"IT WILL ALL BE IN VAIN IF WE DIE."
"MAKE SURE THE GREATER GOOD IS SERVED!"

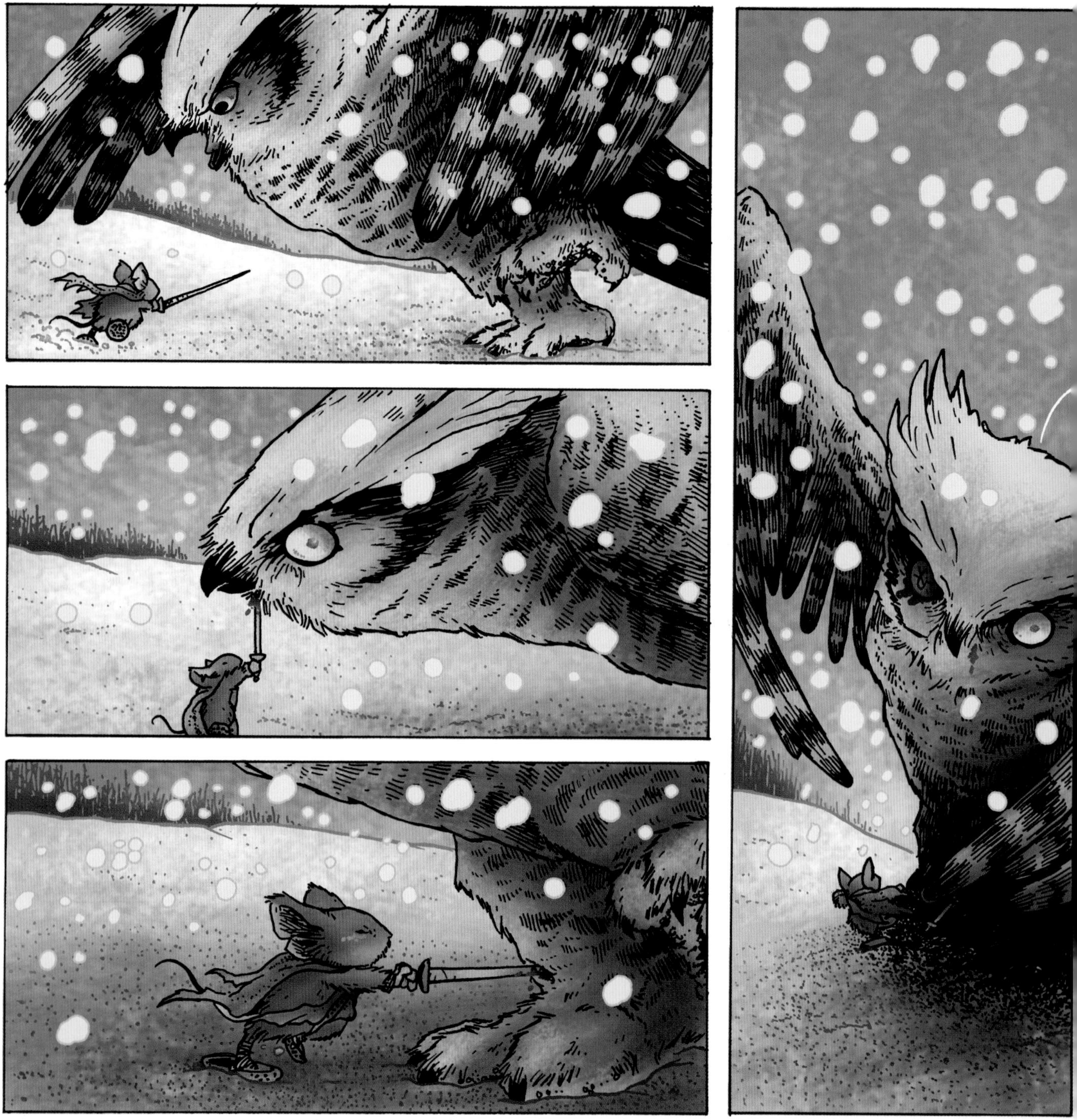

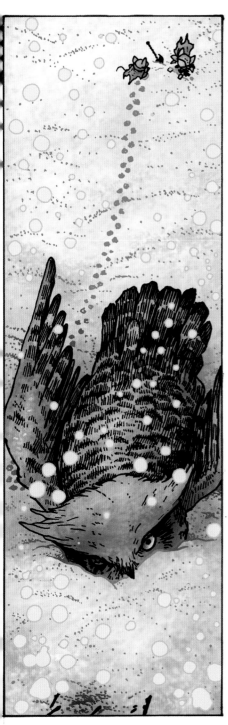

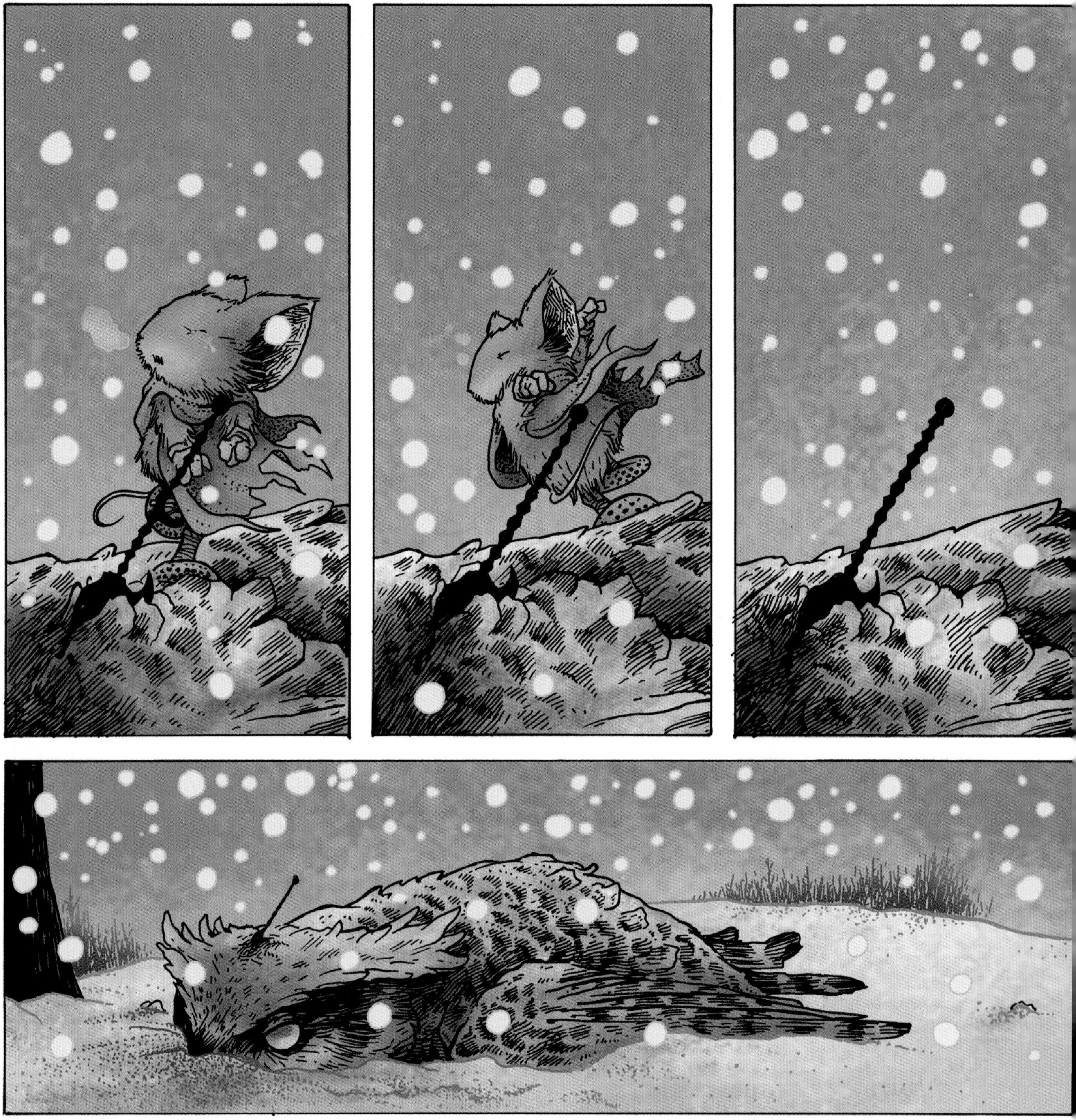

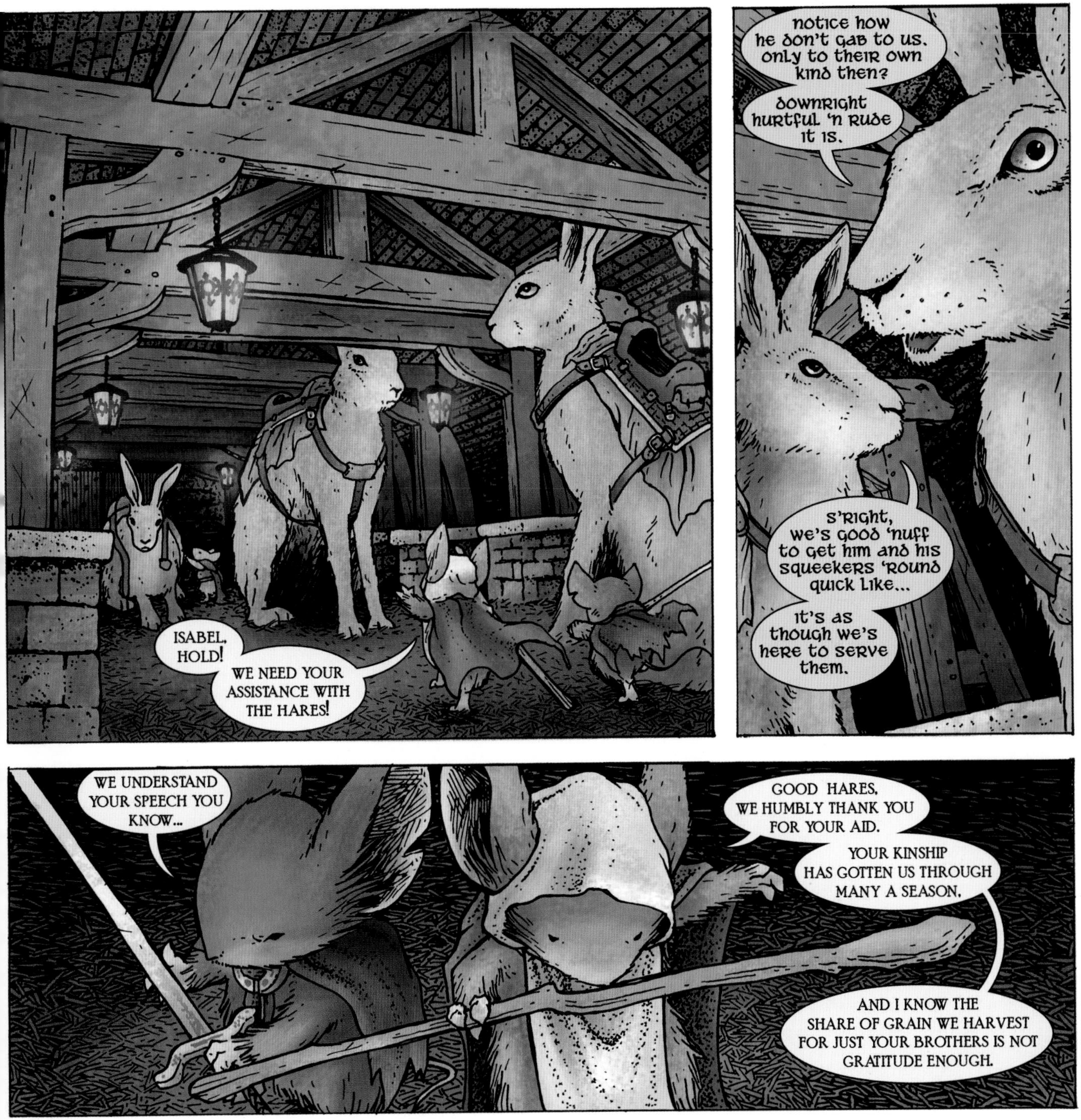
ISABEL, HOLD!
WE NEED YOUR ASSISTANCE WITH THE HARES!
notice how he don't gab to us, only to their own kind then?
downright hurtful 'n rude it is.
s'right, we's good 'nuff to get him and his squeekers 'round quick like...
it's as though we's here to serve them.
WE UNDERSTAND YOUR SPEECH YOU KNOW...
GOOD HARES, WE HUMBLY THANK YOU FOR YOUR AID.
YOUR KINSHIP HAS GOTTEN US THROUGH MANY A SEASON.
AND I KNOW THE SHARE OF GRAIN WE HARVEST FOR JUST YOUR BROTHERS IS NOT GRATITUDE ENOUGH.

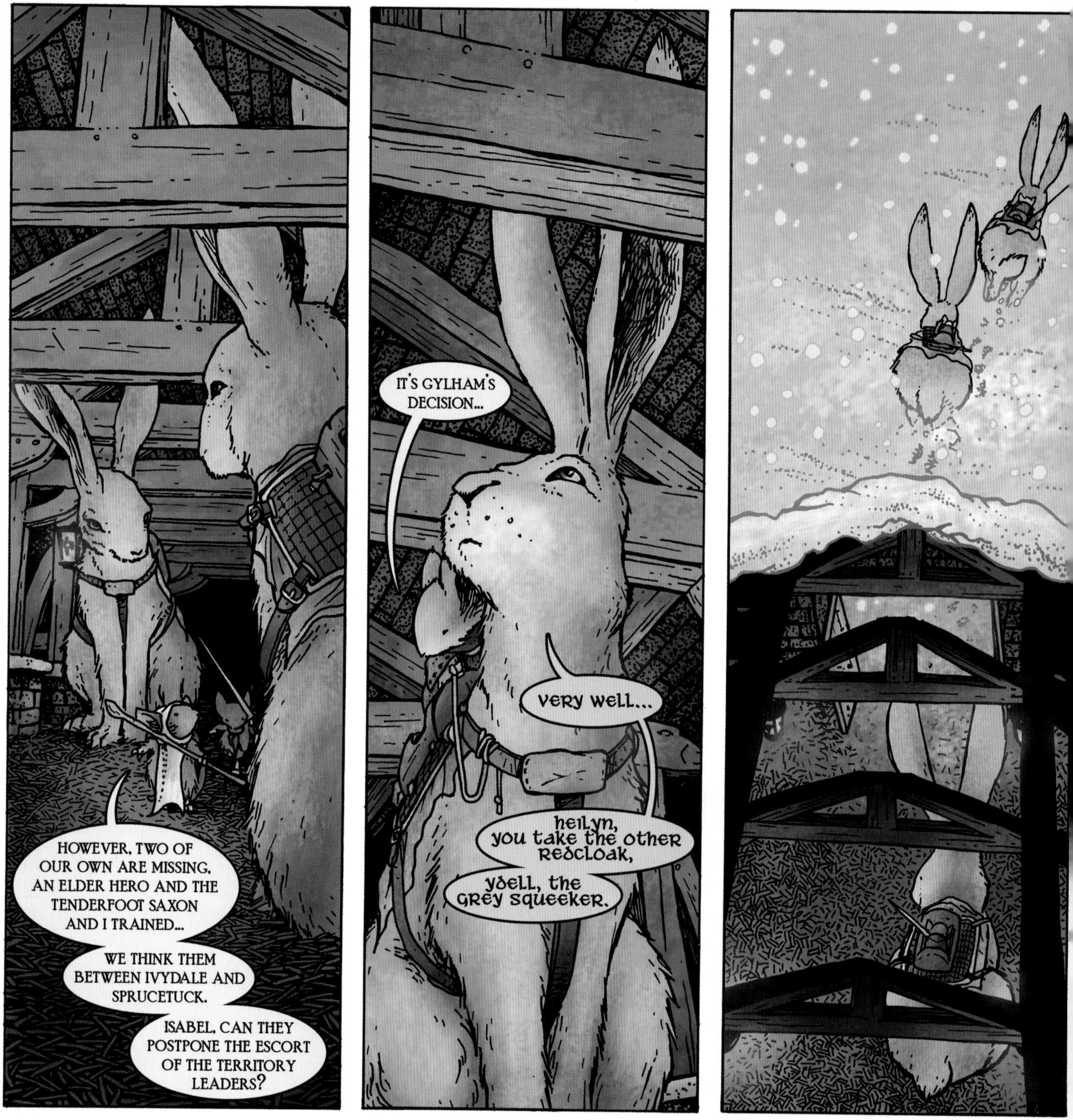
HOWEVER, TWO OF OUR OWN ARE MISSING, AN ELDER HERO AND THE TENDERFOOT SAXON AND I TRAINED...
WE THINK THEM BETWEEN IVYDALE AND SPRUCETUCK.
ISABEL, CAN THEY POSTPONE THE ESCORT OF THE TERRITORY LEADERS?
IT'S GYLHAM'S DECISION...
very well...
heilyn, you take the other Redcloak,
ydell, the Grey Squeeker.

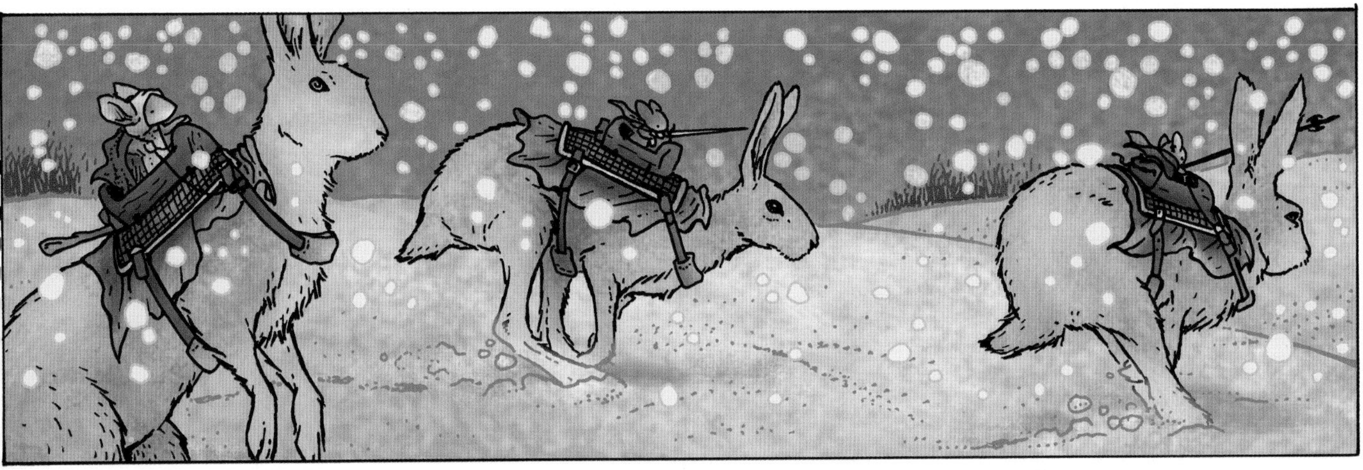
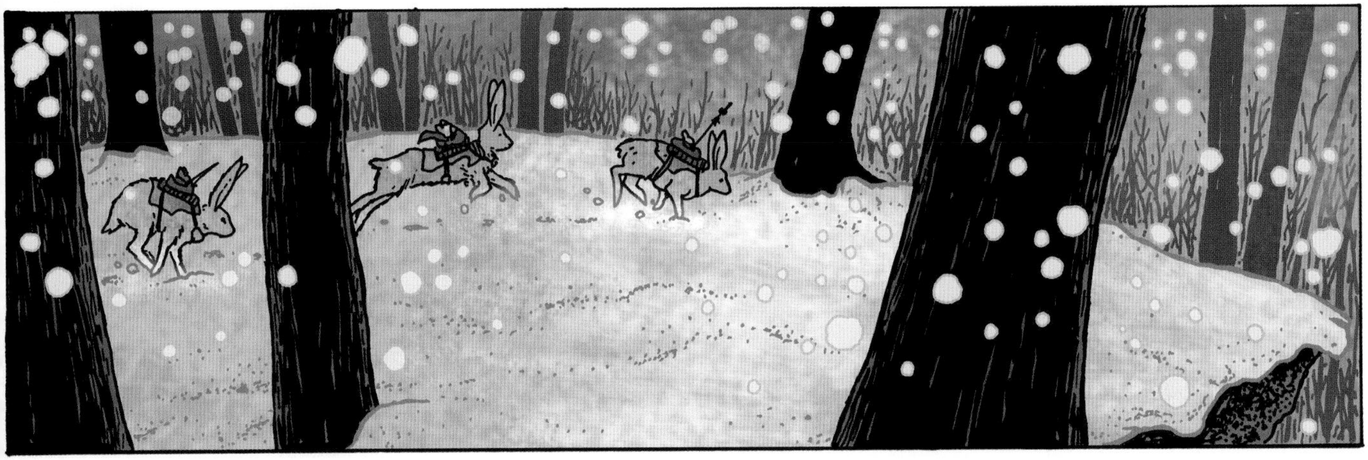
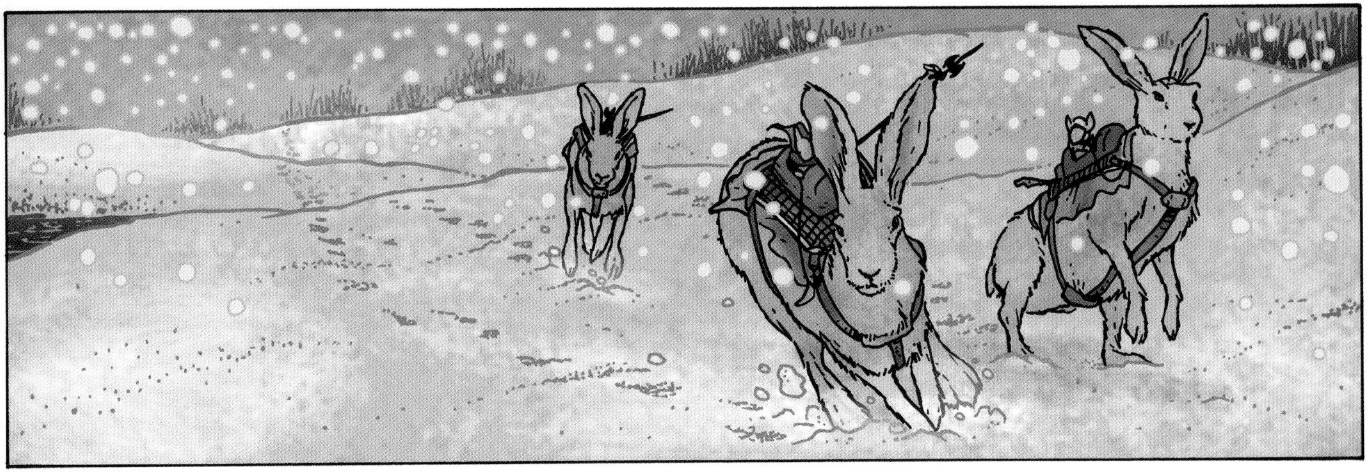

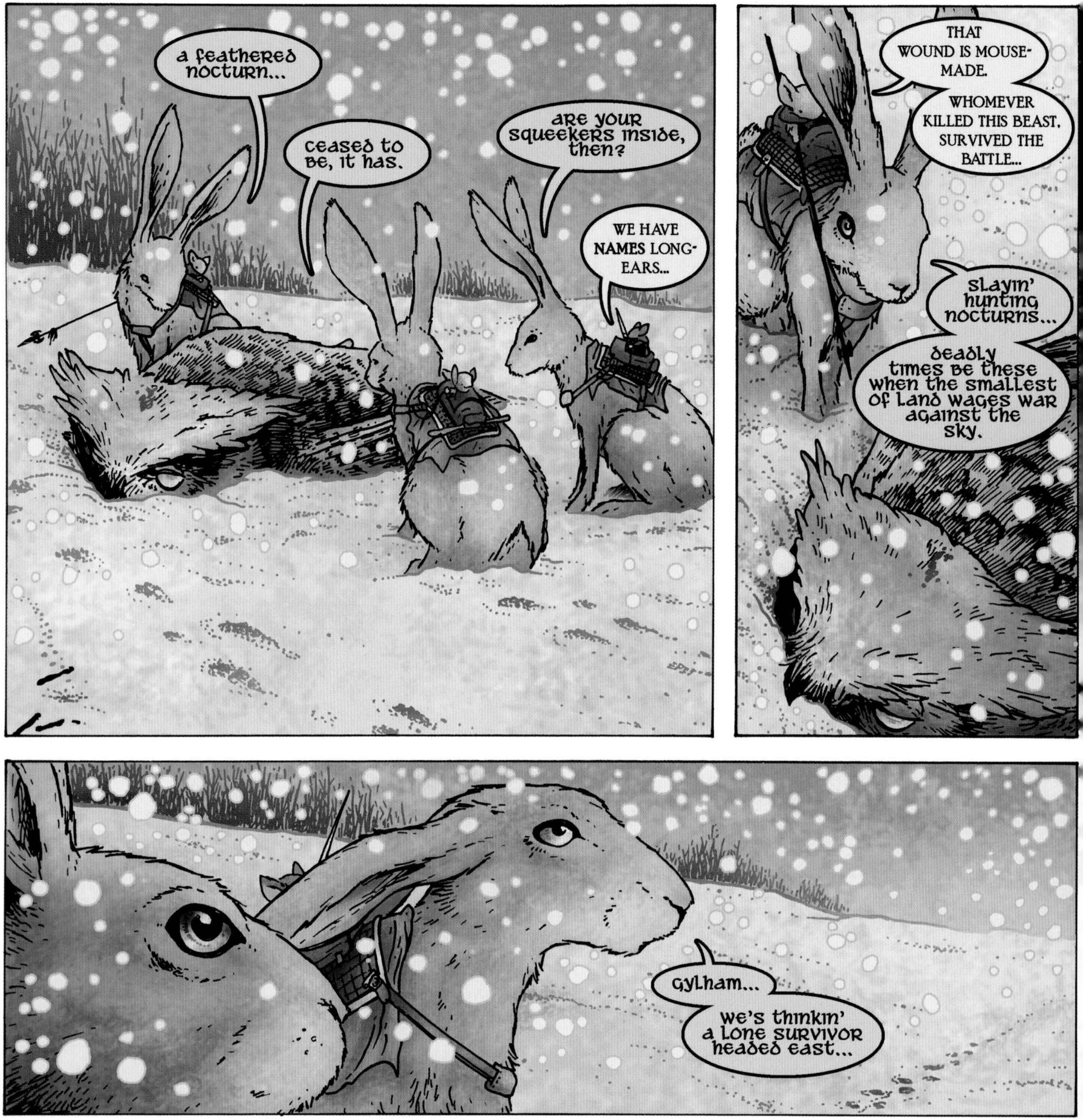
a feathered nocturn...
ceased to be, it has.
are your squeekers inside, then?
WE HAVE NAMES LONG-EARS...
THAT WOUND IS MOUSE-MADE.
WHOMEVER KILLED THIS BEAST, SURVIVED THE BATTLE...
slayin' hunting nocturns...
deadly times be these when the smallest of land wages war against the sky.
Gylham...
we's thinkin' a lone survivor headed east...

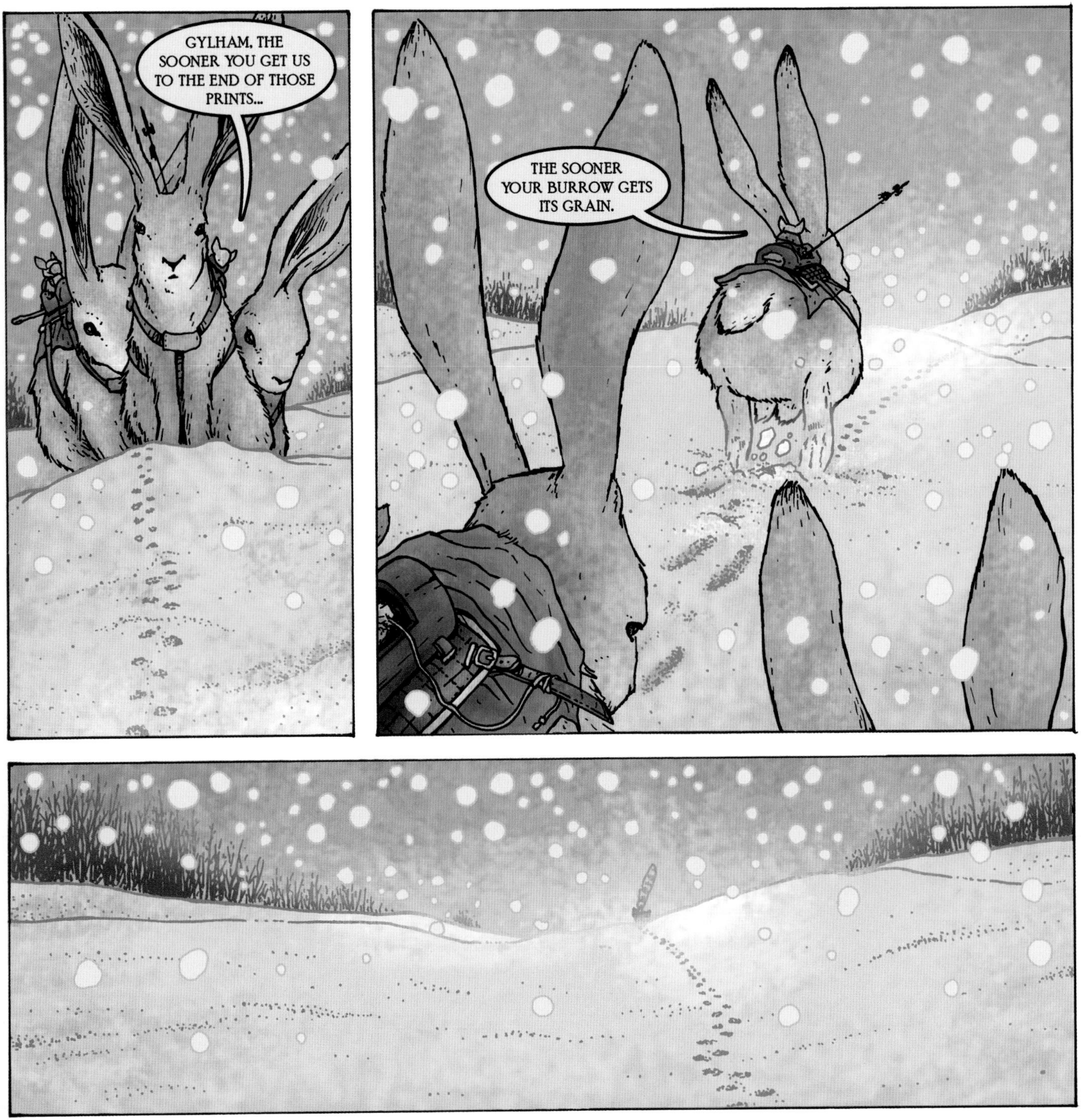
GYLHAM, THE SOONER YOU GET US TO THE END OF THOSE PRINTS...
THE SOONER YOUR BURROW GETS ITS GRAIN.

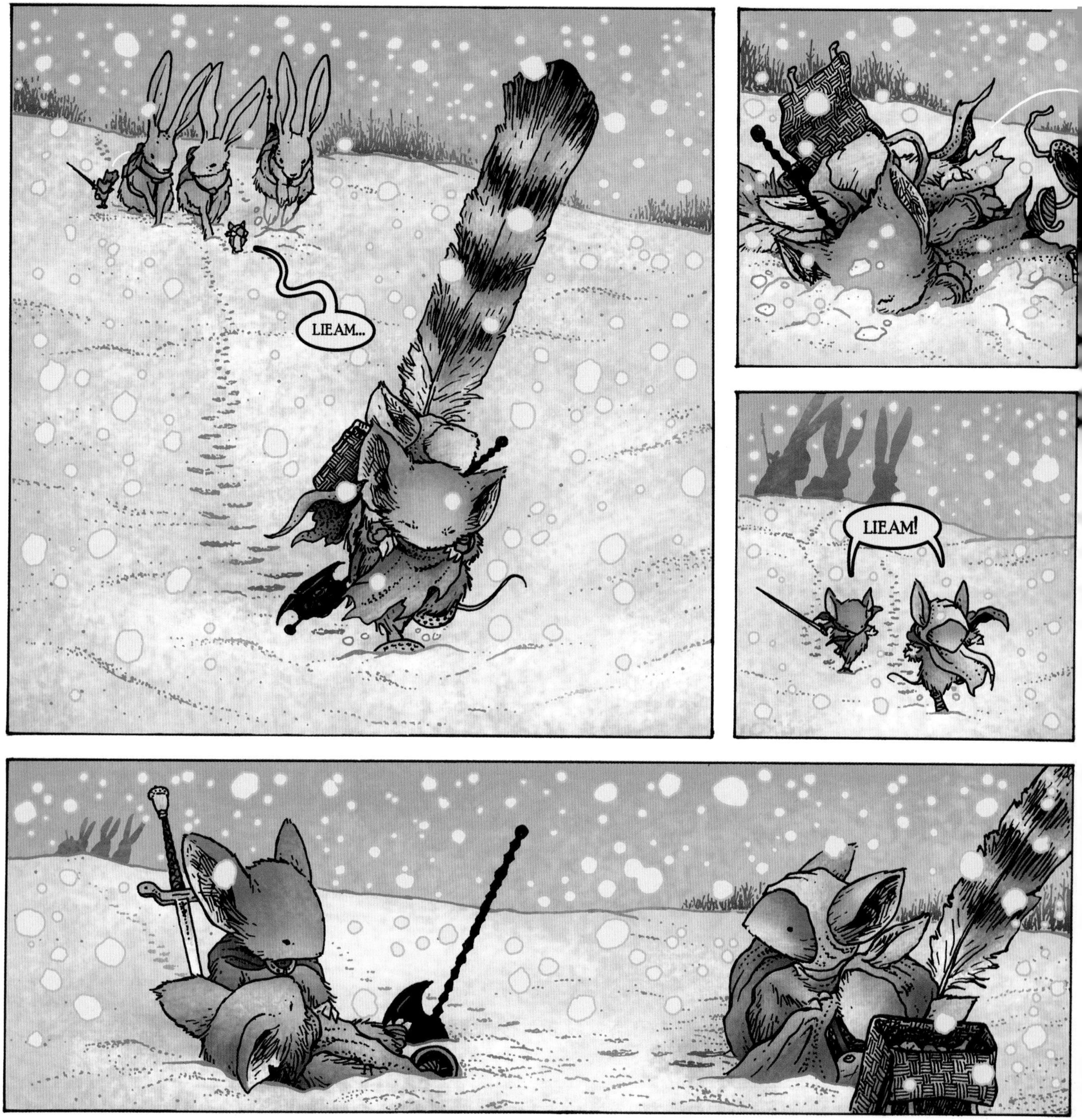
LIEAM...
LIEAM!

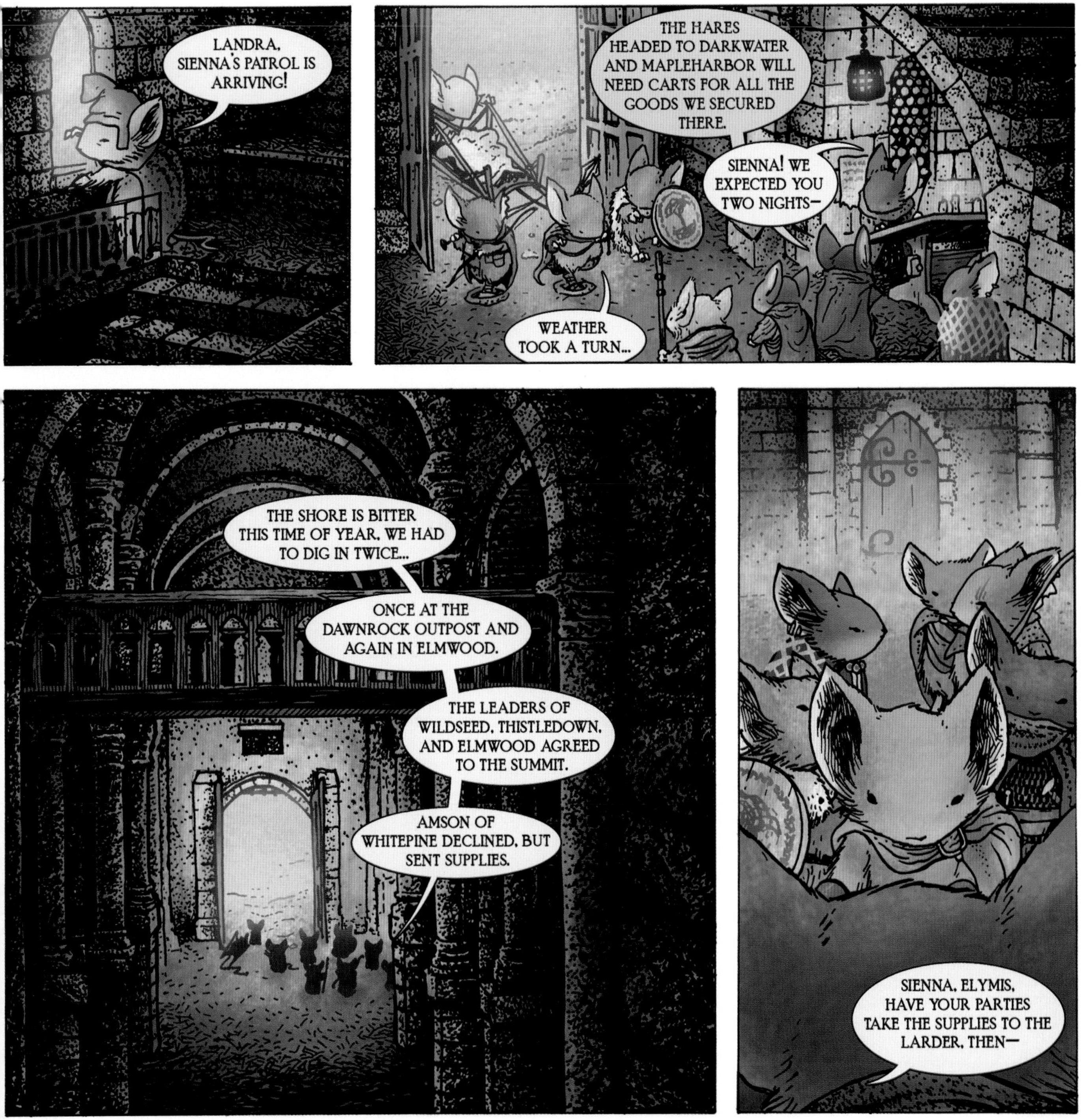
LANDRA, SIENNA'S PATROL IS ARRIVING!
THE HARES HEADED TO DARKWATER AND MAPLEHARBOR WILL NEED CARTS FOR ALL THE GOODS WE SECURED THERE.
SIENNA! WE EXPECTED YOU TWO NIGHTS—
WEATHER TOOK A TURN...
THE SHORE IS BITTER THIS TIME OF YEAR. WE HAD TO DIG IN TWICE...
ONCE AT THE DAWNROCK OUTPOST AND AGAIN IN ELMWOOD.
THE LEADERS OF WILDSEED, THISTLEDOWN, AND ELMWOOD AGREED TO THE SUMMIT.
AMSON OF WHITEPINE DECLINED, BUT SENT SUPPLIES.
SIENNA, ELYMIS, HAVE YOUR PARTIES TAKE THE SUPPLIES TO THE LARDER, THEN—

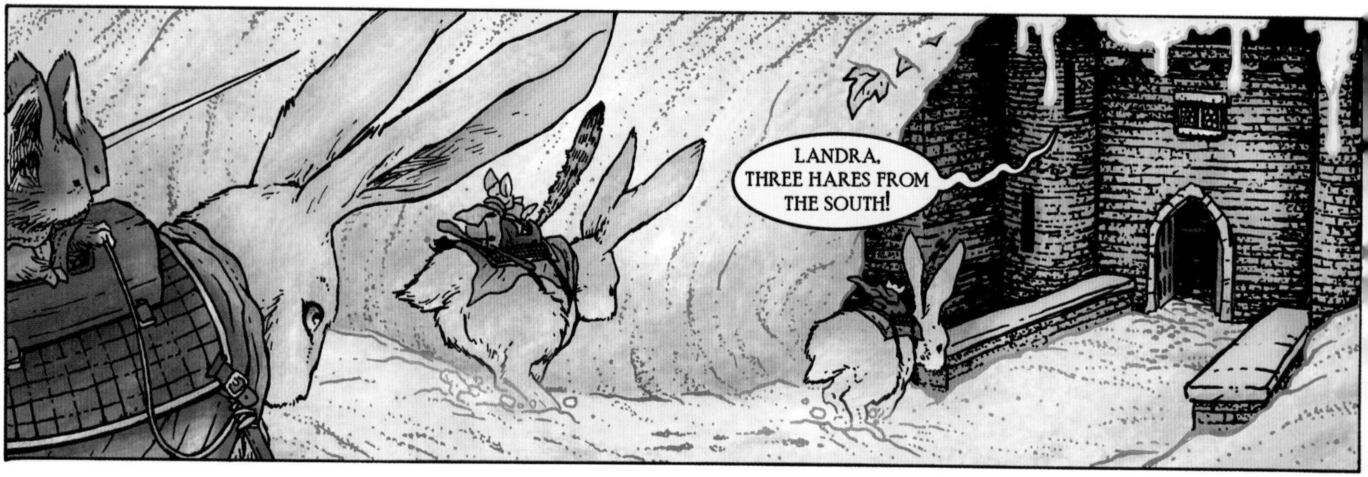
LANDRA, THREE HARES FROM THE SOUTH!

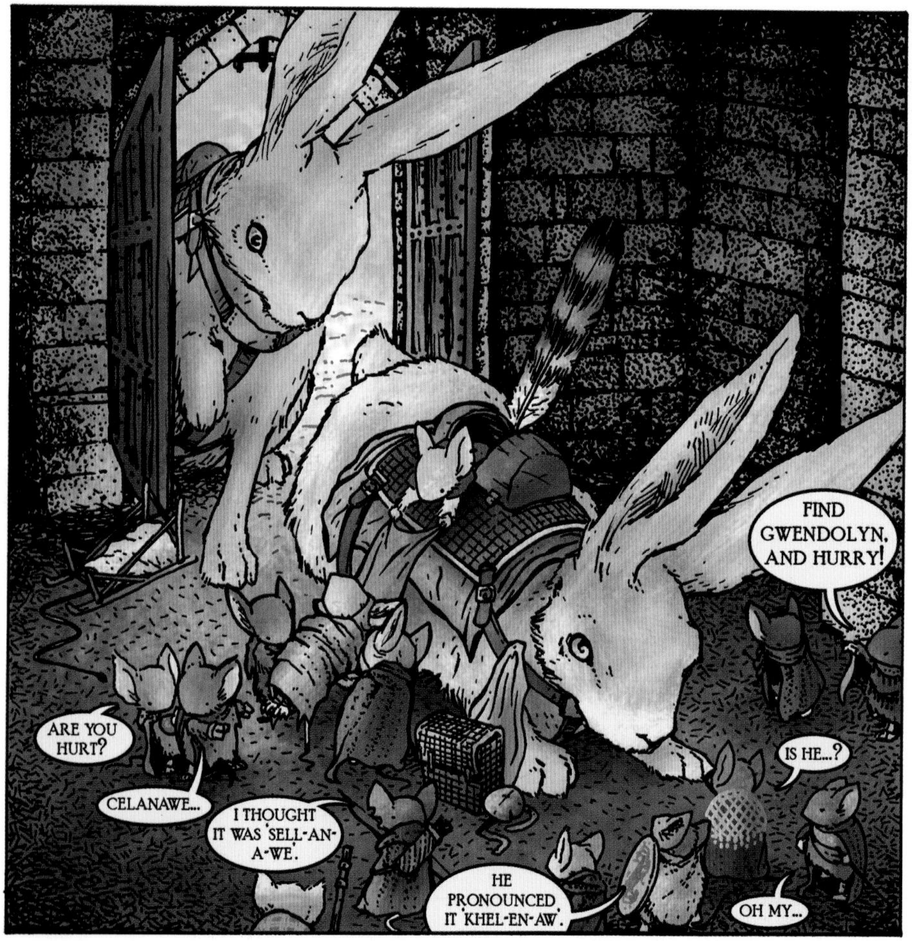
FIND GWENDOLYN, AND HURRY!
ARE YOU HURT?
CELANAWE...
I THOUGHT IT WAS 'SELL-AN-A-WE'.
IS HE...?
HE PRONOUNCED IT 'KHEL-EN-AW'.
OH MY...

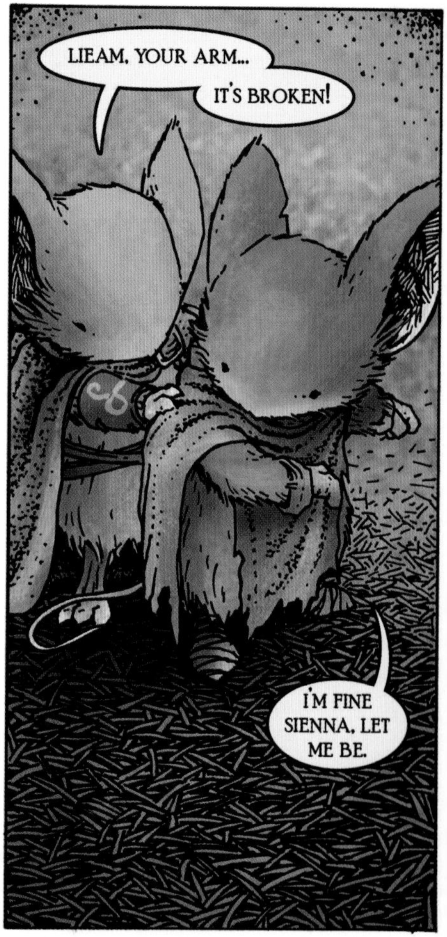
LIEAM, YOUR ARM...
IT'S BROKEN!
I'M FINE SIENNA, LET ME BE.

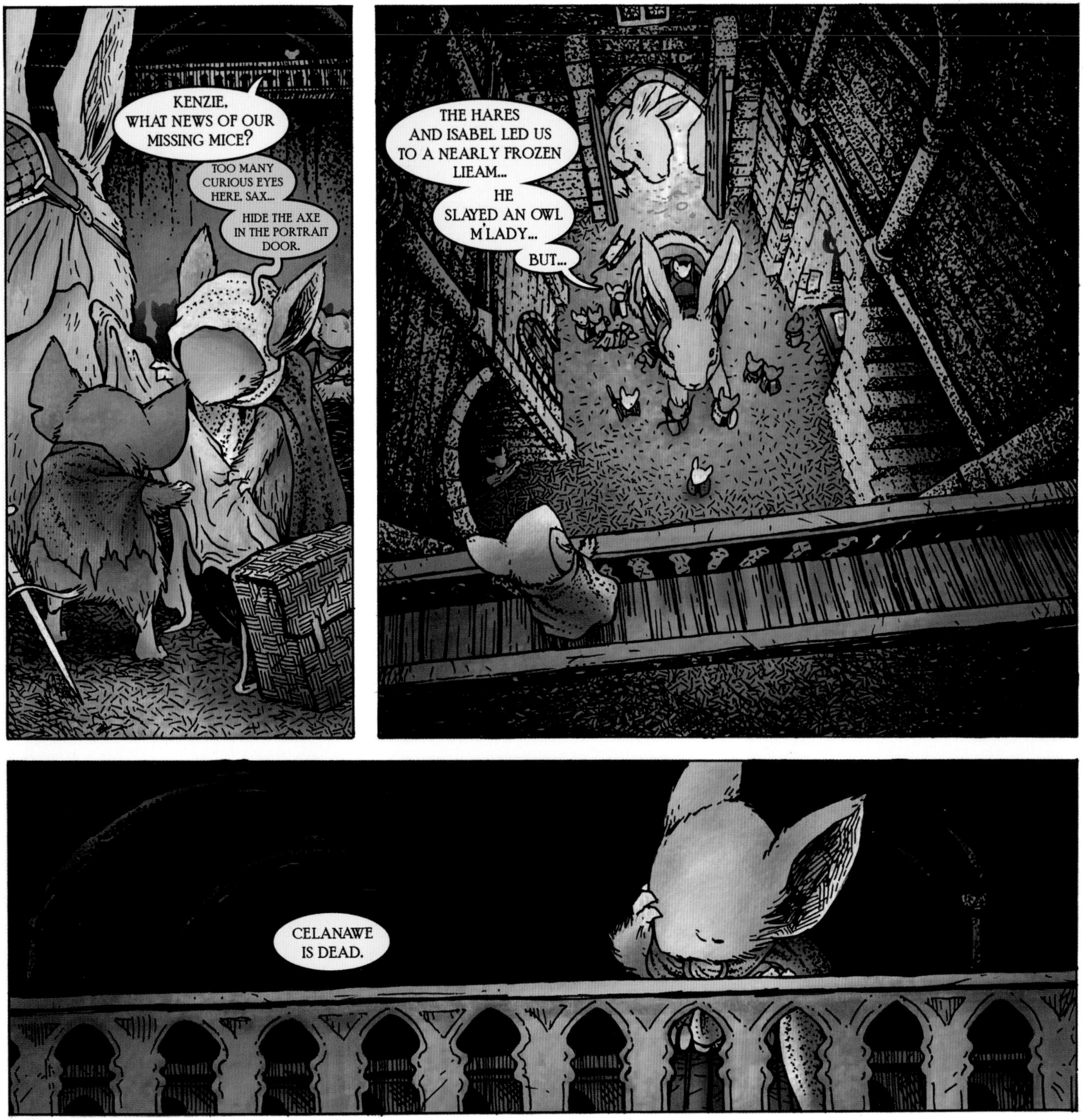
KENZIE, WHAT NEWS OF OUR MISSING MICE?
TOO MANY CURIOUS EYES HERE, SAX...
HIDE THE AXE IN THE PORTRAIT DOOR.
THE HARES AND ISABEL LED US TO A NEARLY FROZEN LIEAM...
HE SLAYED AN OWL M'LADY...
BUT...
CELANAWE IS DEAD.

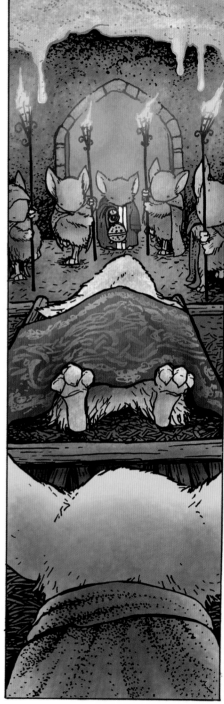

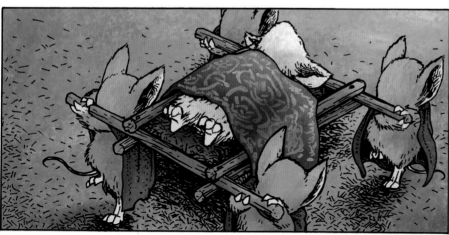

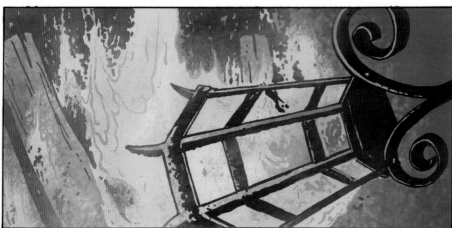

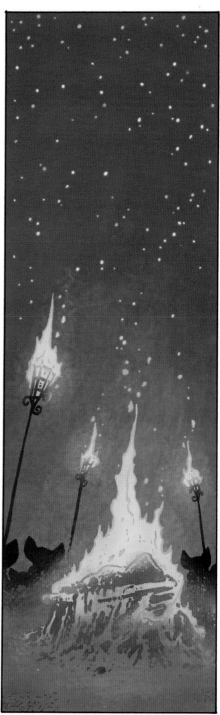

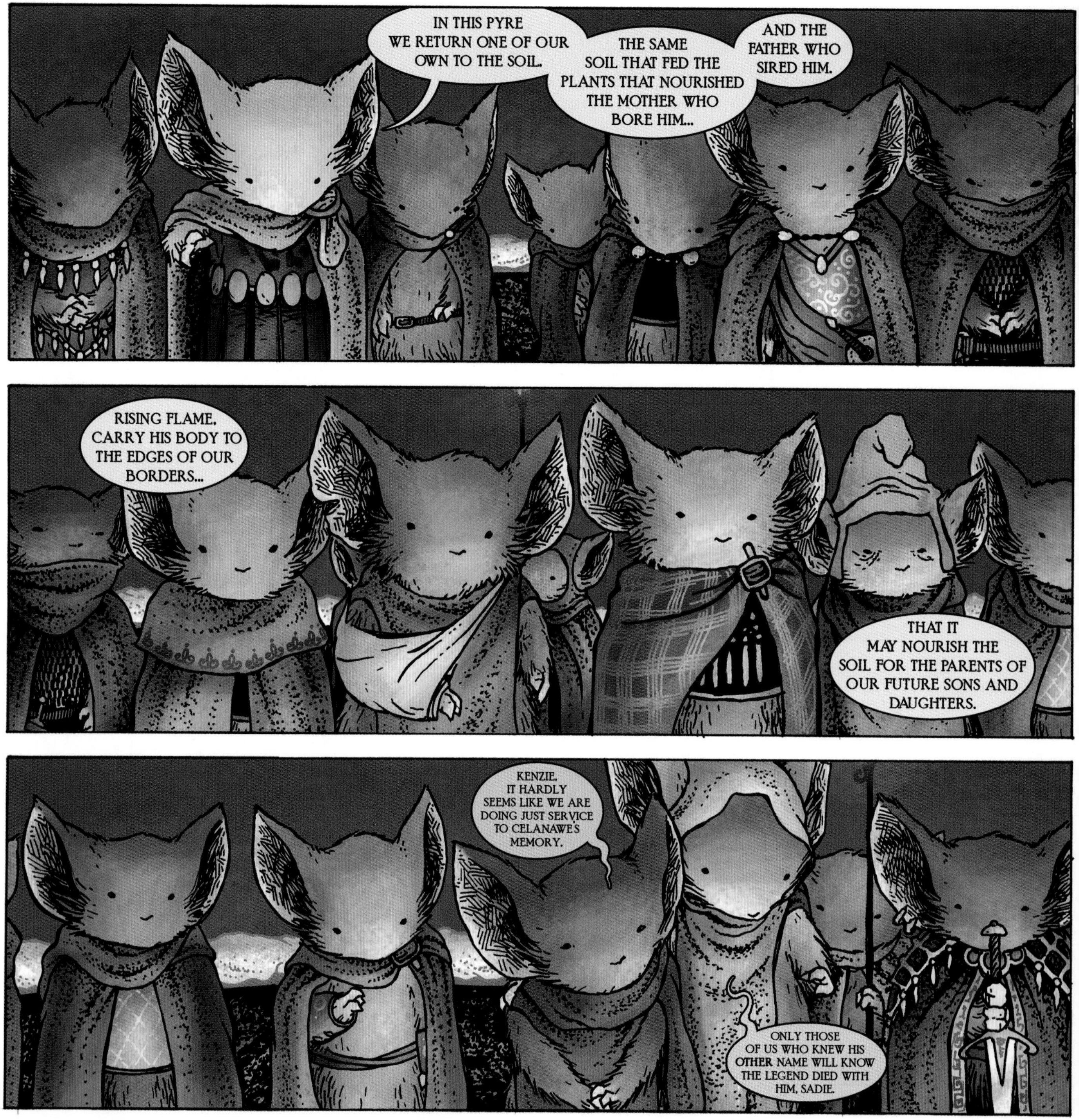
IN THIS PYRE WE RETURN ONE OF OUR OWN TO THE SOIL.
THE SAME SOIL THAT FED THE PLANTS THAT NOURISHED THE MOTHER WHO BORE HIM...
AND THE FATHER WHO SIRED HIM.
RISING FLAME, CARRY HIS BODY TO THE EDGES OF OUR BORDERS...
THAT IT MAY NOURISH THE SOIL FOR THE PARENTS OF OUR FUTURE SONS AND DAUGHTERS.
KENZIE, IT HARDLY SEEMS LIKE WE ARE DOING JUST SERVICE TO CELANAWE'S MEMORY.
ONLY THOSE OF US WHO KNEW HIS OTHER NAME WILL KNOW THE LEGEND DIED WITH HIM, SADIE.

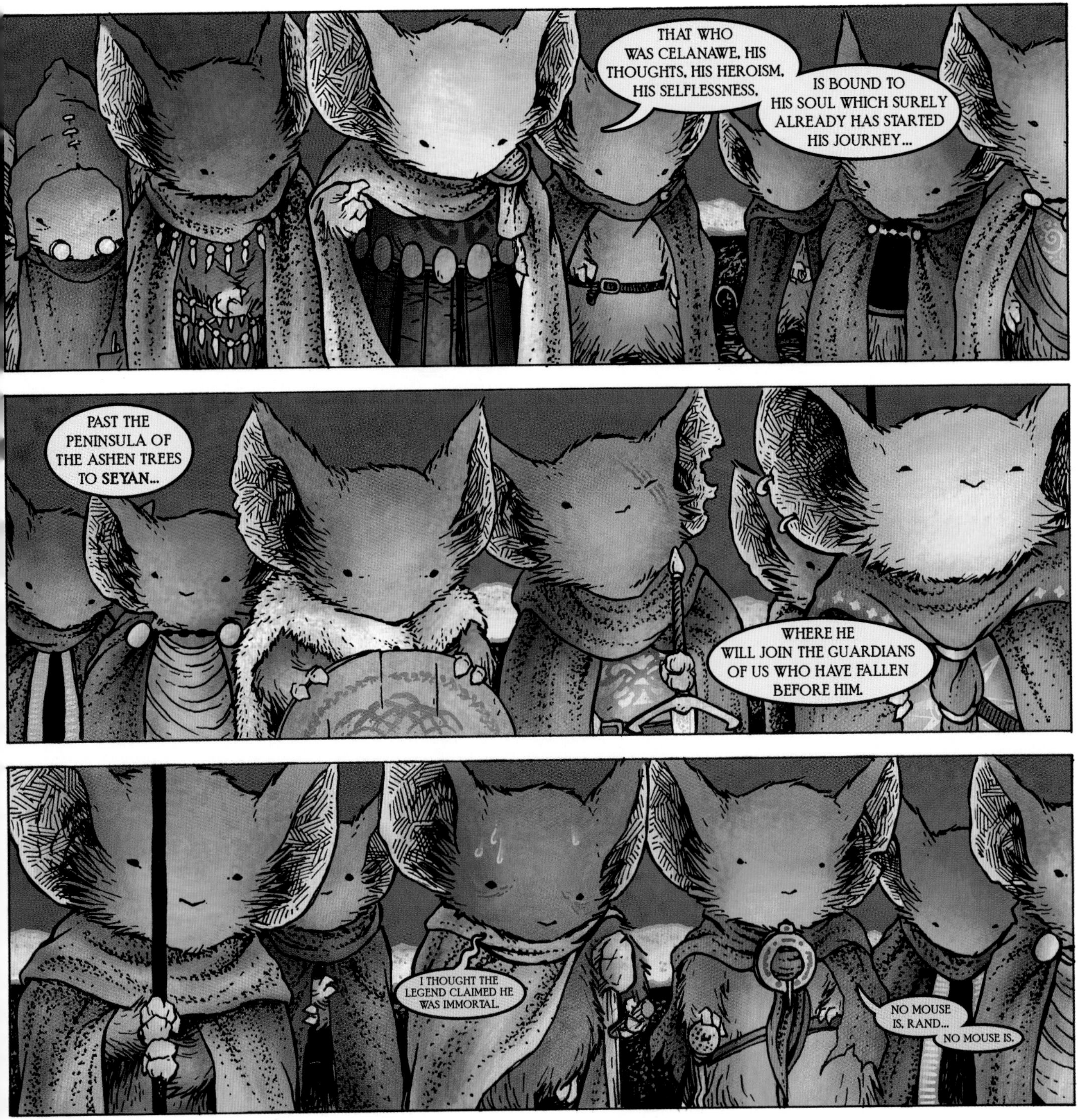
THAT WHO WAS CELANAWE, HIS THOUGHTS, HIS HEROISM, HIS SELFLESSNESS,
IS BOUND TO HIS SOUL WHICH SURELY ALREADY HAS STARTED HIS JOURNEY...
PAST THE PENINSULA OF THE ASHEN TREES TO SEYAN...
WHERE HE WILL JOIN THE GUARDIANS OF US WHO HAVE FALLEN BEFORE HIM.
I THOUGHT THE LEGEND CLAIMED HE WAS IMMORTAL.
NO MOUSE IS, RAND...
NO MOUSE IS.

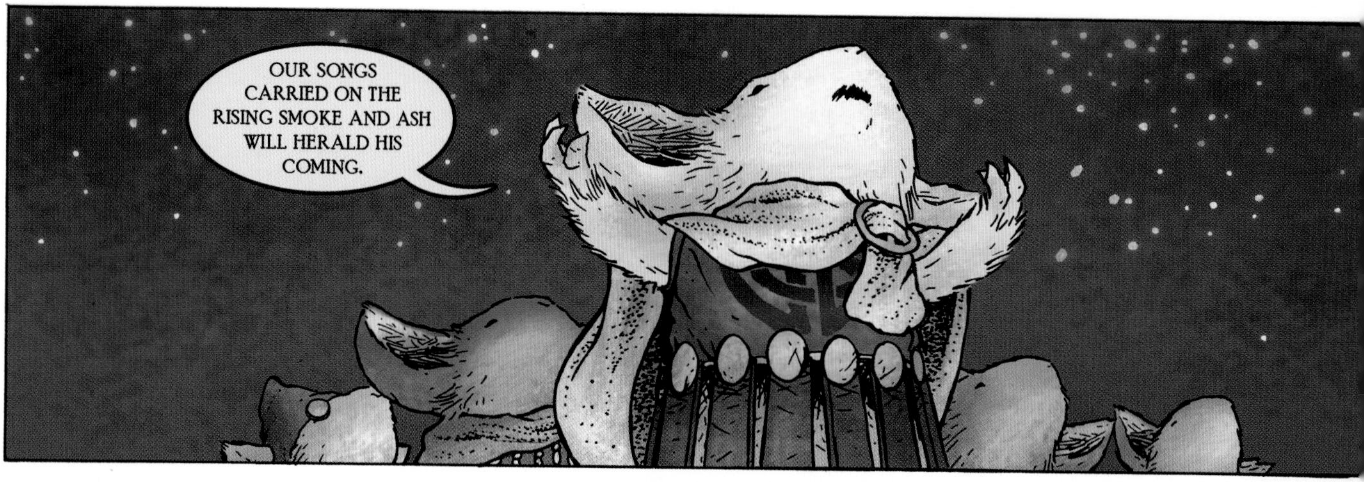
OUR SONGS CARRIED ON THE RISING SMOKE AND ASH WILL HERALD HIS COMING.

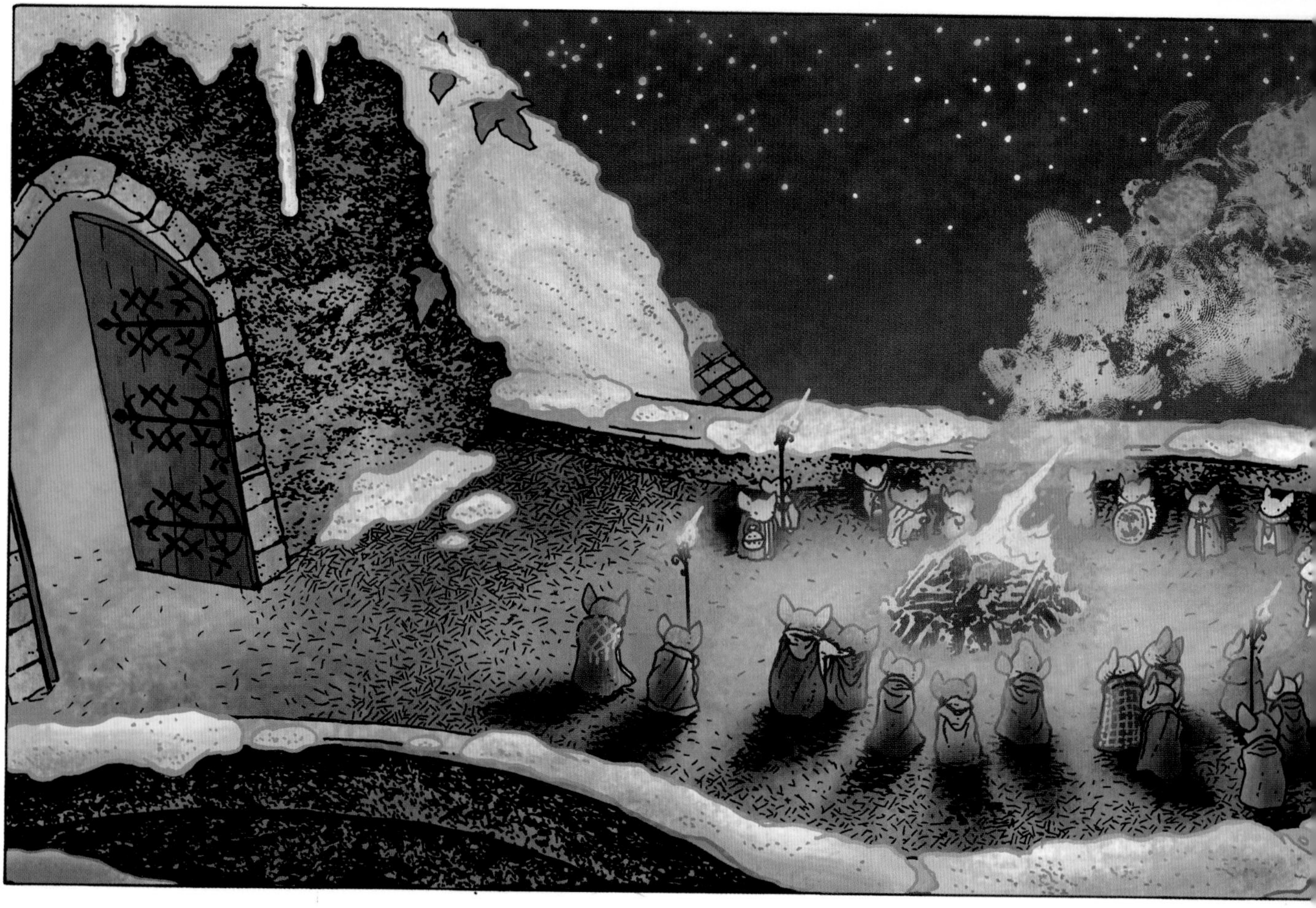

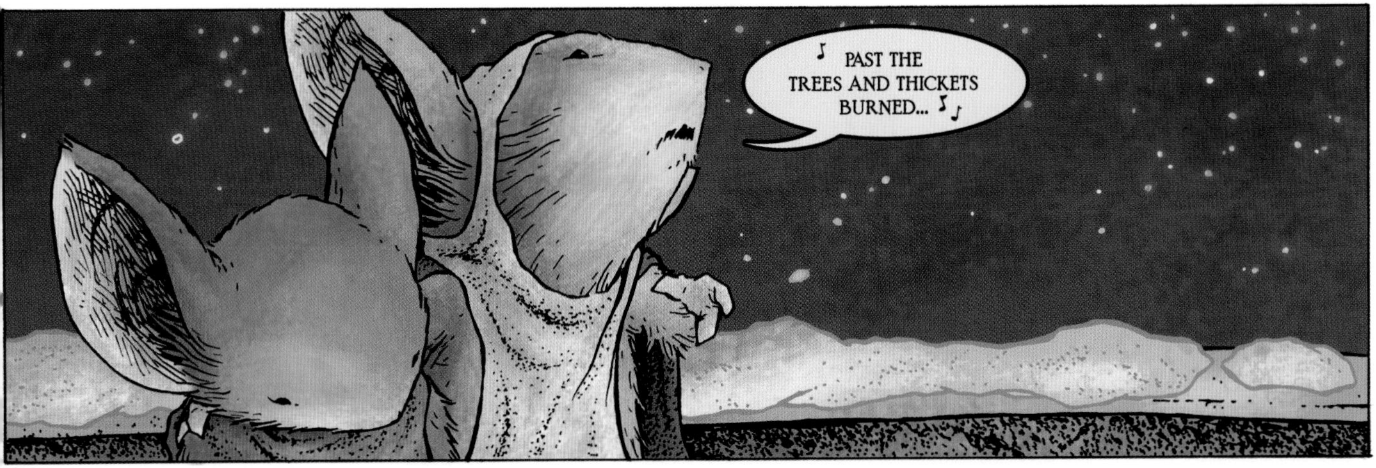
PAST THE TREES AND THICKETS BURNED...

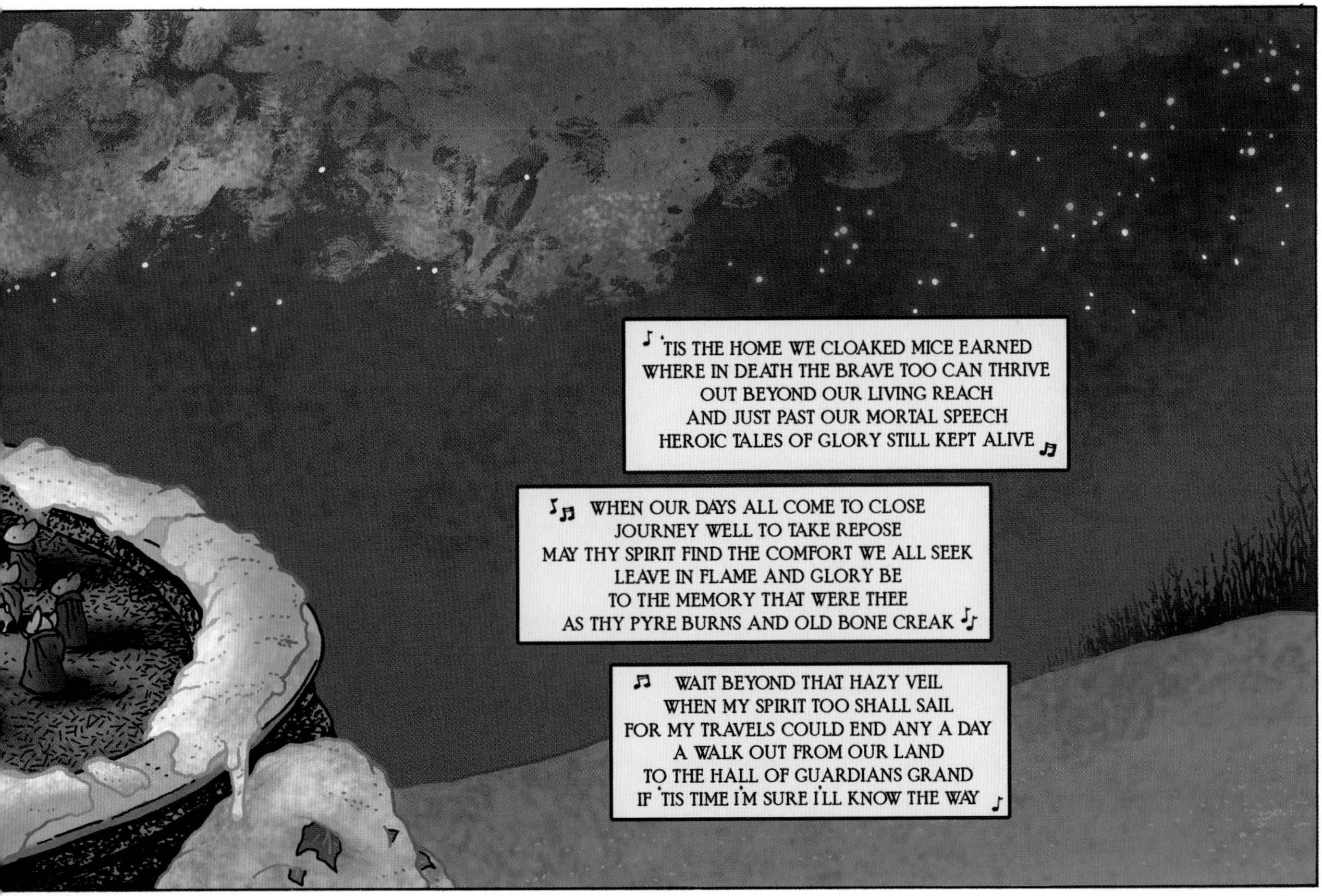
'TIS THE HOME WE CLOAKED MICE EARNED
WHERE IN DEATH THE BRAVE TOO CAN THRIVE
OUT BEYOND OUR LIVING REACH
AND JUST PAST OUR MORTAL SPEECH
HEROIC TALES OF GLORY STILL KEPT ALIVE
WHEN OUR DAYS ALL COME TO CLOSE
JOURNEY WELL TO TAKE REPOSE
MAY THY SPIRIT FIND THE COMFORT WE ALL SEEK
LEAVE IN FLAME AND GLORY BE
TO THE MEMORY THAT WERE THEE
AS THY PYRE BURNS AND OLD BONE CREAK
WAIT BEYOND THAT HAZY VEIL
WHEN MY SPIRIT TOO SHALL SAIL
FOR MY TRAVELS COULD END ANY A DAY
A WALK OUT FROM OUR LAND
TO THE HALL OF GUARDIANS GRAND
IF 'TIS TIME I'M SURE I'LL KNOW THE WAY

SAXON?

M-M'LADY
G-GWENDOLYN...

I HAVE
BEEN TO HELL
AND BACK...

TWICE NOW...

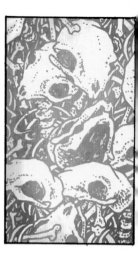

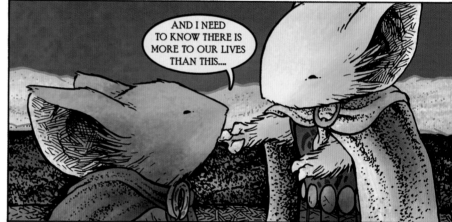

AND I NEED
TO KNOW THERE IS
MORE TO OUR LIVES
THAN THIS....

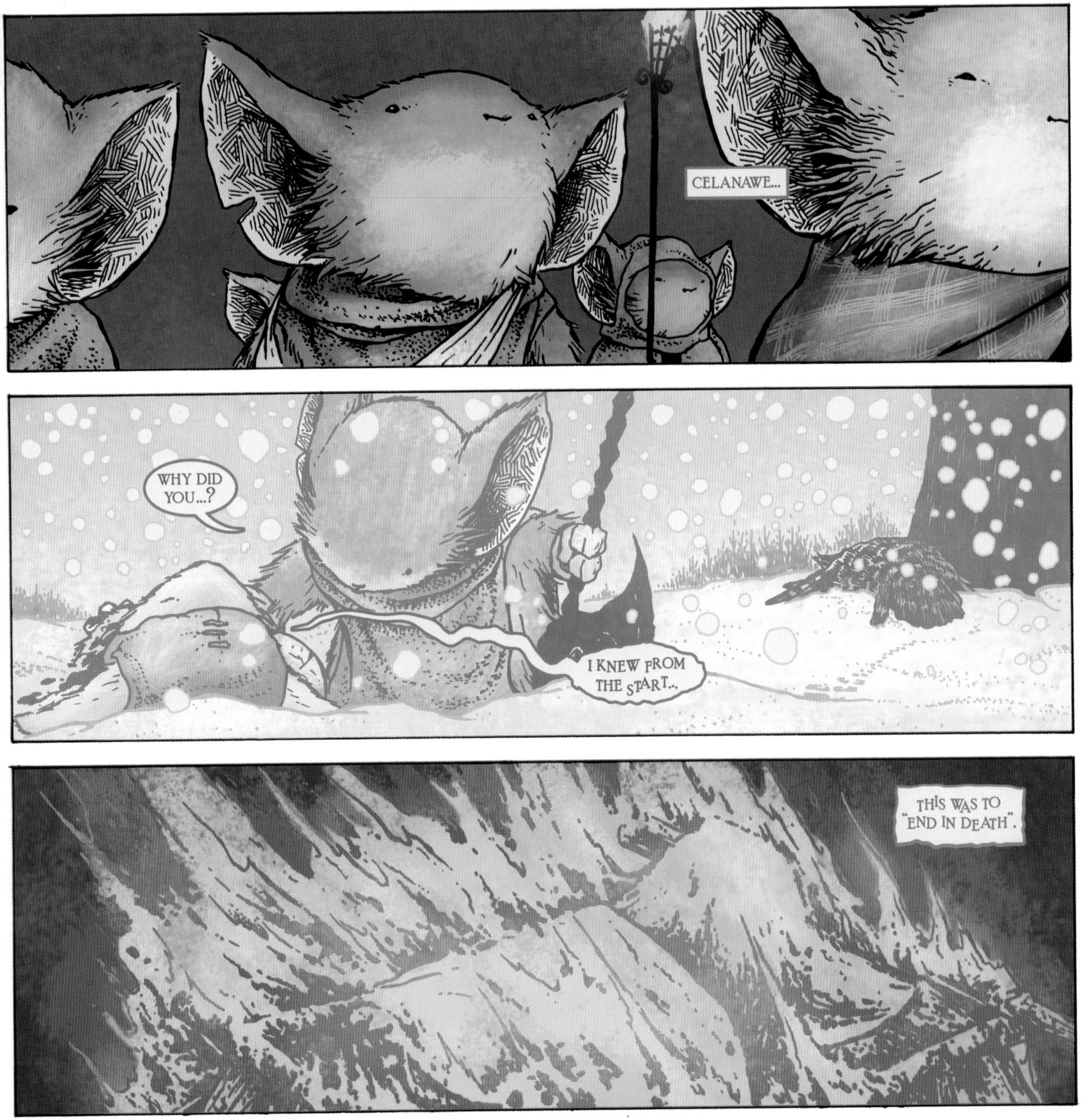
CELANAWE...
WHY DID YOU...?
I KNEW FROM THE START...
THIS WAS TO "END IN DEATH".

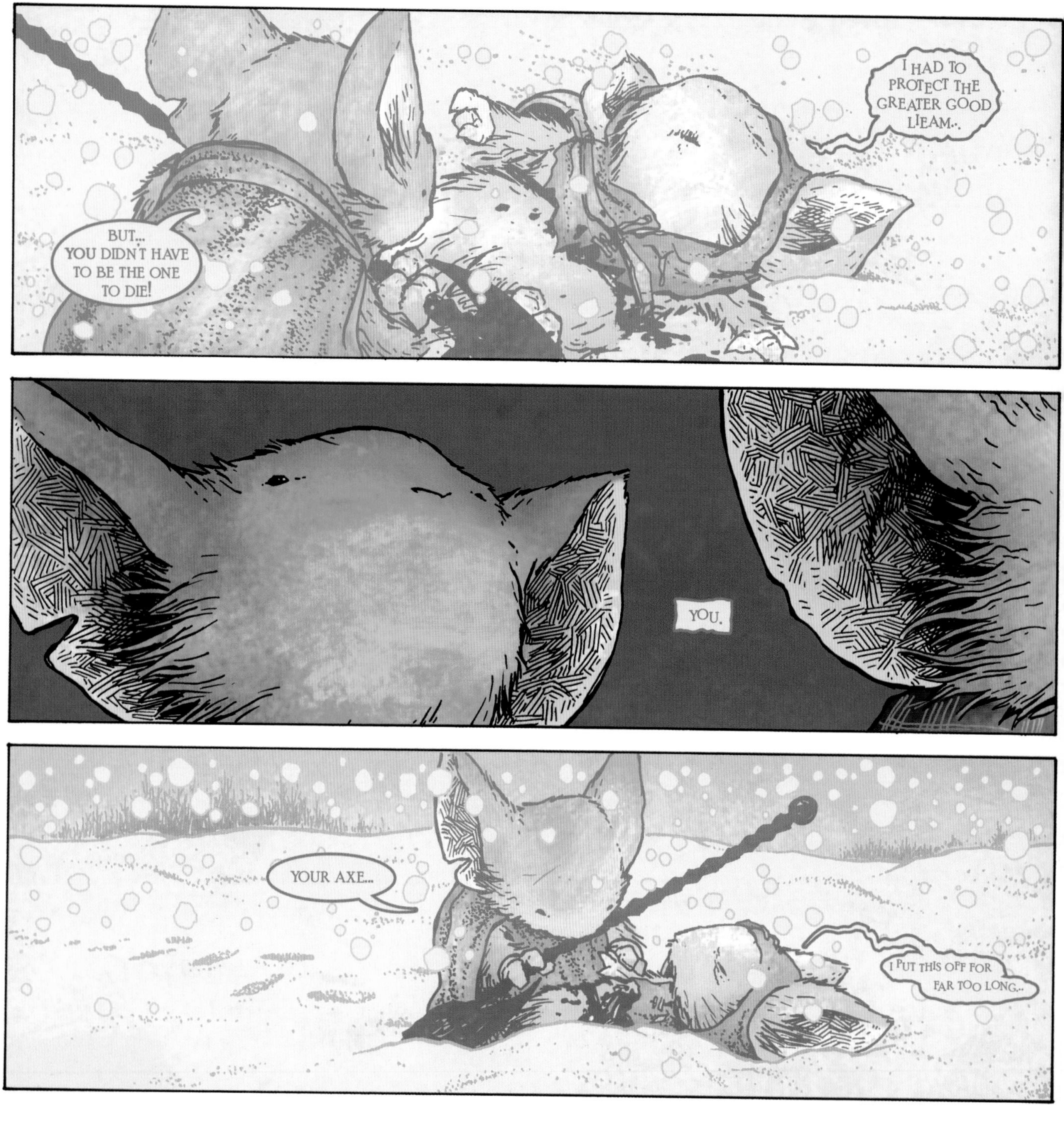
I HAD TO PROTECT THE GREATER GOOD LIEAM...
BUT... YOU DIDN'T HAVE TO BE THE ONE TO DIE!
YOU.
YOUR AXE...
I PUT THIS OFF FOR FAR TOO LONG...

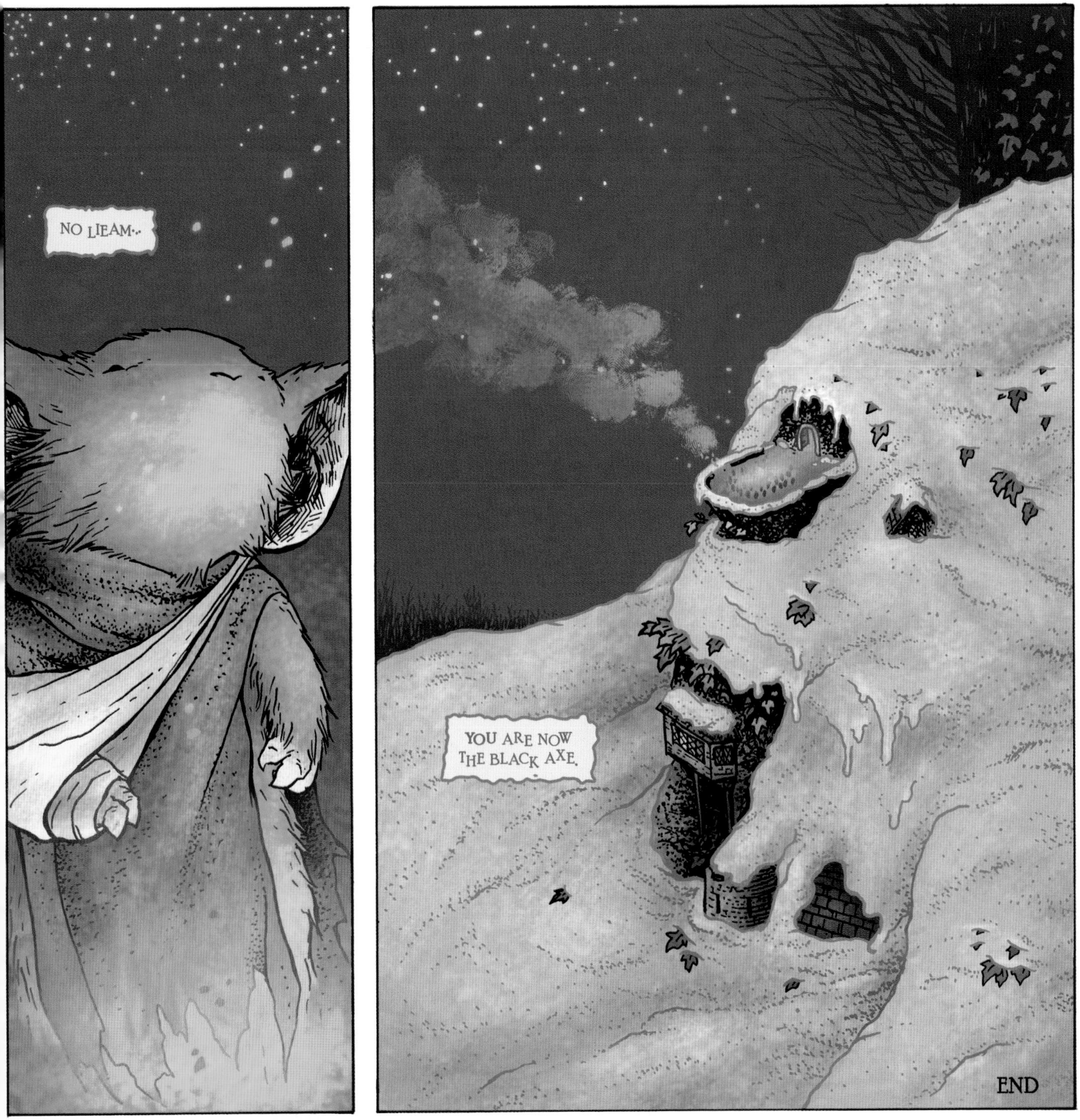
NO LIEAM..
YOU ARE NOW THE BLACK AXE.
END

EPILOGUE

Winter 1152:
The Summit was held three days before solstice.
Mouse leaders from across the Territories arrived
by hare. The discord of the independent cities
played out in full chorus.

Firth of Copperwood started with concern over the balance of power and who should have the weight to sway the Territories.

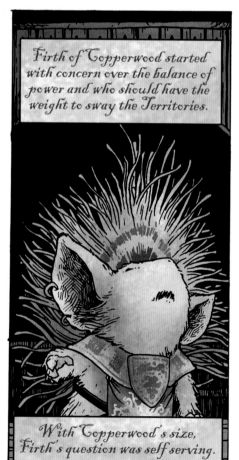

With Copperwood's size, Firth's question was self serving.

We have never superceded or infringed on any city's authority and do not plan to start.

Open country and Lockhaven are all the Guard asks authority over and, in turn, agreed no city shall impose itself over another's laws or importance.

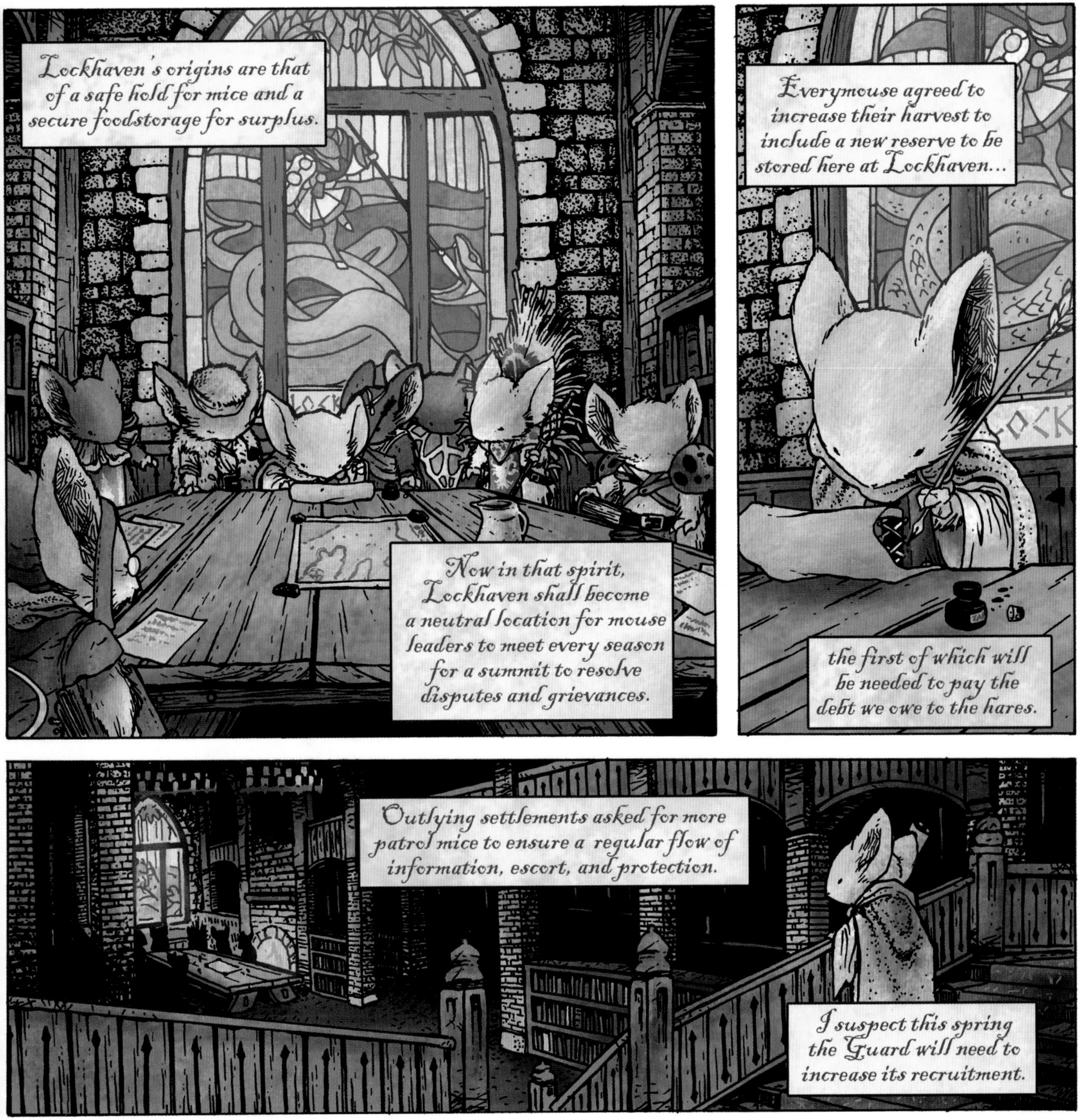

Lockhaven's origins are that of a safe hold for mice and a secure foodstorage for surplus.
Now in that spirit, Lockhaven shall become a neutral location for mouse leaders to meet every season for a summit to resolve disputes and grievances.
Everymouse agreed to increase their harvest to include a new reserve to be stored here at Lockhaven...
the first of which will be needed to pay the debt we owe to the hares.
Outlying settlements asked for more patrol mice to ensure a regular flow of information, escort, and protection.
I suspect this spring the Guard will need to increase its recruitment.

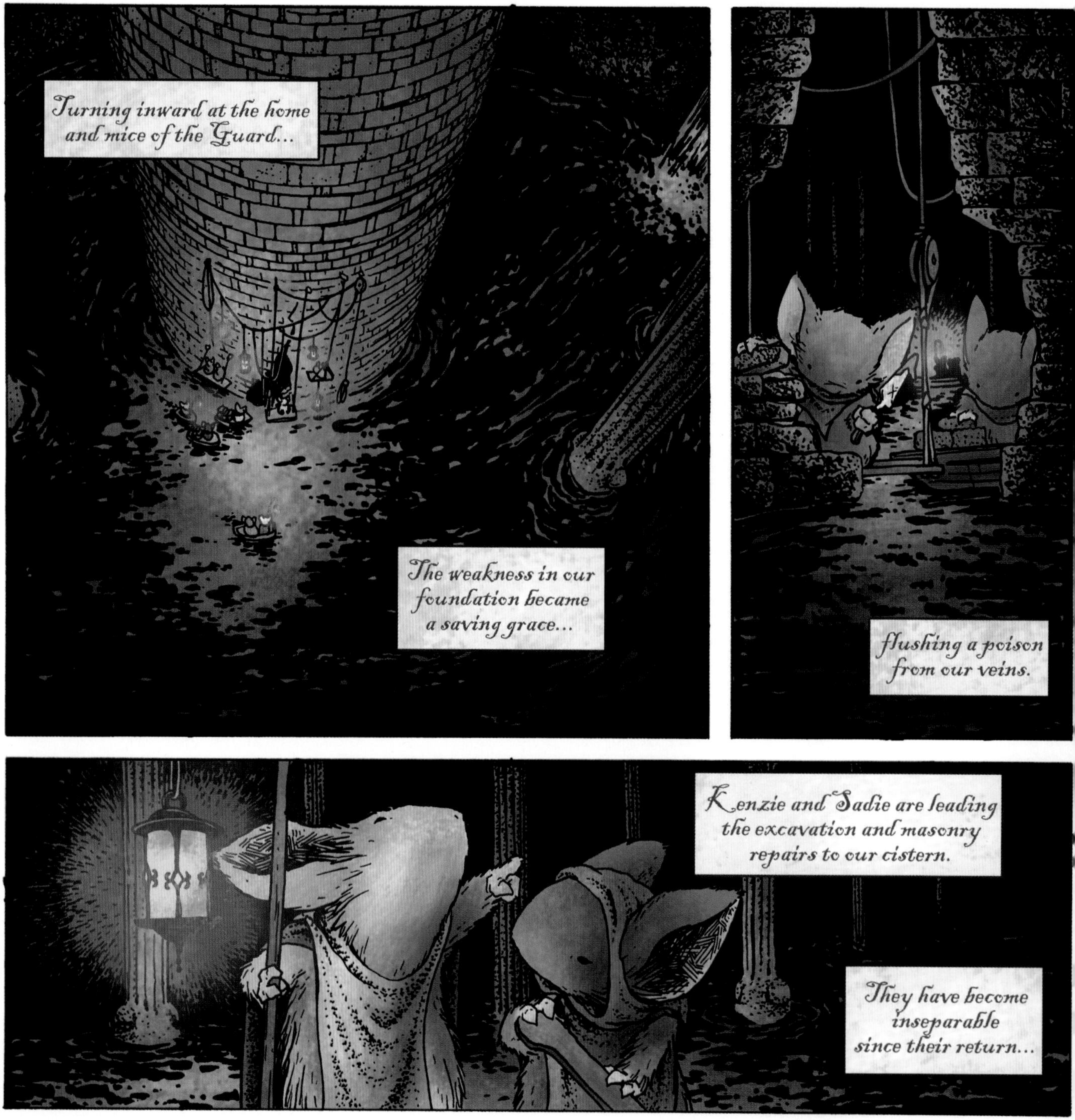
Turning inward at the home and mice of the Guard...
The weakness in our foundation became a saving grace...
flushing a poison from our veins.
Kenzie and Sadie are leading the excavation and masonry repairs to our cistern.
They have become inseparable since their return...

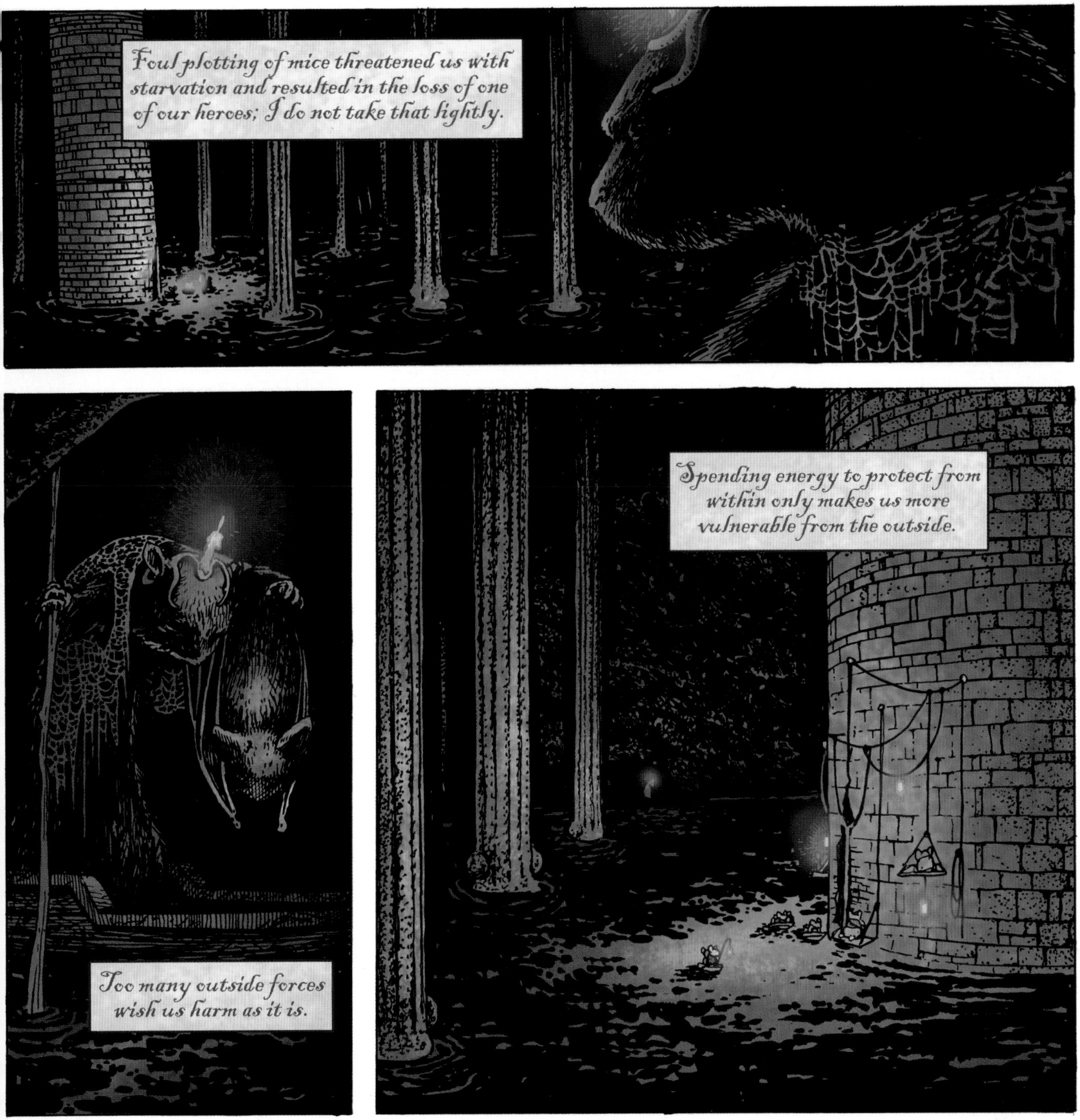
Foul plotting of mice threatened us with starvation and resulted in the loss of one of our heroes; I do not take that lightly.
Too many outside forces wish us harm as it is.
Spending energy to protect from within only makes us more vulnerable from the outside.

Lieam...

He came to Lockhaven with so little, and has lost even more since.

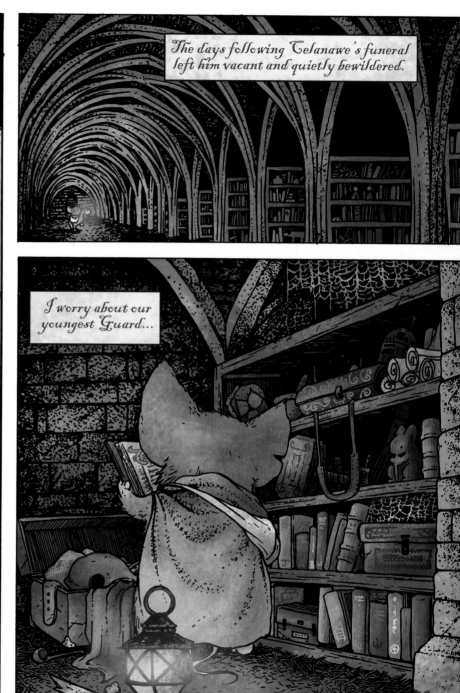

The days following Celanawe's funeral left him vacant and quietly bewildered.

I worry about our youngest Guard...

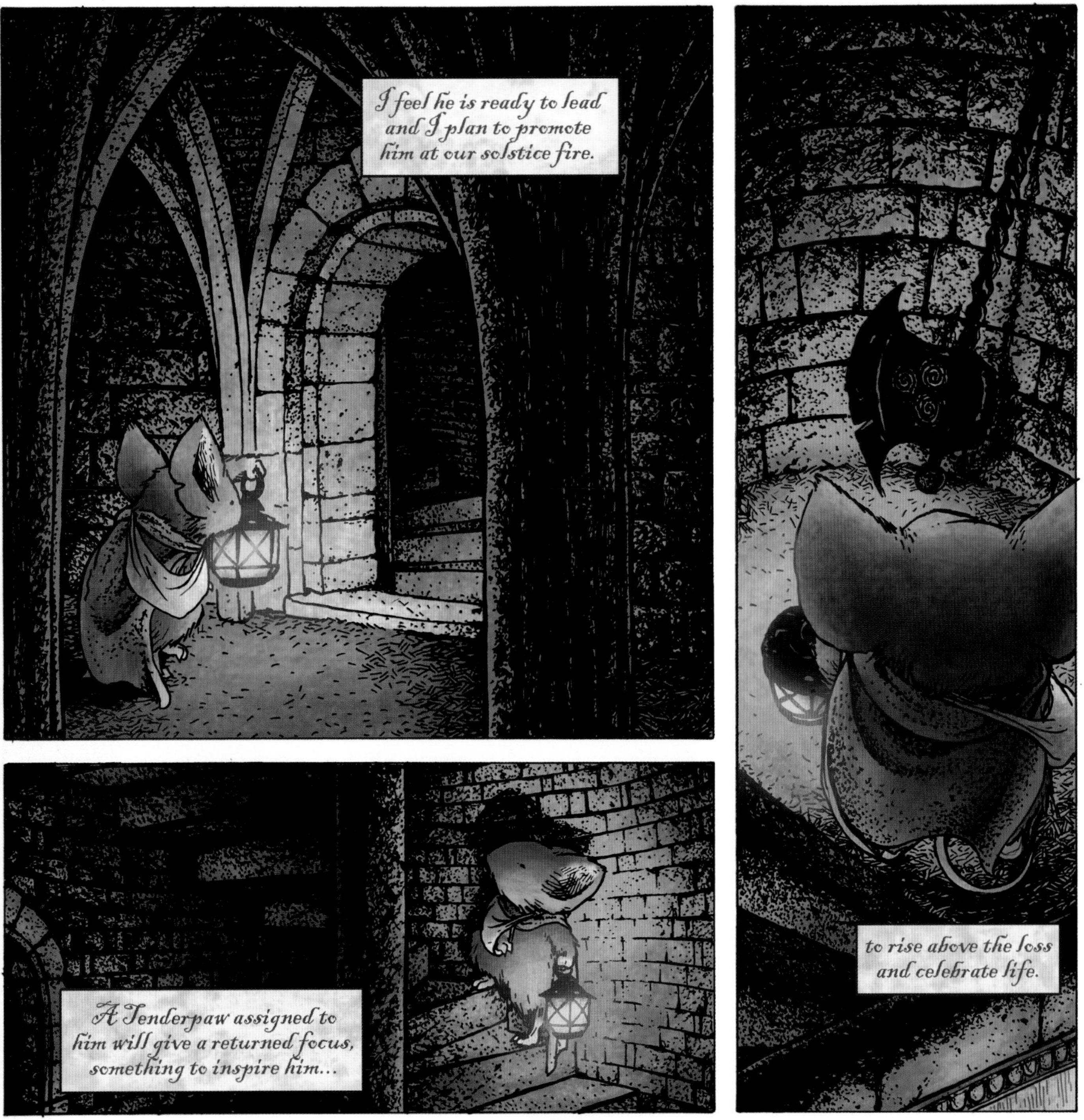
I feel he is ready to lead and I plan to promote him at our solstice fire.
A Tenderpaw assigned to him will give a returned focus, something to inspire him...
to rise above the loss and celebrate life.

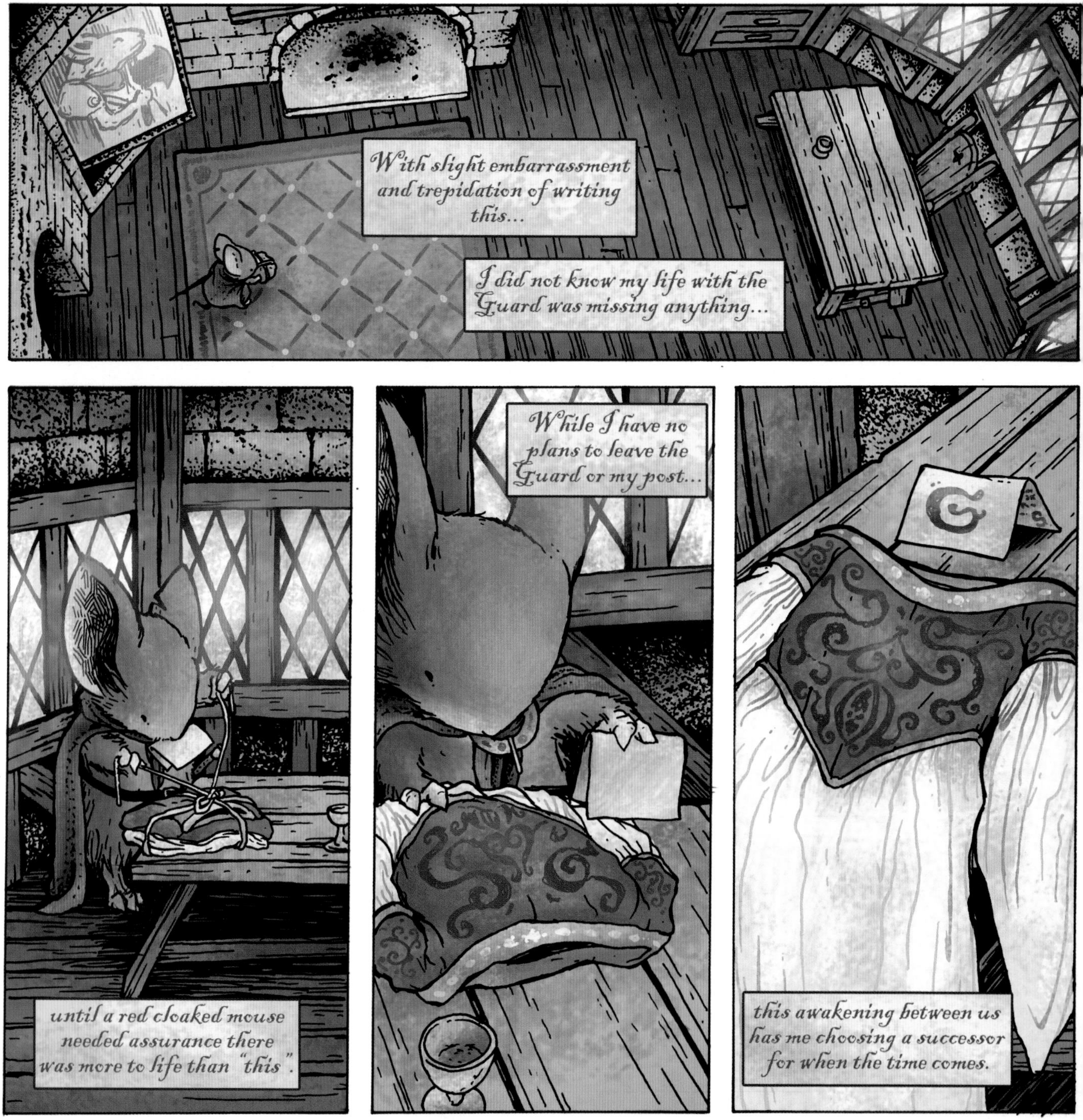
With slight embarrassment and trepidation of writing this...
I did not know my life with the Guard was missing anything...
until a red cloaked mouse needed assurance there was more to life than "this".
While I have no plans to leave the Guard or my post...
this awakening between us has me choosing a successor for when the time comes.

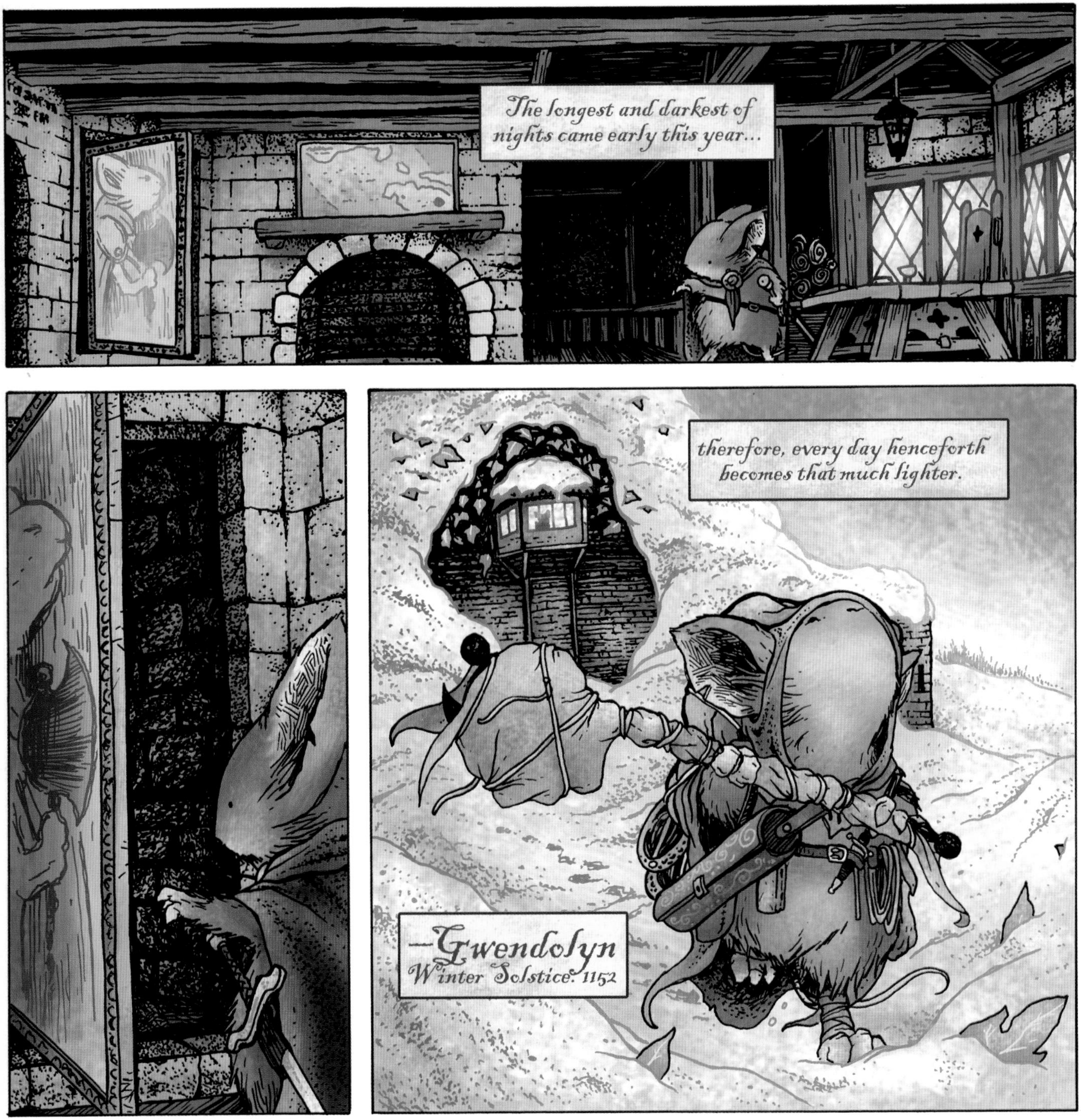
The longest and darkest of nights came early this year...
therefore, every day henceforth becomes that much lighter.
—Gwendolyn
Winter Solstice: 1152

Maps, Guides, and Assorted Extras

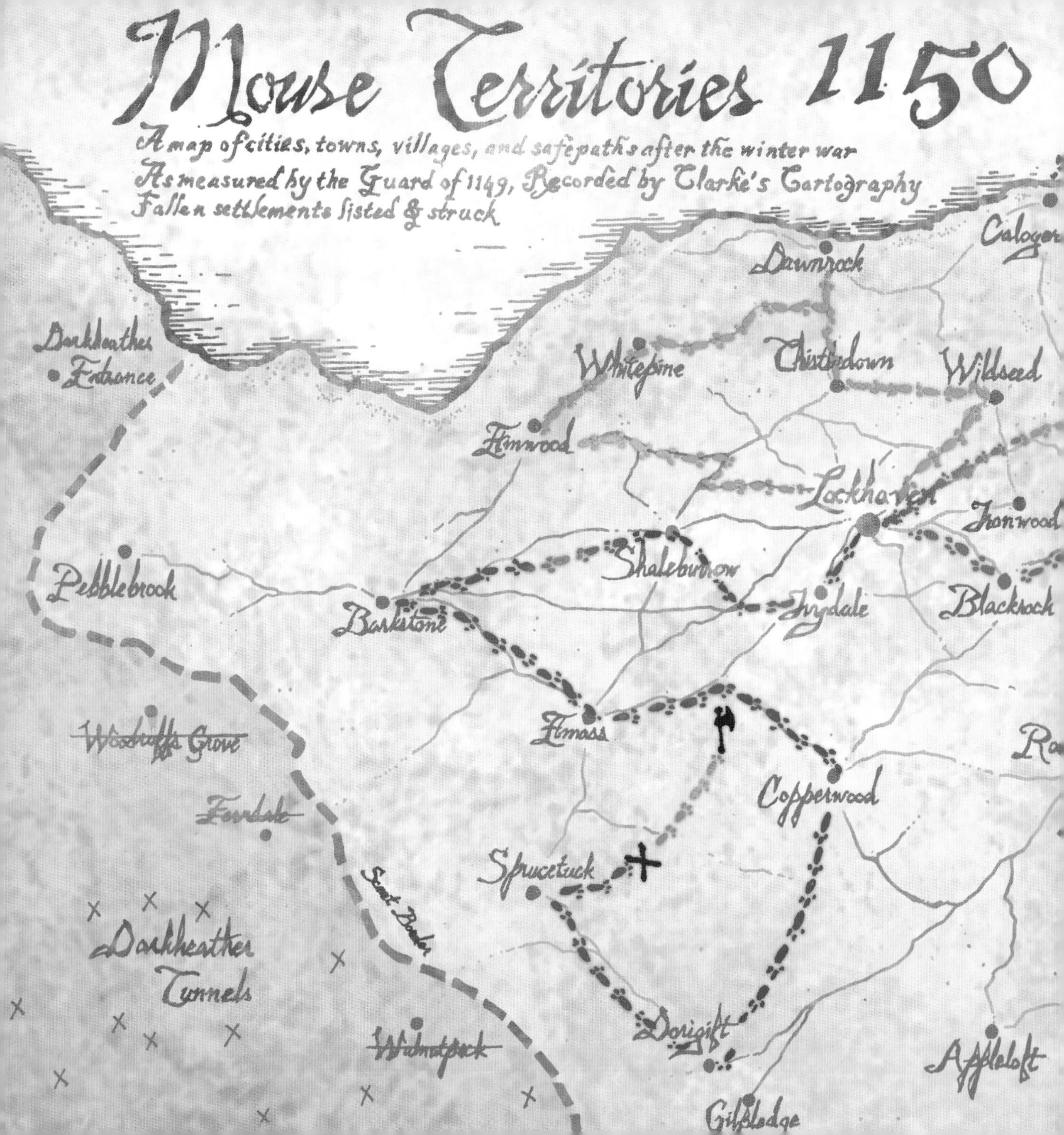

Mouse Territories 1150

A map of cities, towns, villages, and safe paths after the winter war
As measured by the Guard of 1149, Recorded by Clarke's Cartography
Fallen settlements listed & struck

Calogen

Dawnrock

Darkleather Entrance

Whitepine

Thistledown

Wildseed

Elmwood

Lockhaven

Ironwood

Shaleburrow

Pebblebrook

Barkstone

Ivydale

Blackrock

Woodruff's Grove

Elmoss

Copperwood

Ro—

Ferndale

Sprucetuck

Scent Border

Darkheather Tunnels

Dorigift

Appleloft

Walnutpeck

Gilpledge

WINTER 1152 GUARD ROUTES

Route taken by Sienna, Aubrey, Delvin, & Bastian

Route taken by Elymis, Sela, Annika, & Cerise

Route taken by Kenzie, Saxon, Lieam, Sadie & Celanawe

Route taken by Lieam & Celanawe

✕   Darkheather discovery

Frostic

Rustleaf

Port Sumac

Darkwater

Lonepine

Wolfepointe

Grasslake

Burl

Appleharbor   Sandmason

Lillygrove

Oakgrove

Flintrust   Birchflow

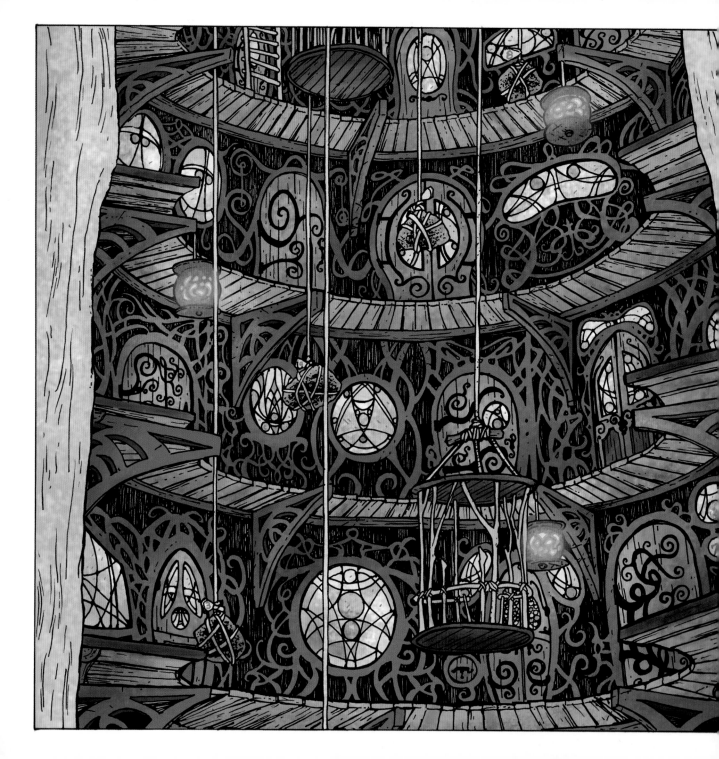

SPRUCETUCK:

A village in the southwest of the mouse territories located inside a tall and old spruce tree. The hollow trunk provides stories of living quarters, apothecaries, breweries, and libraries. Long known as being the elegant home of mouse science, the village also has laborers who harvest sap, tend fire, and haul wood, water, and supplies.

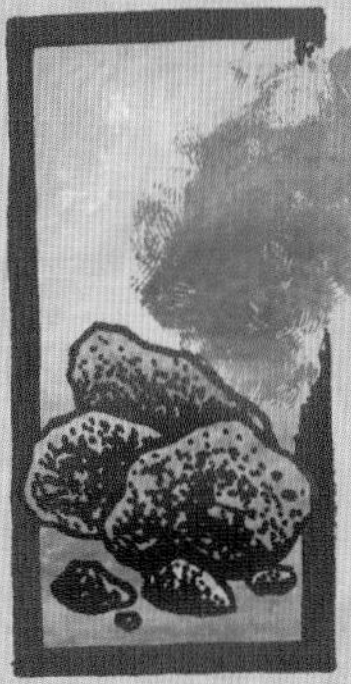

HOT STONES:

In cold seasons, Sprucetuck has a single fire burning in its underground level. Stones are placed in the flame and then carried up to mouse dens to radiate heat. This ensures there is minimal open flame in Sprucetuck.

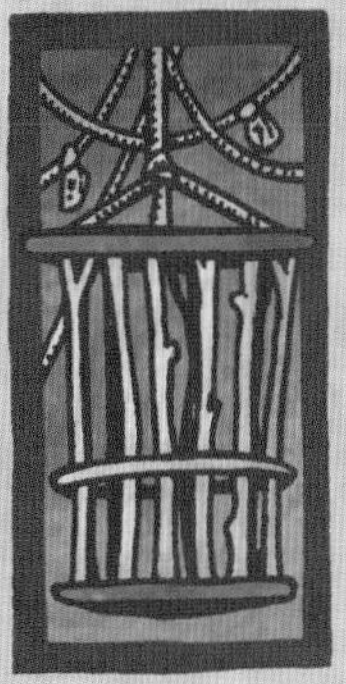

LIFTS:

The central hollow shaft of Sprucetuck is a bustling network of counter-weight driven lifts. Floors, ropes, and weights are all given numbers to help the operators use the correct combination for mice to get to their proper destinations.

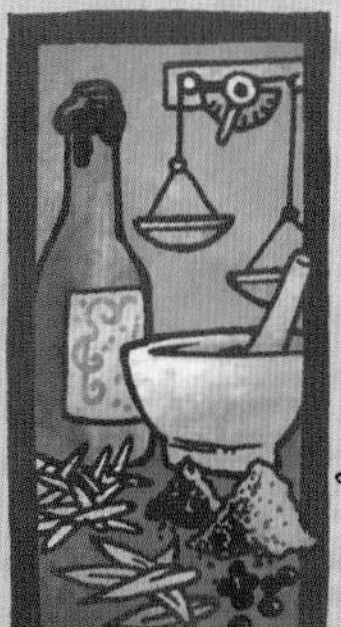

SCIENCE & MEDICINE:

Mice of Sprucetuck pursue science of medicine, harvest, pest control, and metallurgy. The sap from the spruce is the key ingredient in Sprucetuck's own "Spruce Brew Elixer".

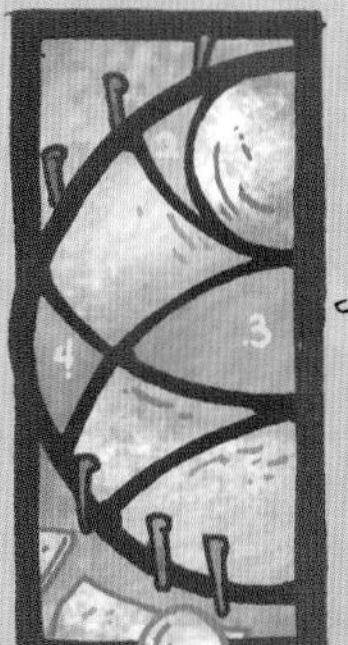

GLAZIERS:

Glass is one of the marvels of Sprucetuck's science. They perfected the recipe for larger and more durable glass. In addition to the glass itself, the village is also known for its mathematically based geometric window designs.

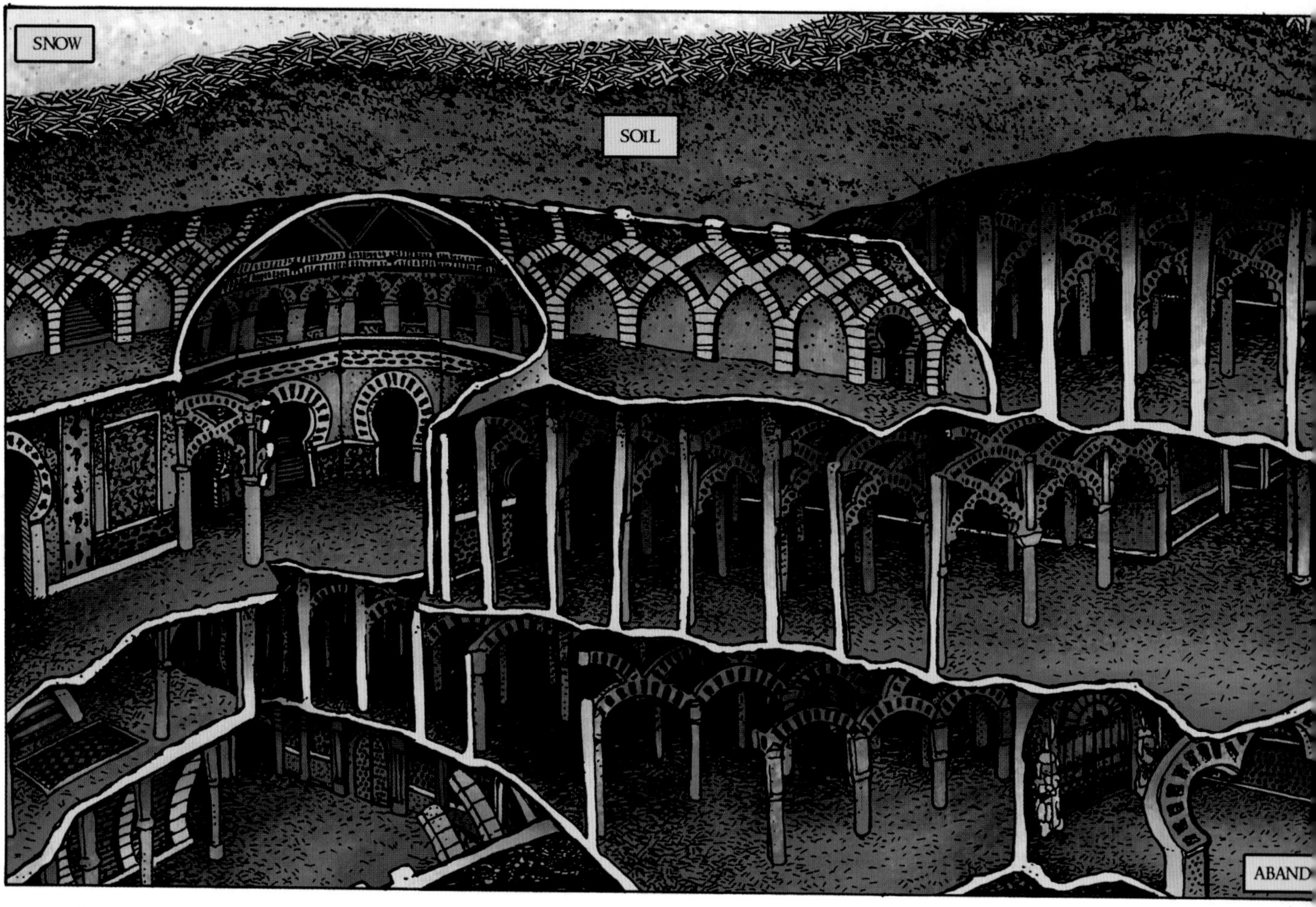
SNOW
SOIL
ABAND

DARKHEATHER: *This abandoned maze of interlocking tunnels stands as a horrible monument of cruelty and greed for the mice of the territories. Much of Darkheather was not excavated by weasels themselves, but were conquered or abandoned burrows and homes of animals long gone. The weasels decorated their new tunnels with tilework and the pelts of their slain foes.*

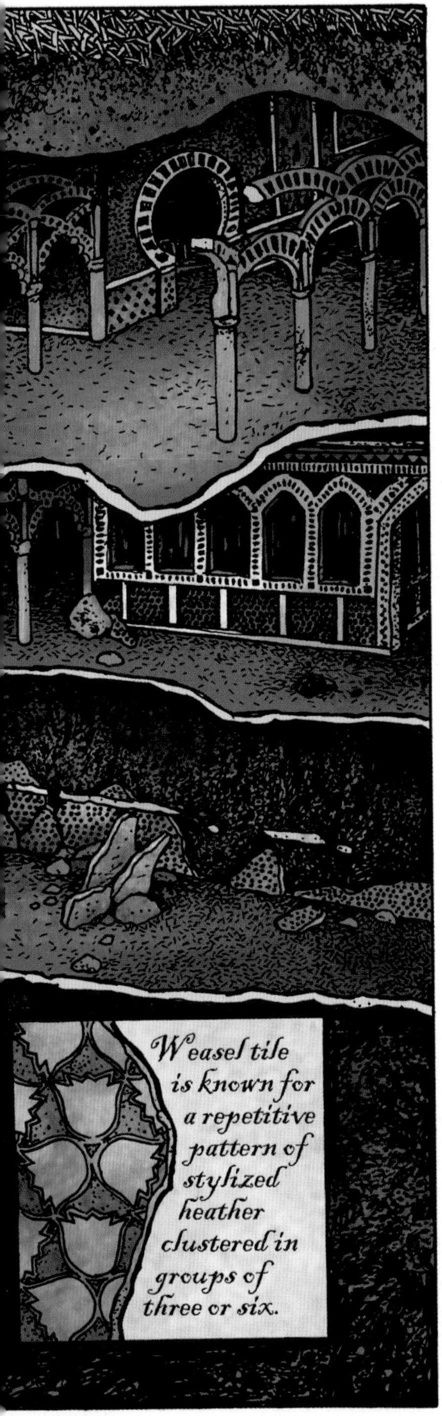
Weasel tile is known for a repetitive pattern of stylized heather clustered in groups of three or six.
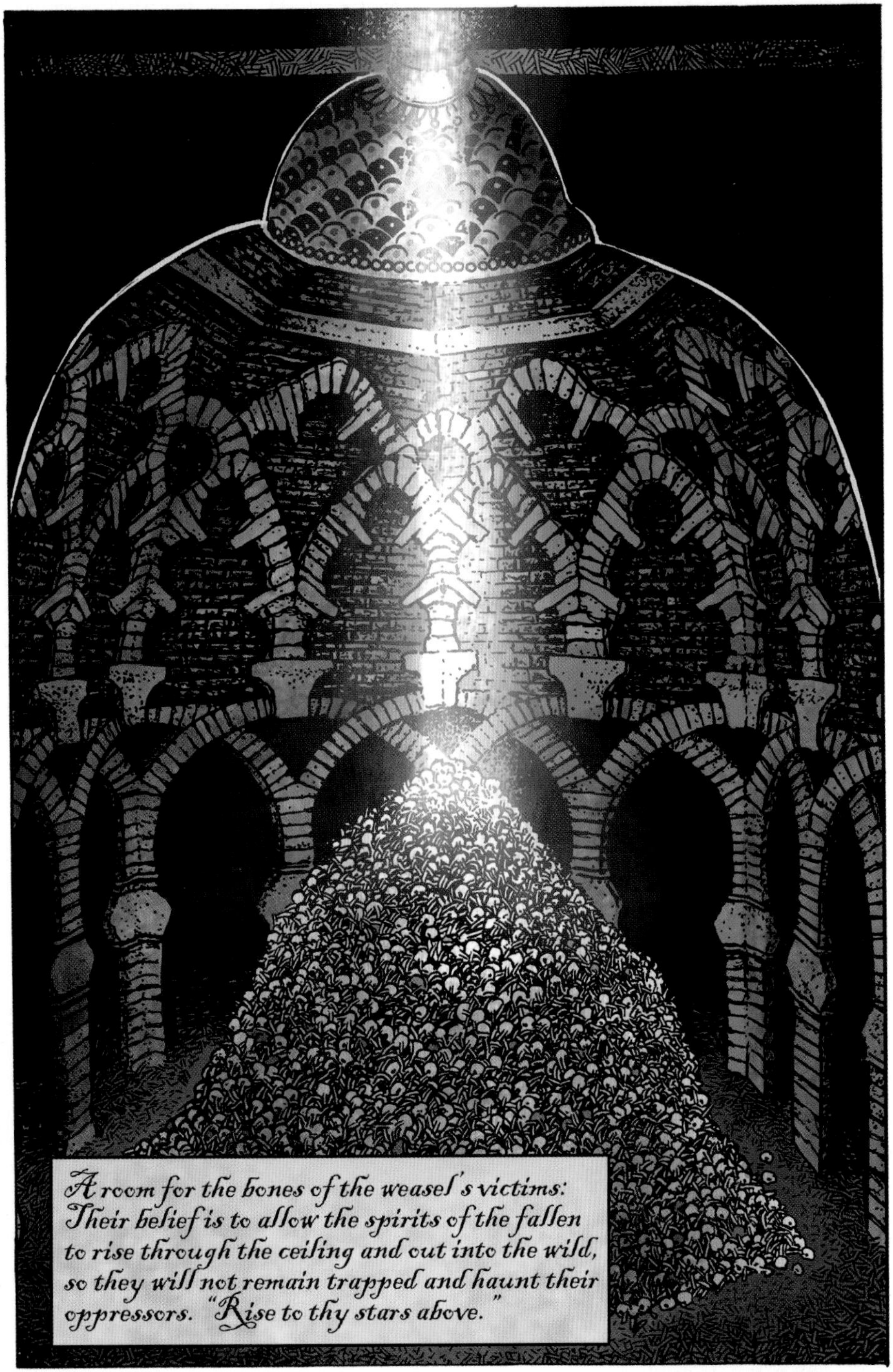
A room for the bones of the weasel's victims: Their belief is to allow the spirits of the fallen to rise through the ceiling and out into the wild, so they will not remain trapped and haunt their oppressors. "Rise to thy stars above."

Common Mouse Trades:

Blacksmith:

Iron, Copper, Steel, & Bronze are all forged by the fires of the blacksmith. Mouse blacksmiths will make every-day items like hinges and nails or larger architectural items like gates or doors. Even some weapons and tools are made by the blacksmith.

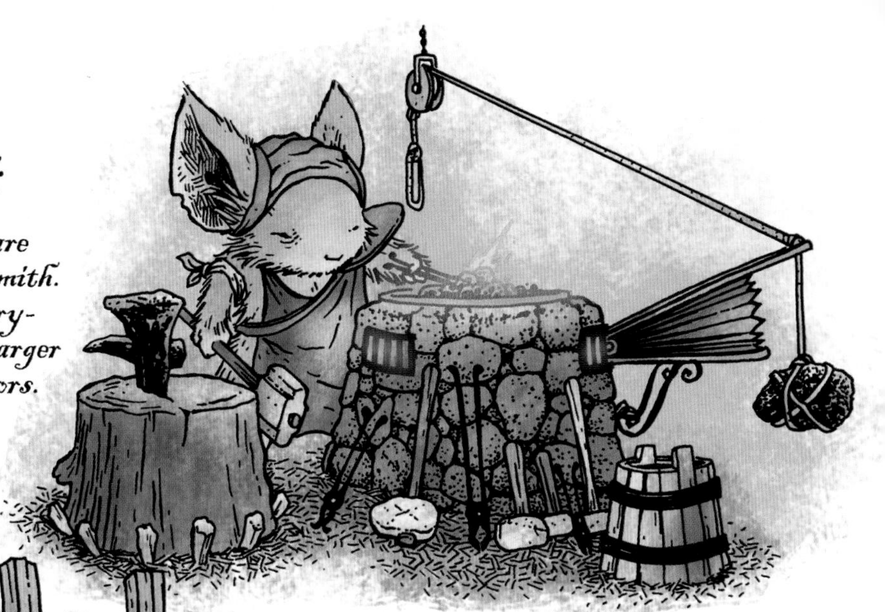

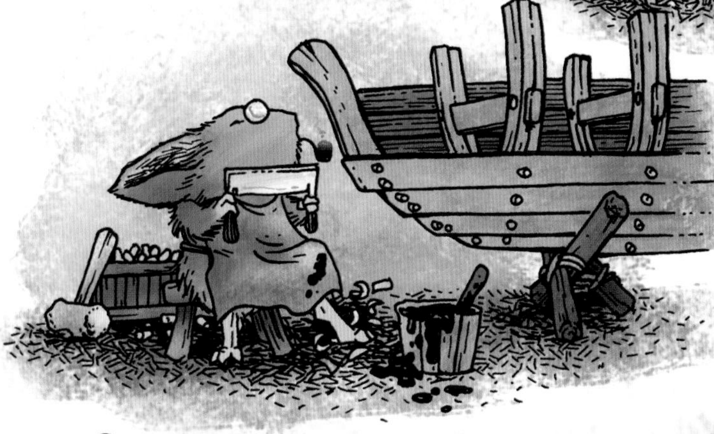

Boat-Builder:

Two types of water vessels are used by mice: those made from scavanged items for a one-time use, and those that are crafted to last a lifetime. To make a boat sea-worthy, this craftsmouse can use elm, wax, pine-pitch, and various other water-proof materials.

Mouse Pagentry & Attire:

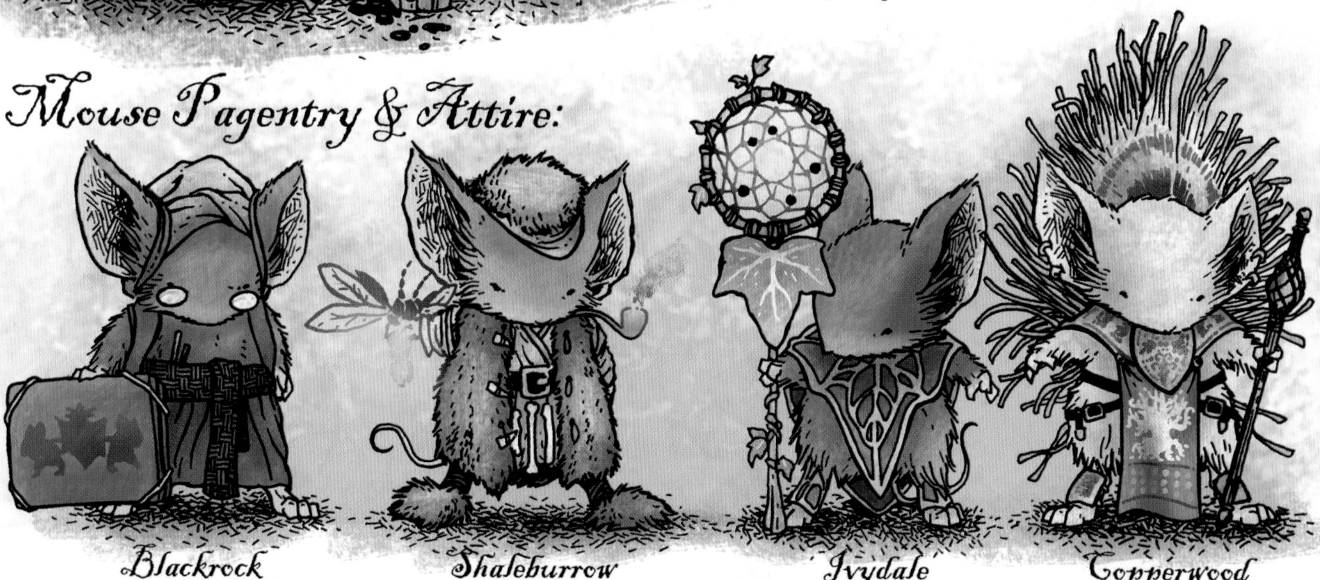

Blackrock Shaleburrow Ivydale Copperwood

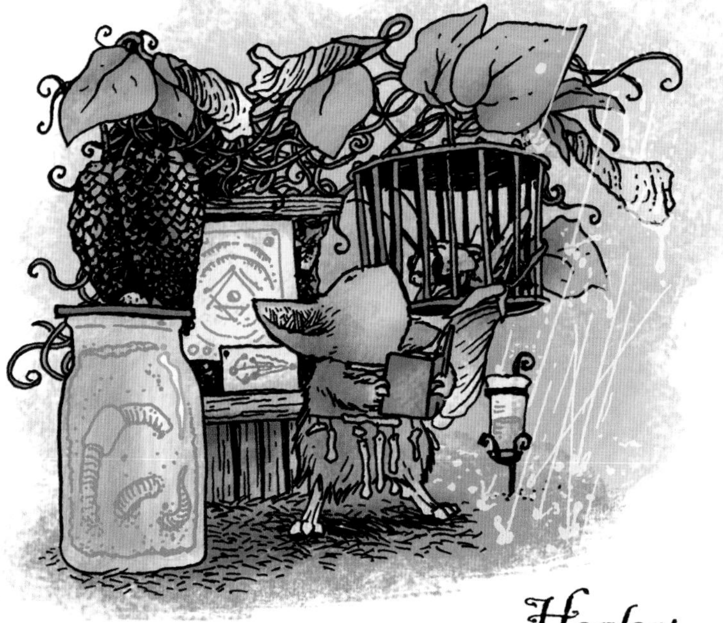

Weather Watcher:

Taking cues from flowers, plants, and insects, it is the Weather Watcher's duty to observe and report on climate changes. Cricket chirps, worm activity, and pine-cone shape can help predict the imediate and long-lasting forcast.

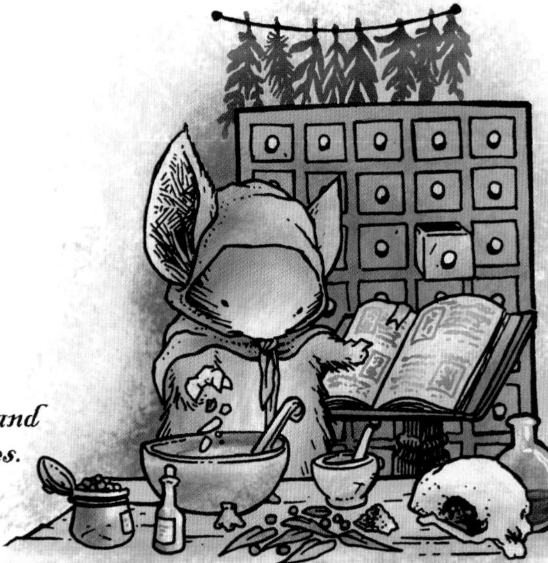

Healer:

A healer uses handed down knowledge of botany and the mouse body to create elixers, salves, wraps, and balms for many injuries and poisons that can afflict mice of the territories.

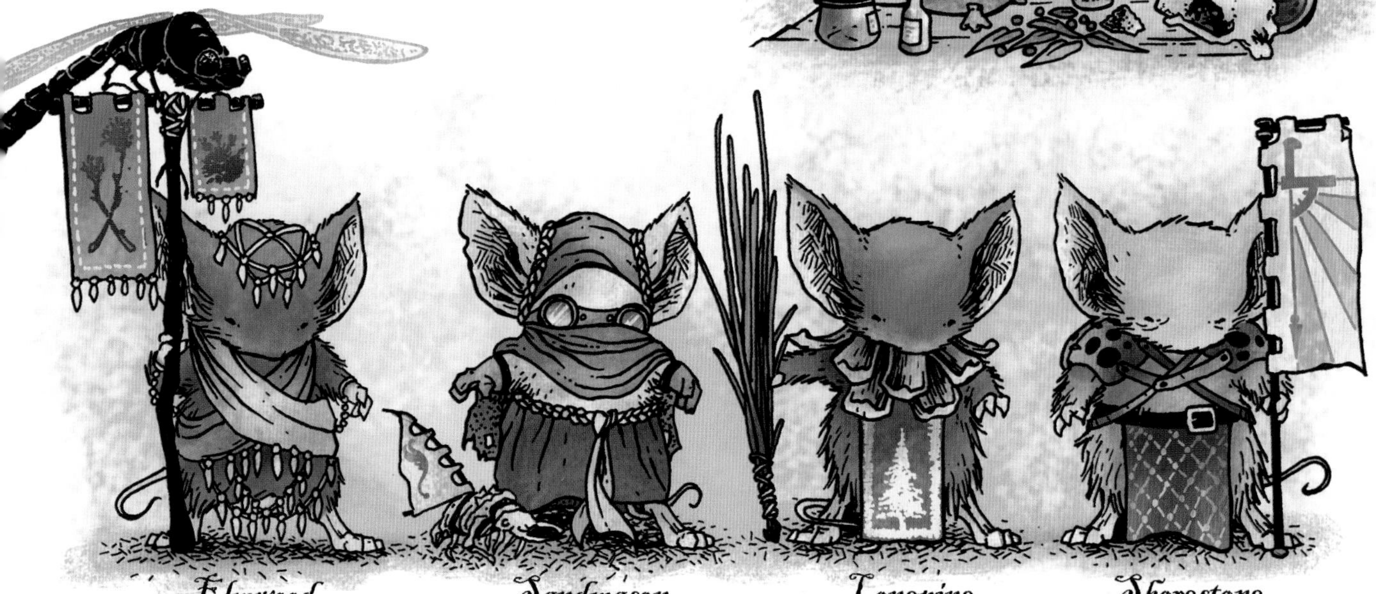

Elmwood Sandmason Lonepine Shorestone

A GALLERY OF PINUPS

BY ESTEEMED AUTHORS & FRIENDS

AS PRESENTED IN THE
ORIGINAL MOUSE GUARD SERIES

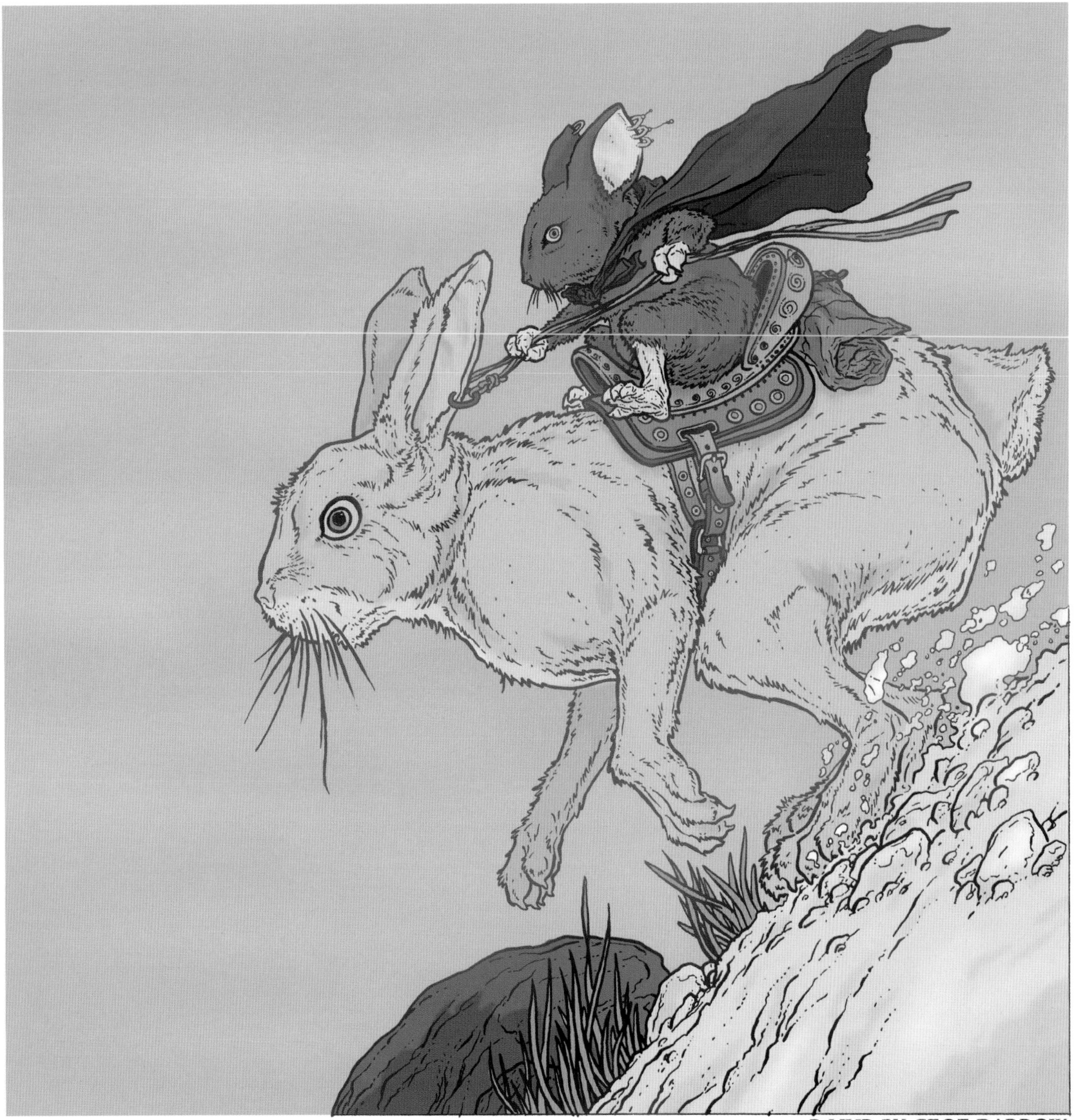

PINUP BY GEOF DARROW

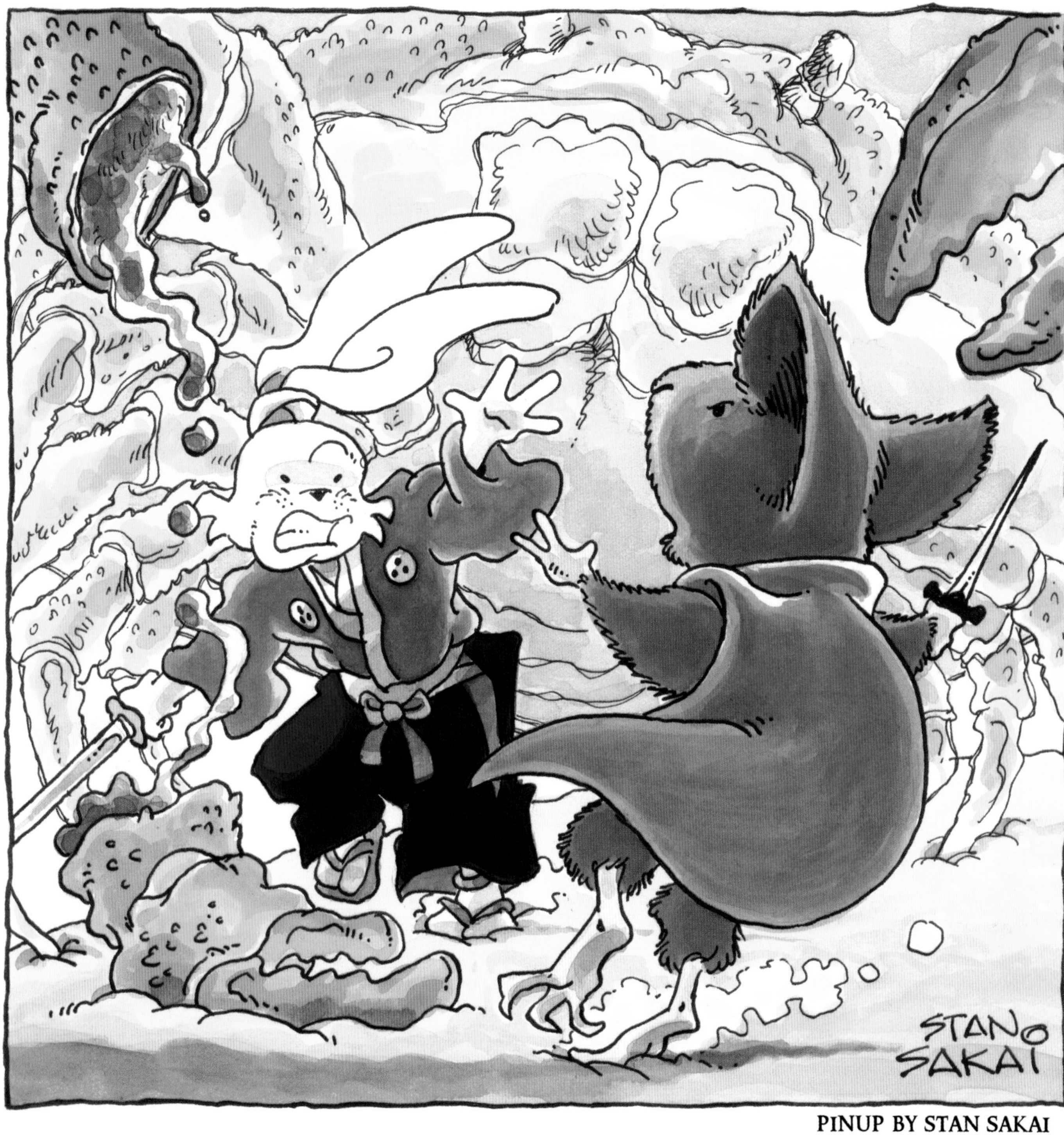
STAN SAKAI

PINUP BY STAN SAKAI

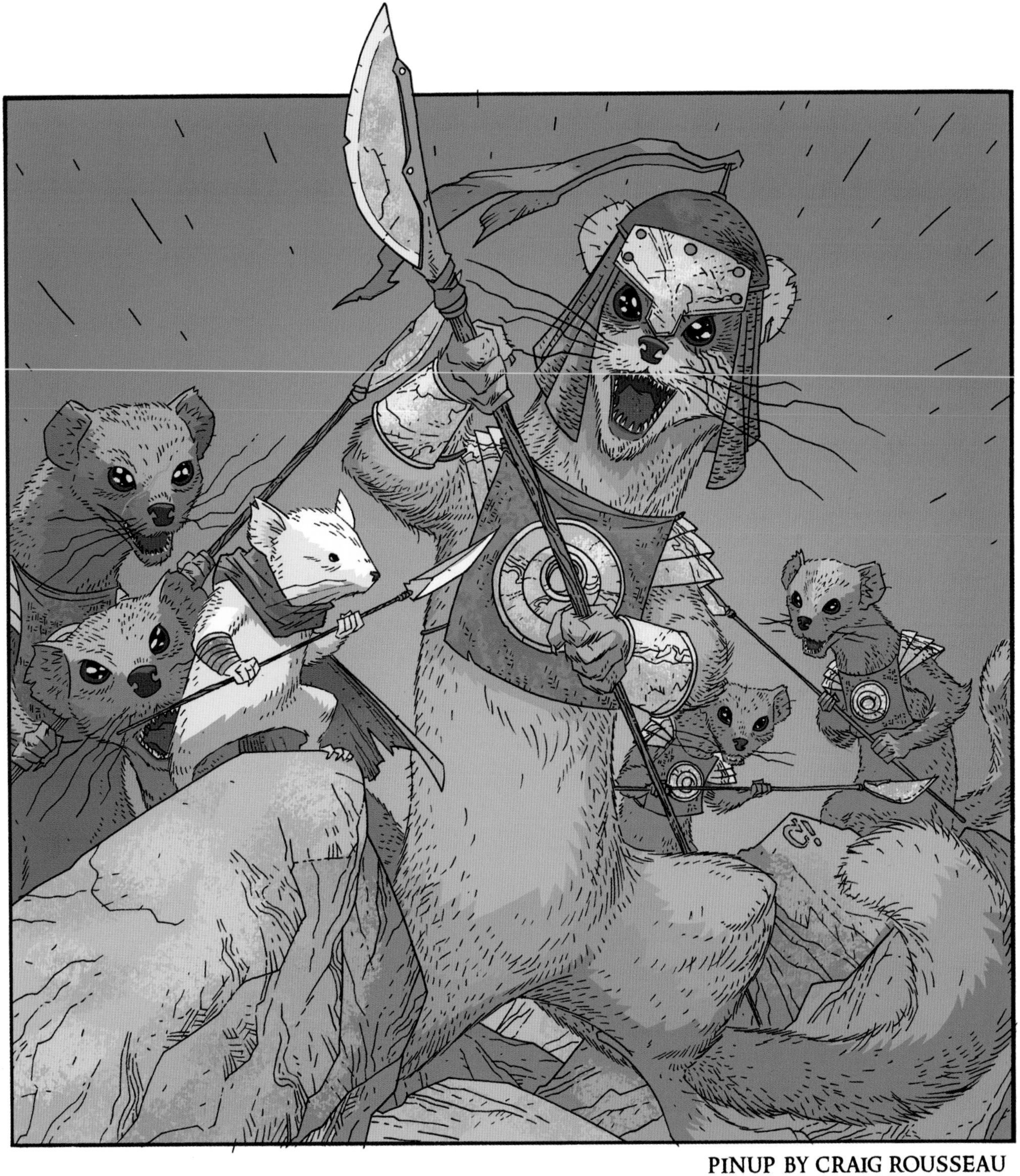

PINUP BY CRAIG ROUSSEAU

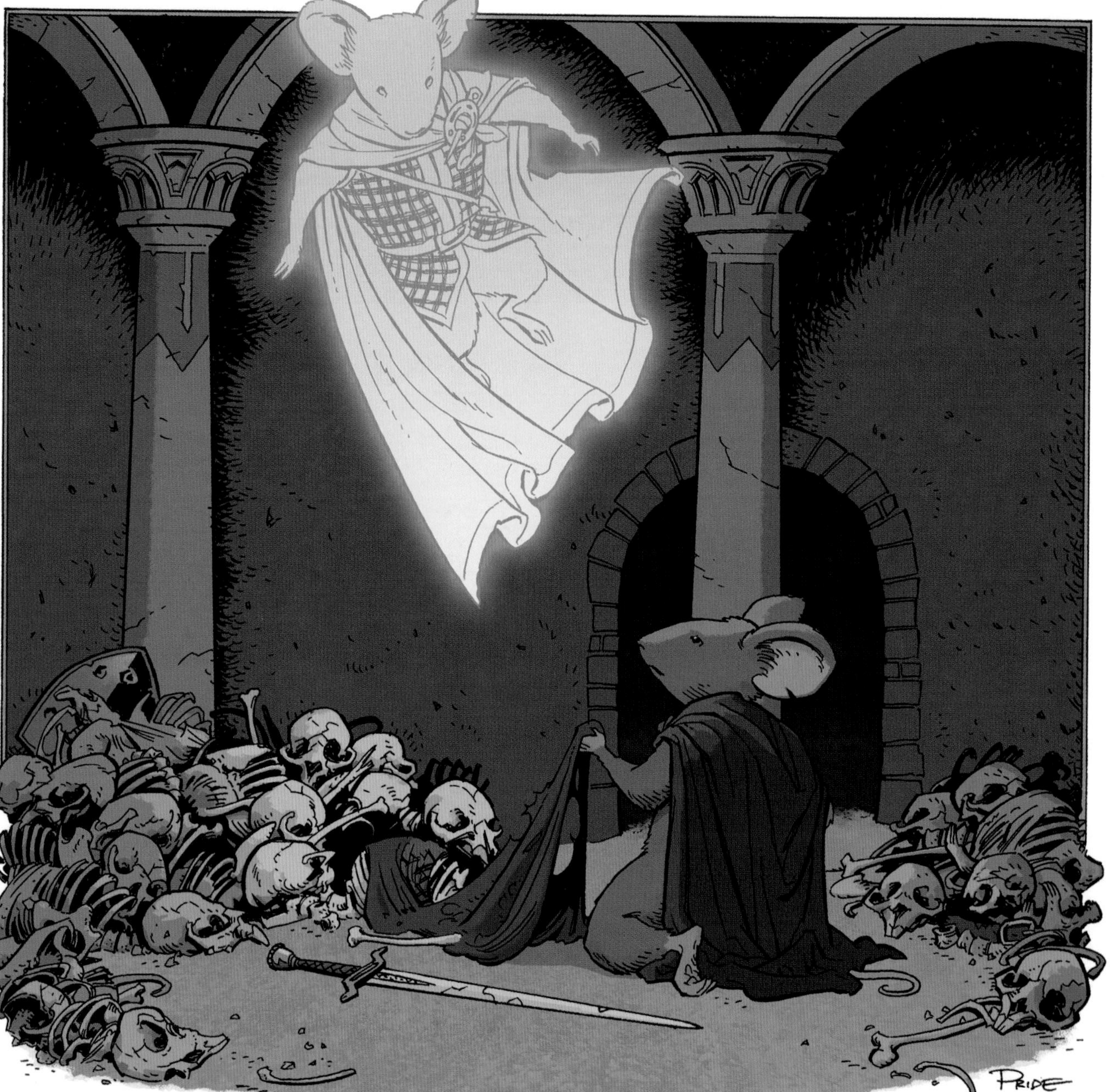
PRIDE

PINUP BY NATE PRIDE

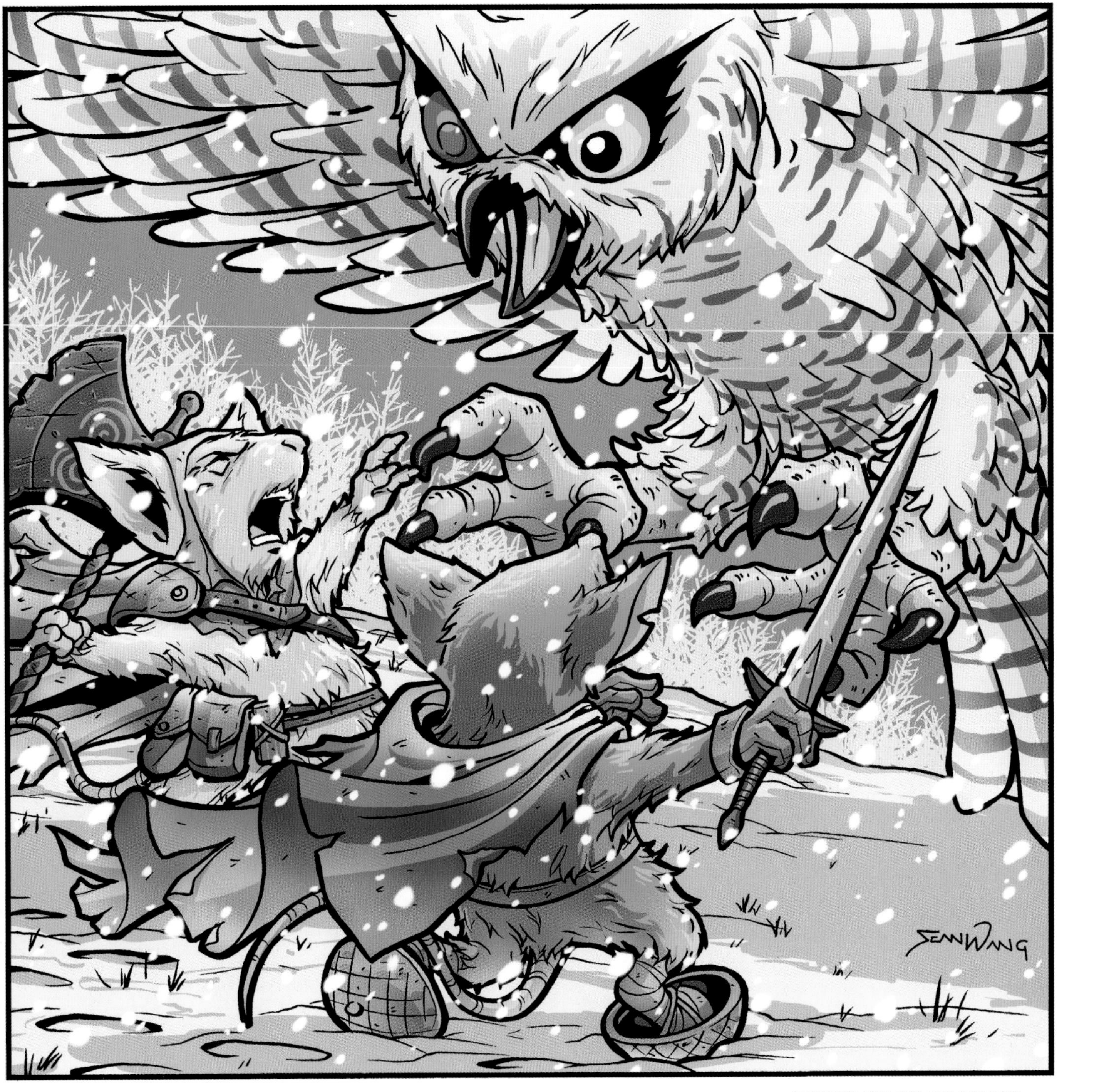
SEAN WANG

PINUP BY SEAN WANG

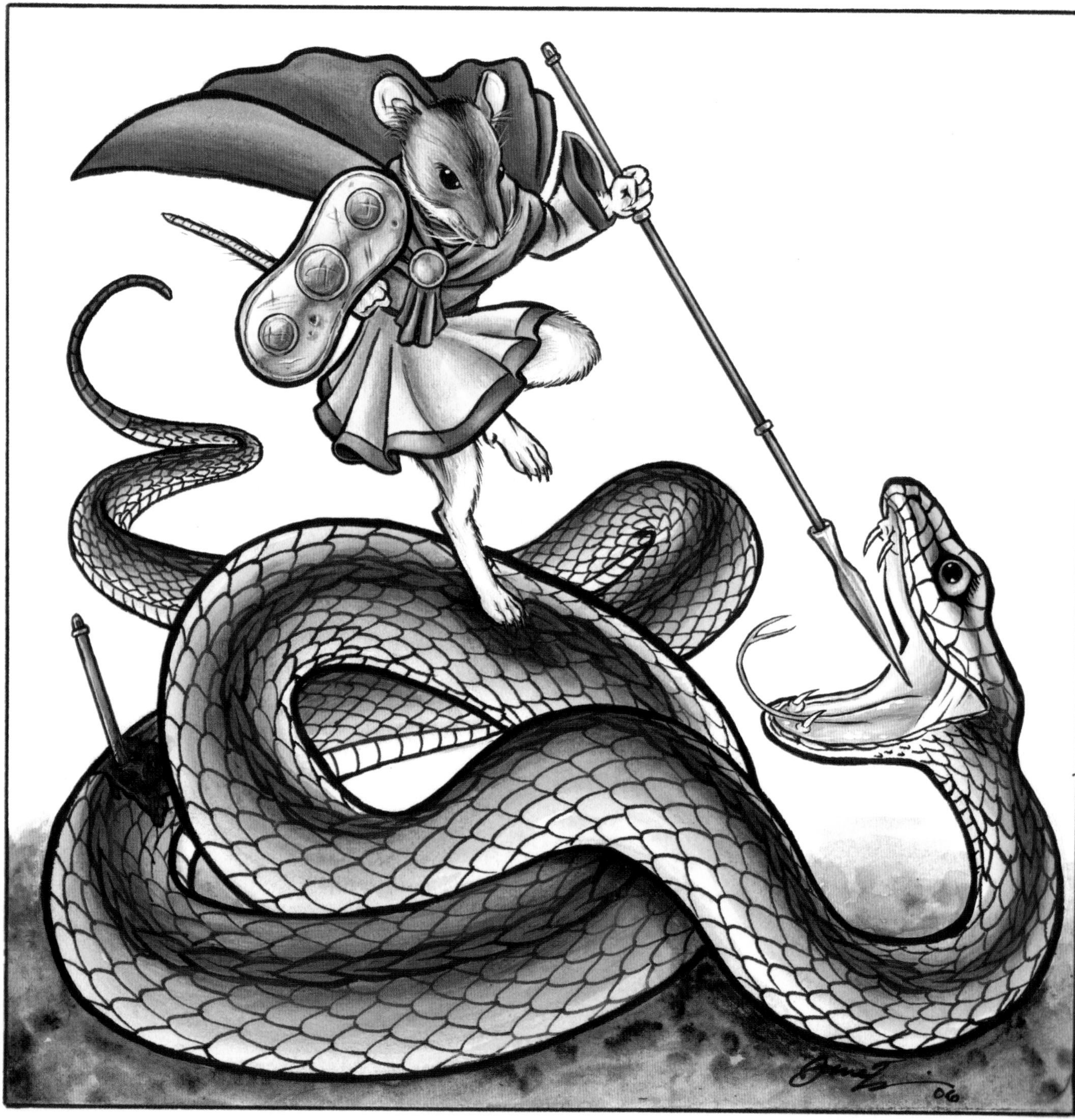

PINUP BY JANE IRWIN

THE NEXT BOOK IN THE

MOUSE GUARD SERIES:

THE
BLACK AXE

ABOUT THE AUTHOR

David Petersen was born in 1977. His artistic career soon followed. A steady diet of cartoons, comics, and tree climbing fed his imagination and is what still inspires his work today. He is a three time Eisner Award winner and recipient of two Harvey Awards for his continued work on the *Mouse Guard* series. David received his BFA in printmaking from Eastern Michigan University where he met his wife Julia. They continue to reside in Michigan with their dogs Bronwyn & Coco.

Mouse Territories 1150

A map of cities, towns, villages, and safe paths after the winter war
As measured by the Guard of 1149, Recorded by Clarke's Cartography
Fallen settlements listed & struck

Calogero

Dawnrock

Darkheather
Entrance

Whitepine

Thistledown

Wildseed

Elmwood

Lockhaven

Ironwood

Pebblebrook

Shaleburrow

Ivydale

Blackrock

Barkstone

Woodruff's Grove

Elmoss

Roo

Copperwood

Ferndale

Scent Border

Sprucetuck

Darkheather
Tunnels

Walnutpeck

Dorigift

Appleloft

Gilpledge